SMOKE ON THE WATER

A MYSTIC BEACH FANTASY ROCKSTAR ROMANCE

AISLINN ARCHER

MYSTIC BEACH PRESS

CONTENTS

Content Warning

Content reviews for all of Aislinn Archer's works are located on her website at aislinnarcher.com. Readers are strongly urged to review these content reviews before purchasing, downloading or reading, and to use their discretion as to whether a given work is appropriate for them. Among other things, this novel includes some steamy love scenes, and is recommended for those 18 or older.

A WORD FROM THE AUTHOR...

For those who are entering the world of Mystic Beach for the first time:

Welcome! Be aware that happenings in and around this little beach town have frequently been described as "odd." And that's an understatement. From mermaids and witches to ghosts, immortal beings, and a deity or two, Mystic Beach is fantastical — literally.

The Mystic Beach "Mysteries" series (conceived first, and publication forthcoming) is in the contemporary/paranormal fantasy genre, featuring many of the hallmarks of urban fantasy — including danger and even deadly consequences — but set in a small resort town by the sea. The Mystic Beach rockstar romances cross over into that genre, blending rockstar romance with fantasy/paranormal romance. They exist in the same world as the fantasy series, sharing some of the same characters, each with their own set of fantastical circumstances. But the danger ahead for our rockstars is more of broken hearts and tarnished careers than of life-threatening run-ins with the supernatural. Mostly.

Each book in the rockstar romance series is a standalone and can be read separately from the others, but they are part of an interlaced story and reading them in series order is recommended. You'll get a richer experience of our guys, their ladies and Mystic Beach itself. Portions of this story have appeared in prior books in the series, from other characters' points of view. But you'll get a new perspective here.

Note: This series — this book, "Smoke on the Water," in particular — does contain spoilers for the first book in the Aurora Carmichael/Mystic Beach Mysteries fantasy series, "Safe Harbour." If you're intrigued by what you read here, you'll want to read the forthcoming sister series to fill in the details. Subsequent books in that series will reshuffle the deck, so you can get to know the charismatic men of aMUSEd now and still enjoy the Mystic Beach Mysteries later.

To John Nigel Taylor and Adam Charles Clayton, who captured
a young girl's heart with the magic of music and amazing men.
Sometimes, the bass player *does* get the girl.

PROLOGUE

David

"How is she even still here?"

Declan slams back a double shot of Jameson.
"I've got to find her."

If you'd told me a couple months ago that today I'd be sitting at a bayfront bar in South Coastal Delaware, consoling my brother over his broken heart — honestly, I'd have laughed. Now, I just find myself glad we never rented a car to use when we came down here to rest and record. I'm not sure what Declan would do if he had the means at this moment to try to chase down Callie, who lit out of here like her hair was on fire the moment she recognized him.

"Don't do anything stupid, OK?"

Declan glares at me. "When have I ever..."

"Just about every night since things went haywire with Callie."

He looks ready to argue with me, but he appears to consider it and stays silent instead.

But he's right — what are the odds his ex-girlfriend would still be here, after all these years? And here tonight, at our friends' private party?

Yeah, Declan's romantic life is a disaster. Well, more like it's nonexistent. But he's Declan Carter — lead singer of aMUSEd, one of the most popular rock bands on the planet. Not having a girlfriend is a plus for him. He has his pick of girls at our gigs, and he likes it that way.

Declan's been a ladies' man since he was 18, after he broke things off with Callie. He disappears most nights we're on tour, a girl or two on his arm, while I... don't. I may be the bass player in our band, as well as his co-writer for most of our songs, but there — aside from our parents and the brown hair and blue eyes they gave us — our commonalities end.

Every once in a while, I find a girl I like, but I want more than that. I want someone special. Someone who gets me. Someone who can look past my awkwardness, someone I really... connect with. After 30 years, you'd think I could find one girl like that.

Nope.

I thought maybe I had. Watching our bandmate Hunter propose tonight to his lifelong best friend and now fiancée, Brighid, has been bittersweet. I'm happy for them, but I feel like I came so close, only to have things fall apart. So maybe I get how Declan is feeling. I mean, I kept things to myself, just like Declan had his past with Callie and the fact that he — clearly — never got over her.

But now Declan's secret is out. Even Brighid's dog knows what went down, and he tries to console Declan in his own way, his head in Declan's lap.

My secret — well, the new one, the big one — rests in a pair of big brown eyes. No, not the dog's. The *girl* with those big brown eyes — *my* girl, if I had my way — now that I've found her, she's very determinedly dodging me.

I feel eyes on me, and I already know exactly who it is. I turn and spot her leaning up against the side of the restaurant, her iPad still in hand, as if she's waiting to see whether we're going to go back on stage. She's hired for the night, so she can't run away from me. Not this time. Not if she wants to keep this job, and I know better than anyone how determined she is to keep this job, especially when her other one is already hanging by a thread. Though that's on me, which is half the reason she's dodging me.

I walk over and I lean up against the wall next to her.

"Are you going to be playing more?" she asks after a minute.

"Probably. I don't know."

She heaves a frustrated sigh.

"No one here is going to report back to Steve that you were talking to me."

"It's a bad idea nonetheless."

"Piper…"

I give a frustrated sigh of my own. Then I grab her hand and pull her behind me to the other side of the corner, out of view of everyone at this little private party. And then I push her up against the wall, my hands going to her face, my mouth within inches of the temptation of her lips.

"You don't have to do this. I'll fix it. I can still fix this."

"It's better this way, David. For both of us. You'll be leaving soon, and I can't leave Mystic Beach. And I can't live with the risks involved. *You* can't live with the risks involved."

My fingers trace up the side of her neck.

"It's worth it to me."

I brush my lips across hers, and I can feel her melt, her mouth opening to me, eyes sliding closed. My hips press into her. There's a clatter as the tablet slips from her grasp.

The moment is broken. She pushes me away, grabbing for the iPad and frantically examining it. Though it appears undamaged, damage is still done — she pushes me away again as I try to get her attention back on me, on us.

"It's not worth it to *me*, David. I won't risk it. I can't."

She scoots out from between me and the wall and walks away, taking my heart with her.

We're a sorry pair tonight, the Carter brothers. It's going to take a miracle for either of us to get a happy ending out of this.

CHAPTER 1

I BELIEVE

Piper
A year ago

"Rónan, I want to do this on my own! There's no accomplishment in it if you buy things, and call in favors and arrange this for me!"

My foster-brother is acting like a stereotypical big brother, even if I'm almost certainly older than he is. He's just been here longer than I have. Not older, but bolder. A leader. I'm neither of those things, which is why my standing up to him over this seems to have surprised him.

"Piper — I know you want to be independent and accomplish things on your own, but we've got to be very careful here, make sure we have some control over circumstances if your employment documents aren't sufficient."

I'd wanted to go to high school, or college, but Rónan didn't want to risk that either. His girlfriend, Rory, said I'd be better off avoiding high school anyway, because most people don't enjoy it. But I could have at least gone to college.

Rónan disagreed. And his word is all but law in Safe Harbour.

"I'm doing the next best thing — arranging for you to have a paid internship in an environment where we do have some control. I have liquid assets I need to invest in concrete, established businesses to reduce the scrutiny on our finances, give us a legal foothold here. It just so happens that I think a recording studio at the beach would be a great investment. And you're interested in the work, and naturally inclined toward it, and putting you in place at the studio solves two problems at once — how to integrate you into the outside world and where to put some of our money."

Rónan has already leveraged the collective resources of Safe Harbour into a modest empire, to the benefit of us all. We have a place to live here now, right on the shore in quiet little Delaware, where our arrival has been taken as just another part of the recent influx of well-off retirees, remote workers and real estate investors in Mystic Beach. Just like he planned. Now it's a matter of integrating more of us into the community. And while it terrifies me, I've not only volunteered to be part of the vanguard, I've demanded Rónan let me make my own way. But he's not cooperating.

"Rónan, I can do this. I don't need your help. I've worked hard to learn everything I can on my own. I'm ready. I want to fill out an application, have a job interview, go in without you as a safety net. Unless you've changed your mind and will let me go to college."

"Mayhap down the road, that will be something we can do with the younglings..." he says, his slight lilt coming through as he dips back into the more formal vocabulary our folk tend to use in private. He's fully integrated himself into the business world here, but he hasn't fully lost the accent that gives a small hint at his origins. "But Piper — we need to get you settled in place here, now, somewhere that's not an unknown variable. You're just going to have to compromise a bit. You can show them what you can do and earn their respect while you're doing the work. Then you can do whatever you want, however you want — within reason..." he adds cautiously.

He worries so much about me, about all of us. Old habits die hard, and the weight on his shoulders has been tremendous, I know. But he can't take on the world single-handed. Rory will help, if he lets her. And I want to help, too. I owe him that, and much more.

If I'm honest, the entire idea terrifies me. I still need to do it. I can do it. I have to, or I'll bury myself inside this little enclave of ours and find myself following everyone else's expectations and not what I want for my life in this new place, where the sky seems to be the limit if you're willing to make the effort.

Under normal circumstances, I'd soon be facing pressure to get married, have children... But nothing here is normal. It's a whole new set of circumstances, a whole new set of rules. And while that means I can choose to remain single, I haven't spent all this time watching TV and listening to current music just so I can sound like a normal American girl when I talk to Rónan and Rory. I'm making the outside world part of me.

"We still have to be very careful here. Even with Rory working with us now, there are still too many people watching us, trying to puzzle out our secrets," he reminds me. As if I don't already have this at the top of my mind. "You're one of the first of us to go out into the world in any significant way. We need this to go as smoothly as possible so that all those who come after you can follow in your footsteps, with a safe path laid out before them. Can you understand that?"

I sigh. I'm not winning this argument, not with our self-designated protector and liaison, and arguing with him is only making things more fraught for both of us. Maybe once he sees me out there he'll realize I really can do this on my own.

"Yes. I suppose... But you'll let me do more on my own, later, after I get established at the studio?"

"Of course, cariad."

I smile, hearing the Welsh term-of-endearment making its way into his speech again. It's good to hear the old merging with the new. It makes me feel a little less like we've lost our history, our culture, no matter how much he wants us to seamlessly integrate here.

"You know I love you dearly. You're like a sister to me. I know you can do this. I know you *want* to do this. And I respect your desire to do it on your own. It's just not prudent to do it that way. Not now. Not yet."

"So, I'm working at the studio five days a week? Am I sweeping and emptying trash bins, or am I actually helping make music?"

"Three days a week to start, when you're needed. Perhaps more if there's a client in residence, rather than just day-rate clients. And you'll be doing whatever they need you to do, which includes helping with the recording sessions. I've made it clear to Steve that I want you trained as any intern would be. And I'm funding the intern position in full, so it behooves him to bend to my wishes in this. But it'll be up to you to prove yourself. If it isn't working, we'll have to pull the plug and start over. So, take this seriously—"

I growl at him. As if there's any world in which I wouldn't be taking this seriously.

"Sorry — I *know* you want this. I *know* you'll take it seriously. But we're in uncharted territory here, and I need you to help me make this work. So much depends on a simple internship and how well you can do in this setting. I can't place anyone else until we know this will work, and I need to get Molly situated. Soon."

Molly. She's only just arrived, and already he wants her out in the world... But she isn't awkward and anxious like I am — the exact opposite, in fact. Everyone loves Molly. Maybe a little too much for her own good, or for their own good, really, considering. But, bottom line, she'd be better at this envoy business than me, if Rónan trusted her enough to send her out into the world. The question is whether he can trust *me* to do this without turning it into an embarrassing disaster.

For a moment, the fear I'm feeling underneath my fake-it-'til-you-make-it bravado bleeds into my eyes, and he, of course, notices it instantly.

"What's wrong?"

"I'm scared, Rónan." In fact, I'm working to rein in the panic that threatens to sweep me away.

"Of what, cariad?"

"People. Outsiders. Our own folk are too much for me at times. How am I going to deal with so many strangers, so many people?"

"You'll learn and adapt," he assures me, tucking an errant strand of dark brown hair behind my ear. "You're one of the smartest amongst us. And you love music."

"Almost more than my life."

"I know. And that's why I picked you for this, to start this integration effort. You have more on the line than just a job, more than how much we're relying on you to do this and do it well — if you excel, it will cement a life for you going forward, doing something you love, where you can share your talents with people who love music as much as you do."

"I know this opportunity is a gift, Rónan. Never think I don't recognize it as such. Even if it's not coming about exactly as I'd like. So, thank you. Truly."

I throw my arms around his waist, giving him a brief hug as he drops a kiss from his 6-foot-3 height to the 5-foot-4 top of my head.

"You're welcome, cariad. Do us proud!"

Chapter 2

No Mermaid

David
Ten months later

"Yo, Davey! You coming up for dinner? Alex is nearly done, and I'm throwing the steaks on the grill, so you know this is going to be good."

Declan has never been short on self-confidence. Some would call him cocky. Some would call him an egotistical asshole. Some would straight-up call him a dick. All of them would be correct. But he's my brother, and I'm kind of used to it at this point. And there's no denying that his charisma and "look at me" vibe has helped get us where we are today.

When we were kids, we vacationed every summer in this little resort town on the Delaware coast, Mystic Beach. We've come a long way in the last fifteen years. From a pair of teenage guitar players and singers just screwing around to the lead singer and bass player of a band with three multi-platinum albums and a handful of singles that have hit the top of the charts.

We kind of owe it to this place — Mystic Beach — because the nucleus of aMUSEd was formed on the beach right here, when we were 15 and 16 and the two of us ran into a local guy, Hunter Graves, who was playing a Beatles tune on the beach and drawing a crowd. Declan started singing along, with me on harmonies, and the next thing we knew, we had a band. We busked with Hunter all summer, until it was time for the two of us to go back home to Northern Virginia for our junior years of high school.

Declan and I aren't twins, even though we ended up in the same grade. I'm actually a full year older than he is. But I had some problems with keeping focused on school assignments when I was a kid. Kept going off and reading things that weren't assigned, not doing what *was* assigned because it was boring, doing homework during class because what the teacher was saying wasn't keeping my brain busy, refusing to work in a group, doing things outside the rules and parameters because my way made more sense to me.

They eventually told my parents I was on the autism spectrum, but the immediate result was that I got held back a year. It's kind of weird, since I'm the "brain" in the family, but I guess I fit that "Aspie" diagnosis. Once I realized the consequences of doing things my own way, I went to great lengths to ensure I went by the rules — in school and otherwise. Straight A student ever since — just me, my books and my guitar filling up most of my time. And I'd already started writing songs and learning bass guitar at the point when we ran into Hunter.

It was synergy. He was a tremendously talented guitar player, singer and songwriter, and we had my bass grooves to underpin what he was doing and my diva of a brother to tie a ribbon on the whole package with what I have to admit — reluctantly — are some of the best rock vocals most people have ever heard. Like I said, Declan's a dick. I know that better than anyone, since his quiet, oddball elder brother was the one he always ran roughshod over, ever since we ended up in the same grade. But he's a brilliant vocalist and frontman. He takes to the stage like it's where he was born to be. Always has. And it's a big part of what's made us as successful as we are today. So the other four guys and I all put up with a lot of crap from him that no one else would. And then we take him back down a few pegs as needed. Which is often. But he does make a good steak. That I have to admit, too.

"I'll be up in a few!" I yell back at him from my spot on the sand in front of the enormous beach house/recording studio where we've come for the summer to write, test and record the music for our fourth album. It's a relatively new studio, a somewhat new concept — a studio designed to offer a band a quiet vacation spot where they'll largely be left alone by fans and the media, and where they can use the state-of-the-art facilities to produce albums that'll soar up the charts. The other guys settled in inside the house when we got here. And now Declan's grilling out on the beachfront deck.

Me — I dropped my bags in my room and walked straight out the sliding glass door, onto the upper deck and right down the stairs, for some long-overdue time chilling on the beach. It's the one place I can totally relax. When I'm watching the ocean, or even just listening to it, my brain finally stops running in circles, fixating on things. I stop the little "stimming" behaviors that the guys don't really notice anymore, like running through bass lines in my head, tapping my fingers on my legs or the table, in place of my bass guitar. I've tapped on my legs or desk since I was little. Now it's bass lines. Declan calls me out sometimes if I'm tapping too loud, but all I can do is try to be quieter. It usually works. These little quirks of mine, they're things other people wouldn't notice in the first place, since they don't see me for long except when I'm playing music — the only other thing that quiets everything down, drowns out the noise of the world.

Vacation time means surfing time for me. My board's sitting under the deck, along with a standup paddleboard and a skimboard. And this stretch of private beach means I can go out whenever the conditions are right and not have to worry about competing for waves or having to sign autographs. Even better, the section of beach to the south of us is also private beach, for some kind of gated residential community, and the beach to the north is the far end of the state park beach — a hefty hike for anyone parking in the public parking lot. So I've been sitting here alone since we got here hours ago. Haven't seen a soul. Just some footprints farther down the beach and some seal tracks from the juveniles hauling out for a rest during their migration.

I hope I can see some of them while we're here. After music, that's my other passion — marine science. If Declan hadn't decided to skip college so we could go all-in with the band after high school, I'd probably be working on my master's in marine science right now. I'd at least have a bachelor's degree in it. Our parents still aren't thrilled about how that came to pass, despite all the objective success we've had as a band because of it. Declan had declared that if Hunter wasn't going to college, why should Declan or I? A delay would only reduce our chances at making it big. Mom and Dad weren't happy. They were even less happy when I decided I agreed with him, rejecting their plans for me and coloring outside the lines for the first time since I was little. So, no — neither of us went to college. But we each make more in a year than a high-powered attorney or a surgeon would, so Mom and Dad mostly got over it. Mostly. And now...

No one knows. I've never even told Declan or any of the other guys. But I've been taking classes online to get that bachelor's degree I missed. I do lab classes during our breaks from touring and recording, and when Declan's out partying while we're on tour, I'm writing term papers and taking tests. Who knows — maybe when we've reached the point where we don't want to tour so much anymore, I'll find a job at UD's marine science lab just north of here and spend my days studying horseshoe crabs, tidal flow, dolphins or seals, or maybe aquaculture or something.

I shade my eyes from the dwindling light as sunset nears and peer out over the ocean. Ah... there she is... My elusive quarry. Phoca vitulina. Big eyes, mottled silvery-brown hair, round head, just peeking up over the swells. Harbor seal. Judging by the size, a young adult female. No pup with her, as it would likely be at this time of year if she had one. I sit quietly, watching, hoping that she'll haul out for a rest so I can get a better look without getting closer than legally allowed.

"David! I'm going to give Rhys your fucking perfectly-cooked steak if you don't get up here and eat it!"

She dips under the water, apparently startled by my brother's booming voice. And who can blame her?

"Keep your pants on!" I yell back at him.

"Women beg me to take them off!" he retorts. "And more than a few men, too!"

If eyerolls were audible, mine would match his bellowing in volume.

"Coming, asshole!" I yell back at him. No point in waiting for her to show herself again. Declan's frightened her off. But maybe she'll come back once the sun goes down.

"You find yourself a mermaid out there?"

Our keyboard player, Alex, is notoriously preoccupied with our relationships and sex lives. I differentiate because most of us have the latter and not the former. Alex had a girl. She dumped him before we made it big, and that seems to have spurred this fixation with what the rest of us are getting up to.

Declan had a girl the last summer we were here, when he was 17. He fucked that up on a Declan-sized scale, and he hasn't even tried since. Just one never-ending stream of groupies. Alex sometimes hooks up with a girl for a couple weeks, but nothing less and nothing that's lasted longer than that. Rhys is known for finding friendly waitresses on the road who can't resist that vibrant drummer personality. Kier, our lead guitarist, was Rhys' wingman in finding the nice girls for one-night stands along the way, but he's kind of soured on that. Hunter's been simultaneously dating a handful of models and influencers, though my theory is he's only doing that to avoid even the semblance of getting serious with anyone. Which brings us to me.

Early on, I'd been waiting to run into someone who'd just have that spark — that connection that I couldn't resist. While I wasn't in Alex's league, I was a bit of a romantic, I admit. But I never found anyone I connected with like that. I have a hard enough time making friends beyond my bandmates. After a while, I gave up. Maybe Declan and I do have something in common besides music and some DNA.

These days, when I'm not studying, I occasionally find a nice girl among the groupies. It's rare enough that the guys have... yeah — basically concluded that I'm in search of a unicorn, or a mermaid, or some other equally unlikely creature, the pursuit of which will inevitably be fruitless. But, barring that kind of magical connection, the truth is that a relationship just isn't at the top of my list of priorities. My bandmates just don't get that.

"You guys didn't see her? Ravishing! Silky hair, big soulful eyes, and a pair of gorgeous... flippers!"

It's the only way to get them — Alex especially — off my ass on the subject.

"No way! This I've got to see! Does she have a friend she can introduce me to? Preferably a blonde?"

There are times when I can't tell whether Rhys is being serious or not. I don't always read other people well, but I'm not alone in my questioning, because the rest of the guys are just staring at Rhys now, too. Well, except Hunter, who bailed on us to go have dinner with his best friend, who still lives here in Mystic Beach.

"What? Are you guys telling me you wouldn't love to check off 'mermaid' on your list of girls you've been with? Mom took me to Florida once when I was little, and on the way to Disney World we stopped to see the mermaids. It was awesome! They had them living in this big tank, like Sea World, but with mermaids instead of dolphins."

I'm trying to decide whether to break it to Rhys that those aren't real mermaids.

"I was kidding, Rhys. No mermaids on the beach here. Just a seal swimming offshore."

"Aw, man..." he whines, clearly disappointed.

"Ma used to tell us stories of the merrows — Irish mermaids," Kier puts in, his accent kicking up a notch from its usual lilt, as it does whenever he talks about home, though I don't think he's been back in more than a decade other than our couple of tour stops in Dublin. "She said they sometimes lured young men into the sea, where they'd stay, enchanted, until the end of their days. She said the merrows that fell in love with men on land sometimes stayed for a while and even had families with humans, but they almost always succumbed to the call of the sea, leaving their human families behind to go back with their people. Tragic. Moral of the story: Don't fall for a mermaid."

"Oh," Rhys says. "I never thought about that. And it would be hard to tour if I was living underwater."

There's silence for a minute.

"Very true, Rhys. You hadn't better meet any more mermaids, then. Just to be safe."

"Sounds like a plan."

The rest of us are trying not to snicker, with varying degrees of success. Rhys is odd, a little erratic, even. But he's an amazing drummer and a vital part of our little band of brothers.

"Studio tomorrow morning?" Alex asks.

Declan and I exchange a look. We're not even close to ready to start working on songs yet. The well has been a little dry after the first three songs we managed to pull together while on tour. I was hoping for at least a week off before we buckled down on the songwriting.

"Let's give it a couple days, man," Declan says. "I want to work on a couple more sets of lyrics before we drag you all into the studio for anything more than rehearsing the first three. Enjoy the time off, chill."

"Now *that* sounds like a plan," I say. "I need more beach time to feed my muse. Great steak, Dec," I admit. "And that corn could have come straight off that farm truck that used to drive through the neighborhood every morning, back before farmers' markets were all the rage."

"They left us a bunch of fresh produce when they stocked the kitchen," Alex says, his inner chef clearly pleased with the options that were provided. "I love having local produce to work with. The spinach, tomatoes and cucumbers for the salad were marked as local, too. And there's strawberries and blueberries for dessert, cantaloupe for breakfast."

"Don't even mention breakfast," Declan retorts. "I'm sleeping until noon."

"And on that note... I'll see you all in the morning," I say, excusing myself for more seal-watching. I hope.

CHAPTER 3

SEALS

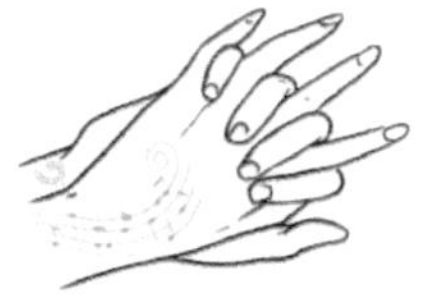

David

I remain irked at Declan. I've been sitting here on the crest of the beach for an hour, and no sign of any seals. I'm going to have to pack it in soon so I can get up early to surf, if the waves cooperate. We'll take a few more days before we start working on new material, but we have to start rehearsing the three songs we already have written. In a few days, we've got our first incognito gig to try them out on an audience.

The sky is completely dark now, the only light coming from inside the house and a near-full moon hovering over the horizon and its reflection on the calm sea. It's peaceful, and I let that peace flow over me, washing away my irritation with Declan and my frustration at not getting my seal sighting.

Just then I spot movement out of the corner of my eye, but it's too quick for me to make sense of it. The beach to the south is private, and not part of our private beach, but I can't resist trying to get another look. I crouch down behind the dune grass and creep slowly toward the movement. I don't want to startle it if it's a seal. There's a flash of movement, but it's not a seal lumbering across the sand.

It's been a little while since I've seen one, but I know what the back side of a naked girl looks like, even though I've never had one run away from me like this one is. I can make out the pale soles of her feet, the soft flash of skin across the curves of her bare back, a dark swath of hair interrupting the pale planes of her shoulders.

Actually, I'm not sure she's running away from me so much as running for the water. There's an arc of light as she dives into the face of an oncoming wave, and she disappears from view, all those curves now hidden below the surface of the ocean. I wait for her to resurface so I can get a better look at my unexpected beachside companion. But there's no sign of her. None. It's like she's disappeared. Maybe she's an exceptional swimmer and she's gone so far out in one dive that I don't see her re-emerge, or maybe she headed straight south and she's beyond my view. Or maybe she hit her head when she dove in and she's now unconscious under the waves.

That's enough to pull me from my spot amongst the beach grasses, and I run straight for the spot where I saw her dive in, stripping my shirt off and ready to go in after her. Trying to find a potential drowning victim in the ocean at night, even with a nearly full moon lighting the water, is a challenge. I need to at least have some idea where she might be. I scan the water, looking for any sign of a human, and there's nothing. Did I imagine it? Has it been so long since I've had a naked girl in front of me that my mind is creating them out of moonlight reflecting on the sand?

There's a flash of movement behind the breakers now, and I approach the oncoming wave, ready to dive in, only to realize that it's not a human, drowning or otherwise. It looks like the same young seal I saw before dinner, only she's looking back at me now, curious about the human intruding on her world. She keeps me in her view even as the swells bob up and down with her upon them, and it's just the two of us, staring at each other across the water, each of us caught up in our curiosity.

She doesn't swim away, or even put more distance between us, even though I'm now standing just meters away from where she floats upright in the water. Her comfort in her natural environment is clear, and curiosity about me seems to be holding her in place. She shows no fear, no sign she's ready to flee, and for a full minute we just watch each other across the waves. I find my feet moving me forward into the waist-deep breakwater, even though I know better than to approach a protected species this close, especially if I might drive her off from a needed rest. I just find myself there, without thought. And still she just watches me, waiting to see what I'll do.

And in this moment, I can't say what that will be. Instinct wars with intellect, my love of the ocean and its inhabitants with the scientist's knowledge that I shouldn't be doing this. My left foot takes another step forward as I'm buffeted by the waves. This is the point of commitment — either I move forward through the breaking waves or I back up to keep myself from getting smashed underneath. There's something so compelling about her as she watches me so carefully with those big, soulful eyes, and intellect is losing the battle with instinct.

Suddenly, there's a flash of light across the water in front of me. I turn to see the source, and it snaps both of us out of our fascination. The seal dives under the water and I find myself staring into a flashlight beam being pointed at me by a short, stout man who looks to be in his mid-50s, wearing what would appear to be a security uniform.

"This is private property, sir!" he says loudly to be heard over the breakers. "You'll have to come back out of the water and go back onto the public beach if you want to swim, though it's too dark now to be safe, especially without a lifeguard on duty."

His expression conveys that it's more than a recommendation focused on my safety. I'm trespassing, and we both know it, even if I had a good reason.

"Sorry — I thought I saw someone go into the water down here and not come up again. I was concerned a swimmer had gotten into trouble."

"There's no swimmers out here tonight, not on this stretch of beach. We keep track of the community's residents when they come out on the beach, and there's no one here for you to be concerned with, sir."

"Are you sure? I could have sworn..."

"Yes, I'm sure. The only living creature I've seen out here tonight is you."

"There was a seal."

"Well, maybe what you saw was a seal. But if it was, you were risking breaking the law if you were going in after it. On top of the trespassing."

He's got an eyebrow raised at me, making his meaning clear. He wants me off his beach.

"Got it. Sorry to have intruded. I'll go back where I'm supposed to be."

I snatch my shirt off the sand and start walking back to the north, the security guard watching me until after I've cleared the line of dune grass between the two sections of beach. He waits until I'm another fifty feet up the beach, in front of the studio house, before he turns and heads back the other way. I glance out at the water and see a pair of eyes looking back at me. No girl. Just a seal. There's another moment of compelling eye-contact between us, and then she dives back into the water, moving away from the shore with a splash of her flippers and disappearing below the surface.

That was... that whole thing was... odd.

CHAPTER 4

MY SPINE (IS THE BASS LINE)

David
Three days later

Is it weird that I'm a little nervous about playing at a place called the Pirate's Cove Bar & Restaurant? I'm used to playing before crowds of twenty thousand or more. That's what we've been doing for the last handful of years. It's been probably seven or eight years since we last played at a place where the capacity was less than 500 people total.

But we're set to debut three new aMUSEd songs tonight, incognito, at this little local bar. It's just a few blocks north on the bay side of the highway — which, like the ocean side where the studio sits, is just a block wide from water to roadway. And for some reason, in this tiny little bar, I'm nervous. Maybe it's trying out the new songs on an audience.

I'm skeptical that we can even pull off this planned series of incognito performances, especially when Declan told them to put us on the marquee as "Rock & Grohl" tonight. If we're lucky, we'll only end up with a handful of Foo Fighters fans here tonight hoping that that other Dave has taken a break from his family vacation to appear at this little dock bar. Hopefully, that'll mean they won't think to connect this unknown band to aMUSEd, even with Declan's distinctive voice. They'll have to work to puzzle it out if they do, though, because we're only doing covers and those three new original songs tonight. No hits, no deep cuts.

I hope that keeps us incognito, because we've got no security tonight beyond the usual venue security. It's a low-key show — no roadies to load in and set up for us, no high-paid touring engineer to handle our sound on the house system. No monitor engineer to keep the sound in our in-ear monitors balanced so we can hear each other and ourselves while we're performing. We're doing load-in and load-out ourselves, and the house engineer — whoever he is — is going to be in charge of what we sound like to the audience and ourselves. All without a clue that he's running sound for one of the most popular rock bands on the planet. So, fingers crossed...

Hunter's friend Brighid, who moved back here after college, has been toting our gear over from the studio in her car — the same one she used to help us tote gear in back when this was a normal size of venue for us. It's a blast from the past. She's a sweet girl and dotes on Hunter, and Hunter's missed her while our meteoritic rise has kept him from spending much time with her at all for several years now. That's half the reason we ended up here for this working vacation, I think.

And now I'm doing something I haven't had to do in years — setting up my own gear. My three Spector basses, amp and multi-effects pedal. It's a lot less to set up than Rhys' massive drum kit or Alex's keyboard "cockpit," which they're in the middle of setting up now. Brighid and Hunter have gone back for Kieran and his "guitarsenal" of Fenders.

"Yo, Davey — you sure I can't talk you into voting for my song?"

Did I mention that Rhys is... odd? We call him "The Madman" because he's crazy good on his drum kit. But he's kind of an oddball, too. And he's back on his idea of a six-minute drum solo going into our setlist and onto the album. We've been saying no to him since he joined the band. We love him, but not enough to subject our fans to that.

"Not happening, Rhys!"

"Come on, man! It'll be awesome!"

"Maybe next time, Rhys. Gotta set up my gear right now."

I tune out whatever else he's saying. It's often the best policy when he gets onto something like this. I adjust my mic, which is farther back on the stage than I wanted tonight. Declan usually owns the front of the stage during our shows. Hunter and Kieran take the sides, with Alex behind Hunter, and me between Rhys' kit, Hunter and Declan's center-stage spot. But we're mixing it up a little for these gigs, sharing lead vocals on some of the covers.

I get my basses set up on their triple stand, tuned and ready to go. My effects processor can do the same job as a massive amount of conventional pedals and modeling amps, and it's been my go-to for a while now. Much less cumbersome than individual pedals attached to a board, and one tap of my bare foot gives me whatever tone I need. But once I've got it set up, I turn around and discover that the mic stand has been moved back where it was. Maybe Rhys is screwing with me because I'm not on board with his "song." He's over at the bar now. I shake my head, move the mic back where I wanted it. Then I adjust my amp, set out my in-ears.

And the mic stand has moved itself back again. I glare at Rhys, who's hard to miss at 6-foot-4 but has some serious catlike reflexes from all of his adrenaline-junkie sports. He shrugs at me. I shake my head and grab the stand again.

"Don't touch that."

I look around for whoever said that, but I can't see anyone. My imagination is clearly running wild. Either that or Rhys has learned to throw his voice. Which I wouldn't put past him. I reach for it again.

"I said — don't touch that."

The voice is coming from behind Alex's keyboard stand and I peer under there to see who's messing with me.

A head of long, dark hair pops up from behind the keyboards, thrown back out of a delicate pixie face full of gentle curves that's wearing an expression so imperious that I instantly feel chastised, even though this girl is a good half-foot shorter than me.

She climbs out from behind the keyboard rack and moves to stand directly in front of me, turning and standing so close that her back is almost touching my chest, and my breath staggers as I catch a whiff of a sweet sea-air smell that has to be her shampoo.

"See that line array there?" she asks, nodding toward the side of the stage.

"What?" I'm still entranced with her scent and the silky dark hair that reaches to the middle of her back.

"Line array," she repeats and sighs, clearly disappointed in me. "The speaker thingy," she explains, like she's talking to a 4-year-old, grabbing my hand and using her own to point it for me. "Several speakers arranged in a line, actually. Hence, line array."

"Yeah..." And now I'm caught up in the feel of her hand on mine. There's almost a hum of energy to it, until she releases me. I shake my head to clear my mind, because she's still talking to me.

"Do you like feedback?" she asks.

"Personally or sonically?"

"I'll save my personal feedback for later. I mean the screechy, ear-splitting kind."

"Of course not."

"Then don't touch that mic. Any farther forward and it'll catch some of the signal from the line array, and you and everyone in the audience will be holding your hands over your ears and cringing, and you'll be looking at me to fix it, which I'll do, but it'll look unprofessional — for you and for me." Her eyes flash. "And I am a professional, so let's just skip the eardrum-stabbing portion of tonight's show and go straight to you leaving the mic stand where I put it. OK?"

"OK."

"Thank you."

She climbs back behind the keyboard rack again. And I'm standing where she left me, my mouth open and all the blood in my body racing straight to my dick.

"What was that?" Rhys asks as he walks back up from the bar.

"I'm not entirely sure. But it was fucking hot."

CHAPTER 5

LOVE IS A BATTLEFIELD

Piper
A few minutes earlier

He's moved the mic stand. I take a deep breath to try to calm my pulse, which is racing at the idea that I'll have to talk to these guys and try to get them to respect my expertise with this stage and sound system.

This has been the biggest challenge of this job for me. Not learning to run live sound, beyond what I've already learned for the studio, but trying to get the musicians to listen to what I tell them about what will make them sound the best here. And doing it without having an anxiety attack that will leave me curled up in a ball on the floor.

After six months working in the studio, I took a chance and sent my résumé in to the Pirate's Cove, hoping they might take me on as a backup for their house engineer. A month ago, they'd called in a panic. Their engineer had moved to L.A. with his band, with no notice, and they needed somebody to run sound that night. I had several hours to learn their system and refresh my mind on what I knew about live sound before helping the band with setup and soundcheck.

It had gone surprisingly well. The band wasn't wild at first about letting "a girl" be in charge of their sound, but they didn't have much choice unless they wanted to run it themselves from the stage, and that never turns out well, since stage sound is a million miles away from what the audience hears. Ten minutes in, the lead singer left the stage during a guitar solo and came out to stand next to me in the middle of the room, listened for a moment, nodded his head at me and went back to the stage. And that was that.

It wasn't the last time that happened. Standing in the middle of the deck with my iPad nearly a dozen times in the last month, I'd been marveled at by the acts, backseat-engineered by random musicians in the audience, and told countless times that I was the first female engineer that person had ever seen. Often with an expression that said my novel profession and gender combination were virtually a fetish for the guy in question. No thank you.

Between that and the bands that just couldn't see how a female engineer could handle running sound for them, I've had to learn to be more assertive and to shift my anxiety-fueled flight response to instead glue my feet to the floor so I can stand my ground. That doesn't mean I'm not feeling the anxiety. But I'm learning to work around it.

So these guys — Rock & Grohl? Really? — messing with my mic setup is a familiar problem, but one that still has me in a state of near panic. Rónan wouldn't have approved of me taking this job, outside the safe confines of a business he had influence over, but he's gone now, and I'm on my own here, making decisions without my safety net. Rory and some of the elders are dealing with the money and legal issues and the other things Rónan had done before he'd sacrificed himself for us... for everyone, really. So I'm mostly on my own. I shake my head and push my grief from my mind, and resolve to instead draw on the strength and self-confidence that Rónan had always demonstrated.

I've already moved the mic stand back to its place twice. But this guy just won't take the hint.

"Don't touch that!" I finally tell him from the spot under the keyboards where I'm plugging them into the cable snake that runs all the signal to the mixing board. He's not taking the hint, so I explain painfully simply why the mic can't be moved forward.

My pulse is already pounding from anxiety over confronting him. But standing up close to him to point him at the line array brings me within the range of his distinctly male scent —

stronger than I'm used to, but normal for one of his folk. It's tinged with saltwater, like he's been in the ocean today.

I have to steady myself and focus on my job. I'm probably more terse with him than I have to be, but it's a layer of distance between us that I need. And even more so once our skin touches as I point his hand at the line array. There's an energy in the sensation, an almost electric hum. I drop his hand as soon as I realize I'm still holding on to it and duck away back behind the keyboards to finish the job.

I sneak peeks at him from below the keyboard rack. He's objectively attractive. Shortish brown hair with natural sun-bleached highlights, blue eyes the color of a winter morning sky, a surfer's body and, oddly, his feet are bare. I haven't seen a musician play a gig barefoot before. It's... intriguing. There's a quiet, restrained intensity to him that's a sharp contrast to his drummer friend, who practically vibrates just standing casually at the bar.

No, this one feels like the ocean on a calm day when the currents are running high. A hidden rip current that could carry a person out miles in minutes. Not that I've ever had to worry about that. But there's a depth and an edge to him under the surface that reminds me of the risk posed by such conditions. I'm wary of him now. And only more so since we've touched. I'm not sure what got into me that I did it, but it was done now and I was warned.

I can feel his eyes on me still, and my cheeks flame in embarrassment. But I was right about the mic, and I stand by it as a professional, even if I haven't been one for very long.

I stand up again, now that the keyboards are sorted.

"Hi — I should have introduced myself earlier. I'm Alex," the keyboard player says. He's taller than the bass player by a few inches, with his deep black hair in a long shaggy cut around his face, his watercolor-blue eyes outlined in black, rings on most of his fingers and heavy cuff bracelets on each wrist.

"Piper — I'm the house engineer. If you need anything special, let me know."

"Shouldn't be much. We've been playing out for a while," he says.

"First time here, though?"

"Yeah. We're doing a working vacation and decided to try someplace new. I take it you haven't been here long, either?"

"No. I stepped in on short notice a month or so ago, but I've learned this system like the back of my hand, tweaked a few things, so whatever you need, I'll make it happen."

"Awesome! We've got our in-ears, so no need for wedges."

"A band after my own heart."

"I know — a lot less hassle."

"And better for your ears as musicians."

He gives me a nod of respect. It's still not standard practice for musicians to take care of their hearing, especially ones that play on this kind of scale. The longer they've played with monitor wedges and the more concerts they've attended themselves, the worse their hearing tends to be — especially in the range of their own instruments, since that's usually what they boost. I'm unusual as an engineer in that I work with earplugs in — pro-quality ones that ensure I'm still hearing the mix accurately, just not as loud, with a slight customization to accommodate some small differences in my hearing range. My ears are my living, so I take protecting them seriously. And a good set of in-ears, properly balanced, will save a musician's hearing.

"That's David, our bass player, and Rhys, our drummer. Hunter, our rhythm guitar player, was here earlier..."

"With the blonde girl?"

"Yeah, his friend Brighid. She lives here, has a shop in town. She's helping us out with hauling our equipment today. They'll be back with Kieran, our lead guitarist, and Declan, our lead singer. He's David's brother, and a bit of a diva, to be honest. Just to warn you in advance. Don't take Declan too seriously. He takes himself seriously enough for everyone."

I smile back at him. Alex seems pretty laid-back. It sets me at ease, which I desperately need after the tension of interacting with the bass player. David. His name is David. I sneak a peek back at him and find that he's watching me interacting with Alex, his pale blue eyes unmistakable in their focus. I slip on my sunglasses, eager to hide my own gaze. Somehow, there's something familiar about him. He *feels* familiar.

I shake myself free of that thought and go back to my work, confirming the proper routing of Alex's keyboards into the snake, and then the mics on Rhys' drum kit into the drum drop. I grab a mic to put on Hunter's amp, which is my usual preference for guitars, rather than running directly into the mix. David's clearly still watching me.

"He prefers his amp mic'd, if that's what you're wondering," he tells me. "Direct is too dry for him. I run directly into my Helix, then the Helix into the board and back into the amp. That goes for Kier, too. So you'll just need to mic-up Hunter's amp."

"Got it. Thanks." I give him a shy smile, genuinely appreciative.

"**M**ore of my vocal in my monitor mix, sweetheart! Nope — too much. Back it off a bit. That's almost got it. Close enough, I guess... A little less lead guitar, though. And back off Davey's mic. I've heard enough of my brother to last me a lifetime..."

Alex was right. This Declan guy is kind of a jerk. I've dealt with formal manners and drunken heathens and everything in between, but I'm not entirely sure what to make of his blend of suave self-assurance and cocky dismissiveness. If anything, he reminds me of one of our young men when he's trying to prove himself in front of some girls. He knows he's good. He's just not sure everyone else recognizes it, and he desperately needs them to. Maybe when these guys have had some more shows under their belts he'll settle into his confidence.

"That's enough, Dec! She's a pro, not your personal audio lackey. Your mix is fine and you know it. Stop busting her balls."

I can't put a name to David's expression as he chastises his brother. Irritated, certainly. Protective? Maybe. I don't like it. It reminds me of Rónan, which makes me chafe under the weight of my newfound independence and also makes me sad. But would David stand up to Declan for a male engineer? Experience has told me he likely wouldn't.

"If she had balls, maybe my mix would be better..." I hear Declan mutter, his voice amplified in my headphones as I tailor his monitor mix as requested.

So Declan's being a jerk because I'm a girl, and his brother is giving me special treatment because I'm a girl. Why can't they just treat me like the pro I am?

"How's that?" I call back at the singer. Declan pauses to listen, does a quick vocal run, and then nods sharply at me. High expectations met.

I glance back at David, challenge in my eyes, hoping he'll get the message that I don't need him to stand up for me. The protectiveness doesn't leave his expression, and I'm doubly irritated to see a little bit of hurt in his eyes.

He clearly doesn't get it. I have to fight for every morsel of respect I can get in this job, because a lot of the bands won't give me the same benefit of the doubt they would a male engineer. I've already lost valuable experience in the studio because Steve won't let me work with some of the acts recording there.

"You'll have to work with the more veteran musicians," he'd told me on my first day. "I can't have you working with the younger bands, because they won't be able to keep their minds on the music if there's a girl in the room."

Nevermind that that attitude punishes me for guys' inability to treat me like a professional, or even just a fellow human, when it's no fault of my own. And nevermind that there's no reason to assume that an older male musician won't be distracted even more than a younger one. It's insulting to everyone involved. But I knew when I decided to pursue this career that it's one still mired in sexism. I just expected better from Steve, since Rónan had vetted the position.

Not that I ever told him what Steve had said. Then, as now, I knew I had to be the one to deal with the pitfalls of my work. Having David jump in now makes me look weak, and I know all too well that those who look weak are the first to be targeted.

I break eye contact with him and double-check the virtual mixing board on my tablet. I've already balanced the system with Steely Dan's "Deacon Blues," — from an album notorious for being so precisely engineered in the studio that it's perfect for balancing a sound system. And now everything is all set, with two hours to go before they start. I lock the physical mixing board to prevent tampering and toggle the audio system back to the house mix of classic and contemporary rock.

Alex said they'll be doing mostly covers tonight, and I'm hoping my extensive listening to a wide variety of rock will ensure I'm on top of the mix, even though I'm not familiar with this band. I've got five vocalists to keep on top of, since Kier is apparently the only one who doesn't at least sing backup. It requires quick adjustments to ensure the lead vocals and background vocals are appropriately balanced from one song to the next. And even with an unfamiliar cover band, it helps if you know what the original song is supposed to sound like.

And as the band breaks for dinner, I'm as ready for this as I'm going to get. From here on, it's all flying by the seat of my pants. Every gig is a rush from start to finish, adapting on the fly and dealing with the unexpected. At least I know I won't be dealing with unwelcome feedback. Of the sonic variety, anyway. With Declan in play, there's no telling what other kind of feedback I'll be getting tonight.

I've got nearly two hours before I need to be back for the band's set. Dealing with their lead singer has put me back on edge, and sitting around the bar for two hours with basically nothing to do is only going to encourage my anxiety. Dealing with strangers trying to make conversation, men looking to pick me up... And David the bass player, who keeps glancing over at me, which is less unwelcome than I'd like to admit. I need to burn off some nervous energy, and I can think of only one surefire way to do that.

It's a quick walk back home, and I make a quick change into a swimsuit in my room before heading out on the beach. The waves are up today, and I relish the adrenaline rush of getting out past the breakers, keeping an eye out on the horizon for larger sets that I'll have to duck under if I don't want to be rolled back onto the beach in a wash of sand.

Out in the swells, I let my feet lift up and I float on my back, gazing up at the sky, where clouds race across a cerulean backdrop. The adrenaline rush is wearing off, and it leaves me calmer than before. Swimming in the sea always relaxes me, and it's become my default way of dealing with my anxiety at the end of the day, and sometimes in the middle of the day, like today.

I'm a strong swimmer, never a concern about getting in trouble, even when the sea is rough, and I read waves like most people read faerie stories in their native language. Short of running into a large and hungry shark, I'm as comfortable in the ocean as I am in my own bed, and I can close my eyes to cement that feeling of relaxation without fear of the unseen.

Until something bumps against my leg.

I go upright and take a few strokes toward shore, ready to seek the safety of dry land should there, in fact, be a hungry shark looking to taste-test Piper as a possible appetizer. (I'm not big enough to be an entree for any shark large enough to consider me part of the menu.)

"Piper... Looking yummy..." I hear a voice drawl behind me. My hard-earned calm flees in an instant.

"Go away, Ramsay." I turn to face him, not trusting him at my back, no matter how comfortable I am in these waters. A half-starved great white would be a preferable swimming companion.

"Feisty little Piper showing her teeth. I think we can find you something better to do with your mouth, little one."

Ew.

"Your overtures have been rejected, Ramsey, and you've been told to leave me alone. Don't make me go to the Elders for sanctions. I know you favor those outmoded ways, but my honor price is high, and I don't think you've got enough to make recompense for the insult."

"Oooh... She's going to sic her daddy on me! Oops — I mean her foster-brother... No — wait! It won't be him now, will it? Maybe it'll be that cute blonde girlfriend of his with all the curves. Now, that's a punishment I could look forward to..."

He leers at me, and I can't help but shudder at the threat he's making against Rory, who can defend herself better than I can, but is nowhere near as much of a force as Rónan was.

"What do you think, boys?" Ramsay asks, relaxing his posture to float leisurely on his back. "Should I risk little Piper's wrath and give her enough 'insult' to make her scream my name?" He rubs his hand over his crotch, making his meaning clear, and I spin around, looking for his friends, who I now realize must be in the water nearby.

There's a brush against my arm below the surface, and Stewart's coal-black hair rises from the water, his predatory grin enough to send chills down my spine. A hand brushes across my thigh, and I spin to find Wylie's nearly colorless grey eyes inches from my own. I backpedal in surprise and bump into Stewart's chest, nowhere left to go.

My thumb goes reflexively to the ring on my right hand, running over the etched surface with its pattern of breaking ocean waves, and Rónan's image floods into my mind, giving me a feeling of calm and strength. I take a deep breath and send that calm from my center outward down my limbs.

"You three are here under forbearance. Safe Harbour will not welcome bullies, nor those who refuse to adapt to changing ways in our new home." Ramsay scoffs. "I do not belong to you, Ramsay MacAulay, and I will never belong to you. Your refusal to accept that marks you as weak and ill-suited to survive here, in this new place. I would suggest you adjust to changed circumstances or find another place for yourself, preferably on the other side of the ocean."

Ramsay's dogs move away as he approaches me, circling in an ever-tightening spiral. I stand my ground, or what passes for ground out here in the ocean swells. Ramsay may be used to weak-willed women, but I know well that the weak are the first ones the predators pick off, and I will not show myself to be weak in the face of this threat. I am Piper, foster-sister to Rónan MacMurchadha, savior of Safe Harbour, and I will not be cowed by one of Ramsay's ilk. The bravado seems to pay off. Ramsay looks uncertain for a moment, like maybe he's thinking twice about harassing me like this, wondering if I still hold enough sway here to ensure he is punished. But in the end, his determination seems to hold the edge over his uncertainty.

"You were promised to me, Piper, daughter of MacGilleMhoir. And that's a promise I will collect upon. Best *you* adapt to *that*. It is inevitable, and I have a long, long time to make sure of that. It will go better for you if you find a way to accommodate me. If you fight me..." A predatory grin eclipsing even Stewart's spreads across Ramsay's face. "Let's just say I'll look forward to that, too."

Ramsay drops below the surface of the water and disappears, his companions following in his wake. I close my eyes again — this time not in peaceful relaxation but with a sinking feeling that Ramsay isn't anywhere close to giving up on his supposed claim on me, which is as much a relic of the past as any family ties I held beyond those formed with Rónan.

But I hold the upper hand now, in this new place, this new order of things. And if Ramsay can't be persuaded to back off, I won't hesitate to play that hand to his severe detriment.

My thumb falls again to my ring, rubbing over the engraving in a gesture that soothes me once more. I tip forward and sink into the oncoming swell, my hair trailing out behind me as I stroke quickly through the water, making my way as far out from the beach as I dare right now. When I return to land, my calm is restored, and I'm ready to make Rock & Grohl sound like they could top the charts.

CHAPTER 6

YOU KNOW ME

David

Piper. Her name is Piper. It fits. She reminds me of the little piping plovers that dart along the shoreline here in the spring. Rare — a threatened species, actually — and almost delicate, with pale, tawny coloring that could make them seem plain if you didn't take into account their tremendous energy, and their ability to start and stop on a dime. Stealthy and subtle, but determined, like the girl who moved my mic stand without me even detecting her presence.

I know Alex warned her about Declan, but he's being even more of a dick than usual tonight. If I didn't know better, I'd wonder if it was nerves.

But Piper gets the mix perfected for us in just a song or two, even tailoring Declan's monitor mix to his satisfaction. Mine's as good as it is on the road with our regular monitor engineer, despite the fact that she's also handling front-of-house. It's impressive, especially given how young she is and that she's only been running sound here for a month. Yes, I was eavesdropping on her conversation with Alex. Do you blame me? I've talked to her once and I'm already fascinated.

I'm trying to think of an excuse to go talk to her, but she got us dialed in so fast that I can't even ask her to tweak something without seeming like as big of an asshole as my brother.

I don't usually have to approach girls — they're all too eager to latch onto me. Sometimes it's to get to Declan, mind you, but I have my own admirers, most of whom are happy to spend an hour or a night with the bass player or try to get below the surface of "the quiet one." And, after more than a decade of playing out, I have yet to meet a girl I wanted to spend more time with than that. On top of it, I'm both too private and too awkward to even feel comfortable with the ones who want that peek below that tranquil surface. I had a couple girls who tried, and tried too hard. It all but sent me running for security. So me trying to approach a girl... It's nerve-wracking.

And this girl... she's beautiful. And ballsy. And polite — she was actually kind of nice about me moving the mic stand over and over, and she didn't even tell Declan where he could stick his mic, which wouldn't have been the first time someone had done that. Will she talk to me just to be nice? I don't think she'll chat me up to get to Declan, but maybe she prefers Alex? They seemed to be getting along well...

"Go talk to her."

Speak of the devil.

"She's nice. Said she was glad we were protecting our hearing with the in-ears."

"Grohl — the real one — said he's lost a lot of hearing from using wedges," I remind Alex. "But he doesn't like the isolation of in-ears."

"We were smart to invest in in-ears early on, and my hearing is more important than a little sonic isolation while we're on stage. Our fans should be wearing earplugs, too. Maybe we can do a PSA with the next tour, remind them they can't hear us if they damage their hearing."

"Yeah — can't replace your ears."

"So, go talk to her about it," he presses.

"I'll just mess it up."

"Won't know if you don't try."

"I also won't embarrass myself if I don't try."

"Being unwillingly single at 30 is a little embarrassing, too, Dave."

Ouch.

"You're single," I remind him.

"I am. But I wasn't always. And it isn't for lack of trying. We're here for a while. Go talk to the nice girl. Give her a chance to get to know you. I've got a good feeling about this."

I look over at the bar where Piper is standing, fiddling with something on her iPad.

"Let's get some dinner, guys!" Hunter says, beckoning us over to a big table on the deck, where he and Brighid are already settling in. "The seafood here is awesome! And they've got chocolate lava cake."

"Maybe *he* can eat as much dessert as he wants, with four models and Brighid all ready to throw themselves at his feet," Declan comments from behind me. "I'll have to work it off in the gym tomorrow. Can't lose two off this eight-pack if I'm going to give the audience what they want!"

I roll my eyes at him. I can't fault Declan's diligence on issues like our public image, but his hyper-focus on superficial things has always reared its head when he's feeling insecure about something. I'm not sure I want to know what's making him feel insecure right now, when we're supposed to be on vacation and only performing in front of a comparatively tiny crowd. But maybe that's it — not a big enough audience to provide the ego boost he needs. He's usually so self-confident on a gig night.

Which reminds me about Piper. Maybe Alex is right. Maybe I should find some balls and see if she wants to join me... us... for dinner.

I slip on my flip-flops and turn to go ask her, but she's no longer by the bar. In fact, she's nowhere to be seen. Missed my window. Crap. Just not meant to be...

The guys spend most of dinner asking Brighid about what there is to do around here. I know a lot of it already, since Declan and I spent our summers here as kids. Plus, I've got my vacation time planned out, and the only place I need to go is just steps from my bedroom door.

"Dave, man — stop the fucking tapping, please," Declan says, incredibly polite for Declan.

I smooth my hands over my jeans to make myself stop. I hadn't even noticed I was doing it, again. I guess I'm a little wound up, though I'm not sure if it's about Piper or because of the change from our usual kind of venue. I don't usually get nervous before gigs. Not anymore.

I tune out the conversation and keep an eye out for Piper. She has to come back. She's running sound. But there's a long break between soundcheck and our set. It only makes sense she'd have something else to do for nearly two hours. The food here is as good as I remembered. I just wish I was sharing it with someone other than Brighid and my bandmates...

"**G**reetings, ladies and gents! We are Rock & Grohl, and we're here to 'amuse' you," Declan tells the audience.

I give him a frown and a glare, the first for the reference to the other Dave and the second for dropping in most of our real band name when he's knows we have to stay incognito. But he's already playing to the audience and doesn't even glance my way.

We have two challenges tonight: to stay incognito and to get the audience moving so we can slip in our originals and get a real impression of how they're received. The set list — nearly all covers — is designed to do just that, with a lot of audience favorites right up front and some indulgence of our individual favorites later on, including my request for some '80s gems and some funky bass parts.

We start off basically a cappella, with only Rhys's kick drum and some claps keeping the beat as Declan takes on the legendary Freddie Mercury. Then Hunt, Rhys and I jump in on background vocals, before Kier tears through an electrifying solo. We've already got audience participation in the bag, cementing our reception with Alex joining in for four-part harmonies behind Declan for "Fat-Bottomed Girls." Hunt is watching our table closely as the four girls brought in for his reality show appear to be needling Bridge, but she's doing an admirable job of ignoring them and, as always, only has eyes for him. I feel a pang of jealousy. Screw the models — I want a girl who looks at me like Brighid does at Hunter.

My eyes slide over to the bar, where Piper is standing, tapping her feet along in time to the backbeats coming from my bass — not the main beat of Rhys' kit, but my take on the funky bass lines of "Brick House." Is she a bass girl?

Everyone's got a sound they love — for some it's vocals, others the smack of sticks on a snare, and for many, it's the scream of a guitar. But for me, it was always the driving undercurrent of the bass. The first time I picked one up, I knew that was me. It's not a thing most people notice when they listen to music — bassists are known for not getting the girls, even if I do OK, considering — but it's what ties the rest of the song to the drums. Without the bass, music becomes hollow. At least for me. And maybe for Piper, too?

I settle into our more aggressive take on the Commodores' song, reveling in the notion that Piper seems to be just as into it as I am. I usually lose myself in it, but my attention is divided tonight, between her and my favorite Doug Wimbish-model Spector, custom-made for me in violet burst. The neck's lightning fast, and I throw in some extra little flourishes on top of Flea's harder take on the originally keyboard-focused "Higher Ground." Showing off? For a girl? Me? Maybe.

This girl — she's got my in-ear mix tuned to perfection, and the audience seems to be loving how we sound. But I notice Piper has stopped tapping her toes along. She doesn't like it? There are little frown lines between her eyebrows. Maybe she doesn't like my flourishes. I rein it back in when we shift into "Dark Necessities," with Alex taking center stage in the keyboard intro. But Flea's slap-pop bass line and the ghost notes embedded in it are the core of this funk-forward song, and pretty soon, it's just me and my bass again.

As much as I love the song — it's the first one we ever played with Rhys — doing "Spoonman" makes me nervous in this context, because Declan's voice is most often compared to that of Chris Cornell. But Declan insisted. It's one of his favorites to cover. Avoiding a diva fit meant giving in to him on this one. And I can't say I don't love the bare little bass riff that leads out of the drum break. But when I look up at Piper as the last bits of guitar fade away, her eyes are wide. She's staring at Declan. And it's not the usual mesmerized-by-his-glory stare I see on Declan's fangirls.

We move into Kieran's much-loved bluesy Arc Angels tune, "Crave and Wonder" — Kier's actually mouthing the words, which is saying something since he never, ever sings. Declan, on the other hand, also loves doing his growly Charlie Sexton impression over top of my harmonies. It's in that moment I realize why Piper's staring. And not just at Declan anymore. She's giving each one of us close scrutiny. I can see the wheels turning in her head. And there's no doubt when we go into the first of our new songs.

What can I say? We sound like aMUSEd. Declan sounds like Declan. I see Brighid glance nervously back at the people behind her, but she seems to settle back down after a moment. Piper, meanwhile, is wearing an expression somewhere between delight and outrage. I catch her eye and make the most imploring expression I can manage, silently begging her not to say anything. She frowns back at me but nods curtly.

I relax just enough to enjoy the rest of our set, including our second new song and my one major request for the set list, The Fixx's "Saved By Zero." Alex and I play off each other, with Declan somehow pulling off a reasonable interpretation of Cy Curnin's elegant, floating delivery in the space in between, and Hunt and Kier trade off on guitar. I see Bridge looking behind her again as we move into our third and final original of the night, and she adjusts her chair to block the phone camera recording. The jig is very close to being up, if it isn't already. I manage to catch Declan's eye and shake my head at him, hoping he gets the message to bring this to a close so we can get back in the dressing room and out of camera range. As soon as the song is done, he thanks a very enthusiastic audience, and we make a hasty exit after some urgent whispered conversation with the other guys.

Alex asks the venue security to station someone outside the dressing room for a bit, just in case, and one of the bouncers takes up a post there. Hunter manages to wait all of ten minutes before he's chomping at the bit to get back out to Brighid. Or is it the other girls? All of them? That whole thing is weird.

"Can you all handle load-out without me?" he asks.

"Girl trouble?" Alex replies.

"God, I hope not," Hunter says. "But I'm afraid if I leave them out there together much longer, there will be a food fight."

"Not with those four," Kier observes. "They don't eat."

"Good point. But I still think I'd better go play referee. All I need is for the cameras to catch my 'girlfriends' pulling out my best friend's hair."

"Bridge has the weight advantage. I'd put ten bucks on her in a wrestling match," Declan says, and Hunt's expression goes furious.

"Is there chocolate pudding involved in this wrestling action?" Rhys asks.

Hunt turns his glare on our drummer.

"What? You love chocolate! Could there be anything better than big, beautiful Bridge and four models covered in chocolate pudding?"

He ducks just in time to avoid Alex's attempted smack to the back of his head. I think it's the first time since Alex joined the band that Rhys has managed to avoid the tough-love mom-style intervention of our keyboard player. He had to know it was coming.

"We've got it, Hunt," I tell him. "Go ahead. Actually — I'll go out with you if the rest of you want to keep a low profile. I need to talk to the engineer."

Declan's eyebrows go up. It's saying something when I manage to surprise my brother.

"She figured it out before we even got to the first original. We're lucky she seems to understand that our identity is a secret."

"How do you know she figured it out when you didn't talk to her yet?" Alex asks, baldly curious.

"Her expression — perplexed, scrutinizing, then shocked and a little miffed, I'd say."

"Sounds like you two are on the same wavelength," he observes. "You always talk about how hard women are to read."

"They usually are."

He looks intrigued, and that's more than enough to send me out of the room in Hunter's wake. Time to talk to Piper.

CHAPTER 7

LETTING THE CABLES SLEEP

Piper

If I was any other sound engineer, I'd be embarrassed beyond belief to have gotten fooled by these guys. But I haven't had time to get familiar with what the popular bands look like. I've spent it all learning their sounds, going back through a hundred years of jazz, folk, blues and rock to pick the sounds apart and learn their acoustic profiles so I could engineer them instinctively.

So I know exactly what aMUSEd — one of the most popular bands of the last decade — sounds like. I'm actually a big fan. But unlike most of their fans, I suspect, I've never seen so much as a photo of the band members. If they don't appear on their album covers, I have no idea what any band looks like, not even my favorites. I can repeat dialogue from my favorite TV shows by heart, but that was research, too. Technically. But I didn't waste any time on band photos or videos or interviews.

And that's the only reason the six members of aMUSEd managed to sneak past me as I helped set up their instruments and ran them through their brief soundcheck. Something started nagging at me while I ran out for a quick swim before their set, and that feeling only got stronger once they started into the covers. They didn't make it to what is clearly a new original song before I knew...

The deception rubs me the wrong way. I know what it is to keep secrets. But my secrets are life-or-death ones.

"Thank you for not saying anything."

David.

I can't help it. I glare at him. Beyond that, I don't know what to say.

"You *can* talk. I didn't mean..." He stammers. "I meant — thank you for not telling anyone who we are, not that you shouldn't talk to me. You can talk to me. I want you to talk to me. If you want to, I mean. I hope you still want to."

He's so nervous that I can't stay mad at him. What rockstar of his caliber is so tongue-tied just talking to some newbie sound engineer at a small local venue? Clearly, he is. But it makes no sense.

"Let's start over," I suggest. He looks relieved, holding his hand out to shake mine. I grasp it briefly, until that zap of energy I felt before makes me drop it again. "I'm Piper Morrison. I'm a sound engineer. I work here a couple nights a week."

"David Carter. I'm a musician — bass player, songwriter, background vocals. I work in studios and stadiums."

"I am not amused."

I couldn't help that either. And we both crack up.

"That was *bad*," he says after the laughter dies down.

"Couldn't help myself. And the least you owe me is a shot at a good pun."

"It's a shame that was a bad pun instead." He grins at me.

There's a clatter behind the bar as the barback drops a tray of glasses.

"Dammit," she says.

"Hardison," David and I both finish simultaneously.

Surprise registers in his face at the same moment it hits my own.

"'Leverage!'"

"I love that show," he says.

"I know. I'm so glad they brought it back."

"Wait. They brought it back?"

"How did you not know that?"

"I've been on the road nearly constantly for almost two years. I watch it from the files I saved on my laptop, the same con jobs over and over again. Otherwise, all I do is play music, write songs, do promos and take tests. And sleep. Sometimes I sleep."

"Sleep is good. What kind of tests?"

"Science mostly. I've finished most of my core classes."

"You're in college?"

"Yeah. But don't tell anyone. No one knows."

"Oh. OK. I guess I'll add that to your tab of secrets."

He gets serious. Uh-oh. Did I mess that up? Maybe I shouldn't have reminded him that I know his other big secret. Maybe he thinks I'll blackmail him or something. I look at my shoes, my cheeks heating up.

"Yeah… Thanks again for not saying anything about the other thing. We're supposed to be flying under the radar, testing out the new songs before we record the next album. Though Declan needs to do a better job picking our fake band names."

"Yeah. 'Rock & Grohl'? Did he think anyone was going to buy that?"

"So you know Dave Grohl, but not David Carter?"

And now I've offended him. This is why I usually do my job and go home, rather than socializing with the bands.

"I only know his name because he's been in two very big bands, and because he comes here sometimes."

"Here, to this bar?"

"No! I mean to this area. Someone mentioned it to me once."

"Oh. Yeah. I knew that. Hunter's friend Brighid mentioned it to me years ago. Talked to Dave about it the last time I ran into him. We're both from Northern Virginia, both vacationed here as kids."

"I don't think you need to worry about name recognition when you can say so casually that you've had chats with the guy whose name I *did* know."

"I wasn't name-dropping."

And I've done it again.

"I didn't mean…"

"It's OK. I'm not upset. I just didn't want you thinking I was. Name-dropping, I mean."

"Oh."

"So are you OK with keeping our identity secret while we're here? I'm not sure how long we can keep the word from getting out, but we want to keep it going until we've tested out all the new songs."

"Yeah. That's fine. It makes sense. I'll keep it to myself."

Not that there are a lot of people I would tell.

There's an awkward silence.

"You want some help with load-out? The DJ is on the rest of the night."

"That'd be cool. Hunter — Graves, in case you wanted to know," he says with a wink, "— he's got a thing..."

He looks over at the table where they had dinner, and there's a ruckus with four very tall women arguing loudly with each other in front of a big video camera.

"Huh... Looks like he got out while the getting was good. Him *and* Bridge."

"They seemed happy together."

"Who? Him and Brighid? They're best friends. Have been since they were little."

"They didn't look like friends."

"Well, you'd have your work cut out convincing him of that. But you're not wrong."

He hops up off his barstool and offers me his hand. It's old-fashioned, gentlemanly. There's that energy again in the contact. I like it. And that makes me blush. Again.

David and I start work, side by side, disconnecting amps, mics, effects pedals... it's companionable. I can't remember the last time I worked in silence alongside someone without feeling a need to say anything. Even Rónan and I chatted when I helped him out with projects. And Steve either keeps up a rambling monologue of instruction when I'm working at the studio or insists on a total silence that wears on you because it's not necessary outside the live room on the other side of the glass from the mixing board.

I stop David with a hand on his arm when he starts coiling cables. There's that electric zing again. We both look down at my hand on his bicep, tension suddenly erupting in the air between us. He shakes his head, and I withdraw my hand. The zing abates, but the tension merely ramps down.

"The cables..." I lose track of what I was going to say about them.

"The cables?"

Coiling cables. We were coiling cables. And I touched his arm... to...

"Oh — there's a better way to coil them."

"Sorry — we haven't... I haven't... We haven't done our own load-in and load-out in years. And no one ever showed me a different way."

"Here," I say, holding my hand out for the end of the cable he was coiling. I'm careful not to touch his skin this time, and he seems to be equally careful in not touching mine. "See — over, under, over, under..." I demonstrate the technique. "It keeps the wires from twisting. Puts less strain on them. Makes them easier to uncoil and lay out, because they lay flat and spool off neatly."

I hand him back the end of the cable, dropping the rest to the floor.

"Your turn. Give it a try."

He starts to coil the cable back up, but he doesn't have the technique down, and it starts to twist as he falls back into his old way.

"No. That's not it."

I go to take it back from him, but he pulls it away.

"No — let me try again. I'm having a hard time visualizing it while watching you from the front."

He steps around behind me and wraps his arms around me, the cable in front of us. I freeze. If that energy we have between us was stunning before, it's stupefying like this. He looks over my shoulder at the cable. But we're both breathing hard. Whatever this is, we're both feeling it. I swallow hard and take the cable from his hand.

"Like this... Over, under, over, under..."

"Over, under," he continues, taking the cable from my fingers and continuing the process.

"You've got it."

He finishes up with this cable and goes to hand it back to me. I can feel his breath on my neck. I turn my head to look at him, and his mouth is right there. My eyes slide up to meet his, and...

"Hey, Davey — you need some help there?"

I duck out from between his arms, taking the cable with me and avoiding looking at anyone.

"Thanks, Rhys. I think we had it handled."

"That wasn't all you had handled there, bro..." Declan says with a snicker as he passes David.

"Ignore them," Alex says quietly as he passes by me and starts unhooking his keyboards from their cables. I take the opportunity to slip under the keyboard rack and start unhooking the cables on that end. My face is burning.

This cannot happen. I've got to work with these guys. These chart-topping musicians. This... thing... whatever it is... with David — it's unprofessional. I have a hard enough time being taken seriously in this job without having people assume I'm playing on my sexuality to get ahead or, alternatively, trying to leverage my job to meet and date musicians.

"He likes you," Alex says quietly as he bends down to drop a cable. "He doesn't usually talk to women. He's kind of awkward."

"That makes two of us."

"All the more reason..."

"I can't."

"Why not?"

"Lots of reasons. Not the least of which is it's unprofessional."

"I don't think you'll find any of us complaining, even if the guys may tease him about it a little. He's a nice guy, and we'll be here all summer..."

The fact that I'm even thinking about what Alex is telling me is a warning sign.

"I can't."

"Boyfriend?"

"No!"

"Fatal illness?"

"No."

"Arranged marriage?"

"Not really."

"Over-protective brother?"

"Not anymore..."

That finally stops him.

"I'm sorry." He touches my shoulder. There's no zing.

"It's OK. You didn't know."

I glance over at David, who's glancing over at me and Alex, surreptitiously, as he continues coiling cables like I showed him, dropping them one by one in a pile by his feet.

"I'll drop the subject. But I think you two should get to know each other. If nothing else, he could use some more friends. He spends too much time on his own."

I look over at David again, and I can see it — there's a quiet intensity about him that almost suggests loneliness. Though how he could possibly be lonely when his band has the high profile they do, I don't know.

A little over an hour later, the guys have all their equipment set to go, and I've put away every microphone, cable and rack in the equipment room, locked the board down again and set the iPad back in its charging dock. All that's left is to get them on the road.

"Uh... you don't happen to have an SUV or something, do you?" David asks.

I live an easy walk from both of my jobs, so I've never needed a car.

"No. I usually walk home."

"We kind of forgot about getting the equipment back to the house when we told Hunter he and Brighid could leave. We really aren't used to having to haul our own gear anymore. Brighid used to help us out with that, so we didn't even plan beyond that once she offered."

"Oh. Sorry. I can see if any of the staff can help..."

"No. Don't worry about it. We'll call Hunt and get them back to help. He wasn't really tired anyway. Just wanted to get away from the girlfriends and the TV camera."

"'Girlfriends'? Plural?"

"Yeah — Hunt is kind of commitment-phobic. But he's not much on groupies anymore. So he has several ladies he dates. The four that were arguing over there when they left..."

"He's dating four women. At the same time..."

He looks a little sheepish about it, even though he's not the one with the unusual dating behavior. Some of our folk are polyamorous, but I know it's not something most people are comfortable with. And it seems Hunter's girlfriends may not be either.

"Yeah. I know — it's weird. That's how he got himself roped into this reality show on his dating life. Not that he wants any part of it."

"Then why is he doing it?"

"The label's making him. Pushing him to choose one of them."

"The label can make him do a reality show on the women he dates? And stop dating all but one?"

"Apparently. Makes me glad I'm not in his shoes..."

I want to ask him if he means he's not dating anyone or if he's just not dating four women at the same time. But that would suggest I'm interested in *his* dating life, and I've already concluded that can't happen. Regardless of what Alex said.

"Well, if you're sure you can get him and Brighid back to transport your equipment..."

"We could give you a ride home if you want to wait around..." he suggests tentatively.

I wouldn't mind spending some more time with David Carter. And that's a clear indication I should avoid doing just that.

"I've got a long weekend ahead of me. More gigs here. And then more work on Monday. I really should get some sleep, see if I can get in a swim..."

"You swim?"

"Don't most people?"

He's got that nervous look again.

"I mean — I mean you swim for fun?"

"I live at the beach. It'd be a waste if I didn't swim."

"I swim. And surf. And skimboard. And paddleboard. That's my vacation plan."

"I thought you smelled like..."

Uh. Awkward. Now he knows I was paying attention to his scent earlier. He waits for me to finish.

"'Like...'" he prompts when I don't.

"Like the ocean."

"I took a swim before we came over."

"I took a swim after your soundcheck."

"Oh! So that's where you went!"

"Yeah."

"So we both swim."

"It seems so..."

"So we have that in common."

"Yeah."

"And music."

"Yeah."

"And 'Leverage.'"

I just nod.

We're dodging each other's eyes, though my reticence is matched by David's barely contained enthusiasm over this discovery.

"Maybe we can go swimming together sometime..."

"Uh... I, uh — I don't think that's a good idea."

"Oh. OK." He looks... crushed.

"It's just... I need to keep things professional if we're going to be working together."

"Oh. Right. Of course. And we've got more test gigs coming up."

"I assumed so."

"Well, probably best we don't go swimming, then."

"Yeah. Probably."

Why am I *feeling* crushed? I'm the one who insisted we keep things professional.

"I should go..."

"OK. Uh — have a safe walk home. I'll see you next week probably. If we've got more songs ready."

"You're amazing." Wait. Did I just say that? David is looking at me with hope in his eyes, and that wasn't at all what I meant. "The music, I mean. The new songs were great."

"Oh," he says, deflated again. "Thanks. Declan and I wrote those. We need to finish a bunch more. I just haven't been feeling very inspired."

"Well, maybe you'll find some inspiration on your vacation."

"I'm sure I will," he says, and the statement is heavy with meaning as he looks in my eyes.

"Goodnight, David."

"Goodnight, Piper."

I turn and start walking, because if I don't, I'm not sure I won't end up caving in to him. David Carter. Rockstar, student, "Leverage" fan and swimmer. And most definitely not an option.

CHAPTER 8

BREAKFAST AT TIFFANY'S

Piper
Monday morning, several days later

Steve called last night to tell me there was a band in residence at the studio and that I should stay out of the living areas, but I should make sure the studio was ready for them to record scratch tracks first thing in the morning, just in case they wanted to get started before their producer arrived.

I would not be needed for recording until the producer was ready, he seemed to take great delight in informing me.

Fine. It's not like I was expecting to be called in until I was absolutely needed. Steve and his concerns about my "distracting" the bands...

So I'm here extra-early this morning, well before any pro musician is likely to be awake, let alone in the studio, to make sure the lights are on, the studio equipment and instruments in good working order, fresh recording drives in the system and the facilities stocked.

That last bit was my first task. There's now bottled water, fresh fruit and other snacks in the refrigerator, a selection of chips and candy in the cupboards, coffee and tea ready to go, with a fresh jar of local honey to soothe overworked vocal cords. It's actually Safe Harbour's honey. Rónan insisted we keep our own hives, as had been tradition for many of our folk. All the better to keep the musicians healthy and recording at their best.

Studio next...

But the lights are already on, the board lit up, and the sound of an acoustic guitar drifting from the open door of the live room. I start to turn around and leave to give the artist their privacy, but there's something about the song they're playing that stops me and lures me forward to the door. It's definitely one I haven't heard before, with a liquid, shifting quality that reminds me of the waves lapping on the shore at sunrise on a clear summer day, like today. A quiet hum of melody drifts over as the phrase on the guitar is repeated, words now emerging from the formerly lyricless tune...

The voice I hear over the water
Thrilling me now to let go
Touching me
Taking my hand as I lead in the dance of my soul

I'm drawn forward into the doorway by that voice, the words... something familiar...

Feel the wind as it slips through your fingers
Just like the sands of time have come and gone
Never looked back

I look up from the fingers on the guitar to the face of the person crouched over it, eyes closed, immersed, focused... Until they pop open, apparently having sensed my presence.

Pale blue, like a winter morning sky...

"Piper? What are you doing here?"

David Carter.

Of course.

He's here to record — aMUSEd is here to record. They're the band in residence. And Alex said they'd be here all summer.

Any plan I had to avoid David Carter and the temptation to get to know him was just blown out of the water... Gods help us all.

"Piper?"

It snaps me out of my head. He wants to know why I'm here.

"Uh... I work here."

"At the studio?"

"Yeah. Paid internship. I just run live sound on the side. I've been working here for nearly a year."

"Wow. That's a coincidence."

"I guess so... Steve called me last night to ask me to set things up for a new band that would be in residence. I don't think he realized you'd gotten to the point of recording yet."

"We haven't. Just scratch tracks. I know enough — we all do — to record scratch tracks without an engineer or producer. Malcolm Fisher is going to join us here in a few weeks, if things stay on schedule. Right now, we're still writing and arranging."

"Sorry I interrupted you. I didn't realize anyone would be in here this early. I didn't think any normal musician would be *up* this early."

"Surfer, remember?"

"Yeah. It's flat today."

"It is. Which is why I'm sitting here in my board shorts and not out on the beach."

"Right..."

He and I are just looking at each other, that tension starting to rise again.

"Hungry?"

"Huh?"

"Are you hungry? It's early, I know, but as we've established, I'm an early-riser. And I make a mean omelet. Alex taught me, and he's halfway to a chef."

"I'm not sure... I'm supposed to be... Steve..."

"Isn't here. And what else did you need to do?"

"Set up the drives for scratch tracks."

"Already done. I laid down a couple guitar tracks the other day, shortly after we got here. The drives were already ready to go."

"I leave them that way when we finish a project. I just like to make sure they're still fresh when a new artist comes in, just in case Steve or someone came in to noodle around."

"Well, they were still fresh. So, that task is done. And you can come eat breakfast with me."

I can't think of a good excuse not to. It's just breakfast. It's not like it's a date. And the rest of the band is here somewhere.

"Steve likes me to stay out of the living areas when a band's in residence." There. That's a good excuse.

"Well, the label has paid for us to have the run of the house and studio, and since I have the run of the house, I can invite you up for breakfast. In fact, that makes me Steve's boss for the moment, so I can countermand that rule."

"That would make you my boss's boss. Which would make you my boss..."

"And you can't have a meal with your boss?"

"I... I'm not sure..."

"Piper."

"Yes?"

"Come eat breakfast with me. It's eggs. And coffee. Or tea if you prefer."

"I brought over some honey. We... my family makes it... well — the bees make it. We help."

"Then let's get this Piper's Family Honey and go eat breakfast together."

"OK."

He gets up and sets his guitar on a stand, grabbing my hand and leading me back out of the studio proper. I pull free as we reach the door to the studio kitchen, plucking the jar of honey from the counter. I hesitate when he reaches for my hand again, but I let him take it. Every time. That same electric charge...

He leads me up the stairs and into the residence kitchen, where he gestures at the bar stools at the kitchen island.

"Have a seat. Two omelets coming up..."

"Should I make coffee?"

"Do you want coffee?"

"I usually have tea."

"I figured, since you mentioned the honey. Go ahead and make two cups. Won't hurt my throat to have some tea with your magical honey..."

What? How?

"You OK there, Piper? It's just tea. And honey. The tea's in the cupboard by the sink, and the cups are in the next one over. I usually just use the coffee pod thing to heat the water."

"Yeah. That's fine," I reply, shaking myself out of stunned silence. He didn't mean...

David sets about making omelets while I get two cups of tea ready. There's no honey dipper handy, so I find a spoon and drizzle a spoonful into my tea just as David sets down two plates containing beautifully rolled omelets. I catch the end of the drip with my finger so the honey doesn't get on the counter.

David snatches my hand up, and I'm jarred by that zing again. Enough that I don't resist when he pulls my finger to his mouth and licks the honey from it. And then I'm incapable of thought.

His eyes are on mine as he sucks my fingertip into his mouth. My lips part in an unconscious mimicking of his. And his eyes drift down onto them, our joined hands left to fall between us as he leans in...

"Oops! Sorry, Dave — didn't realize you had company this early..."

I yank my hand free and step back away from David, glancing over to see Alex enter from the living room.

"Piper! This is a surprise!"

"To everyone, apparently."

"Piper's an intern here," David explains. "She came in early to make sure the studio was ready for us to record scratch tracks."

"A little late on that," Alex says.

"Yeah — sorry. Steve didn't tell me anyone was here to record until last night."

"I think we got into the studio sooner than he expected, since this is technically our vacation," Alex acknowledges. "Not a problem. No reason to expect we'd be in that fast with no producer scheduled for weeks."

"But Declan and I usually record scratch tracks when we're still in the writing phase, before we bring the other guys in."

"How's it going on that front?" Alex asks him.

"I'm working on a couple more. I had one come to me this morning. I was trying to get it down when Piper unexpectedly arrived."

"I hope I didn't throw you off track there." I'm not sure I apologized before. I should now, just in case. "I know it can be hard to pick up where you left off if you get interrupted while writing."

"No — not at all. I've been feeling inspired the last few days. The music is coming more easily than it had been."

"Gee... I wonder why..." Alex mumbles, seemingly to himself, though the smirk on his face hints that he wanted us to hear. I'm blushing again at the implication.

"So — breakfast for two?" he asks, gesturing at the omelets.

"I can make you one, too," David offers.

"Oh, no — you two go take your breakfast out on the deck. Enjoy the fresh air. I think I'm going to go extra-fancy this morning and do a soufflé omelette. I spotted a hinged pan in the cabinet last night. It's been a while since I had one handy. So, shoo — I've got some eggs to separate."

David hands me my plate and I pick up my teacup.

"Don't forget the honey!" Alex calls behind us, and David goes back for the jar, which still has the spoon sticking out of it. The look he gives me is heavy, liquid, like the honey itself. I shudder and resume my walk toward the sliding glass doors that open onto the deck, balancing my teacup as I use one hand to open the doors.

I set my plate and cup on the outdoor dining table and then go back to close the door behind David. When I turn around, I stop to take in the view. I haven't been out on the deck here before. I've been in the kitchen to restock the refrigerator, but I went about my business and left. The view of the ocean here is spectacular — less occluded than the one at home, though offering less privacy. Not that it's as much of a worry for the studio guests, even if privacy is something most of them value, given their occupations. But it is a private beach, next to a private beach, so they likely get all the privacy they need and get to enjoy the view, too.

"Beautiful," David comments. Only he's looking not out at the ocean but back at me. I've either got to stop blushing or to get a mild sunburn to hide it better.

As I approach the table, he holds the chair out for me. Such old-fashioned manners on this one. I haven't seen many men recently who even think to perform these tiny little acts of respect, reverence. I've also known men for whom it was a way to assert superiority over women, to imply they were incapable of handling simple tasks on their own, but David doesn't seem at all like that. I take it as a gesture of respect when it comes from him.

He is such a study in contrasts — the self-effacing, awkward guy peeking out from the facade of the performer, the rockstar. And the unsure suitor who at times reveals a suave would-be seducer residing under the surface. I really don't know what to make of him. Moreover, I know what I shouldn't be making of him, and that's anything resembling a non-professional relationship.

We sit and eat quietly, stealing glances at each other when we think the other one isn't looking. Only we are, and we keep catching each other doing it.

"This is delicious," I tell him, trying to break the silence and the pattern of stolen glances with it. "Thank you."

"It's Alex's expertise. Basic recipe. Since I'm the early-riser in the group, he wanted me to be able to feed myself. Mom never taught us to cook. I don't think she particularly liked cooking herself. Plus, I think she thought she had a few more years before we'd move out on our own. But then we skipped college and moved to New York as soon as we got signed."

"That had to have been a big change for you. And then touring all the time."

"It has been. But these guys are like extra brothers to me. Except Alex — Alex is a mom, for sure," he adds with a laugh.

"He seems very motherly."

"He's always been that way. And he loves to cook. Loves food in general. I think he'd have ended up as a chef if he hadn't turned out to be a virtuoso on the piano."

"You're all very talented."

"Thank you. The other guys blow me out of the water. But it works, the six of us together."

"You're amazing in your own right."

"Thanks."

"Six is an unusually large number of members for a band."

"I know. It was three of us — me, Declan and Hunter — needing a new drummer, so we got Rhys. And then Alex came along and was too mind-blowing to pass up. The keys became a signature part of our sound."

"And then Kier."

"It's a long story. Kieran didn't want to be part of the band — any band. And especially not to tour. Never did really tell us why... But he changed his mind after the label made him an offer. They — well, several people — said we needed more guitar than just Hunter, and Declan never got very proficient at it and, really, he just likes being out front."

"He's good at it. One of the best frontmen I've seen. Not that I've seen a ton..."

"Why's that? You seem like you really love music. You know your stuff..."

"I..."

"Piper! There you are!" Steve is suddenly standing in the doorway, clearly unhappy. "I thought I asked you to stay out of the residence while a client was here. I apologize..." he says to David. "She shouldn't have..."

"I dragged her up here," David replies firmly. "She was setting up the studio as requested, and I was the only one up. I asked her to join me for breakfast so I didn't have to eat alone. In fact, I insisted. We do have the run of the house and studio, don't we?"

"Oh... Yes. Of course. Well, I suppose it's alright this once, so long as she got her work done and didn't distract... uh... disturb you."

"She had everything sorted out before I even realized she was there. Very efficient. And quiet. Both good qualities in an engineer."

He's telling Steve something here, and I'm not quite sure what.

"She's only an intern."

"Her skills behind the board suggest otherwise."

"I'm sorry — behind the board?"

Oh, no. Steve doesn't know I've been moonlighting at the Pirate's Cove. David's going to get me fired.

"She ran sound for us the other night at one of our little incognito test gigs."

Steve has gone from flustered to livid. He's redder now than I was after David's compliment.

"Piper? You didn't mention you had a second job. I thought you were focused on your job here and learning the ropes at a professional studio."

"I am, Steve... But you usually only need me a few days a week, and you haven't asked me to come in on the weekends or evenings since I started. So I offered to fill in if the engineer at the Pirate's Cove needed a backup. And then last month he quit with no notice."

"Sean was supposed to be their first call if they needed someone else to run sound there."

Wow. This somehow just got worse. Sean is Steve's son, a notch above me on the intern ladder, even though he's usually too busy to be here doing the stuff Steve has me doing, and hasn't shown any real talent for engineering that I've seen. But he does like to schmooze with the clients.

"I'm not sure what to tell you, Steve. They had my résumé on file for months before they called me and needed someone the same night. Maybe Sean already had a commitment that night. I don't know. But they were happy with my work and asked me to take the job. It's only part-time, and I haven't had any conflicts with working here."

"Until now..."

"I'm sorry to butt in — but how is her working at the bar and interning here a conflict? Seems to me if you want a well-trained intern, she should get all the experience with sound that she can get."

Steve looks like he wants to say something but is biting his tongue because David is a client he can't afford to offend.

"Of course," he finally says. "I just need to make sure she's available to be here if I need her, and that she's focused on learning. That's why the position was created for her."

Leave it to Steve to imply that I wouldn't have this job if I hadn't had Rónan funding it. Even if that's probably true, just because Steve would have handed Sean the opportunity exclusively and never allowed anyone else to even apply. David gives me a curious look but doesn't say anything.

"Well, she's clearly learned a lot in the time she's been here. She gave our tour engineers a run for their money, and she was running monitors and front-of-house at the same time. She's got a real talent for it."

Again Steve seems to be holding his tongue.

"It's good to know she can handle live sound on her own, in a very small venue. I've certainly made an effort to teach her the basics she'd need. And the experience will certainly come in handy when she starts looking for a job elsewhere..."

I hear the threat implied and cringe.

"Sometime down the road," Steve adds, though I question his sincerity there.

"Well, we're very happy to have her here working with us. She's already proven herself very valuable. And since she's already aware of our identities, it means one less person we have to take into our confidence."

"So she knows who you are?"

"Figured it out while we were still doing our covers. She's sharp. Good ears."

"Well, then... I'll look forward to seeing her demonstrate her skills sometime soon," he says. "Piper — when you get a minute, I'd like to go over the schedule for aMUSEd's stay with us. I'll be down in the office."

If looks could kill...

CHAPTER 9

RULES AND SCHEMES

David

I don't like the look on Steve's face when he leaves, and I don't like the look on Piper's face either.

"Did I mess this up for you? He's not going to try to fire you, is he? Just for moonlighting?"

"Probably not. Not now, anyway. Not just for moonlighting..."

"What aren't you telling me?"

She's stiff. Not just awkward and unsure like she's been a few times in the short period that I've known her. Stiff, like all that's keeping her from falling apart is the steel ramrod of her spine, clutched with a death-grip.

Her eyes slide closed.

"I can't lose this job. I promised I wouldn't lose this job. If it was just about me, that would be one thing, but people are relying on me. I can't let them down."

"Piper — it'll be OK. I'll talk to him again."

"No!" Her tone is alarmed, enough that I'm alarmed in return. "You can't get in the middle of this. Sean's his son, his heir-apparent, and that's only made this worse. I have to handle it myself. I'll find a way to fix it. I have to."

I reach over and squeeze her hand. She recoils. Stands up. Takes a deep breath.

"Thank you very much for breakfast, David. I appreciate the praise for my work. I think it's best if we keep things professional from this point forward, as I said."

I can hear the reproach in her words. She asked me to keep it professional, and I didn't listen, and now her job could be on the line.

"Let me know if you need anything while you're here, at the studio," she emphasizes. "Whatever you need to get the album recorded successfully. That's my job."

"Piper..."

She looks at me for the first time since I touched her hand to try to comfort her. Those huge brown eyes of hers are liquid with unshed tears. I feel compelled to jump to my feet and hug her tight. But I resist the urge. Because this is my fault.

"I'll see you later, David. Have a good day."

She turns on her heel and heads back inside at a near-jog.

I look across the table at her empty chair, her half-eaten omelet mocking me from its place next to that jar of honey, her tea gone cold. Just like she did.

"Something go wrong?" Alex asks from the doorway, a cup of coffee in his hand.

"Yeah. *I* did."

"Somehow I doubt that."

"I accidentally told her boss that she's moonlighting at the bar, which is apparently a job she got over his own son. And that's on top of the fact that he'd told her to stay out of the residence and I dragged her up here so I could have breakfast with her."

"Oh."

"Yeah. 'Oh.'"

"He's not going to fire her, is he? Just for moonlighting? For breakfast?"

"She said not. But I'm pretty sure that was just to make me feel better."

"I'll talk to him."

"No, don't. She asked me not to."

"Look — she can get another job. She's a gifted engineer. Give her a glowing testimonial."

"This is the only high-end studio in the area. And she's just an intern. She might get more work running live sound, but there are only so many days in the week when there's a live band playing. I think I really screwed this up for her."

"What were you thinking when you told him she'd been moonlighting?"

"I know, right? Why did I have to even bring it up? Stupid."

"No — I mean, what was your intention when you spoke the words?"

"I don't know... to impress upon him how good she is at her job and how much we'd already valued her work for us, even if it wasn't here at the studio."

"Then it will work out fine."

"How can you say that? He could be down there firing her right now!"

"I doubt it. Not with you having sung her praises and us having done basically no work on the album here yet. We could pull out tomorrow and find another studio. He won't risk pissing you off, pissing us off."

"You didn't see his face."

"I saw it when he came up and when he went back down. That was an angry man who'd realized he was between a rock and a hard place. He'll make things hard for her for a while, but he knows which side his bread is buttered on. If he pisses us off, he doesn't just lose one client and months' worth of work, he loses dozens of clients when we tell people how unprofessionally *he* behaved."

"I hope you're right. If she loses this job, it's my fault. And... she's got people depending on her, she said."

"If it comes to that, we'll make it up to her. This wasn't her fault."

"No. It was mine. See — I told you I'd screw this up. I couldn't even have breakfast with the girl without fucking something up."

The feel of her finger in my mouth flashes back to me, the taste of sweet honey and Piper... I'm not sure what came over me. It was either the most incredibly smooth thing I've ever done or the most awkward one. She didn't seem to mind, though, now that I think about it.

"But you didn't fuck it up with her," Alex argues, breaking me out of my reverie. "You made the girl a nice breakfast and praised her work to her boss. That's the kind of thing that gets you a girlfriend."

"Yeah, if you don't get her fired in the process."

"Give her some credit. She's not a wilting flower. She called your dumb ass out on moving her mic stand around."

"And on lying to her about who we were."

"Oh, she did, did she? I missed that."

"I apologized. She said she was 'not amused.'"

"Ha! I knew I liked this girl. She'll keep you on your toes, Dave."

"She's not going to want to have anything to do with me after this."

"I think you're wrong. But we'll see..."

Piper

"Have a seat, Piper."

I don't think Steve's told me to have a seat since I first met with him about this internship. This does not bode well. At least I managed to stifle the tears I almost let go in front of David. There's no crying in engineering. Not if you're a girl, anyway.

"I'm sorry, Steve. I understand having breakfast with a client wasn't the most professional behavior. It won't happen again."

"No, it won't. I can't fire you over it with your defender up there ready to throw himself in front of you like a human shield. I can't afford to offend him or his band. But I want to make it very clear to you — this is not your personal pickup spot to snag yourself a rockstar. This is a business, and you are expected to behave like a professional, not a co-ed out at a bar on a Friday night..."

"I understand."

"And that brings me to my next issue with your professionalism... You should have gotten my approval before you took outside work in the same field. We don't have a non-compete in your contract for this internship, but it's good business etiquette to get approval from your primary employer before you take an outside job. I may not have had you working nights or weekends so far, but that could change at any time, and I can't reschedule a platinum-selling recording artist who's ready to cut tracks just because my intern is off running sound for a local cover band at a bar."

"I understand."

"That said, you're now going to be running sound for aMUSEd when they play out locally, and you owe them the same kind of professionalism there as you do here. That means no chatting with your friends about the famous band that's in town, and it means keeping a professional distance from the band members. Am I understood?"

"Of course, Steve. No more breakfasts with David."

"Or any of them. And I'm a little uncomfortable with this degree of intimacy between you."

"We're not..."

"Doesn't matter," he interrupts. "It looks bad. You having breakfast with a client in residence is a far cry from me or Sean taking a client out for dinner."

I'm not entirely sure why, but since he's already threatened to fire me over this, I'm not going to argue the point.

"Now — is all the other prep work done for their early studio time?"

"I restocked the kitchen, and I was headed in to load up fresh drives in the studio when I ran into David..."

Steve cringes. Does he expect me to call him "Mr. Carter"?

"He said they'd already started scratch tracks last week, right after they'd arrived, and the drives were clear at that point."

"That's fine, then."

"I told him if they needed anything... in the studio," I emphasize to him, just as I did to David, "to just let me know and I'd see to it they got whatever they needed."

"I'd like Sean to be their first point of contact."

"OK. I understand. I'll make sure David has his cell number."

"I'll take care of it."

"Alright. Is there anything else you wanted me to do?"

"The cleaning crew didn't do a great job with the kitchen and restroom this week. Can you go over those areas again, make sure they're up to aMUSEd's standards?"

Oh, boy. He may not have fired me (yet). But Steve's going to make me pay for this...

"Piper? What are you doing?"

David's standing in the doorway to the studio kitchen, watching me. I turn my attention back to my work before I answer.

"Scrubbing a sink."

"I can see that. Why are you doing it?"

"Because Steve asked me to."

"I see."

He's standing close behind me now. Too close.

"I'm sorry. Do you want me to talk to him?"

"Please, don't. I've got to get this all back on the rails. I'm the only one who can do that."

"If you're sure..."

"I am."

He sighs deeply enough that I can feel his breath on my neck.

"He told me to call Sean if we needed anything."

"I know. He told me."

"I'm really sorry."

"It's not your fault."

"It really is. I insisted you come have breakfast, and I'm the one that spilled the beans about your other job."

"You didn't know it would cause a problem. You were being nice."

I turn around to look at him. I really don't want him blaming himself for my mistakes. His lovely blue eyes are full of regret.

"It's OK, David. Really. I'm sure it'll be fine. And I really do appreciate how nice you've been, and under other circumstances, the praise for my work would have been very welcome."

"But not in this circumstance."

"No. Steve's very adamant that I've been unprofessional, and he's going to correct that by bringing in Sean. And that's his right. He's the boss."

"No, we're the boss — aMUSEd is."

"That's not the same. And I think you know that. But it's OK. I'll scrub a couple sinks and make coffee for a couple weeks. I'm sure he'll get over it."

That is patently not true. Not even vaguely. Steve's a petty tyrant. He doesn't like being challenged in his demesne, especially not when his own flesh and blood is getting shortchanged as a result. I had the upper hand when Rónan was here to rein in the blatant favoritism, nepotism, sexism, narcissism... lots of -isms involved here. But David doesn't know that and doesn't need to — shouldn't — know that.

Still, he looks skeptical. He'll have to live with his doubts. I've got sinks to scrub. And he's got songs to write.

David

"**C**rap!"

This is the second guitar string I've broken today. Maybe it's the salt air. Or maybe it's my overly aggressive playing technique. I'm taking my frustrations out on my guitar. Only now I've broken a second high-E string, and I don't have any spares left.

"What's up, Davey?"

Alex is standing in the doorway of the live room, the same place I spotted Piper this morning before I sent the entire thing off the rails.

"Broke a string."

"Isn't that the second one today?"

"Yeah."

"Same string?"

"Yeah."

"Burr on the saddle?"

"You know there isn't. I've been playing this guitar for five years. The saddles are in perfect shape."

"So, it's a rough spot on the frets, then..."

I glare at him.

"No. It's not a rough spot on the frets. It's me."

"I see."

"He had her scrubbing the kitchen and the bathroom this morning."

"That sucks. But she can handle it."

"She shouldn't *have* to. She didn't do anything wrong."

"So, tell him to lay off."

"I can't. She told me not to."

"And you always do what you're told, don't you..."

Strictly speaking, he's not entirely correct. But mostly he is.

"I didn't go to college when my parents insisted."

"No, you didn't. But *Declan* told you not to, and still you regretted that decision, didn't you?"

"A little. At times."

Alright — I regretted it a lot. Frequently. That's why I started taking classes online. But no one knows about that. Except Piper. I'd told Piper within hours of meeting her. Totally unlike me.

"So, are you going to do what Piper told you?"

"That's different. It's her boss, her job."

"And it's easy to just let her take the flak for your mistake... especially when she told you to."

"What the fuck, Alex? I thought you told me not to blame myself?"

"But you're doing it anyway. Proof that you can do something other than what you're told."

He's right. But I don't want to make things even worse for her. She's holding onto her job by the skin of her teeth right now. If I confront Steve about how he's treating her, he could just decide to fire her, and he might even be able to excuse it by citing my intervention as evidence of her unprofessional relationship with me. Damned if I do; damned if I don't.

"You want to get her back here?"

"Of course I do!"

"Well, you need strings, don't you?"

"Yeah."

"So ask Sean to bring you some strings."

"How does that get Piper back here?"

"I think you overestimate the work ethic of the pampered offspring under the influence of nepotism."

Ah... I see where he's going with this... and it's brilliant.

CHAPTER 10

REACH THE BEACH

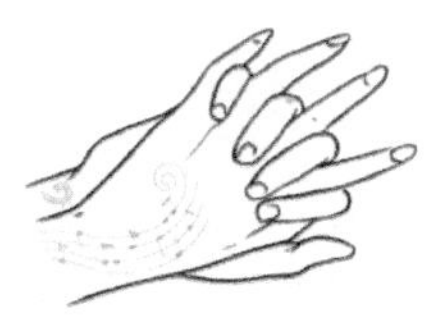

Piper
Three hours later

How many strings can one guitar player break in a few hours? And why on earth do they have to be of an odd gauge and manufacturer that only one music store in the entire area carries? One that's 45 minutes away?

Sean, you suck. Lazy so-and-so... and you have a car!

Two Lyft rides, two and a half hours in transit and in the shop — where they had to dig into the stock room for this special gauge of strings that someone, presumably Hunter or Kieran, needed, along with a few sets of more standard strings — I'm finally back in Mystic Beach, strings and a takeout order from Panera in-hand. Because that was the other thing aMUSEd had requested, and I could get both in one trip.

Sean had called me 20 minutes after he'd gotten the call from the band.

"I have plans tonight," he said. "You'll have to go get their stuff for them."

"But Steve said he wanted you to be their contact-person..."

"And I am. They contacted me, and I'm contacting you."

"I don't have a car. You do."

"Figure it out. I've got a girl I'm meeting at Fager's."

So, that's how I end up here, back at the studio, at 7 p.m., with a bag of guitar strings and someone's dinner. Even though

Steve clearly wanted me to stay away from the band, and David specifically.

I let myself in the studio entrance. I can hear someone playing electric guitar down the hall and follow the sound into the live room. Only it's not Hunter or Kier — it's David.

"Great! I've been waiting for those all afternoon!"

"*You* were the one who needed the guitar strings?"

"Yup. That was me. Strangest thing — kept breaking strings this morning."

"Well, I'm sorry it took so long. They didn't have the ones you asked for at the local shops. I had to go to Salisbury. Was the sandwich order for you, too?"

"Yeah. Had a yen for Panera. There's one near my apartment in New York, but we've been on the road so much that I haven't had it in a while."

"OK... Well, here's your strings and your food."

I hand him the string bag first.

"Oh," he says as he looks inside.

"What? Tell me I didn't get the wrong thing..."

"Well, I think it was probably my mistake. This one is the gauge I usually get for the electric-acoustic, not the straight acoustic. I might have given Sean that instead..."

David Carter should never play poker.

"You 'might have given Sean' the wrong gauge of strings... the ones he had me go get because no one local had them and he had plans..."

"It's possible that the correct gauge — this one," he says, holding up the other strings, "— would have been easy to find locally... and Sean didn't strike me as someone willing to go the extra mile for me, literally or figuratively."

"So you gave him the wrong string gauge, knowing there was a good chance that he'd pass the arduous task on to me..."

"Maybe."

"And the food?"

"It's dinner time. And I'm hungry."

"And Alex doesn't cook dinner?"

"He does. He will. In a few hours, when the guys get back from their outing to the amusement park."

"And you ordered enough food for three people to eat now because..."

"Thought Sean might be hungry after all that running around."

"I see."

"I think you do."

He's looking at me very intently now.

"You want to get me fired, don't you?"

"Alex reminded me that I too often do what I'm told, and that sometimes it's better to not do that."

"And you think I should not do what *I* was told."

"Well, I was more thinking that I shouldn't do what you told me — when you said I shouldn't intervene with Steve."

"Tell me you didn't..."

I'm imploring him, though now I'm wondering if I'd be better off telling him he *should* go talk to Steve.

"I didn't."

I sigh in relief.

"But if he keeps busting your balls, I will. And if I have to, I'll go over his head."

"He's the manager, part owner. There *is* no one over his head. Not anymore..."

That's something I'm not going to get into with David. Not unless I have to.

"I think you'd be surprised how much Steve has over his head..."

Apparently, two can play at the cryptic game. But I'm not going to ask. I don't want to know.

"Regardless," he says, "you're here, and you did me a big favor—"

"All part of the job. Literally."

"Well, Sean didn't think so. And now you're the one here with me and all this food. What do you say — beachside picnic?"

My stomach picks that moment to growl.

"I'm taking that as a yes."

David grabs a beach blanket from a closet in the residence kitchen, a bottle of white wine from the wine fridge below the counter and a pair of glasses from the cupboard, and we head out across the dune, laying the blanket out on a relatively flat spot well above the high tide line.

He's ordered several different sandwiches — one meat-heavy, another all veggies, another gooey with cheese and fresh vegetables.

"I didn't know what you'd like. I wanted to cover my bases."

"You were really sure Sean wouldn't come through with the strings, weren't you?" I observe, taking a quarter of the cheesy-tomatoey melt between slices of chewy bread.

"I was pretty sure, though it was Alex's idea."

"Mom's a keen observer of human behavior."

"That he is."

"And a busybody."

"That, too," he admits with a laugh.

"How about your actual mom? Your parents? Any other siblings?"

"Mom and Dad are great. A little too traditional to be thrilled with their sons becoming rockstars, and they were never the warm-and-fuzzy type. More the raise-them-right-to-prove-we-can type. And, no, no other siblings. Just me and Declan. Though Declan was probably as much trouble as three kids put together."

"And you were the good boy — the one who minded his manners and colored inside the lines."

"Right up until I refused to go to college as planned and followed Declan's lead in putting the band first."

"That paid off."

"It did," he says, taking a bite of the multi-meat monstrosity.

"But you came to regret it."

"A bit. Only in that I put the other love of my life — marine science — on the back burner. The closest I get now is when we stop someplace by an ocean and I can go surf or paddleboard. Or, it was until I started taking classes online."

"It's nice that you found your way back. You didn't have to give up one dream in the pursuit of the other."

He's staring at me.

"You're the first person I've met who seems to really understand that."

"I've had to give up on a few dreams in my life, find others."

"And now you have engineering."

"I do. That's the big one now."

"What about you? Your family, your parents?"

"My parents are long gone," I admit. That's true. An understatement of epic proportions, but entirely true. I hesitate to elaborate...

"I'm sorry," he says, his face full of compassion. "No siblings? I can't imagine being an only child. My life would have been so different."

"I would bet. Life would have to be a lot less dramatic for a lot of people with no Declan Carter," I reply with a smile. Belatedly, I re-think it, wondering if he'll think I'm trashing his brother and get upset that I said anything negative. I look down at my feet, waiting for a harsh response.

"It would have been," he says quietly. "A lot. But also probably considerably less exciting in good ways. I'd probably be spending my time sitting in a lab or on a boat, rather than performing for thousands. But you didn't answer me, about siblings?"

I'm relieved that he wasn't upset at what I said about his brother. I wish he'd been distracted enough not to ask again about my family.

"I had a large extended family."

"Had?"

"They're all gone now."

"You're an orphan?"

"After a fashion..." This is so hard to explain without telling him secrets he can't be told. His expression is curious, and I don't think I can avoid giving him some kind of answer. "I don't have any living siblings, no close cousins or other family members who are still around."

"That a lot of loss for someone so young."

"I'm older than I look."

That's the truth, too, but it's a messy one.

"What? Twenty-two?"

"Older."

"Twenty-five?"

"And a bit more."

"You're right. You look much younger than that."

"But I'm not. People don't remember that when they look at me. I get treated like a kid when I feel ancient."

He chuckles at that.

"How old must I seem to you at 30 when 25 is ancient?"

"You're not old — 30 isn't all that old. I just mean that people treat me differently because they don't realize how old I am. Being small doesn't make that any better."

"I get it. I know what it's like to be underestimated because people take you at face value."

"Oh?"

"People always assume I'm some vapid rockstar only interested in fame, women and money, and not a brain cell to spare past playing my bass."

"But you're not."

"You say that like you know that for a fact."

"It's obvious to me."

"That's nice to hear. I'm the quiet, brainy brother. The quiet, brainy band member. I don't carry across well in interviews. I don't carry across well with strangers, really."

"Then that makes two of us."

"I just don't read people well, don't know how to interact normally."

He hesitates, and I wait for him to finish the thought.

"I'm on the autism spectrum. They used to call it Asperger's syndrome, or high-functioning autism. Now they call it 'low support needs' autism. I guess it's kind of trendy to identify as an 'Aspie' these days, but it means I do stuff that some people find annoying, like tapping bass beats on my legs—"

"I haven't seen you do that," I interject. He shrugs.

"I do it a lot less when I'm at the beach, even if I'm inside. There's just something about the way it feels here..." He sighs — a sigh that sounds like relief, not dismay. I like how that sounds, how his shoulders relax when he does it. "And I don't do it when I'm playing, of course, because the bass is right in my hands."

He looks up at me, hesitating.

"But I have problems dealing with people I don't know, whose mannerisms I haven't learned, who don't know how I think. Even the people who know me sometimes don't understand me. I got Hunter in huge trouble with Brighid once — Declan asked about this song they used on 'Sesame Street,' and I just answered him, without thinking about it, just because he'd asked, but he was kind of making a joke about Brighid, and then Hunter joined in, and Brighid overheard him..."

He looks up at me, clearly still regretful.

"She didn't speak to him for two years."

"Wow."

"Yeah. She was pretty mad. I can't blame her. As soon as he was talking to her again, I apologized. And she was very cool about it, took me at my word that I hadn't meant anything by it at all. But that's the kind of thing I do sometimes, not noticing the context of social situations. I just blurt things out, even if it's something I shouldn't say. Makes it hard to make and keep friends. Now, Rhys — Rhys has no filter. At all. If it comes into his head, he says it — every word. Doesn't matter how ridiculous or offensive it is. I'm not *that* bad, but I still usually just try to avoid saying anything unless it seems important. I don't want to fuck things up again, for anyone, though I kind of did that already with Steve and you..."

He looks guilty, and unsure of himself, like he's waiting for me to react to his confession about being... different. And then the fact he's apparently waiting for me to react makes *me* anxious. What's the right thing to say to him? I have no idea, and I don't want to get it wrong. He's being very open with me, making himself vulnerable, sharing his secrets. I have to say the right thing in response... My brain races in circles, trying to figure it out. But that also means I understand a little bit of how he feels, I think.

"I don't communicate very well with strangers, either," I finally say. "They call it social anxiety disorder, I guess. But everyone used to just say I was shy. Painfully shy."

"Wow. I mean, I can see it now, but I wouldn't have guessed that about you that first day we met. You looked ready to smack my hand with a ruler if I didn't stop moving my mic stand."

I smile, my cheeks reddening with embarrassment.

"Sometimes I overcompensate a little... or a lot," I admit ruefully. "But I've really had to learn to be more assertive, even when I'm ready to crawl under the mixing board and hide. Especially as a woman."

"Yeah... Declan wasn't cool that night. I'm sorry about that. He's got something that happened to him. It's changed how he interacts with women. He can come off a little hostile at times, makes snap judgments. And not to make excuses for him, but being here has reminded him of that situation, so it's been worse than usual. He's pretty on-edge these days. And you might remind him a little..."

He hesitates, shakes his head.

"Anyway... I don't think he even does it on purpose. He's just more used to dealing with guys on a professional level at this point. I chewed him out after we got back from the gig that night."

"Thank you for trying to defend me. But please don't. I have to deal with guys like that, and like Steve, and it makes me seem weak if another guy has to stand up for me."

"Oh. I didn't even think about that. Sorry. I didn't mean to imply you weren't capable of standing up for yourself. I just felt responsible for the conflict with Steve, and I often feel responsible when Declan's being a dick."

"You're not your brother's keeper."

"No, but he definitely needs one," he admits with a laugh.

"It's OK. I know how brothers are..."

"I thought you were alone?"

Oops.

"I am. But I had a foster-brother who used to look out for me. A little too much at times."

"Had?"

I'm twisting the ring on my right index finger — the one Rory gave me that was made to match Rónan's ring that he had given her. She'd given the original back to him, for luck, before... "Strong as the ocean, Deep as the sea, Song on the waves," the inscription on the inside reads, just as his had. And after he was gone, she'd had a copy made for me, like a sister-in-law might. And that was how I thought of her these days. If Rónan had survived, I'm certain they'd have gotten married. He loved her very much, and she him. I think it took them both by surprise.

"He died. About six months ago."

"Oh, wow. I'm so sorry. What happened? If you don't mind me asking..."

"There was an... accident, at sea. We actually never found his body."

And we'd looked. With all the resources available to us, all of the deep-diving folk we had among us, with Rory's journalistic contacts in the local police departments, the Coast Guard... We couldn't tell them exactly what had happened, but they'd looked... we'd looked... and nothing...

There's a tickle on my cheek, and I realize it's a tear. Before I can react, David reaches out and wipes it away, the contact of skin on skin once again buzzing between us. He swallows, hard, before pulling his hand away.

"I'm sorry. I didn't mean to upset you."

"It's OK. It's still a little raw. Six months isn't a lot of time in the context of my life."

"You being ancient and all," he jokes, trying to lighten the moment. It's sweet, and I find myself smiling back at him.

"You said you'd be in a lab or on a boat if Declan wasn't around?"

"I wanted to be a marine scientist, back before we realized we could make it as musicians."

"Oh. So you wanted to study fish?"

"More marine mammals — dolphins and seals. I've actually seen a harbor seal offshore here a couple times since we've been here. I was hoping to get a better look, but she just floats out beyond the breakers, watching me. It's a little odd, to be honest. They're supposed to be migrating, so I'm not sure why she seems to be hanging out here."

Danger. Danger, Piper Morrison. This is not a safe topic.

"How do you know it's a female?"

Apparently, my anxiety isn't strong enough, at least where David Carter is concerned, to keep me from saying unwise things.

"I don't for sure. But she's small, and I just got the feeling that she's female. I don't know. It's been kind of weird. She seems very curious about me."

"Oh."

"The guys keep joking about me needing to find a mermaid." The brief smile he gives me is a little sheepish.

"What for?"

He blinks and stares at me for a moment. He has no idea how complex the topic could get...

"For a girlfriend," he explains, and I get it now. "Because... I don't date."

"Oh."

"I don't read women well. Even worse than men. I'm not really comfortable around them in that context." He seems uncomfortable admitting that.

"You're not... Surely, you've... I mean — all those women who must throw themselves at you..."

I'm stammering now. Our folk aren't circumspect about sex, and you don't reach my age without having it and discussing it pretty freely. But this is different. With David, for some reason, it's different.

He turns red.

"I feel silly being embarrassed talking about sex at 30. But — yes, I've had sex. I'm not *that* awkward." He laughs. "But it's just sex. I haven't found anyone I liked well enough to... get involved with."

"Oh."

I'm either stammering or monosyllabic right now. There's no in-between. And he's looking at me...

"So..."

Oh. I'm supposed to share, since he did...

"Are you seeing anyone?" he asks.

Oh, thank the gods... I was afraid he was going to ask whether I was a virgin. That would also be hard to explain without getting into trouble.

"No. Our people... uh... my family doesn't usually settle down until we're older."

"Probably wise. Human brains don't finish developing until we're around 25. Everyone I know who got married before 25 got divorced before they were 30. The one who wanted to get married at 17..." He cuts himself short.

"It's not a commitment to take lightly."

"No. I think you have to wait until you find someone you really connect with, who can appreciate you for who you really are... and I just haven't met anyone like that..."

The silence is heavy between us. We're both glancing across each other, avoiding eye contact while trying to figure out what the other one is thinking. Our gaze connects for a moment, and I look away, nervously biting my lower lip.

David's thumb slides across it, and I look up to find him staring at my mouth. His eyes shift up to meet mine, and it's like lightning across the water. He wraps his hand around the back of my neck and pulls me toward him, his lips pressing against mine. I moan, the shock of it dissipating under the wave of heat that rolls through me. David's lips part and his tongue flicks against my upper lip, encouraging me to open up to him.

"Davey! Are you out there humping a mermaid again? Throw her back and come inside! I've got a melody to run past you!"

He and I pull apart, both of us breathing heavy, though I couldn't say whether it's from being startled by Declan's bellowing or from the need that was on the verge of breaking free in both of us.

Regardless, the moment is gone. I look into David's eyes and see regret, and I know things have gone too far. Unfairly far, given all he does not know about me, and inappropriately far given that we're going to be working together for weeks to come. This was not a good idea, no matter how wonderful it felt in the moment.

I clear my throat.

"I'd better get going. You all have songs to write."

He pauses.

"You could come in and give us some feedback. You've proven you're fully qualified to give us some input."

His expression is earnest, almost pleading, but it's also marked by hesitation. He's unsure about what he's asking me to do.

"I think I'd better let you two figure things out. Steve asked me to come in tomorrow and line up some more drives for recording, since you all are further ahead than he expected. I'll... I'll see you then..."

I pick myself up off the blanket, gathering up the debris from our picnic, and David quickly follows, but he's looking deep into my eyes, as if he's waiting for an answer to a question he never asked. My breath catches again, and I force myself to look away.

"Did you need a ride home?"

He sounds almost hopeful, though I know the band members don't have any cars here, so I'm not sure what he's hoping for.

"No. It's an easy walk from here," I tell him. "I'll be home in no time."

"Oh." He sounds disappointed. I don't tell him that my walk home is only a few dozen yards. It's one of the secrets that help keep us safe. But I know I'll be thinking about him tonight, knowing he's so close and yet still out of reach. Because I can't... we can't... do this. No matter how right it feels. Too much depends on keeping my secrets. And I already know that keeping secrets from David is going to be a challenge the more time I spend with him. Best not to spend more time with him than I have to.

For once, the overbearing Declan Carter has come in handy. Saved by the bellow.

CHAPTER 11

SHRED OF EVIDENCE

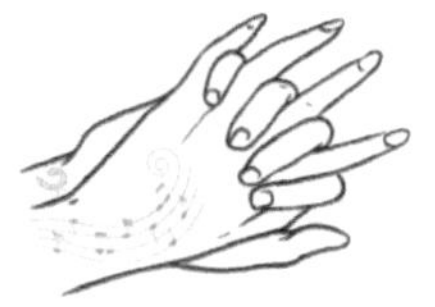

David
The next day

I've got to get Declan to stop scaring off girls, of the human or seal variety. I mean, those decibels he throws at our audiences are impressive, but shouting at me from the deck has been counterproductive at least twice already since we got here, and last night had to have been the worst timing ever. I'd finally gotten the chance to kiss Piper, and it was amazing, and then — poof! Engineer on the run! I could only hope she'd make her way back to me, like the seal had. If she didn't...

So far, she hadn't. She'd been in the studio all morning, but she was showing great skill at avoiding me without actually having it be blatantly obvious that she was avoiding me.

Just after dawn, she'd sneaked into the control room while I was in the live room playing around with the new song from yesterday. I'd been hoping I could somehow entice her into going for a swim with me, since that was a thing we had in common. It was early. Chances were Steve wouldn't be around for hours, and Sean hours after that, if at all.

But the only reason I knew she'd actually been there was that there was a fresh batch of drives for the recording system sitting on the rack by the mixing board that hadn't been there when I'd gone into the live room an hour earlier.

I went straight to the office to see if she was in there, and she was. Only, the moment she saw me, she said she needed to test and inventory all of the cables in the equipment room, and she took off, locking herself inside. Short of demanding she open the door so I could talk to her, I'm not sure what else I could have done.

Declan wouldn't be up for hours, so I was at loose ends. Two months ago, I'd have had some reading to do for classes. But this was time I'd normally be spending on lab classes that couldn't be done remotely. So I fell back on my usual therapy: I went outside and sat on the beach, just watching and listening to the waves pounding on the sand. It was overcast and too choppy to surf, and while I'd brought my skimboard down to the water with me, I just wasn't feeling it.

There were some new seal tracks on the beach to the south, but no sign of any seals in the water or actually on the beach. This day was turning into a total bust.

I hear voices behind me and spot Piper talking to Alex. I'm on my feet in a split second, but I don't get three steps before she's bolted again.

"Piper!" I call to her retreating back, but like those little shorebirds, she starts and stops on a dime and scoots out of reach before I can even get close.

"She's flighty today, isn't she?" Alex observes.

"I think Declan scared her off last night."

"So Sean did flake on your errands?"

"As you predicted. She went the better part of an hour away, via Lyft, just to get what she thought *Hunter or Kieran* had requested, while the daddy's boy had a hot date."

"Was she pissed when she realized you'd set her up?"

"Actually, no. She seemed mildly amused. And hungry."

"So, you managed to feed her again? That's always a good sign. Food is a love language."

"We had a picnic out on the beach — blanket, wine, sandwiches... And she talked to me, told me about her family..."

"She mention her brother?"

"Her foster-brother?"

"She said she'd had a protective older brother who'd passed away. Recently, I assumed."

"Yeah — her foster-brother. Boating accident about six months ago. She's basically on her own now that he's gone.

Though she said yesterday morning that the honey was her family's... I guess they're distant cousins or something... She said they're relying on her — this job's really important to her."

"Why wouldn't it be? What would you do if something threatened to take away the band?"

I don't answer that. Because I've got a quick answer right on the tip of my tongue. And that makes me realize how much more she has at stake here. Not only are people relying on her, she's got one single career she loves with all her heart. I have two, either of which would make me happy to pursue for the rest of my life. I would never want to live without music, but as long as I could play, I'd be happy working as a marine scientist in some capacity.

Moreover, she was being deprived of the full value of her internship because of her gender. Whether it was the favoritism Steve already showed his son or the extra scrutiny and scutwork he'd dumped on her to punish her for socializing with a client, she was being held to a higher bar and pushed down at the same time. I'm not sure I'll be able to hold my tongue the next time I see Steve if this continues. I get why she feels she needs to take this kind of treatment and just deal with it. But it's not right.

"Dave?"

"You're right. I'm not going to let them take this away from her if it gets to that point. I can respect her wishes until then. But this is partly my fault. I can't have her pay the price for my mistakes."

"Does that mean you're going to stay away from her?"

"Fuck no! If anything, it pisses me off all the more that there's a double standard that's keeping me from spending more time with her."

"Good."

"Good?"

"Yeah. Sometimes you've got to fight for what's important, what's real and authentic and part of who you are. No matter what tries to stand in your way."

I get the feeling Alex isn't just talking about Piper, or relationships, or even our music or Piper's career as an engineer. He's staring out at the water now, preoccupied. I let the silence continue for a minute, but he's not volunteering anything.

"Did you need me for something?"

"Huh?" he replies, snapping out of it. "Oh — Declan was looking for you."

"Nice of him to finally get his ass out of bed."

"We *are* on vacation, Dave. And not all of us work equally well at dawn as we do at midnight."

"Yeah. I know. My fault for being the early-riser... I'm just still pissed at him for interrupting me when I was with Piper last night, and out watching the seal before that."

"Well, if you want a few hours of quiet at night, tonight's your night. He said he's going out clubbing in Ocean City."

"Shit... He's going to get himself recognized, and then we're going to have paparazzi all over us."

"I'm not sure Hunter's girlfriends aren't going to make the whole area Insta-famous before they even get the show filming done. So the problem may not end up being Declan. Anyway — he's going to be out until the wee hours, I'm sure, so seal-watch away tonight. Unless you were making plans with Piper."

"I can't make plans with Piper when I can't get within 30 feet of her without her taking off."

"Ouch. Sorry, man... Just give her some time, let this all settle down a bit. It's not like you to be impatient, anyway. Try some classic David passivity."

"You've got to make up your mind, Alex — am I supposed to be fighting for her or being passive so she can have more time?"

"That's a very good question. One only you can answer."

I roll my eyes at him and his pop psychology. Or is it "mom" philosophy? Either way, I need to go find Declan and see if we can get some writing done, since it doesn't look like I'm going to be spending my afternoon getting things sorted out with Piper.

I t's almost 9 o'clock, and the sky is finally dark, which should give me an advantage in spotting any seals in the water, especially if it's the pale, tawny-grey female I've seen several times now. I'm stationed at the south end of our section of beach, eyes and ears peeled. My mind, meanwhile, is wandering, and keeps following what seems increasingly like a road that inevitably leads back to Piper, no matter which detours I keep trying to send it down.

I get the image of her sweet little pixie face stuck in my head and give up trying to pry it back out again, lying back on the beach and closing my eyes, recalling the feel of her lips under my thumb, watching her chocolate brown irises as they dilated in arousal when I leaned in to kiss her, that almost electric zap of energy whenever we touch. Even just coiling cables together, the chemistry between us is just off the charts.

The nearly-full moon comes out from behind a cloud, shining on the water, which has settled down a bit since this morning. The waves are waist-high now, but clean. If I was wanting a night-surf, this might be the night. But I'm taking advantage of Declan's absence for my seal-watching. Maybe it'll help get my mind off of Piper.

There's a flash of light from down the beach, and I lie back down amid the beach grass to avoid being seen by that security guard. The light shines across the shoreline between us before swinging to the west and then back south. I start to sit up but drop back when I see more movement in that direction. I peer through the clumps of grass and see someone moving quickly toward the water... too much moonlight reflecting off skin to be the security guard or any normal — clothed — swimmer.

She — and it has to be a she, with those curves — darts toward the water and makes another elegant dive into the face of the wave. I'm up on my feet in a flash, tossing my shirt onto the sand and darting down to where she entered the water. That whole incident has been nagging at me for days. There had to be an explanation for her near-instant disappearance, other than my imagination running away with me. Maybe it's the scientist in me, but I want an explanation, something tangible that'll explain what happened so I can get that one nagging question out of my head. And get back to focusing on Piper. And seals. And maybe writing some music.

I stand exactly in the spot where I saw her go in this time. There's even a set of footprints from someone running from up the beach to the water line. There — tangible evidence that I at least saw someone this time. I peer out into the water, expecting to see a head of dark hair bobbing atop the waves or at least someone stroking down along the beach. But there's nothing. Again.

Is this girl some kind of free-diving champion who can hold her breath for minutes and minutes on end? I mean — I can hold my breath for longer than most people. I could top three minutes when it was just a surfing skill I wanted to develop, but Gryffin, our head of security, is a retired Navy SEAL, and he gave me some extra tips based on his training. I'm up to just over five minutes, the last time I timed myself. But there's no way this girl is swimming so far out or up the beach in one breath that I wouldn't be seeing her. Unless she really is a champion free-diver.

Or maybe I really am seeing things. But hallucinations don't leave footprints. Neither do ghosts, right? Assuming you believe in ghosts. Which isn't the most scientific thing to do. Because there's no tangible evidence. But I have no tangible evidence that I saw what I think I saw — twice now — except my memory and a trail of footprints that could, possibly, have been left earlier in the day. Maybe. What's the more likely scenario: world-class breath-holding swimmer, or a phantom, or David Carter is losing his mind?

Right now, it's a close call. At least as far as David Carter, scientist, is concerned. And, honestly, I'm not sure who else I'd tell if I wanted an outside opinion, because chances are whoever I told about this disappearing swimmer would conclude my cheese had slipped off my cracker.

I concede defeat and walk back toward the studio house. I stop to pick up my discarded shirt and give one last glance down the beach. No seal. No phantom swimmer. No Piper. Not even an idea for a song. Today really was a bust on all fronts. Maybe I should have gone out with Declan.

OK. Now *that's* crazy talk. Thankfully, I didn't voice *that* thought to anyone else. They'd know I had lost my mind.

I shake my head to clear whatever cobweb spawned that nonsense, and I dismiss the flash of light I catch in my peripheral vision as the result of that movement. Until I look more closely and see it resolve itself into a human form, this time racing from the water up the beach. Pale skin, curves, dark hair... I take off after her, determined to put this mystery to rest once and for all. It's not my beach, and I don't care if she's trespassing to skinnydip, but I need to prove to myself that I'm not imagining things.

I'm twenty yards behind her and gaining when she reaches the fence that runs along the bottom of the massive structure, partly covered by a deck four times the size of the one at the studio house, huge pilings supporting it over the sand. And it's one of those pilings that trips me up.

I go down, catching myself on my elbows and then popping right back up, just as if I was popping up on my surfboard — but I've lost sight of her in that instant. There's nothing to indicate my mystery woman was even there, except more footprints, which disappear amidst the dune grasses along the fence. Where can she have gone? Is she some kind of superhero-mutant-ghost, holding her breath to swim for miles, becoming invisible at will and leaping over 10-foot fences?

The evidence would suggest that's the case. Either that, or I really am losing my mind.

CHAPTER 12

HUMAN

David
A few days later

I'm determined to prove to myself that I'm not losing my mind, seeing things that can't be real, like phantom skinnydippers. I'm going to find proof, whatever that takes. My determination has nothing to do with my frustration that I can't get Piper to talk to me other than to tell me she's busy with her work. Nothing at all. I'm sure I'd still be planning my own beachside episode of "Mythbusters" even if Piper was sitting next to me in a bikini...

And *there's* an image I'm not going to be able to get out of my head. I've only ever seen her in her engineer gear — head-to-toe black with a cute little skirt over leggings, girly and practical all at once — but my mind's eye likes the idea of her in a swimsuit, her lush curves no longer hidden but framed to perfection in a few scraps of fabric...

Where was I? Right. Naked ghostly swimmers. Honestly — I'd rather see Piper in a swimsuit, or even just in her practical wardrobe, than catch this skinnydipper. But since I haven't seen Piper at all today, I'm going to funnel my energy into this little exposé so it will stop driving me nuts. Or at least more nuts than I apparently already am...

The moment it's dark out, I'm down on the beach amidst the dune grass again, my eyes focused on the space between the breakers and the dry sand. Did I mention I didn't sleep very well last night, between the frustration over this mystery and the even more infuriating frustration of having Piper dodging me? It's really no surprise that I nodded off.

I jolt awake with no idea what time it is, except it's still dark out, so nowhere near morning. Did I miss her? Would she even have come out again tonight after having me chase her up the beach last night? She seems pretty bold, making use of a guarded private beach for her little nude swimming habit, but was she bold enough to try it again after her last run-in with me?

I scan the beach and the water, but there's no sign of anyone.

Correction — there's my seal. And she's coming ashore.

Well, if I can't catch my phantom, at least I can get a good look at this seal, finally. She rides the waves in until she's on solid ground, hauling out from the receding wave, galumphing along on the sand with the rocking-lurching motion of a species of true seals, whose short front flippers don't allow for the "walking" motion a sea lion would have. The waves push along behind her, washing over her, with her mottled grey-brown coat the perfect camouflage amid seafoam and sand.

I stand up to look closer but I lose sight of her in the churning shorebreak.

Wait — there's my phantom swimmer, emerging from the ocean at nearly the same spot and time. In an instant, I weigh approaching the seal closer than I should against resolving this swimmer mystery once and for all. Either way, I'm trespassing, but then so is this woman. And the seal will come back if I — we — frighten her away, right?

With no more thought than that, I take off at top speed down the beach to the water. In my desperation to ensure the woman doesn't take off and give me the slip like she did last night, instinct takes over and I throw myself at her, using my body weight to make sure she can't get her feet under her. Then, determined to get answers that won't evaporate between my fingers, I grab hold of her arms and flip her over on her back, still pressing her into the sand to avoid another disappearing act.

"What the hell?" My eyes go wide with disbelief. "Piper?"

My brain is trying to catch up, but it's having problems putting the things I just witnessed together into one cohesive picture.

Seal emerging from the sea.

Wave washing over.

A dark head of hair, luscious curves and an extraordinary expanse of bare skin.

And I instinctively threw myself on top of her to prove to myself she was real. Only to have her roll over and discover a very naked, very female sound engineer trapped under me.

"What... How... Where?"

"David, I need you to get off of me. Now. Before the guard comes and finds us here like this."

She nods down, where her bare breasts are crushed under my shirt. And suddenly, my dick is all-in for whatever this is, while my brain still insists that none of this can be happening.

"David! Please! Now!" she pleads urgently.

I snap out of my fog and hop to my feet. I reach down for Piper's hand to help her up off the sand, but she's clutching a tawny length of cloth to her chest in some semblance of modesty. It must have been caught under her when I landed on top of her. She climbs to her feet, careful to keep herself covered.

Only then does she take my outstretched hand, pulling me behind her as she hurries up the beach, away from the surf. I try not to gawk at her, bared from heel to head and appearing not to care that I can see her shapely ass, the tops of her thighs and the smooth taper of her waist, with not a stitch of clothing between her body and my eyes. She's skirting along the edge of the beach grass between us and the studio house, scanning down the beach with her eyes while very determinedly pulling me along in her wake.

As we hit the toe of the dune, her path is blocked by the fence and I expect her to turn us around and take us back onto the studio's private beach. Instead, she reaches through the dune grass and fiddles with a spot on the fence. A gate I didn't even realize was there swings open, and she pulls us both through, securing it behind us.

"Piper — I don't think we're supposed to be here. This place is private, and they're kind of serious about keeping it that way," I whisper urgently at her.

"I know, David. Just trust me. Stay quiet."

She pulls me along, under a low deck that allows me just enough clearance not to bump my head, and approaches a clapboard-covered wall. Once she reaches it, she presses her fingers to the wall and it springs back toward her, a hidden door opening to allow access inside this massive structure, which is both several times the size of the studio complex and much bigger than I would have guessed from the profile it has from the beach.

Piper tugs me along behind her once more, her bare feet padding along a floor made up of tiny pebbles compressed together inside a strip of compacted sand. The sand falls away from our feet as we move down the long, dimly-lit hallway. And if a storm surge managed to overtop the dune and inundate the ground floor, the water could just filter away afterward. Ingenious design.

When we reach an intersection, Piper pulls me down a side hallway and up a short flight of open stairs, then presses her hand to a panel above a doorknob. There's a soft click and she again drags me forward through the doorway. She finally comes to a stop in the dark room and gives me a firm shove. My arms windmill, instinctively looking to break my fall, but instead I land on my ass on top of a thick towel that sits atop a bed cloaked in sheer curtains.

Piper steps away and reaches for a robe hanging on the wall nearby, clicking a switch that turns on a dim light next to the bed. I watch wordlessly as she pulls the silky robe around her shoulders and fastens it at the waist, finally shielding her bare back side from my eyes. The piece of tawny-colored cloth she'd clutched to her chest is lying next to me on the bed, and I reach out to touch it.

It's not cloth. It's fur. Like legit fur-coat fur. Like... like... seal fur...

"This isn't..." I venture in the persistent silence.

Piper turns to look at me and heaves a sigh, closing those big brown eyes of hers, as if she can't bear the sight in front of her.

"It looks like..."

"Seal fur."

"Yeah."

"What did you see, David?"

"Uh..."

"On the beach, David... I know you're probably in shock, but tell me what you saw."

I review it in my head, still not able to make sense of it.

"The seal — that one I've been seeing... she was coming onshore, and then a wave washed over her, and I saw a person, a woman, there instead. No seal. She'd disappeared. But the woman looked like she might be the one I'd seen last week, who I was worried had drowned, because she'd just disappeared in the ocean while I watched. I didn't want her to disappear again, so I grabbed for her..."

"You saw a woman you thought had drowned days ago and you decided the reasonable thing to do was to throw yourself on top of her..." She sounds skeptical. She sounds skeptical of my sanity, actually, and I'm not far from that skepticism myself.

"It was instinct. I didn't exactly think it through. Kind of like when I almost walked into the ocean to follow the seal the other day, even though I knew better. My feet just took me there."

As I work to recall the incongruent scenes from just minutes ago, the details start to become clearer, the picture more complete than the one my mind had processed in the moment. The memory plays back in slow motion on the mental screen in my head.

Seal.

Seal overwashed by surf.

Woman overwashed by surf.

Woman emerging from the surf.

Me falling on top of said woman.

Woman under me.

Piper under me.

Naked.

With a seal fur under her.

I run a finger over the soft speckled fur, and there's an energy to it... like... like when Piper and I touch.

"What *are* you?"

Piper's sigh is pure dismay.

"You saw, didn't you? The seal, and me. You remember, and you've put it together."

"You are the seal. The seal is you."

I can't quite believe I'm saying those words. This is not possible. It defies everything I understand about science, biology, physics... reality... But I'm sitting here next to the fur coat of the seal I've seen repeatedly in recent days, and the woman who emerged from the sea with that coat in her hands is standing in front of me, wet and naked under a thin robe.

The preposterousness of this idea doesn't stop my dick from recovering from the earlier shock and going into "Hello — hot girl nearly naked and within easy reach" mode. I shake my head free, leaving the other active portion of my anatomy to do what it will.

"What *are* you?" I ask again, more insistent this time.

Piper approaches me, but instead of answering, she picks up the piece of fur and lays it carefully across a small table near where her robe had hung. She sits down next to me on the bed and takes a deep breath, clearly steeling herself.

"Most people call us selkies." For the first time, I notice the slightest lilt in her voice, calling into question one more thing I thought I knew about this girl. "We call ourselves 'sluagh rón' — seal-folk."

"So you... you're really a seal."

"No. We're not seals. But we have dual forms — human-like and seal-like. Both and neither, all at once. We're creatures of legend to most humans. Fairy stories they tell their grandchildren, about the fisherman who took a selkie wife and hid her seal coat away from her so she couldn't go back to sea. Kept against her will, she pines for her freedom and dies, or she schemes to take back her seal coat and leaves him and their children forever, or until the child taps into its selkie nature and joins its mother in the sea, transforming for the first time. Humans have made the legend into movies before. It's a beautiful story if you're not living it. And it is true, after a fashion. It has happened. It's our major vulnerability — if we lose our coats, we cannot transform back into seals. So from the first moment we transform and gain our coats, we are very careful with them. Mine won't stay there where it sits right now. I'll hide it safely away once you're not here to see where I put it."

"So, if I took your seal coat, you'd be stuck as a human?"

She shudders.

"It's a cruel thing to do to someone, David." That hint of an accent — Irish? Scottish? — gets stronger as her voice takes on more emotion, as I've often heard Kieran's do. "And you're not a cruel person, so let's skip the hypothetical nightmare scenario and agree that that would be bad."

"Of course."

I don't know what else to say. She's presented me with a story literally out of legend and told me it's true. Not only that — I've seen it with my own eyes, even if my mind didn't want to make sense out of it at first. But I know it happened. A seal transformed into a woman, and I wasn't only there when it happened — I had her in my hands, under me. It was real.

"I'm... uh... I'm sorry about ambushing you there. I don't normally throw myself on top of naked women... not without their permission, at least."

I give her a sheepish grin, and finally, I see something other than frustration and despair on her cute little face, because she smiles back at me. My heart is suddenly about a hundred pounds lighter. I don't like that I made her unhappy. In fact, I realize I enjoy making her smile. She's a seal-woman, and it's more important to me that she's smiling than that my sense of reality has been completely rewritten in the space of half an hour. OK. I can accept that. I'm good with that. Somehow.

"I've never had someone throw themselves on top of me in the middle of a transformation. But if it had to happen, I'm sort of glad it was you."

Her smile is small and a little embarrassed. It makes her seem more like the young woman I've been getting to know, a little unsure of herself underneath the bravado. I'm tempted to run my thumb over her soft lips again to feel that smile in a more tangible way.

"I'm sort of glad that it was me and not some other guy lying on top of you naked."

The small space between us instantly heats up. Nothing I discovered tonight has dulled my physical reaction to this... woman? Seal? Selkie? Whatever I call her, my body has no doubt she's a woman.

The silence stretches, and I look around me. It's a small room. Not much more than a bed, a small seating area and a bathroom, like you'd find in a standard hotel room. There's a television, a laptop computer and a high-end stereo system with studio-quality speakers and pro-quality headphones. That alone declares this space to be hers.

"What is this place? Are there more of you? More seal-folk?"

"This is Safe Harbour. Literally. It's a refuge, for seal-folk and others like us who have been displaced from their traditional homelands or homewaters. It's an outpost where we try to begin to fit ourselves into the human world as much as we can or want to. For some, that's not at all, and they will live here in seclusion, protected from the human world and other threats. For others, we will try to find a place in the human world, to support Safe Harbour and help keep the other Hidden Folk safe."

"Hidden Folk?"

"That's what we call ourselves, this ragtag community of refugees. It's a reminder that our existence must remain a secret. Failure to keep that secret would spell disaster for us all."

"I saw 'Splash.' I wouldn't want you dissected, either." I gesture at the television, my eyes going again to the studio monitors and headphones by her stereo. The sound engineer at home, with her seal coat nearby.

"It's a sweet movie. Not entirely realistic, but that's one part of the plot I fear would really happen if scientists or the government realized what we are. They'd hunt us for the secrets to our transformations, our long lifespans, the abilities we have that humans don't. And I don't mean my awesome engineering skills," she adds with a smile.

And in that moment, it hits me. Our sound engineer is literally a legend. Our sound engineer isn't *human*... And this girl I've been so drawn to isn't a girl at all.

CHAPTER 13

NEVER GET OLD

Piper

"You're not 25, are you?"

"No, I'm not. In my defense, I said I was 25 'and then some.'"

"How much is 'some'?"

Here's where we find out exactly how much truth would-be marine scientist David Carter can take...

"About ten-fold that."

He blinks. Several times. For the better part of a minute, actually. He's not looking directly at me, but I can feel the wheels turning in his head: How? What does that mean beyond the number? Am I telling him the truth, or is this some kind of elaborate joke on the celebrity? Is he being punked?

"You're 250 years old..."

I nod slowly.

"Give or take. We don't count years past the first hundred or so. We just mark milestones in maturity. Among our people, I really am the equivalent of about 25 years old — an adult, fully matured, but not yet in the prime of my life."

He takes that in.

"So, like in 'dog years,' but for selkies, you're 25."

"Yes. Thereabouts."

"So you'll live until you're what... 750? 800?"

And here's the only thing harder than explaining what I am and how many years I've been on this earth...

"No. We don't age like that."

"Faster? Slower?"

"Much slower in terms of appearance. We age faster when we're younger. I will look more or less like I do now for many centuries."

"And how old is 'old' among your people?"

"The eldest among us here has seen more than three millennia. There are stories of those who are older, but they didn't come here with us."

"Three thousand years old?"

Now he's incredulous. Stunned. I can tell his brain is refusing to make sense of this now, and part of me wants to take it back, to not have given him honest answers to his questions, even if it feels like he's earned it. Can his mind, with three decades of existence stored away, come to terms with something so fantastical?

After a few minutes of silence, he looks at me, digesting the details of my appearance, and presumably how different my actual age and my apparent age are from each other.

"We must seem like children to you."

There's a note of resentment in his voice, and it hurts my heart to hear it. I reach for his face and slide my hand gently down his cheek.

"Oh, no — not at all. Humans age on a human scale. Toddlers are toddlers and elders are elders. As a species, you're young. But as individuals, you're as varied as the pebbles on the beach. You're each as mature as your soul is, seen through the perspective of your experiences."

"So I..."

"It's a human cliché, but you're an old soul, David. I knew that the first time we talked. Regardless of your issues dealing with other people sometimes, you're a mature adult human with deep insight. Many humans die of old age with less maturity of vision. You're not a child to me. Not at all."

Please let him hear the affection in my voice...

"But I'll grow old and die in what is effectively the blink of an eye to you."

And that's the crux of this. I don't want to think about that. But it is the way of nature. As unnatural as we may seem to humans, we are intricately entwined with the natural world.

"All humans die, David. It is the nature of your species. It just makes it all the more vital to live while you have that time. Every moment is precious."

"Of course."

He's quiet again. I'm trying to read his expression. He wants to ask me something...

"How long will you live?"

My heart breaks a little. This may be the hardest thing for him to hear, of all that I have told him thus far.

"Barring accident or intentional acts, selkies are immortal."

His eyes go wide.

"So, a few thousand years is nothing."

"It's not nothing. Most of us don't end up living that long. We have enemies, human and otherwise, and we have predators who think nothing more of killing us than they do our animal brethren. They can't even tell us apart most of the time. And eternity is a long time. Not all of us choose to endure that."

"And your foster-brother?"

"Rónan wasn't one of the seal-folk. He was... something else. I don't think *he* even knew the truth of his nature, which is why he was so willing to throw himself between us — the world — and things that sought to destroy us. You have no idea how close they came... Rónan didn't know for sure that he wouldn't be able to survive it. He hoped he could, I'm sure. He didn't want to leave Rory, or me, or the rest of our people. But he was our protector, and he died protecting everyone."

"If he wasn't a selkie, what was he?"

"His father is one of the old gods. A sea god, though we never knew which one. His mother was what you would call a sorceress — not fully human but not immortal either, though she badly wanted to be. There was no telling which of them his biology would favor."

"He was a demi-god."

"In essence, yes. Though I doubt he ever thought of himself that way — not when he didn't know whether he was immortal or how long he'd live if he wasn't."

"How old was he?"

"I never asked. It's not a thing we measure. He was born sometime after I was."

"So he was *younger* than you. This protective 'older' brother."

"In years, yes. But he matured faster than selkies do. His nature put him on land, in contact with humans more than we are, more than we ever have been. He functioned as a bridge between our worlds, eventually making his way here, where he helped us establish our refuge and guided those of us who sought shelter here in beginning to integrate with the human world. Not all of us can. But he could and did, and I... I've started. I was part of the vanguard, the first of us to really go out in the world."

"Is that why you have problems dealing with people — with humans? Because we're new to you?"

I chuckle for the first time since he raised the question of my age.

"I wish that's all it was. I'm the same way with our own people, too. Shy, anxious, awkward. I've found that, in a way, it's almost easier to deal with humans. And some humans more than others..." I let that confession stand between us, unexamined. "You don't have expectations of me, especially as Rónan's foster-sister."

"Those sound like big shoes to fill."

"I'm not the one filling them, at least not most of it. The Elders have taken on some of Rónan's duties. And his girlfriend..."

"Another selkie? Or is she a demi-god like him?"

My face erupts in a broad smile.

"She's human, actually. Like you, she managed to stumble into our secret, and helping him deal with the threat, they got close, fell in love." I blush, realizing the precedent that set and that I've unintentionally laid it out like that to David. "What she did to try to save us, to save him... she's one of us now. And as a human, she's better suited to some things than even Rónan was. She's become an elder sister to me, even though she's younger than you."

"And how did they deal with that difference between them — the human woman and the demi-god? Knowing that she'd eventually die and he might be immortal?" Again a note of near-hostility from him, and my heart quavers.

"Rónan fought what was between them, at least at first, and she did for a time, too. But they were fated to end up together, no matter what their heads told them. I don't think they had enough time together to really think about the long term."

Overwhelming sadness hits me. I lost my brother. Rory lost her mate. We all lost our protector. And now we'd have to make things work without him. And here I am getting attached to a rockstar who'll not only live a comparatively short life but who won't be here more than a few months anyway. I look at my feet, my eyes swimming again.

"I'm sorry. For both of you. All of you."

He reaches out and rubs my shoulder. It's an innocent gesture of consolation, but that zing of connection returns. Now it's *my* brain that refuses to do its job. I look up into those pale blue eyes, and he's *right there*, emotions naked, raw. How does anyone have a hard time understanding this man? All that he is is right there for the world to see. Sweet, caring, intelligent beyond belief. And creative to boot.

I'm in so much trouble here.

"David — you can't tell anyone any of this. You understand that, right? Not your brother, your bandmates — no one. Lives are at stake. Safe Harbour must remain safe, the Hidden Folk hidden away from the human world."

He takes a deep breath, and for a moment I wonder if he really believes any of this enough to make such a solemn vow.

"I won't tell anyone, Piper. I promise. I'm not sure anyone would believe me if I did," he adds wryly. "But I'll keep your secret."

"Thank you!" Flooded with relief, I throw my arms around him. He freezes, and I pull slowly back. Oops. Obviously, what he has learned about me tonight will have put distance between us, one of us human and the other... not. My touch is unwelcome now. I have to let go...

But then I see his face, and it's not discomfort displayed there. It's pure heat. He's feeling this thing between us, too, and, somehow, learning my secrets hasn't erased that.

We're staring at each other, icy blue eyes to earthy brown. So different and yet so much in tune. My pulse and breath speed up, and I can see his chest rising and falling faster than it was moments ago. His scent, human and oh, so male, washes over me, and I'm drawn in, like a cartoon bunny floating airborne on the tantalizing scent of a carrot.

I lean in toward his lips, but his hands grasp my shoulders, holding me back with just a few inches between us. I've overreached. Again. Despite this attraction between us, he can't see his way past the differences in our natures. After all the teasing about falling for a mermaid, a real selkie is a bridge too far. My eyes slide closed and I sigh.

Fingers trace down my cheek, and I open my eyes again to see an expression of wonder as David looks at me from so tantalizingly close. My breath catches with the intensity.

"You don't eat your mates or anything, do you?" he muses with a smile. I laugh out loud.

"No. The worst selkie women do is go back into the sea."

"Like the Irish mermaids..."

I blink in surprise.

"You know of the merrows?"

"Kieran told us a little of the stories his mom told him when he was young. Wait — are mermaids real?"

"Actually, yes."

"I owe Rhys an apology.," he says, shaking his head.

"There are some merrows among us, and other creatures humans might call mermaids."

"Do *they* eat their mates?"

I chuckle heartily.

"No. You watch too many fake cryptozoology documentaries." Now he laughs.

"Not horror movies?"

"You're a scientist. You'd be watching documentaries, even fake ones, before you'd spend time on a horror movie."

"Is that how you learned to act human? TV?"

"We mostly act human anyway. But it helped me get used to how things are here. And learn to speak English like a modern American. A lot of things. I learn quickly, adapt. It's one of the reasons I was one of the first to go out in the human world. And I've gotten a unique perspective on human behavior from my favorite fictional grifters," I add, garnering a smile from my fellow "Leverage" fan. "Though I'd probably spend most of my time watching MTV if they actually had any music on there."

"That's why you didn't recognize us when you first saw us!"

"I'd never laid eyes on aMUSEd before. Not so much as a photo. I don't usually research the artists I listen to. I couldn't tell you who the band members are of *any* of my favorite bands.

But I can tell you which pedals the guitar player is using. And I can tell the difference between coated bass strings and uncoated ones."

"Wait. You can hear a difference? From the coating?"

"My hearing has a slightly different range. Somewhere between seals and humans. My earplugs are designed to compensate, as well as protect my ears, but I can still hear some things humans can't. You play Elixir Nanowebs — light/mediums. Hunter prefers Elixirs as well, but uncoated and heavier gauge. Kieran plays extra-lights on most of his guitars, coated."

"So, you couldn't have recognized us with us standing right in front of you, but you know which strings we all like."

"I do," I admit, suddenly feeling shy again.

"You really are extraordinary."

I laugh out loud.

"So, you discover that I'm 250 years old, immortal and can change into a seal, and the thing that impresses you is that my ears can tell what strings you like. You are definitely a musician above all else."

Now we're both laughing. Until we're not. Heat sparks between us again as David traces his fingers down my other cheek. He starts to lean forward and hesitates.

"No, we don't eat humans. I promise. I much prefer fish." I smile gently.

"I'm not sure I can make the same promise," he drawls. "I'm pretty sure at some point I'm going to be eating you..."

I blink, confused.

"Wait — is that not something that your people do? Oral sex?"

"Oh. Oh!" I blush deep red. "No — we do that. We just don't call it 'eating.' I'm afraid I've got some gaps in my vocabulary with things that aren't commonly said on TV."

"Well, I'm happy to help you expand your vocabulary for all things sexual," he teases, pulling me into him.

"I'd like that."

His lips finally brush across mine, and I'm instantly riveted. There's something about David Carter that just calls to me. I start to see why it is so many of my kind take human mates, if not usually forever. Or maybe it's just David. I wrap my arms around him, pulling him close.

"What is it about you?" he muses aloud, apparently as inexplicably drawn to me as I am to him. His lips trail down my neck, gently exploring, tasting. "You're not a siren, are you? Using your magic to draw me in?"

"Selkies don't have that kind of magic. And there are no sirens among us that I know of." I pull back, looking him in the eyes. "Are you concerned I'm bespelling you, compelling you somehow? I don't want..." I can't bring myself to finish, suddenly feeling self-conscious.

"Hey — no," he says holding my face between his hands. "I was teasing. I trust you to tell me the truth. You've been more honest with me about your secrets than you had to be. You've trusted me to keep those secrets. The least I can do is trust you in return. And I want this... want you. And it seems like you feel the same way."

"I do. I've never felt like this..."

"About a human?"

"About anyone."

I'm two centuries old, and this is the first time I've felt anything like this. No one else, human or otherwise, has ever drawn me in like David Carter. Immortal I may be, but in this moment I feel nothing but vulnerable.

David stares deep into my eyes for a moment, tenderness in his expression.

"Me, either," he says, kissing me sweetly, and then harder. And then we're consuming each other in earnest — mouths, tongues, lips. His fingers tangle in my hair and I slide my hands through his shorter strands. He lets go of me long enough to grab the back of his shirt and strip it off over his head. He pulls my hands to his chest, encouraging me wordlessly to explore, and I do, tracing the planes and lines of his surf-chiseled body as if learning a language composed only of sensation.

His hands trace down the center of my robe, sliding under the edges and playing in my cleavage. I moan into his mouth, pressing my breasts toward him. He pulls at the tie holding the robe closed, and it comes loose. I shrug my shoulders free, and he pulls the sleeves down my arms, leaving me bare from the waist up and covered below only by virtue of the fact that I'm sitting.

David's lips drift downward until he takes my breast into his mouth, sucking gently on one nipple while he runs his callused fingertips across the other one. I arch my back, pushing my breasts into his hand, his mouth. He moans against my breast, the vibrations causing a shiver down my spine.

I pull his mouth back up to mine, feasting on him as he pulls my fingers to the waist of his board shorts. I untie the tie by feel, fully engrossed in his mouth, and then pull the fastening open. He guides my hand down his stomach and below the fabric, and it seeks the hard length of him under velvety soft skin.

He pushes into my hand with his hips, pulling the shorts down as he does so, until he's lying naked on my bed, pulling me on top of him. The robe, now untied, slides down across my hips and onto the floor, leaving the two of us pressed together, nothing between us but this overwhelming attraction.

David absently traces his hands up and down my sides as he kisses me, and I writhe my hips against him. His hand delves between my legs, rubbing lightly until I'm soaked.

"Piper," he says breathlessly. "What about protection? I don't want to get you pregnant."

"Can't get pregnant right now. Wrong time of the year," I reply, just as breathlessly. "We have an annual cycle."

"I'm clean — no infections or diseases. Haven't been with anyone in a while."

"Can't get those kinds of human infections, either. The theory is our DNA is too different. Viruses and bacteria can't adapt fast enough to survive our immune systems."

"I'm starting to think that I should get a degree in cryptozoology instead of marine science." He laughs. "Sounds fascinating."

"We don't have any scientists or doctors, just healers, and they don't do things the way your doctors do. But we've started keeping track of your science, too. There is some overlap."

"Speaking of overlap... Now that we've got the practicalities sorted out..." He grins at me.

"Hmm..." The sensation of his hands on me is entrancing. But suddenly he rolls us both over, sliding me up onto the bed and covering my body with his own. His erection presses into my center, hard against soft, silky against slick as my body makes its desire clear to us both. His hands grip my hips, his lips diving for mine and taking possession.

This David is more aggressive than he's been during our conversations or the time I've seen him in the studio, more sure of himself. He's in tune with his body and mine, and there's no insecurity about how he's reading me, no thoughts of social cues he might be missing. And I find myself wanting to let him take the lead. Our extraordinary age gap doesn't factor in. He's a rockstar in his sexual prime, and he knows how to use his body to make a woman — human or otherwise — feel very good.

I want to let this attraction between us run free and find its own way. So I shift my focus from thought to feeling, reveling in the sensation of his skin on mine, his lips dotting soft kisses along my shoulders and then down into my cleavage. My hands sweep up his back and into his hair, connecting us. His hips roll against mine, pressing his cock against me once again, and my thighs wrap around his sides, pulling us into closer alignment.

His hand reaches between us and sweeps along my lower lips, diving into the moisture growing there and trailing up to the apex, where he circles before sliding himself along the slick channel. He catches my eyes, glints of delight in his that I know must find their match even in my dark umber ones.

"I've never been inside a woman with nothing between us. I'm not sure how long I'll last, but I'm going to make sure we both enjoy every moment of it."

It's a touching sentiment, made all the more impactful because I know there's more here than just sexual pleasure, more than the physical. And as David presses his tip inside me, slowly sinking himself into me, it's like nothing I've ever experienced. Sweet, warm, gentle, exquisitely perfect as he slowly fills me. I've never had a human lover before. Maybe that's all this is — some quirk of chemistry between selkie and human. But as David sheaths himself fully within me and our eyes meet, I know it's more, for both of us.

He begins a slowly building dance, withdrawing and then pushing back inside, tantalizing and teasing but with a persistent, driving rhythm that mirrors his bass lines. And it feels as good between my thighs as his bass does between my ears. His talented fingers play against the skin of my neck and shoulders, his mouth moaning against mine, making a sound as delightful and tuneful to me as his harmonies on stage.

I give myself over to my senses, losing myself in the taste and scent, the sounds and touch of this extraordinary human, who may well have ruined me for any other man the moment his body became one with my own. It's a reminder of what stands between us, but also a testimony to how each of the moments of his preciously short life has been distilled into a gift he is now giving to me.

I cannot conquer time on his behalf, but in this moment, I know I would put myself between David Carter and anything or anyone who would seek to harm him, just as Rónan did for Rory, for me and for so many others. A tear slides out of the corner of my eye, and I can't say whether it is a tear of mourning for Rónan's loss or of joy in David's presence in my life.

Sweet David catches the tear with his fingers, his gaze questioning.

"Are you OK?"

I smile at him.

"More than OK," I assure him, pressing my lips to his before our tongues once again dance together. The interchange mirrors the increasingly fierce merging of our bodies below. I wrap my legs around him again, pulling him deeper within me, and he groans, his eyes sliding closed in concentration, and my own follow, leaving me to revel in the sensations of his body sliding in and out of mine.

The tension inside me builds, circling closer and closer around a looming peak, tantalizingly just out of reach. David's rough fingertips rub across one of my nipples, and my head is thrown back, my hands gripping the comforter. He swivels his hips as he plunges back into me again, and that's it — I fall over the crest, crying out his name as he sucks hard on the skin of my neck and my muscles grip him with rhythmic spasms.

His movements are frenetic now, hitting hard within me, deep and delicious, and I run my hands up along his spine, reveling in the slide of muscle beneath the skin of his back, his hips, his rear, as he loses himself inside me. There's a growl growing within him, nearly ready to break free, and then it does, as he pulses inside me, pouring out his essence within.

He collapses atop me for a moment before taking my lips once again with his. Again those pale blue eyes peer into me, and it feels like he sees so much more than just the brown of my irises.

His expression is full of delight and wonder, and it conveys the feeling that I am something precious to him. Part of me wants to retreat from these feelings, knowing I will not be able to keep him, but I cannot bring myself to do anything other than cherish this time with him. Every moment is a precious pearl to be treasured, just like the look on his face as he gazes upon me.

"Piper..." he breathes, brushing the hair away from my face. "I *so* wanted this..." He presses a kiss between my eyes before sliding off to the side, still breathing heavily from his exertion.

I've never had a human lover before. I'm not entirely sure what is customary afterwards. But David seems to sense my uncertainty, pulling me against him, my back against his chest, and snuggling his head into the crook of my neck. I sigh contentedly.

"It was way more fun being on top of naked you the second time. I can't wait to see how good the third will be," he says, and I can feel his smile against my skin as the thrill of arousal courses through me once again.

I laugh, my heart unbelievably light after the potentially awful results of his discovery tonight. I don't know exactly why, but I trust this man with my heart, and I trust him with our secret. Time is our enemy now, in the short term or the long one. But the only way to fight it is to enjoy every moment we can.

I sigh contentedly and place my arm over his where it circles my waist, lacing our fingers together. Every moment is precious. So precious...

CHAPTER 14

EYES CAN'T HIDE

Piper

I wake with a start, realizing instantly that I am not alone. I can't remember the last time I awoke and was not the only person in the room, let alone my bed. But I can hear gentle breathing near my ear.

David Carter.

David Carter, human, rockstar, bass player, scientist, is in my bed.

I have a lover. And he's human.

Well, that's unexpected. Not the most likely thing to come out of his discovering my nature.

Oh.

He knows what I am...

Oh, my.

I slip gently out of his grasp, immediately going to the table where I'd left my skin. It lays there, just as I left it, and I heave a sigh of relief. Not that I expected David to have taken it, or even have touched it. But I am used to hiding it before I go to bed, and not having done so makes me feel like I've been careless.

I check to see if he's still sleeping soundly, and he is. The sight warms my heart and instills a sense of peace in me. I like having him here, sleeping in my bed. It feels safe, like we're each there to protect the other from whatever challenges we may face.

Before I lose myself in reverie over his sweet sleeping countenance, I pick up my skin and cross the room, stashing it quickly in the hidden space inside the armchair. When I turn around, he hasn't moved a muscle, and I allow myself to absorb the peaceful expression before climbing back into the bed with him and pulling a blanket over us. He stirs but merely pulls me back against his chest once again, settling right back into sleep. That sounds so appealing that I follow him.

Lips trace their way down my back, and I arch into them.

"Mmm..."

"That feel good?"

I sigh contentedly.

"Very. You're very good with your mouth. Talented."

"You ain't seen nothing' yet..."

David flips me onto my back and slides down between my thighs, his blue eyes peering up at me across my mound.

"I'd hand you a notepad to take notes for our vocabulary class, but I want you to focus on the demonstration portion of the lesson first."

"Oh! So..."

"Yes, this is known as 'eating you out.'"

His lips find that little bundle of nerves at the top, and my thighs instinctively move up to cradle his face. He presses them back down on the bed.

"Need access to all of you," he says, sliding his hands under my rear and burying his face between my legs. My head goes back, my eyes rolling up... just far enough to see the clock on the wall.

"David..."

"Hmm?"

"David... Oh! Oh gods..."

"You can keep saying those words over and over. But only those. I'm aiming for speechless here. Give me just a minute..."

"That's just it... Ahhh! Oh, you've got to... we've got to..." I'm mewling now under his attention, no intelligible words coming from my lips, just as he wanted.

"There you go," he mumbles approvingly against my mons. "Just like that... let go..."

Would that I could. It's tempting, but...

"David! Stop!"

He pauses and looks up at me, realizing I mean business. And I do — literally.

"Look at the time!" I nod toward the clock.

"Almost noon. Plenty of time before the guys will be missing me."

"Plenty of time before *they* miss *you*. But *no* time before Steve is missing *me*. I'm supposed to be over there now, restocking the studio kitchen. I can't be late. I can't lose this job. Rónan warned me..."

"Steve may be in charge of the studio, but it's the band and the label calling the shots. It's fine. I'll tell them I held you up. It's the truth, after all," he says, smiling mischievously and lifting my hips back up to his face, licking me from my opening upward.

My hands go down to cradle his head, but my sense of urgency makes them wrap in his hair instead and pull him gently away.

"Not going for that, huh?"

His expression is hope dashed.

"Tonight. After you're done in the studio."

"It's not like we're ready to lay down tracks. It's just scratch tracks and rehearsing."

"And it's just my job. One I can't replace with live sound jobs that will dwindle over the winter. Especially if Steve fires me for not showing up on time. Hard to get a good reference that way."

"I'll give you an *amazing* reference," he says, smiling mischievously again as he licks up the inside of my thigh.

"David! I don't have time for playing around. I should be over there already. 'Early is on time, and on time is late.' Rónan was very adamant about that. And I promised I wouldn't let him down."

His expression goes serious and he tilts his head, considering me.

"Well, we'd better get you dressed and on your way to work, then. The commute is grueling, so prepare yourself!"

"You realize we're a minute's walk away, right?"

"Yes, Piper. That was sarcasm. You seal-folk have sarcasm, right?"

"Oh. Yes. I'm not thinking. My brain is still stuck on 'eating out.'"

"I could make sure the rest of you has eaten out, too... I just need five minutes..."

I like those little laugh lines that crinkle around his eyes when he's feeling lascivious and mischievous. I trace my fingers over them. And then I sigh.

"Nope. Gotta go."

David sighs, too, acknowledging that I mean it.

"I cannot promise that I will not demand a break from rehearsal every hour on the hour just so I can throw you onto my bed and make you sing my name so loud the guys will assume I really have bagged a mermaid."

I chuckle and then go solemn.

"David, they can't know."

"I promised I wouldn't tell anyone your secrets."

"No — I mean they can't know we're lovers."

"Is that what we are? I like the sound of that. Maybe I'll write a song..."

"Title it 'Secret Lovers,' because that has to be a secret, too, David."

"There's already a song by that name. So, no, no 'secret lovers.' Just lovers."

"Steve can fire me for fraternizing with a client, David. He's already threatened to do it. It makes me look unprofessional regardless. I can't afford to look bad when I'm already under scrutiny as a female engineer. And I'm not even a full engineer at the studio, just an intern."

He sighs heavily now.

"I don't want to hide us, Piper. I don't want this to be a dirty little secret. So long as I'm keeping your secrets, I don't want any others hanging over us."

"I understand, David. And I'd love to be open with everyone about us, but I can't. And it's not just the studio I have to worry about. No one else among the Hidden Folk has taken a human lover."

"Except Rónan."

"Except Rónan. But he was the exception to every rule. He *made* the rules. And not everyone approved of his relationship with Rory, nor does everyone in Safe Harbour entirely approve of her taking over some of his leadership role now that he's gone. And they'll be very concerned about whether you know our secrets. If they think you might... I can't promise you'd be safe. Rónan tried to make Rory forget what she'd seen that first night.

"Make her forget?"

"Some of us have abilities... they can be used to muddle or fabricate memory. It didn't work on her anyway, but only because she's different..."

"Different how?"

"She has some unusual gifts."

"She's psychic or something?"

"Something like that. But the point is I'm not sure some among the Elders wouldn't decide that you should forget we ever met. And there's a good chance it would work on you. I don't want you to forget me..." The idea makes me miserable.

"I couldn't forget you, Piper," he says, moving up to touch my cheek. "Even if you were human, I couldn't forget you."

It may be that he'll *wish* he could by the time he has to leave here. But I'll cross that bridge when we come to it.

"I'll *never* forget you, David. And that's saying a lot when never means eternity."

He kisses me sweetly on the lips.

"OK — our secret. You, this place and us. But I still can't promise not to carry you away during breaks and make you come over and over again. We'll just have to be quiet."

I chuckle.

"As long as I'm working when I'm supposed to be, that's fine." I give him a soft smile and then hop up out of the bed. I grab another set of my standard engineer "uniform" from my little closet: long black T-shirt, heavy black leggings and a full black skirt that comes just short of my knees, a belt buckled over my hips.

"Have I mentioned how much I like those little skirts of yours? Just a touch of girly atop the engineer gear." He fingers the hem of my skirt, his fingers tracing underneath and up my thigh.

I smile.

"Very perceptive, Mr. Carter. I may have to work extra-hard for the same respect a male engineer gets, but I refuse to erase my gender in the process."

"There's no erasing your gender, Piper, no matter how hard you try."

He wraps his arm around my waist from behind, kissing the spot between my neck and my collarbone. My eyes drift closed.

"David... I have to go..."

"You sure?"

I turn and give him a stern look.

"That look would be a lot more intimidating if you didn't look like a 20-year-old college student."

I roll my eyes at him.

"I'm eight times your age, mister. You will respect your elders."

"Or what?" There's that glint again...

"Nope. Not going there. If I do, I'll never make it to work."

"That would be a darn shame..." he says, nuzzling my ear.

I growl and pull free of his arms.

"You are incorrigible! This is a whole new side of you, David Carter. What happened to the quiet, rule-following elder brother with his nose in a book, watching the world go on around him?"

"What happened to the shy girl who couldn't bring herself to ask me whether I sleep with groupies, but confided she was looking for someone she connected with, right before she bolted off into the dark?"

"Some guy threw himself on top of her when she came out of the ocean naked, and it turned out he was the someone she connected with..."

His light tone is turned on its head. I've just confessed something that makes me vulnerable again. I'm looking at my feet, half hoping he didn't notice and half begging the gods that he'll tell me he feels the same way.

His hand grasps my chin and lifts my eyes to his.

"And she was the someone he connected with. Finally. I may have only waited 30 years to feel that connection, but it felt just as long and just as important to me as 250 years of waiting did for you."

"This is real, isn't it?"

"I think it is."

"We're going to have to figure out a few things..."

"We are. But that's what couples do." He's very sure of this for a 30-year-old human just starting his first serious relationship. And I'm very *un*sure for a woman who's been around for 250 years and had a number of lovers, if casual ones. This human-selkie thing is complicated...

"We're a couple?"

"I want us to be."

"I do, too."

"We can figure out the rest later. For now, it's just us. That's all that's important," he assures me.

"Yeah. It is."

It's a long, sweet kiss between us this time, before we finally concede defeat to the clock ticking on the wall. But that's the only battle victory I'm ceding to time where David Carter is concerned. I'm going to figure out a way to win the war.

David
Later that day

"**D**avid! Someone's going to see!"

I've got Piper pinned to the wall in the studio kitchen. Steve isn't here, but the guys are in the control room across the hall, listening for the fifth time to the playback of the song Declan and I have been working on. And I can't help myself. I can't focus on the music when I'm sporting an erection that feels like it's the size of the neck on my bass. Just from knowing Piper was down the hall, filling a cabinet with pretzels.

"Then we should take this to a more private location," I tell her, pressing into her with my hips.

She can't help herself, either, tracing her fingers along the front of my shorts.

I grab her under her thighs, and she wraps her legs around my waist. That's all the permission I need. I'm headed straight for the stairs up to the second floor of the residence and down the hall to my bedroom, the sun shining through the sheer curtain that is all that separates us from that ocean view. It's a stark contrast to the intimate, almost cavelike, feel of her room at Safe Harbour, which seems designed to contain its secrets and keep the outside world safely outside. Here, sunshine lays everything out in the open, and as I strip Piper out of her clothes, I find new appreciation for the luscious curves I'd seen glint in the moonlight and softly lit by the lamp next to her bed.

We may still be a secret from everyone, but just having her here, in my space — temporary though it may be — feels like staking a claim, to her and to our relationship. We certainly have challenges ahead of us, but standing up to strip off my own clothes and watching her coquettish posing atop my bed as she gets a show of her own, I know I'm all-in on this girl. And that word makes me chuckle now. Not a girl — a woman, a *seal*-woman. But nonetheless holding all of the enthusiasm and feeling of exploratory delight as a human girl of her apparent age.

I take her mouth in a slow, sensuous kiss as I lay myself on top of her, ready to sink myself deep inside her but determined to draw things out just a little, to enjoy the sight of her here, her dewy skin alive in the sunshine, the warm light reflected off the ocean catching glints in her eyes. I roll us both over, leaving her on top of me, and that sweet smile of hers widens to a sexy smirk as she straddles my hips, no words needed for us to communicate what we both want from each other.

She raises up and positions me at her opening, then slides slowly down over me, until we're pressed as close as can be. My hands slide up to cup her breasts — a perfect complement to her slim waist and round hips. She's petite, but overtly feminine, undeniably sexy. And she's mine.

Piper writhes against me, setting a steady pace that seems all too aware of the fact that we'll be missed if we're gone too long. I can accept that, enjoy it, so long as I can make love to her leisurely once our workday is done. My hand slips down between her legs, to the spot where we're joined, and I circle her clit with my thumb, determined to make this hurried bit of afternoon delight pay off for both of us. I've been hard since we left her room two hours ago, and her mutual level of arousal is evidenced by the moisture I can feel on my fingers. The added stimulation sets her to panting as she rides me hard and fast, and within moments, we're both nearing the edge. I moan as she slams herself down on me, hard, and she whimpers before quickly putting a finger to her lips to remind us both, it seems, that we have to keep this quiet.

I grasp her hip with my other hand, continuing to rub her clit with my thumb, and I push my hips up to meet her increasingly desperate thrusts, the air filled with the sounds of our panting breaths, the slapping of flesh against flesh and the small whimpers and moans that are the minimum expression of pleasure we can manage.

I capture her glance with my own as I feel that tingle at the base of my spine, my orgasm approaching just over the horizon, and we're locked together, body and soul, frantically chasing release that crests suddenly in both of us. She throws her head back and my eyes screw shut as I come inside her, her muscles creating a strong rhythm that milks me dry as she collapses on top of me.

I caress her back as she recovers herself, tracing my face with her hand. Her eyes are filled with delight that I know is mirrored in my own, and I take her mouth in a slow, sensuous kiss that has me ready to do this all over again, even if I know we have to get back down to the studio. We clean up quickly and dress in silence, smirking at each other in recognition of the fact that we've successfully carried off this little secret escapade.

I take her hand as we head back down to the studio, kissing it as we approach the door to the control room and then reluctantly dropping it as she pauses out of view while I go inside.

Declan and Alex are sitting at the mixing board, with Rhys stretched out on the sofa, while Hunter and Kier are testing out some variations on the guitar part I laid down previously. Alex gives me a glance as I come in, but no one seems at all suspicious about my absence. Piper crosses the doorway on her way back to the kitchen, and we share a secretive smile.

Just over an hour later, I drag Piper out of the office, where she's filing paperwork, alone. I pull her down the hallway to the equipment room, locking the door behind us before pushing her up against it, face-first, my hips pinning her to it from behind. I lick a trail up the side of her neck, and she's already panting in anticipation. As much as I'd like to fuck her up against this door, I know it would make too much noise and give the game away to anyone in the studio.

"I want you to come on my hand," I whisper in her ear, grabbing the shell of it between my teeth before pulling up her skirt with one hand.

She moans, wordless with instant arousal, belatedly nodding her assent as she places her palms against the door. I pull her leggings down her thighs and her panties with them. I run my hand up the inside of her thigh, teasing and tantalizing but not touching her where she wants me to the most. Not yet.

I slide my other hand up under her shirt, pulling her breast free of the cup of her bra and tweaking the nipple between thumb and forefinger. She bites her lip to keep herself quiet, and that sight is all I can take. I dive into her center with my finger, spreading her arousal up to lubricate her clit. Then I press two fingers inside her while my thumb presses against that little button. I work her with thumb and fingers together, my other hand still caressing and teasing her nipple. She lets loose a little moan. It's quiet but might still be heard through the door if someone were to pass by, so I take her mouth with mine, muffling her response as I fuck her with my fingers, circling her clit as she swiftly rises toward her climax, riding my hand with a feeling of desperation. She wants this badly, wants me to make her come on my fingers while my bandmates continue working down the hall, and I'm going to relish doing it.

She's panting hard now, and I stroke her deep, tapping against her clit in time with my strokes and curving my fingers to reach that one little spot inside her. She cries out, silently, against my mouth, her jaw opening wide, and I plunge my tongue inside, sucking on her own. She's so close. I can feel it... A little harder, a little faster, a little more pressure on her clit... and there!

Her pussy contracts around my hand, her thighs clamping me between them, and she mewls into my mouth. She's boneless now, collapsed against the door. My hand between her thighs is the only thing keeping her upright as her spasms continue on, strong and fast, while I keep stroking her through her orgasm. When they slow and wane, I tuck her breast back into her bra before pulling down the collar of her shirt and sinking my teeth into her shoulder in a spot where only the two of us will see the mark I leave on her. She shudders against me, then sighs as she comes down from her sexual high. I press a kiss to her cheek and then pull up her panties and leggings, and then set her skirt back to rights. She's still collapsed against the door, and I smile in satisfaction before turning her to face me.

"That was fun."

"Ummhmm," she murmurs, still wordless in her pleasure. She looks up at me, almost shyly, then a look of cunning spreads across her face.

"I'll meet you back here in an hour. Then it's your turn to come — quietly — up against this door..."

She dots a kiss on my chin, checks that her clothes are straight, unlocks the door and steps out into the hallway, leaving me slack-jawed behind her, eminently glad that my shorts are loose, because I'm hard as a rock, and it's only going to get worse in the next hour.

CHAPTER 15

PRECIOUS STONE

David
Later that night

It's dark out when we get done in the studio for the day. Normal hours for a rock musician, and I'm wide awake. Moreover, I'm antsy, wanting to see Piper again, wanting to make love to her again. It's been a few hours. That's a long time, right? I don't know. Give me a break — she's my first actual girlfriend. And my sense of time has been confounded by all this talk of eternity and my comparatively brief lifespan. Makes me want to cram as many Piper orgasms into a day as physically possible.

She left a couple hours ago, while we worked on the set list for the next incognito gig. She'll get the final list later, since she's inside the bubble on our secret identity now. That's turned out to be useful — no more worrying about the live engineer at the bar figuring out who we are after a few gigs and letting it slip to the press or online. We have her loyalty from her work at both the studio and the bar. Moreover, I know — even if the other guys don't — that if anyone can be trusted to keep a secret, it's Piper.

Whenever I haven't been in the middle of a song, or getting my hands and mouth on Piper — or *thinking* about getting my hands and mouth on Piper — I've been thinking about Piper's secret. I'm still running through what I saw last night, like it's on a loop in my head, repeating over and over in slow motion. It's allowed me to fill in some of the blanks that remained after those very confusing minutes.

I didn't actually see the seal transform into Piper in her human form. They were — she was? — washed over by a wave in the brief moment that took. But there was too little time involved for there to have been any other explanation. Well, other than me losing touch with reality, which I'm still not fully prepared to discount.

I step out onto the beach in front of the studio, letting my eyes adapt to the dark. It's cloudy now, so even with the moon out there's not a lot of light. But there's enough to spot a flash of skin near the water at the border between the Safe Harbour beach and this one. It's not a naked woman this time. It's a mostly clothed one: Piper, dressed in shorts and a tank top, watching the water.

I walk up behind her and wrap my arms around her waist, kissing the side of her neck. She stiffens in surprise before relaxing back into my hold.

"You OK?"

"Yes. You just startled me. I'm not used to having anyone be able to sneak up on me like that. Between my hearing, sense of smell and my self-preservation instincts, I usually know someone's nearby long before they get within touching range."

"Is that a good thing or a bad thing?"

"I'm not sure. It's disconcerting to think my instincts have dulled. But I think it's more likely that I've already learned your scent and sound, and my instinct tells me those sensory patterns are safe and welcome."

"I like hearing that." I smile against her shoulder, pressing my lips to the mark I left near her collarbone before swiping my tongue along the depression there. "I like knowing that I've become part of your life already."

She takes in a deep breath and tilts her eyes to the dark sky. She seems troubled.

"David — we haven't talked about where we go from here. And the most pressing problem is that you're due to leave at the end of August. Or sooner, if the album gets finished early."

"You can come with me. We've got a spot for you on the crew. You can be our monitor engineer when we go on tour. Our last one just retired."

"Even if I wanted to take a job you gave me because I'm your lover, I couldn't leave Safe Harbour, David. Not for long. I'd fade away if I was away from the ocean for very long. We dwindle without it. That's why the theft of our skins is so devastating."

"How long is 'very long'?"

"A few days away, a week or so at most."

"So you can't tour."

"Not unless you're only doing coastal venues with short jaunts in between."

"Oh."

"I can't leave Mystic Beach, David. They're relying on me — not just to support Safe Harbour financially but to help the others integrate. As much as I'd like to pretend I'm a normal 25-year-old, we both know I'm not. I have responsibilities that I can't abdicate, especially not with Rónan gone."

"I understand." I don't like hearing it, but I know the pressure she's under. "They're as reliant on you as the band is on me, or any one of us. Without one of us, it all falls apart."

She turns in my arms and loops her arms over my neck.

"Thank you for understanding. I know this isn't what you want."

"All I want is you."

She gasps.

"David — don't say that. You've got a life in New York, with the band, on the road. You can't put me first."

"That's my decision to make. When it needs to be made. Which isn't yet."

I look deep in her eyes.

"Give us the time to figure this out. Don't shut us down. Don't shut me out. Please. Don't give away the time we have."

"Every moment is precious."

"Just so."

I plant a kiss on the top of her head, and we stand quietly in each other's arms, listening to the waves breaking on the beach. After a while, I ask her the thing I've been wondering about all day. I just hope she doesn't take offense.

"Piper — what I saw last night... the transformation..."

"You want to see me change again, to understand it better."

"Is that stupid? Offensive? I don't want to treat you like a sideshow act."

She scrutinizes my expression.

"Why do you want to see it again?"

"Well, part of me still wonders if I'm losing my mind."

"You're not. But I understand why that would be a concern."

"And... I want to understand more. About you, about your life. And this is a big part of your life. It's your very identity. And I don't know anything but the most basic concept of what happens."

"I can't explain the physics of it, David. I'm not sure what the physics of it would even be. I'm not sure it even complies with physics as you know it. It's just part of my nature."

"I don't care about the physics. Not really. I mean — I'm a science nerd, but that's not why I'm asking... Does it hurt? Like the werewolves in the movies? Are you self-aware when you're in seal form, or do you think like a seal until you change back?"

"You want to make sure I'm not in pain when I change... that I don't lose my thinking self..."

"Yes."

"Because..."

"Because I care about you. I'm not sure what I'd do to protect you if it did hurt, but if it doesn't, at least I can stop worrying about that. And if you're self-aware, maybe I can worry a little less about you getting attacked by a shark or something."

I feel very silly right now. Maybe none of this is an issue and I've just made a fool out of myself. But I need to understand her, her life.

She scans my face, and I see her eyes well up.

"What? Does it hurt that badly?"

"Oh — no, David. It doesn't hurt at all. I just... That you thought to be concerned... that you asked because you care..."

I can see now that she's overwhelmed with emotion. I pull her into my arms and hold her tight.

"I didn't mean to upset you."

"You didn't. I'm just so... touched. I don't know what I should have expected from a human lover, but this wasn't it."

"That's so strange to hear — your 'human lover.'"

"I don't mean it that way. We've both had other partners before, if casual ones, short-term. But something about this... about us..."

"We're different. Together, we're something else... something new."

"Something precious."

"Yeah."

"We'll figure this out, David. We just have to be careful for now, and just try to enjoy what we have."

"So..."

"You want answers to your questions..."

"Yeah. If you don't mind telling me about it."

"No, it's fine. First — no, it doesn't hurt. It's a physical and mental effort, like sprinting down the beach on dry sand. But once it's done, you feel free, on both sides of the transformation. Like you are just as you should be."

"So you're aware when you're a seal?"

"My mental processes don't really change from one form to another. It's like the difference between walking on land and swimming. You make a conscious choice to be doing one or the other, and your body — assuming you know how to swim — just does its thing and adapts. From there, it's totally natural, instinctive."

"And if an orca or a shark started chasing you?"

"Seals haul out on dry land when the threat is in the water. We do that instinctively. But we also have a deeper ability to plan ahead, adapt, strategize — it's the best of seal instinct combined with human-style reasoning. Sharks don't think much and definitely don't strategize beyond the obvious. Orcas... their brains are far more similar to ours. They're dangerous predators when they're hunting. They work together, teach successful skills. They're nearly as much of a threat as humans."

"So you need to stay away from orcas."

"Yes."

"That wasn't a suggestion. I'm telling you you have to make sure you stay away."

"Oh. I try. But I'll try extra-hard from now on."

"Thank you. I don't want to lose you."

I hug her tight to me, as if my arms alone can keep her safe. I know they can't, but I would do anything to ensure she was safe.

"Did you want to see it again? The transformation? Up close?"

"Only if you want to."

"I want you to be able to understand, to know it's real, that *I'm* real."

"OK."

"Wait here. I'll be right back."

I pace in small circles on the sand near the water, unaccountably anxious, even though I know this is an everyday thing for Piper. A few minutes later, she's back, the piece of fur — her seal coat — in her hand.

She pulls me down to the very edge of the water, looking discombobulated.

"You don't have to do this."

"No — it's fine. I'm fine. I just usually make a run from my room to the water with the coat in my hand... and no..."

"Naked."

"Yes."

"Well, let me help."

She looks torn.

"You can hand me your coat, or you can hold onto it and I'll take your clothes. Might be more fun that way..." I add with a wink.

She chuckles, shaking her head at me, and raises her arms over her head. I follow the unspoken suggestion and strip her tank top over her head, sliding the arm openings over her arms and the seal coat in her hand. She pulls the coat to her chest as I drop her top on the dry sand above the water line. At my smirk, she moves it back away, leaving her breasts bared. I place my hand on the waistband of her shorts, unfastening them and dropping them down around her ankles. She steps out of them and I place them higher up on the beach, with her tank top.

I pull her against me, her seal coat between her bare chest and my T-shirt, and my dick, already starting to harden just from stripping her out of her clothes, pressing against her belly. The scrap of lace covering her is next to go as I slowly slide them down off her hips and she steps free, not a stitch of clothing on her and only the seal coat remaining. I glance back up at the house, making sure the guys aren't outside, and I peer down the other way, hoping the guard patrol is slow tonight.

"It's safe. They're on a break. I told them I was going to the studio for a couple hours. No one else will be out here for a while. Not on this part of the beach."

I pull her hard against me again, sliding my hand over her bare ass, reaching behind the fur to rub her nipple with my thumb. She writhes against me with a quiet moan. I shake my head in pure wonder. With a quick peck on my lips, she steps toward the water.

"Watch closely. This is as good a view as any human has likely ever had of one of us changing form. Commit it to memory, because we probably won't get another chance like this."

I nod solemnly and give her a soft smile.

Taking a deep breath, Piper wraps the seal coat around her shoulders, the edges covering her sides. Her eyes close in concentration, and suddenly it's like someone has blurred a lens over her image. She's no longer in sharp focus before my eyes. She drops to her knees, bending forward toward the waves until her elbows, too, are on the sand. The seal coat appears to stretch to cover her, the spots of bare skin disappearing beneath it like a child hiding under a blanket. The top of her head is the last bit to disappear, the sharpness of the image blurring even more in my eyes before resolving into a more distinctly seal-shaped blur and then refocusing once again to reveal that same tawny, spotted harbor seal that I'd been seeing since the first day we got here.

It really was her. Piper.

She hesitates for a moment, allowing me a second to take her in in this form. I experience that same unconscious pull toward her, only now more explicable as I recognize that I'm drawn to Piper in both of her forms. I close the distance between us slowly, afraid of startling her, despite her statement that she retains her human-style awareness even in seal form. When I'm within arm's reach, I crouch down and ease forward, my hand outstretched. I hesitate as my fingers reach within inches of the seal's muzzle, and she seems to grow impatient with me, pushing her cheek into my hand and nuzzling against it. I realize I've been holding my breath during this long approach and finally remind myself to breathe again. She cocks her head at me, seeming to ask if I'm OK, and I have to laugh, because it seems like I should be the one asking that question. So I do.

"Are you OK, Piper? Is this OK?"

Her response is to grab my thumb in her mouth, gripping it just loosely enough between those predator teeth to make me gasp at the damage I know they could do to my fingers, which are my living, and my joy... my other joy, now that I have Piper...

She licks my thumb and I get the impression of cheeky humor in her eyes — huge and soulful as they had been every time I'd seen her in her seal form, only now providing some explanation as to why the impression of self-awareness was so strong. She bites down again — not enough to hurt or break the skin, but with a solid grip on my thumb, and pulls as she moves herself farther into the water. She tugs almost hard enough to pull me over from my crouch, then releases me again before moving into the water, looking like any other seal returning to the sea after a break on land.

There's a sharp pain. Not my thumb, which is unscathed by her seal teeth, but in my heart as I realize this is probably the last view many a human has had of his selkie mate as she leaves her home on land for the last time and returns to the sea, never to be seen again. The sensation feels like being torn in two, and I resolve never to let that happen. I already feel lost without her, and she's just stepped into the ocean for a brief swim. At least I think that's what she's doing.

I see her head bobbing just beyond the breakers, watching me, just as she had all those nights I'd watched her from the beach, knowing I shouldn't listen to that compulsion to follow her into the water. But this isn't a seal. It's Piper. And while she may look like a seal right now, she's not. She's still Piper. And then I realize what that tug on my thumb was meant to convey. I pull off my T-shirt and toss it on the sand with Piper's clothes, and I make a running dive under the breaking wave, emerging in the swells where I'd seen Piper — Piper the seal — just moments before.

It's unnerving when I feel something large brush against my leg. My surfer instincts are to pull my legs out of the water, but I have no board. And my rational mind insists that there is no threat. So strange to have my rational mind being the part of me that insists that this marine creature bumping against my leg in the ocean on a dark night is actually my girlfriend. And then I realize how preposterous that idea itself is in the context of my life. It's no less incredible that I have a girlfriend than it is that she's a magical seal-person. And the thought makes me smile as I tread water in the ocean swells.

Again a bump, only this time against my hand and not a glancing touch but an intentional press of soft fur into my palm. My hand emerges from the surface of the water, carried aloft by the head of a seal. She moves closer, floating inside the arc of my slowly paddling arms, coming right up against my chest. I feel her rear flippers swish in front of my shins, her small stature in human form also present in her seal form. She tilts her head to look at me from up close, then she moves even closer, pressing her seal nose against my mouth.

It's strange and wonderful all at once. Kissed by a seal. Who is also my girlfriend. Can I marvel again that after 30 years and hundreds of random hookups, I have a girlfriend? And that I really am not bothered in the least that she spends a good portion of her time as a seal? I shake my head and smile.

Piper slips below the surface and noses at me, investigating me below the water in a decidedly seal-like fashion. She brushes against my legs like a cat seeking affection, and I reach out to run my hands over her soft, smooth fur. It feels just the same as her coat did when it lay on her bed. This should not be surprising, and yet somehow it is. She re-emerges in front of me, watching me for a moment before using her rear flippers to boost herself higher in the water. She waves a front flipper at me before diving below the surface and disappearing from view.

Was that goodbye? My heart clenches, even though I know it's most certainly just a temporary goodbye at most. When she doesn't re-emerge within my view after several minutes, I decide to make my way back on shore to wait for her. I sit back on the sand, watching the water for any sign of her. There's nothing for the longest time, and then I spot her, riding in on a wave before hauling out on the sand. There's no surf washing over her this time, and I stand up to approach her once more. She cocks her head at me with a questioning look, and I crouch down within arm's length of her, watching as the process of transformation reverses itself, the bizarre blurriness resolving into a human-like shape before revealing a woman draped in a seal-fur coat. I reach down and scoop her up out of the surf, carrying her up to dryer ground near our clothes and setting her down on my discarded shirt.

She hasn't spoken a word, and I briefly wonder if she's still finishing the transformation process and unable to speak, before I remember just how vociferous she was the other night when I threw myself on top of her just as she'd come onshore in human form. Maybe she's waiting for me to say something?

Instead, I sit down next to her on the sand and pull her into my lap, stroking her damp hair and enjoying the feel of her curves, cushioned by the fur coat, pressed up against me.

"Did I mention that I have a girlfriend?" I ask her with a grin. She looks confused for a moment. So I clarify. "She's cute and curvy, with this amazing brown hair and these incredible dark eyes that look like they contain the entire universe inside, and she has the most amazing set of... engineering skills that I've ever seen."

She swats me playfully on the shoulder.

"And only slightly less amazing than the fact that I have this amazing girlfriend is that she's immortal and changes into a seal. She's pretty wonderful all around, actually."

Piper smiles shyly at me, pink in her cheeks from embarrassment and not from her swim.

"I think her boyfriend is pretty amazing, too," she says. "Caring, creative, trusting, talented, spectacularly handsome and more than a little bit gifted in the bedroom."

"They sound like a perfect match. The hot seal-lady and the sexy rockstar."

"I think they are. They really should take the time to enjoy each other before morning arrives."

"True. They could get in at least two or three rounds of orgasms before recharging for a few more."

"That sounds like an excellent idea."

"They should do that, then."

I set her on her feet, the seal coat still clutched to her chest, and I gather up our discarded clothes.

"Race you to the bed!"

"On your mark, get set..."

"Go!"

She races ahead on her own premature start, and I resist the urge to call out her cheating in favor of staying quiet to avoid being discovered. I close the gate and hidden door behind me and pad quietly down the hall to her room. I drop the clothes just inside the door, peering around for her, only to be slammed into and falling on my back on the bed with a 250-year-old sound engineer between my legs, pulling my board shorts down in urgent movements. I give her a hand, and she wraps her hand around my dick, which stands at full attention and ready for duty.

"So, is this also 'eating out'?" she asks, giving an all-too-brief lick to the head of my cock.

"We call that a 'blowjob.'"

"Humans blow on each other for pleasure?"

I laugh out loud.

"It's kind of a weird name for something that involves much more sucking than blowing, isn't it?"

"Oh! So it *is* done how we do it, then! English is confusing. Irish makes more sense."

"You speak Irish?"

"And a few dozen more languages. I wanted to be prepared in case I ran into someone who didn't speak English, Irish, Manx, Welsh, Cornish, Scots Gaelic or Breton, which covers most of our native tongues."

"Oh. I see... I guess 250 years gives you a lot of time to learn an extra language or twelve. And speaking of tongues..."

Piper's tongue flashes from between her lips, tracing up the length of my cock.

"We should really do language lessons more often. The more demonstration sessions the better."

"I think that can be arranged," she says, taking me into her mouth and demonstrating quite clearly that selkie blowjobs are at least as amazing as human ones.

OK — I admit it. They're way better. Or maybe it's just my girlfriend... I'm good either way.

CHAPTER 16

DON'T BE SCARED

Piper
The next afternoon

"Y ou've been a very bad girl, Piper..."

Ramsay's leaning against the wall right outside my door, his demeanor casual, but he's got a cat-ate-the-canary grin on his face, and that alone sets off alarm bells.

"Go away, Ramsay. I'm not going to keep telling you. You've gone way over the line, and I'll go to the Elders if you don't stop harassing me." Once again, my oft-practiced false bravado comes in handy even when I'm not in a work setting.

"Why don't you do that, then?"

Something's off here. I can tell.

"I will. Or you can apologize now and never bother me again."

"I think I'd much rather see you go have a chat with the Elders."

I give up. I'm not in the mood to deal with this cryptic unspoken riddle of his.

"Why is that, Ramsay?"

"Because then you'll have to explain to them why it is you've got a human coming and going from your room at all hours."

My blood runs cold. If anyone was going to discover David and I were lovers, Ramsay was the worst-case scenario. By far.

"Why do you think that?" Maybe he's bluffing. If this is all a bluff and I fall for it, whatever happens next will be my fault, because I will have as good as confessed.

"Because I've seen him. And Stewart has seen him, and Wylie. Several times."

"And you think that's something that would concern me?" He's not bluffing. Let's see how good *my* pokerface is.

"I *know* it would. Because it's just like you to get attached to a creature who'll be dead in fifty years, like some kind of pitiful pet, and to spill all your secrets as easily as you spread your legs for him."

My stomach lurches, threatening to empty itself. It's tempting to not fight it and just vomit all over Ramsay. Maybe he'd find me less desirable after that.

"Who I take into my bed is no concern of yours, Ramsay. Especially as short-lived as humans are."

"They're also very... fragile..." he reminds me, showing his teeth in a way that clearly conveys menace.

"That would be an unwise threat to make. A suspicious death of a human so close to our enclave would bring in law-enforcement or wildlife experts, or both. And that would not only put us all at risk, it would lay the blame on you in the eyes of the council. You'd be banished. Or worse."

He appears to consider this for a few moments. Perhaps this is something he hadn't thought of.

"I won't have to touch your precious little pet if the Elders decide he's a problem. And even the great Rónan MacMurchadha—" sarcasm drips as he says the name "—was prepared to take severe measures to ensure no humans were aware of our presence here. If he hadn't developed a soft spot for that plush ass of hers, she'd have been dead long ago."

The threat, the insult to Rory, brings anger that thaws the chill created by his threat to David, and my mind spins faster, trying to think of a way out of this vise Ramsay seems determined to trap me in.

"But she's not. In fact, she sits on the Council of Elders now, in Rónan's stead. And any sanction against me would require her support, which I can promise you she would not give, since she is already fully aware of my dalliance with the human and has given her approval on behalf of the Council."

I want to savor the look of shock on his face, but now is not the time to get cocky or gloat. How he responds now will determine my path forward, if I have one at all.

"She's aware you have taken a human lover and let him watch you transform?"

I school my expression, because he's just confirmed that he was never bluffing at all. In fact, he had more evidence to leverage against me than he initially let on. Bluster is the only way through this.

"Of course, Ramsay. Do you think I'm a fool? After all she and my brother went through, do you think I would not have sought Rory's advice and approval before taking a human into my bed and bringing him into my confidence? You're short-sighted and impulsive, Ramsay. I am not. Humans are careless with their secrets, and I know enough of his to ensure he'll hold his tongue. Moreover, I am a key part of our efforts to integrate here, so naturally I have been granted more leeway with my associations."

It's pure bluff. And now we see which of us is the better player in this game.

Ramsay scrutinizes my face, looking for any indication of weakness or deception. David's life is on the line here, and it's with that in mind that I steel my expression in confidence that barely covers the surface and beg several gods to shore it up from underneath. Today, I find their favor.

"Be very careful, little one. You are playing a very dangerous game — one that could end with you in much the same shape as your little pet will be in a century. As I warned you before, I have a very, very long time I can play out my part in this game, and someday you'll be in a position of weakness, and then no human will stand between me and what is mine. And make no mistake — you are mine."

"You are the one who is mistaken, Ramsay — in this as in so many things. My position here is one of strength, and that will not change. The winds of fortune will only shift further in my direction as time passes, and you will find out very quickly how far they have turned against you should you continue to challenge me and mine."

"We shall see, Piper, because I plan to be around to see the look on your face when you realize you have no one left who can save you. Then, you can beg me for my favor, because your fate will be solely in my hands."

I find Rory in Rónan's office, sifting through a thick sheaf of papers, a pair of reading glasses resting low on her nose.

"Your brother had the oddest filing system I have ever seen. Was he filing these receipts according to company name translated into Irish?" It's a mirthless chuckle she gives me, and I know she's feeling his loss strongly, sitting behind his big desk, still steeped in the affection she held for him and also lamenting that he's not here to handle the tasks that have now fallen upon her strong shoulders.

"It's more likely to have been Welsh," I acknowledge, half-serious. She looks up at me, trying to ascertain whether I'm joking.

"You're amused, but not being untruthful. He really would have used a Welsh filing system with American companies whose names are in English?"

"I can give it a look, if you want to know for sure whether that's the case."

"You're serious." She shakes her head in wonder. "How on earth did that man manage to build a financial empire of this size when he couldn't even keep his files in English?"

"So many of us are polyglots that I'm not even sure what language he thought in. There's a good chance it was Welsh."

"I'm going to have to learn Welsh, aren't I? I mean, I'm already taking Irish 102 and a Scots/Manx Gaelic intro class... Why not add a language from an entirely different branch of the Celtic language tree? French wasn't on offer at the Hidden Folk School of Languages?" She sighs in frustration.

"Je parle français aussi," I mumble, looking down at my feet. I think I spent all of my bravado on Ramsay. It'll take me weeks to recover, and I don't have the luxury of that kind of time before I have this conversation.

"OK — who's dead?"

She says it as a joke, and then catches herself.

"Sorry — I didn't realize how bad that would sound until the words came out of my mouth. I'm tired, but that's no excuse."

"It's fine. I knew you were joking. And you're no less sensitive about it than I am, so I take no offense."

"OK, then. Who's pregnant?" She cracks up with laughter before rubbing the space between her eyes.

"No one that I'm aware of. The selkies, at least, have another two months or so before our mating season."

"I don't know if that's an advantage or a disadvantage, and I truly am too tired to care right now. So long as *you're* not pregnant..."

"No. As I said..."

"You're very somber, Piper — hence my poor taste in broaching the issue of what's brought you here. Clearly, it's something serious."

"I fear so, Rory. And I apologize for having created this mess and for having brought you into it, without your knowledge, even. Rónan would have been very unhappy with me, and you have every right to be as well."

"Spit it out, Piper. I can't deal with preamble tonight."

"The band I've been working with at the studio, it's the same band who I ran sound for last week."

"Wait — I thought the band at the studio was some big-name act that has the studio for the whole summer..."

"They are, and they wanted to try out some of their new material under a false name while they're here."

"I see... Who's this big-name act? I haven't been keeping track of the details with the studio, I admit. It was one of Rónan's holdings that he'd left in others' hands."

"It's aMUSEd."

Rory blinks and shakes her head in disbelief.

"Wow. I would have been less surprised if you'd said Godsmack or Kaleo or Halestorm... I knew the facility was good, and it's a brilliant concept. I just didn't expect it to bring in a band of that caliber. ...Oh!" She smacks herself on the forehead. "Wait... Hunter Graves grew up here. Of course they're here for the summer. Lyric's friend Brighid is a friend of Hunter's."

Lyric is Rory's best friend and former housemate, mother to her godchildren. Our world suddenly seems very small, especially given the depth of the secrets we're keeping.

"Sorry — I interrupted you, Piper. It's my music journalist's enthusiasm carrying me away. There's a problem with aMUSEd, I take it?"

"Not with aMUSEd as a whole... It's their bass player..."

"David Carter, right. The quiet one. Especially in contrast with his brother, Declan. Oh, boy — *there's* a focal point for problems if I've ever seen one... But his *brother*? What on earth could David Carter have done that's got you so upset?"

It all comes out in a rush.

"He kept moving his mic stand, and then he lied to me, and then he asked me to go swimming, but I said no, and we had breakfast instead, which got me in hot water with Steve — literally, since he made me scrub the kitchen and bathroom..."

"Wait! Steve gave you cleaning duties to punish you for having breakfast with one of the band members?"

"Yes."

"I see." She doesn't ask for more details. I can see her filing away the information, and I'm kind of glad in this moment that I'm not in Steve's shoes. It almost makes me smile.

"Anyway... David asked Sean — that's Steve's son — to get him some guitar strings, but Sean had a date, so I did it instead, and we had a picnic on the beach afterward, and I told him about Rónan being gone, and he kissed me. And then I avoided him for a while, but he'd seen somebody swimming at night and thought maybe she'd drowned..."

"I take it that somebody was you."

Sheepish barely covers my expression. In fact, it covers it better than I was covered up those nights that David spotted me. I nod solemnly.

"Piper... you have to be more careful!"

"Well... uh... That's kind of the thing... You remember the night you first came to investigate the guard's heavy-handed enforcement of the private beach, for your article?"

"Oh, no. Tell me he didn't see you. Tell me he didn't see more than he should have."

"I wish I could."

She's rubbing a spot in the middle of one eyebrow, her eyes focused on a spot on the ceiling where even my vision can't discern a single blemish or bump.

"This gets worse, doesn't it?"

I nod.

"Just spit it out, Piper. I need to know what level of awful I'm dealing with."

"He saw me transform — clearly enough that as soon as he thought back through it, he put it together. In fact, he kind of threw himself on top of me just as I changed back to human form."

"And he'd already courted you and kissed you, so I'm guessing naked Piper was more enticement than mythological creature was a deterrent."

I nod again.

"So you've followed in your brother's footsteps and taken a human lover. You are lovers, right? Not just a one-time checking of a box on the sexual checklist for both of you?"

I nod more enthusiastically this time.

"So you filled him in on Safe Harbour and the Hidden Folk, and your nature…"

"I needed to make sure he understood how important it is to keep the secret, that it's not just my own, and that lives are at stake."

"And did you tell him your brother tried to have my memory erased to keep that secret?"

"I did."

"And that a number of people would rather I wasn't sitting here at this desk, but lying down six feet under?"

"I did."

"And he agreed to keep the secret?"

"Without a second thought. He had far more of a problem with the idea of keeping our relationship secret."

"Which speaks well of him."

"But, unfortunately…"

"Oh, no… Someone's found out already, haven't they? Tell me it's just Hunter, or someone I can at least hold hostage with the threat of paparazzi."

I shake my head gravely.

"Piper, you're scaring me."

"Ramsay."

"Crap."

"He threatened to tell the Council that David is now aware of our secrets, and that we're lovers. I think he hoped that would force me to stop seeing David and to give in to his demands."

"Which, of course, we will not do."

"Thank you." I expected she'd say that, but it's still a weight off my mind.

"You're living in a democracy now, Piper. You may still be under the influence of a council of elders and some pretty antique attitudes, but Rónan understood what living here meant for you all, and he wholeheartedly believed each of you had the right of self-determination. If you want to date David Carter, that's your choice, though I can already see some issues on the horizon there, even without Safe Harbour's secrets being a factor. But there's where we run into some serious concerns that impact you, David, me, the studio, the band, the Council and on and on..."

"David will keep our secrets. I know he will. I trust him."

"Do you trust him with your life? Because that's what you're doing."

"I do. I don't know why, but I have no doubt he'll keep his word and protect our secrets."

"I'd feel a little better if we were relying on something other than your selkie instincts, even if you are 250 years old. You've had very little exposure to humans and how our minds work."

"Rónan trusted *you*."

"He didn't have any choice early on. I'm not sure what he'd have done if I'd been ready to expose all of you. A less-ethical human might have put career ahead of your lives, or even her own."

"But you're not a less-ethical human, and Rónan knew that very quickly. Just as I know I can trust David."

"I know you believe that. For all of our sakes, I hope you're right."

"What are we going to do about Ramsay? About his threat and the Council?"

"What did you tell him?"

"That you were already aware of the situation and had given me your approval to take David as a lover and to let him in on our secrets. And that I knew some secrets of David's that ensured he'd keep silent."

"Do you?"

"I know a couple things about him that no one else knows. He trusts me as much as I trust him. But none of it would keep him from telling our secrets if he wanted to."

"I have to admit that I'm relieved about that. If you're going to put your trust in him — put our lives in his hands — I'd rather he was someone who wasn't carrying horrible secrets of his own."

"He's sweet, Rory. Awkward, like me. He's not at all the stereotype of the rockstar. I'm his first actual girlfriend."

She blinks at me.

"I'm trying not to be skeptical of that. Surely, he's been awash in lust-crazed fangirls for the better part of a decade?"

"He has. But as I said, he's awkward, so no girlfriends. Ever."

"And now he's got a girlfriend who's a 250-year-old immortal straight out of 'Roan Inish,' secret and all."

She chuckles and shakes her head.

"Well, if you had to get tangled up with one of them, I'm glad you picked the quiet one in the band. I can't imagine what we'd be dealing with if it was his brother. Or, god forbid, that drummer of theirs... As it stands..."

"Can we salvage this situation? I don't want to put David at risk."

"David has put himself at risk, and all the rest of us, with your help." Her frown is repressive. "But I think we can mitigate the risk. Give me a little time to consider our options. If Ramsay continues to pressure you or threaten David, tell me immediately. I'll try to figure out a way to defang him, and if we can't, we'll consider other options."

"What other options?"

"Let's just hope we don't get to that point. For your sake, and especially for David Carter's. And for me, because I don't want to be the person responsible for destroying a really good band."

CHAPTER 17

RED SKIES

David
The next morning

I awoke before dawn this morning with more of that song in my head, and I left Piper sleeping sweetly in her bed to come back to the studio and work it out on my guitar. I'm sitting on a stool in the live room, pen between my teeth as I test a chord change for the bridge, when I hear knocking. On the studio's front door.

I'm not sure who'd be knocking here, let alone at this hour, and I'm tempted to ignore it in case Declan's barhopping last night got him trailed back here by a fan. But the knocking is pretty insistent, and I don't want it to wake the guys. So I open the door.

There's a tall blonde woman standing there, looking a little irritated. She's got her sunglasses in her hand and — except for her bare feet — is dressed for "casual Friday" in an office, though today is Tuesday. Her brown eyes are a shade or two lighter than Piper's but equally expressive. Yeah, she definitely seems irritated.

"David Carter?"

"Uhhh..."

I'm not sure how she knows David Carter would be here, or whether I should even confirm I'm him.

"No point in denying it, David. I know what you look like, even though not everyone on the planet does. It's my business to know."

"I'm sorry — who are you and why are you here?"

And in an instant, my fears are realized.

"Aurora Carmichael." She offers me her hand, and I shake it reflexively. "I'm a reporter with the Mystic Beacon. I cover the music beat, so I'm very well aware what the members of aMUSEd look like."

"Listen — we're here on a working vacation," I tell her, my hands raised up defensively. "We're not doing any interviews. This is all hush-hush so we can get our new album done. If you like, I can refer you to our PR person, and they can consider doing something with your paper once we've finished the album."

"I'm not here for an interview, David." She shakes her head at me, like I'm missing an obvious point. "Well, no — I *am* here for an interview, but not for the paper or any kind of publication. I'm here to interview you so I can ascertain whether my little sister is right about you, that you can be trusted with our secrets. Safe Harbour's secrets."

It's so unexpected that I just stand there, dumbfounded.

She brushes past me, walking past the reception desk and down the hall to the control room, like she's been here before, and I follow, finding her seated on the sofa. More like she *owns* the place.

"I did a feature on the studio when it first opened," she explains, accurately reading my puzzlement. "I spent the better part of a day here, going over the project with Steve, who has turned out to be exactly the misogynist I feared he was under the surface." She frowns deeply.

"I'm sorry... I'm lost here. You're a reporter for the Beacon, and you know about Safe Harbour..." My hackles are up. I like reporters even less than the rest of the band. Except Kier, that is. Nobody is more media-shy than Kier. "Are you writing an exposé?"

She scoffs, a hint of amusement in her smile.

"If I was going to do that, I'd have done it a year ago, David. It's definitely ironic that a year later, I'm one of the ones doing my best to keep their secrets secret."

Suddenly I realize who this must be.

"You're Rónan's girlfriend. Rory?"

She flinches at his name, confirming that that's exactly who she is.

"As I said, I'm Aurora Carmichael — my friends call me 'Rory' for short."

"Piper didn't mention that you were a reporter."

"Well, at least she managed to keep that to herself, even if she's apparently powerless under the influence of your charms, rockstar."

"Hey — Piper is strong, fierce..." I rise to her defense, ironically, given I'm championing her strength.

"Yes, she is. I'm glad you can see that. Not everyone does. Even Rónan underestimated her. Should have sent her to college, rather than putting her in Steve's hands..." She shakes her head with clear regret.

"So..."

"David — you're now one of just three humans who know about Safe Harbour and the Hidden Folk. One of a tiny, tiny few alive today who even know the selkies and their like actually exist in more than myth. That's like having the government clearance level of the White House chief-of-staff. And the only background check you've undergone is my little sister's instincts about people. And she's not exactly unbiased where you're concerned, thanks to that charisma of yours."

I don't think anyone has ever said that *I* have charisma. Did she confuse me with Declan?

"Umm... Thanks?"

"It's not a compliment. Rónan had it, too, which is why he got away with so much for so long, and why things got harder for Safe Harbour recently."

"I'm sorry for your loss."

I see the same grief reflected in her eyes as I've seen in Piper's when she talks about her foster-brother. If anything, it's even more intense.

"He died protecting us. It was his mission in life, the essence of who he was. Would that he'd favored his father's nature more. It might have saved him. Not that he ever favored that mother of his at all, thankfully." She shudders.

I want to ask her to explain, but it doesn't seem like the time to ask for more information, not when she's clearly unhappy I'm already aware of some of their secrets.

"Piper said she'd told you about how I stumbled onto the secret and how Rónan had tried to make me forget."

I nod.

"What she didn't tell you, because I've never told her, is that their methods for doing so were less than pleasant. I probably endured it longer than you would, since they kept trying until it was clear they'd failed. But unless there's something to you that I can't see, you'd fold — sooner, rather than later. Like origami."

"I won't forget her." This isn't a promise — it's a fact.

"You may find yourself wanting to, if it comes to that..."

Sadness and frustration is plain on her face.

"I won't. Ever. I love her." And as the words leave my mouth, I realize I mean them. "I'd never let anyone or anything harm her. I'd protect her with my life."

"I really hope you mean that, because it could come down to exactly that." She gives me an assessing look and then sighs. "There are certain factions within Safe Harbour that are... displeased... with some of Rónan's rules and his plans. Some of them would very much like me gone. And I don't mean like a restraining order against an unwelcome former girlfriend — I mean dead. I wouldn't put it past them to try again in the future."

"Again?"

"I've had a few self-defense classes. Let's just say it was one of my story assignments that's come in very handy."

Her blasé attitude about people trying repeatedly to kill her sends a shiver down my spine. What have I gotten myself into?

"Is Piper in danger?"

"Less so from them. She's a natural focus with Rónan gone, but she's one of the harbor-seal selkies, and they're generally much less aggressive than the grey-seal clans, so people largely underestimate her. And she's only seen a quarter-millennium, so they still consider her a kid."

"You realize how weird that sounds, right?"

"You know the line from the Alice-in-Wonderland story? Where the queen says, 'Sometimes I've believed as many as six impossible things before breakfast'? Welcome to my life."

Her grin is wry.

"The love of my life was a demi-god, and he still ended up dead, David. As you know, Piper is immortal, but she's *not* indestructible. There is a reason very few of the selkies alive today are more than a few millennia old, and it's not all from humans hunting seals. It's clan wars, factional conflicts, political assassination. They're a very old species with a very long memory. Their society doesn't change as quickly as ours does. And there's a reason why all the tales are of selkie women taking human husbands and not of human women taking selkie husbands... What little about selkie men that is in our tales describes them as aggressive, violent, territorial, ugly — which most people take as meaning they're physically repugnant, but what I've seen tells me it wasn't their looks that they were talking about, especially not where the grey-seal clans are concerned. And we have a few of their kind here, on a provisional basis..."

She looks me in the eye.

"I wasn't thrilled about it, but Rónan was determined this place would be a refuge for those who sought it. So they've been given a chance to prove themselves."

"Are they a threat to Piper? I asked her about sharks and orcas. I didn't even think to ask her about her own kind."

"At the moment, I would say no. There were some old covenants that she was apparently tangled up in when she first arrived, but Rónan set aside nearly everything that came before, to give everyone a chance at a new life here, to make of themselves what they wanted. Some of those who would prefer Rónan's human mate was gone with him would also prefer that those old ways returned. But they're a small minority, unlikely to challenge the community or its Elders, which somehow has come to include me. And I'm not going to let anything happen to Piper or to Safe Harbour — not while my heart still beats."

"And you want to make sure that I'm not only not a threat to them, but willing to make the same pledge to protect them."

She nods.

"If you're not, David, you need to cut all ties with Piper. Right now. Before anyone else realizes that you know."

She swallows hard, giving me another assessing look.

"You've got a very appealing life waiting for you when you leave here, and no one would blame you for going back to it and leaving all of this behind, like a strange dream. Including Piper." The mere idea makes me frown. "You — *we* — only have a handful of decades to live our lives. They'll be here long after we've fed the trees, as they say. Someday, she'll have to go on without you, and she knows that. Every selkie who's ever taken a human lover knows that. They accept it when they cling to those ties instead of breaking them. In the back of her mind, she's already mourning you."

"I..."

She cuts me off.

"That sounds morbid, I know — but what it really means is that you can break things off with a clear conscience. She'll miss you, but they're better equipped to handle loss than we are. It's their nature, with lives that long."

"I don't want to break things off with her. I really do love her."

"You've known her what... a week? Two?"

"About that."

"And you're sure?"

"I've never felt like this about anyone before. It feels like I've been waiting my entire life for her, for Piper specifically."

"Well, then you're fucked." She smiles and chuckles. "Been there, done that," she adds in response to my surprised expression. "No gift shop at the end of the ride from which to buy the T-shirt."

"'I made love to a demi-god and all I got was this lousy T-shirt'?"

She barks a laugh.

"Yeah, that would be kind of a letdown. Most humans who sleep with divine beings end up with a superpowered baby or transformed into a swan or something. Me, I just inherited a little sister and a colony full of mythological refugees."

"Makes your day-job seem like a day at Disney World, I would bet."

"Man, I need a vacation..." she says, shaking her head.

"But David — I'm serious. You've got to be all-in on this thing with her, because I'm the 'good cop' in this scenario. And you really, really don't want to meet the 'bad cop.'"

CHAPTER 18

TROUBLE ME

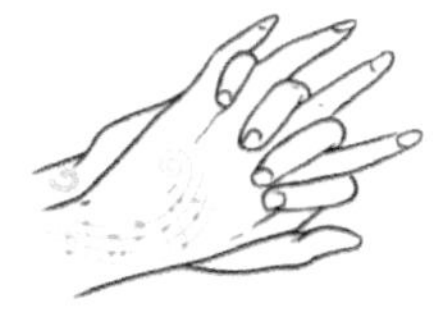

Piper

"Piper, can I speak with you for a moment, please?"

I'm sitting in the control room, tweaking the EQ on David's acoustic guitar as he noodles in the live room, ready to put down a scratch track on his new song. None of the rest of the guys are even up yet, and I wasn't expecting Steve to arrive for at least another hour. But there he is, standing in the doorway, looking... unhappy.

"Sure." I wait, expectant.

"In the office, please." He turns and walks down the hall without waiting for my reply. Uh-oh.

"David," I say into the talkback mic that feeds into the live room. "I have to deal with something in the office. Do you want me to start the recording so you can just keep going while I'm gone?"

"Yeah — I've nearly got this melody down," he says, smiling warmly at me through the big glass window between the two rooms. "I can come back in there to do playback for myself once I've got it nailed."

I start the recording, give him a thumbs-up and head to Steve's office.

"Have a seat."

This is a trend I don't like. My anxiety ramps from fifty to ninety in an instant.

"I thought I asked you to keep away from David Carter."

I think fast.

"That wasn't what you asked me to do. You asked me to stay out of the living area, let Sean be their first point of contact and behave like a professional with the clients. I was in to do my usual morning checks, and David was up, wanting to record some scratch tracks, and he asked me to man the console for him so he didn't have to run back and forth between the live room and the control room. Doing that for a client is the definition of professional."

As I point this out, Steve's face is getting progressively more and more red. I don't mention that David and I walked over to the studio together this morning after waking up in each other's arms, sharing my shower and getting dressed for work. What Steve doesn't know won't hurt him.

"That wasn't what I had in mind. I expected you to do your daily checklist and stay out of the studio until the band is ready to record and we need an extra hand in there."

"That's not what you told me. I followed your instructions to the letter."

Steve's lips purse, and I'm afraid he's going to start sputtering. I break eye-contact, looking down at my feet.

"Obviously, I should have made my request clearer," he said through gritted teeth.

"Should I have refused to help David when he asked?" I'm careful to keep my tone neutral.

He's quiet for a moment and then sighs.

"Of course not. We are here to serve the clients' needs, day or night."

"That's what I was doing this morning." I manage to keep a straight face when memory flashes in my mind an image of the other needs of David's I was attending to around dawn, during that shower.

"Next time, call Sean and tell him to come in when something like that happens. You're the junior intern, and that really should be his job to do."

"But Sean is never here before noon..."

"Don't argue with me, Piper! Next time, call Sean."

There's a knock at the open door, and David is standing there, now also wearing an unhappy expression.

"Sorry to interrupt, Steve. I didn't realize Piper was in here with you," he says carefully. "I actually came over to tell you that I really appreciated you having Piper in this early so that I could get some scratch tracks recorded before the other guys wake up. I do my best work early in the morning, when it's quiet and no one else is around, but it's a little tedious to go in and out of the live room every time I want to scrap a take I don't like."

"I realize that, David. We can have someone in here whenever you need them. But Sean's the senior intern."

"How far away does he live, Steve?"

"About twenty minutes?"

"How far away do you live, Piper?" he asks, turning to me, though he already knows the answer to that question.

"About two minutes."

"So, Steve — you're telling me you want a client who's got an idea for a potentially Top 10 song waiting around for eighteen unnecessary minutes to get that track down, when the idea could get lost at any moment, just so you can have the senior of your two interns record it?"

"It would be more than that." Oops. Did I say that out loud? Maybe it was quiet enough that...

"What did you say?" Steve asks, an edge of irritation in his voice.

I swallow and glance at David, who nods his head, encouraging me.

"It would be more than twenty minutes for Sean to get here if David's waking him up this early in the morning. He's not exactly a morning person. He'd have to get dressed, and he always stops for coffee on the way in, and then..."

"You've made your point, Piper."

"And it's a good one, Steve," David says. "She's made my point for me. She can throw on some clothes and be here inside five minutes. Sean might get here after half an hour. We're paying a premium for 24/7 access to the studio, and while we aren't recording final tracks yet, some of the value in that arrangement is that we can record scratch tracks at a moment's notice. If it takes six times as long for Sean to get here as it would Piper, clearly, Piper's the better choice for that."

"But she hasn't been here as long as..."

"Is she trained enough to run the console for recording scratch tracks?"

"Yes, of course. I make sure all my staff are trained in the basics before they even meet our clients. They aren't unskilled labor."

"Interesting," David says. "Because you seem to be using Piper as if she was unskilled labor and not a professional sound engineer, which she is — since she's being paid for her skills both as an intern and in her live sound work."

Now Steve splutters.

"David... I don't—" I start to say, looking nervously at Steve and wanting to defuse this conflict before I end up out of a job, paid, trained or otherwise.

"No — I think this is an issue we need to address before we get any further into the recording process. Is there something Sean can do for me, for this multi-platinum, award-winning band, that Piper cannot also do? Because if Piper is qualified to assist with scratch tracks, and she's much closer 24/7 and can be available whenever we need help, why are you inconveniencing both us and Sean by refusing to let her do her job?"

Looking at Steve, I can see he doesn't have an answer for that. At least not one that doesn't start with, "She's a girl," or "Sean's my son." And I am doubtful that realizing that is going to make him any less inclined to fire me. Especially once aMUSEd has finished recording and David is no longer here to confront him about it. This is why I asked David not to defend me with Steve.

"David, I appreciate your support for my work, but Steve's right — Sean's the senior intern, and if he thinks it's more appropriate to have Sean doing the work... I'm sure Sean can just plan to be available early every morning so he can be here when you're up at dawn..."

Steve makes a strangled noise. It's almost like he knows that Sean won't ever do that. He could. But he won't.

"David — you're the client," he finally says, deflated, "and if you prefer to work with Piper, especially at odd hours, when she's the one who's most likely to be available on short notice, we can accommodate that. But you'll be working with *me* once Malcolm Fisher arrives. Piper isn't qualified to engineer a project of this magnitude, even with Malcolm sitting at the console with her, and I'm contracted for your album."

"Of course, Steve. I'll look forward to it. In the meantime, I'm ready to get back to this song, and I could use Piper's help with the scratch tracks. Is she free to go?"

Steve frowns briefly, clearly having wanted to dress me down once David left the room. But he puts a cordial, if artificial, smile on his face.

"Of course. You're the client. We'll provide whatever you need."

"Thank you," David says, his smile real, if determined. "I'll look forward to working with you."

He grabs my hand and pulls me along behind him, back into the studio. I can't help but smile myself as that zing once again erupts with our skin in contact. But I'm not three steps down the hall before I realize that, even if I'll have a short reprieve while aMUSEd is still here, David Carter probably just got me fired.

David

"**D**avid! What did you just do?" Piper's voice is hushed but shrill.

"I solved a problem. And it felt good. Now we don't have to worry about him interfering."

"Why couldn't this be one of those times when you decided to not say anything?" She wonders aloud.

I pull her into the live room with me, closing the door behind us and pushing her up against it so we're not visible from the control room. And because having her pressed against me feels amazing, and I can do both at once this way. Yeah, I like touching my girl. So, sue me!

"Because he's being blatantly unfair, and if there's one thing I can't stand, it's people treating others unfairly." I run my fingers through her beautiful brown hair to ground myself, but I'm still so wound up about how Steve treats her... and I want her to know why.

"The other kids at school always treated me like I was a weirdo, some kind of super-awkward super-nerd. And I didn't *do* anything to ostracize them. It was just me being me. And once I got diagnosed, Mom and Dad explained to Declan that my brain just worked a little different because of the autism, and that I was having a hard time following the rules because of that. And then Declan and I were in the same grade, and they started calling me 'Rain Man,' because he told his friends I was autistic, and one of their parents told them about the movie…"

"I don't know that movie," she says slowly.

"It's a movie about a higher-needs autistic man — a math savant, who can do amazingly complicated math in his head. But he's been in an institution since he was young, and then his little brother — who never knew he even existed — gains custody of him and takes him to casinos to count cards, and…" I can tell I'm losing her.

"The point is that was the other kids' parents' idea of what an autistic person was — I don't blame Declan, because he didn't realize at that age that it might be used to tease me — but the other kids then expected me to be like that. And I *was* really good at math, and for a while I played along, until I realized why they thought it was funny. With my shitty social skills, it took me way too long to realize they were laughing at me and not with me."

"That's… that's mean. And unfair."

"Yeah, it was. The teacher caught them throwing math problems at me one day at lunch, like I was some sort of circus act, and the entire class got a lecture. They called my parents to tell them what had happened, and I thought I had fucked up somehow when they took me to the principal's office. A couple weeks later, we had a school assembly where they taught all the kids about autism and other 'special needs,' and encouraged them to make friends with people who might be different from them. And I knew it was because of me."

"That had to be uncomfortable."

"It was. But between the lecture and the assembly, the kids stopped teasing me, stopped calling me 'Rain Man' — for the most part, anyway. And while they didn't stand in line to become my friend, at least they left me alone to just do my thing."

"You didn't have any friends?"

"I did. I had a few other kids who were kind of nerdy and liked science, and once we'd done a couple after-school projects together, they realized I was pretty normal after all. And when Declan and I started taking guitar lessons, started talking about forming a band, suddenly I was cool, too, just like Declan had always been. Well, cooler than I had been, anyway. Like I said — I didn't date." I chuckle, if a little mirthlessly.

Piper's eyes are wet, and she grabs me into a rib-crushing hug. Do selkies have super-strength or something?

"It's OK, Piper. *I'm* OK. I'm part of a world-famous band now, and people usually just assume I'm cool, at least until I prove otherwise," I add with a laugh. "And now that I have this amazing, talented girlfriend, I've got everything I've ever wanted. Well, except that marine biology degree. But I'm working on that!"

I kiss her lips, and she returns the kiss, then suddenly stills.

"Steve's still going to fire me."

"No, he's not. We just got that established."

"No, you got that established, that while you're recording scratch tracks, I'm supposed to assist you. After that... And once you're gone..."

"You're not going to get fired, Piper. I'm going to make sure of it. Especially if Steve is being hard on you because of me."

"I think you underestimate Steve."

"I think *you* underestimate *me*."

"I don't, David... It's just..."

"Trust me, Piper. You've already trusted me with so much, so much important stuff. Trust me with this, too. OK? I can handle this. It's at least partly my mess, so I'm going to take care of it. Just trust me. Please."

She looks deep in my eyes, as if some kind of additional assurance can be found there, something more than my words. After a minute, she nods.

"Now, let's get back to work, show Steve how much of a pro you really are."

CHAPTER 19

THE FLOW

David

I keep losing my place in this bass riff, catching myself staring out the sliding glass door, looking at the beach, wishing Piper was here with me. But with Steve already scrutinizing her every move, we agreed it was better to have her go home after we'd finished the scratch tracks and a rough mix this morning.

Let's be clear here — I don't ever lose my place in a bass riff. They're as natural to me as breathing. That's why when I stim, it's usually bass riffs. My brain gets caught up in them, and it pulls me out of wherever I am and into a place of quiet focus, where the sensory stimulation of the rest of the world is tamed, controlled. It's one of the reasons I dove head-first into music — rock might be noisy, but it's a singular focus, and it opens a door to a place where I'm most comfortable being myself. I'm just lucky that I'm good enough at it to make my living doing it. So, my love of marine science aside, I'd never want to lose my music.

Only bass riffs aren't keeping my mind off Piper, and I smile as I picture her, in control behind the console, melting into me when I have her pressed up against a door, smiling mischievously when she drops to her knees in the shower, her hands gripping the sheets as she comes, her profile against the setting sun, her softness as she brushes my leg when she swims by.

I'm startled out of my reverie by my phone ringing, and I drop the bass back into its case to grab the phone and answer.

Marina Matthews.

The CEO of our label is calling me directly?

"Hello?"

"Good afternoon, David. This is Marina Matthews. I just wanted to check in and see how things are going down there."

"Uh... Fine?"

"You can elaborate a bit more, David — this live-in studio is a new experience for you and for the label, and the studio is new enough that I wanted to see how it's working, even this early in the process."

"Well, it's going pretty well. We're just getting started with the material, of course, but I got some scratch tracks down today that I think the guys are going to love."

"Is this one of your songs?"

"Yeah. I've been feeling kind of inspired since I got here."

"That's great! It's exactly what I was hoping for when I sent you down there to record. So the working vacation is offering a nice balance for you after being on the road?"

"Definitely. I love this place, with the beach and everything. People leave us alone, no paparazzi, no groupies."

"And the facilities? The staff at the studio?"

"They've been pretty great. The studio has everything we need that we didn't bring with us. I haven't worked with Steve in the studio yet, since we're just at scratch tracks, but his intern is *amazing* and also ran sound for us out at the one show we did with the new material, and the audience loved it. So that worked out really well."

"Was that Sean, or Piper?"

I know Marina Matthews has a reputation for being hands-on with her bands, but I never expected she'd have learned the names of the interns here at the studio.

"Piper. She's very talented, very easy to work with, always willing to help."

"Excellent. I like seeing young women getting opportunities to succeed in this business. It wasn't easy for me to make my way up the ladder in what is still a very male-dominated industry, so I keep an eye out for success stories like Piper's."

"Well..."

"David? Is there a problem?"

"It's just that Piper's not being used as effectively as I think she could be. Steve has all these rules about her working with us, not wanting her to socialize with us, wanting Sean to work with us instead. I'm not sure she's being given a real chance to learn and use her skills. I had to push him to even let her work on scratch tracks with me this morning."

"I see."

Her tone promises trouble, and I start to see why Piper asked me not to confront Steve, because now I'm the one worrying about the consequences. A shot of adrenaline hits my bloodstream as that worry takes hold.

"I mean, it's Steve's studio. He's the manager. But I just don't like the way he's treating her, making her scrub the bathroom because she had breakfast with me..."

I totally did not plan to say that. This is why I stay quiet most of the time.

"He did what?"

I swallow, hard, because I know I've messed this up now.

"He'd asked her to stay out of the residence while the band was here and keep things professional with the clients. But I was up early and she came in, and I dragged her upstairs to have breakfast with me."

"And Steve objected to this?"

"Yes. And to her working part-time at the bar we played at."

"But she's been available whenever you all needed her in the studio?"

"Yeah — she's doing a great job. I've hardly seen Sean, even though Steve made him our contact person."

There's silence on the other end of the phone.

"Thanks for telling me, David. As part owner of the studio, that's valuable information."

"Uh... I didn't realize you were an owner."

"It's one of my personal investments, along with a few other investors. Steve is a minority owner."

"Oh. OK."

"Please don't share that information with anyone, David. I'm asking you about this as an owner, not on behalf of the label, and it's best people don't know the CEO of a label has an ownership interest in a studio — every unsigned band will want to book time there, hoping I'll hear their EP and sign them to a big deal."

"Like you did with us."

"After a fashion. But I'd rather the focus was kept on the music, rather than contracts and dreams of fame."

"The music is definitely the most important thing."

"I'm glad you agree." After a second, she asks, "Are you happy, David? I'd like to think being signed to my label helps bring my artists the lives they'd dreamed of, but I know it can be a challenging lifestyle. And you boys have been on tour for a long time."

"It was a long tour. And, yes, I'm happy. Very grateful to you for all you've done for us. We needed the vacation, though, and now that I'm here, I'm really not sure I'll want to leave."

I say it with a chuckle, but I mean it. I could easily see myself living here in Mystic Beach, maybe getting a cute little cottage with Piper, surfing whenever I get a chance, writing music... Seal-watching has a totally different feel now that I know what I know, but it would be a great place to get my feet wet in marine science, maybe volunteering with a conservation group when I'm not on tour.

And there comes reality, crashing into my daydream. I'm going to have to leave. We're going to have to go back out on tour, gone for months at a time, for more than a year. Hunter hadn't even managed to see Brighid for nearly two years because of this last tour.

Even with Siren Song's generous revenue-sharing in our contract, we still make most of our money from touring. It's not like it was for bands decades ago, when record sales were the bulk of the bands' revenue and touring was done to promote the albums. Now, bands essentially release albums to get fans excited about the tours, because streaming bites into royalties and most record labels don't exactly rain what revenue they get down onto their acts.

Marina Matthews is the exception there. We got extraordinarily lucky she took a liking to us and was so generous in our contract. Even if she's making Hunter do this dating show...

"David? David? Did I lose you?"

"No! I'm sorry. I was thinking about touring, and..."

"What, David? What about touring?"

"It was a very long tour."

"And you would prefer a shorter tour in the future? More time at home?"

"I think so, yes. If that could be arranged."

"I'll see what I can do, David. No promises. But as I said, I like to keep my artists happy, and if more time at home would make your lives better, then I'll definitely look into it."

"Do you think it would be an issue if I left New York?"

"You're thinking L.A.? London? We could accommodate the distance with the corporate jet, though you'd have to be prepared to stay near whatever studio you're recording in for at least that length of time. Or if the band prefers, we could set them up temporarily in London or L.A."

"Actually, I was thinking of Mystic Beach..."

"Ah..." I can practically hear her smile through the phone line. "You've fallen in love."

"It's not—" I object, wanting to throw her off the track of Piper and me being together, but she talks over me.

"That little beach town is a wonderful place, David. I spent a little time there when I bought into the studio project. It's an easy place to fall in love with. And it certainly would make it easy if you wanted to continue to record there in the future. I think that's a lovely idea." She does? "Just remember that you're still going to be on the road again this fall."

"I know. I'm just not looking forward to leaving."

"You just got there, David. Give it the rest of the summer. Enjoy your vacation, put together a great album. Then you can come back refreshed and ready to go back out on tour."

I'm not sure a summer is going to be enough. Not if I have to leave Piper behind.

Feel the wind as it slips through your fingers

••• *Just like the sands of time have come and gone*
Never looked back
Timeless
Senseless
Faceless
And you know it's only a dream
Fly so high over the rainbow

Colors before never seen through eyes forever blinded to the whole mystery...

The song fills the control room as the guys sit around on the sofa and chairs, listening to the playback of my scratch tracks from this morning, engineered by Piper. Yeah, I got the guitar and the vocals recorded with her at the console. It flowed like... Well, like the tide coming in, washing notes and lyrics up onto the beach, where I just plucked them up and laid them back down onto the recording.

Maybe Alex was right. Maybe I have been inspired since I got here, or at least since I met Piper. And having her on the other side of the window made me feel so comfortable, so at home. No nervousness of what the studio engineer was thinking of these raw tracks, whether I might hit the wrong note in a new song I've barely started to learn. And she was *good* — no, she was *great*. It's the best my scratch tracks have ever sounded, even when recorded in a top studio in New York. She just seems to get my sound, our sound, like it's native to her. She manipulates frequencies like she's grabbing hold of tangible notes and tweaking them this way or that.

Maybe I'm biased. I probably am, at least a little. But the test of that is right now, as the guys listen to what Piper and I created together in just a few hours this morning, before any of them were even up. She's gone home now, resting up before she has to run sound at the Pirate's Cove for a local cover band. She was kind of in a hurry to get out of here once I suggested that we let the guys hear the song. I think she was nervous about how they'd respond, what they'd think of her work. She shouldn't have been.

...And should you go off on your own
Never lose sight of your home
When you think that it's all just a game
Remember my name
I've taken you home through the wind
And I've taken you home through the rain
I've helped you along
In your weakness I helped you be strong
And I carried you home at the end of the day
Now, too soon, the feeling is gone
In the daylight it all looks so wrong
Just a false sense of reality...

"I've got a vocal break and a guitar solo in mind here," I tell the guys, pausing the playback and looking expectantly at Kieran.

"I've already got the wisps of an idea," he says, nodding enthusiastically.

"This is great stuff, Dave," Hunter says. "The rhythm part is strong, and I can already hear Kier lighting it up with a blazing solo."

"It's just scratch tracks," I emphasize. "We can change things up, if you want to, along with adding the drums and lead guitar. And Declan's vocals should fit perfectly, as usual, since he and I sound so much alike in that range."

"I think you should sing this one," Declan says, and my jaw drops. Declan has never suggested I sing lead vocals. Ever. "It's upbeat, but it's a ballad, and — frankly — this is the best I've ever heard you sound on a scratch track. The emotion's there. I don't think I could sell it to an audience any better than you did, just on the scratch track. And you did this just this morning?"

"I started working on it a week or so ago. But I finished it this morning and laid down the scratch tracks."

"You sure you weren't an engineer in a past life?" Hunter asks, not sounding entirely like he's kidding. "These sound way better than our usual scratch tracks."

"I had some help. Piper was the engineer. I just played the tracks from the live room. She did all the equalizing and mixing. It's just a quick-and-dirty mix, of course. They're just scratch tracks."

"Yeah, but they're the best scratch tracks we've ever had," Alex says, adamant. "She's extremely talented at a mixing board. Can't believe she's just an intern."

"I know, right?"

"Do I detect a note of more than professional admiration there, Dave?" he asks.

"Oooh... Davey's got a girlfriend!" Rhys singsongs.

Heat rises to my face, and it makes it really hard to believably deny it. And I don't want to. But I overheard enough of Steve's lecture to Piper this morning to know that not even the guys can know — yet — that Piper and I are together.

I shake my head. "We're working together. That's it, guys."

"Sure, Dave..." Declan replies, smirking at me.

"So, do you all want to start working on the rest of the parts and the arrangement?"

"No hot date tonight, Dave?" Hunter asks.

"I should ask you the same thing, Mr. Reality Dating Show Star."

"Ouch." Rhys mimes a shot to the heart. "He's got you there, Hunt."

Hunter looks uncomfortable — like really, really uncomfortable.

"You guys know I wanted no part of this. The label's making me do it. And it's for charity. But this whole thing is weird. I was already having to deal with these girls competing over me, and now they're jealous of Brighid..."

The rest of us exchange a look. We know something went down at the shoot last week, after the rest of us had gone out to grab some dinner. Something that has him dodging Brighid, while Holly seems to have taken precedence for these dates he's filming for the show.

"What? What's that look?"

"Hunt — are you sure you and Brighid are just friends? Still?" Alex asks gently. "I think there's a reason the other girls are jealous, and it's not just because you and she took off together from the bar that night after our gig and left them hanging."

"Hey — we've talked about this before. I'm not going there with Brighid. We've been friends since we were 6."

"And she's like a sister to you..." Kier suggests. "A sweet, Irish-speaking sister..." he adds wistfully.

"Who still looks at you like you are the sun in her sky..." Rhys adds. "Man, I wouldn't mind a girl looking at me like that, a girl like *her* looking at me like that."

"You said that before, Rhys," Hunter says, "like a decade ago. And the answer is still no. You don't go anywhere near Brighid. None of you," he adds, giving Kieran the same stern look.

"Thou dost protest too much," Declan says quietly. Uncharacteristically quietly and non-confrontationally for Declan, and all of us notice it, looking at him with expressions ranging from surprise to concern, though Hunt seems prepared to argue.

"Drop it, guys," Alex says. "Let's start working on Dave's song. What's it called?"

"'Remember.'"

"Cool," Rhys says. "I'm ready to get in some beats."

"I'll go get my bass." It's still up in my room, where I've been noodling on it while Piper's working at her live sound gigs. I'd love to go with her, but she's working, and I don't want to risk someone seeing us together and telling Steve. Especially not now, now that she's got the chance to really do some engineering in the studio, even if it's just for scratch tracks. Getting to work with her every morning is like a gift from above, and I'm not going to risk losing that now that I have it.

I stare out at the view, watching the waves caress the beach. It's lousy surfing conditions, but it's a gentle, sensuous sight that makes my fingers itch, and for once it's not my bass strings they're longing for, but Piper's soft skin.

CHAPTER 20

CRUEL SUMMER

Piper

It was a good gig. The acoustic trio's lead vocalist and bass player were both women and greeted me enthusiastically, both surprised and glad to see a female sound engineer. And since it was just an acoustic group, and just three of them, setup was quick, with the electric-acoustic guitar and bass just needing to be plugged into the system. And I mic'd up the minimal drum kit in no time flat.

On the other side, after accepting the band's thanks for a set of unique covers that the audience loved, it was a quick breakdown and load-out, and I'm on my way home just after midnight, the sound of the DJ in the inside bar blaring as the door opens for a customer.

I cross the highway, putting in the code of the gate that keeps outsiders from driving into the Safe Harbour compound, and the gate swings open.

"Welcome home, little one." The tone of the voice belies the sentiment. Ramsay. Of course. "Did you have a good night at that 'job' of yours? Did you enjoy all those drunk human males pawing at you?"

He stands off to the side of the sandy driveway, easy to miss in the evergreens he's standing against, with no moon out tonight and outside lighting anathema at Safe Harbour. Most of our folk see quite well in the dark, even in near pitch-black, so it's not usually needed, and we are conscious of light pollution and its impacts on animals such as sea turtles. So no lights outside. That's the only reason I missed my nemesis standing around waiting for me as I arrived home.

"Ramsay, don't you have anything better to do than harass me? Aren't you supposed to be learning some skills so you can get a job and help support Safe Harbour? Wasn't that part of your agreement when you came here and asked for refuge?"

"I need no 'refuge,' girl. I have other plans for the long term." This is news to me, and I'm not sure it wouldn't be to the Elders, too. "I came here to collect my bride. If I have to stay here a bit longer than I intended in order to accomplish that, I will. I have all the time in the world, unlike your human," he says derisively.

"You leave him alone, Ramsay. He's under my protection and that of Safe Harbour. You can't touch him."

"What would you do about it if I did? He's awfully fragile... awfully mortal." The menace in his tone is clear, and I try to control the shudder that erupts down my spine.

"I can guarantee that if you harm a single hair on his head, you'll never come within a mile of me again, because Rory will see to it that you're evicted from Safe Harbour."

"Ah, yes... Your foster-brother had a little human pet of his own... She's mortal, too, you realize, no matter her pretense of filling her late lover's shoes. At some point, one of our folk is going to have to step up here and take charge of this sad lot of flotsam and jetsam, get the order of things set to rights. No humans coming and going from Safe Harbour at all hours..."

There's something to his tone... he's saying that now for a reason.

"What do you mean by that?"

"Oh, just that I saw your pet human come and go from your room several times tonight, appearing to be up to no good, as humans are wont to be, sneaking around in the dark. I'm surprised anyone would trust them with secrets — especially those who leave their valuable possessions in a room that such a human has free access to..." he drawls.

He's trying to make me think David's not trustworthy, but I know better, and I'm tired of this farce.

"I'm tired, Ramsay, and your threats, your harassment and your intimations about that human are so far over the line at this point... Be very wary. People are watching you, too. And you are here on sufferance. It would take very little to have you removed."

"Promises, promises, little one," he says slyly, flashing his teeth in an aggressive smile.

I push past him and hurry into the main building of the compound, where my room is. I narrowly avoid running, but I can't afford to let him think I'm afraid of him, even if I am. Nor do I want to alert anyone else who might see me and follow me to my room. Because I don't know if David is here or not. Ramsay could be lying, but I don't want anyone else aware of David's presence inside Safe Harbour, should that be the case.

I take a deep breath and unlock the door, dropping my bag and toeing off my shoes. The low light on the table beside the bed reveals a human shape under the blankets. I sigh, both relieved and concerned. Why would David come here without me? It's risky, at best. And the fact that Ramsay was telling the truth about David being here makes me wonder what Ramsay's game is now.

Just to reassure myself, I move quietly to the hidden compartment beneath the bathroom sink, where I left my seal coat this morning. David's never seen me hide it, so he has no idea all these little hidden spots exist within my room. Not even Rónan knew exactly where they were — just that I had them, as do all of the selkies at Safe Harbour. None of us know where the others' hiding spots are, except those who are mated, and not even some of them.

I breathe a sigh of relief when I feel underneath the sink and the hidden compartment is closed and latched as I left it. I spring open the latch, and it drops down. Empty.

Panic. Instant panic. Racing, mind-blazing panic. I've never been without my seal coat. Not since I was very little and my mother stored it away between uses so I didn't try to swim off on my own, into waters too deep to be safe. We transform that first time and gain our coats when we return to human form, and from then on, we learn to hide our coats well, to always know where they are. It's second-nature to us, even as children. Now, it's like a hole has opened up in my heart, and my spirit is pouring out through it like a waterfall.

Think, Piper. Did you put it in a different place this morning? Did you just misremember which spot? Maybe this was yesterday's hiding spot.

I race out into the living area, popping open the hidden drawer in the decorative front of the bookshelf. Not there.

"Piper? Is that you? Are you OK?" David calls sleepily from the bed.

That little niggling thought... Was Ramsay right? Would David have taken my seal coat to keep me with him? After all I told him? He's human. Maybe he didn't fully realize...

I scramble to the armchair by the bed, barely glancing at him, already feeling guilty for even wondering whether Ramsay's obvious lies were true. The false panel under the cushion pops up and into my hands, but I can tell before I even remove it that there's no soft, furry coat inside.

"Piper, what's wrong? You look... panicked."

David sits up in the bed, now wide awake.

"My seal coat is missing."

"Are you sure? Could you have left it in a different spot?"

"I've checked three places already. I'm still looking."

I move to the bedside table, reaching under the base to slide back the bottom panel. The coat should just slide into my hand. But it doesn't.

Every empty hiding spot is a jolt to my system, ramping my panic higher and higher. I'm panting now, on the verge of hyperventilating. When David's hand brushes against my back, I startle, turning on him with bared teeth, seal instinct overriding my human form. He jumps back, startled himself.

"Piper, it's just me," he says evenly, his tone intended to be reassuring, but my panic won't take that bait. "It's OK. It's got to be here. We'll find it. I'll help you look."

"You shouldn't even be in here, David! What were you thinking, coming into Safe Harbour, into my room, without me? What if you'd been caught by the guard? I warned you about what they tried to do to Rory. Was it worth the risk of forgetting you'd ever met me? Because I wouldn't have been here to stop them, and Rory's staying with Lyric's kids tonight so she can write, so she couldn't have vouched for you, either."

He looks taken aback, though I'm not sure if it's by my rapid-fire lecture or from realizing the risks of what he's done, after I've pointed them out.

"I'm sorry, Piper — I didn't think. I've come in and out so many times, it just felt natural to come over to wait for you. And I was so excited — I wanted to tell you how much the guys loved the tracks we did this morning, and then..." he says in a rush. "We finished the song, Piper! Our song — yours and mine. And it's amazing! And then I realized I'd forgotten the flash drive with the song on it, so I went back to get it so you could hear it. I don't think anyone saw me. I'm sorry!"

I turn away from him without comment, moving to check the compartment in the little bench. It's all very plausible, what he's said. And I want to trust him, to trust his word for what happened more than I trust Ramsay's, which is not at all. But he was telling the truth about David being here, and having come and gone and come back... And my coat isn't in the bench.

Could David really have taken my seal coat?

"You talked about being worried about me when I'm out in the water in seal form, about sharks and orcas and... You didn't do this to keep me from swimming out there, did you, thinking that you'd protect me from those dangers?"

"I wouldn't do that, Piper. Ever. I know how much your coat means to you. I'd never keep it from you. I wasn't here all night, but I fell asleep an hour or so ago. I guess it's possible that someone snuck in while I was asleep. I was tired after being up so early this morning. I might have slept through someone coming in and out."

"David, no one has access to my room except me, Rory and emergency access for the healers. And now, you."

We'd added his touch to the lock sensor just the other day, just in case someone was in the hallway when he was leaving and he needed to duck back inside my room to avoid being seen. I'd never dreamed that he'd just come over and let himself in when I wasn't here. Maybe someday down the road, if we could get the full council's approval for him to be here. But not yet.

"I can't explain it, Piper. I just know I didn't touch your coat, let alone take it. Are you sure no one else could get in here without you knowing?"

I think about it. I know what Rónan told me about these locks, which are as much magical as they are mechanical, and he was certain that they were absolutely secure. So do I trust Rónan's certainty and Ramsay's claims on the one side, or David's claim of innocence, when I know he might have found reason to do it, even if it was well-meant?

David's pale blue eyes are imploring me to believe him. And in my heart, I do, but my head... my head has relied on Rónan's wisdom and protection for much of my life, both here at Safe Harbour and before. And the fact is my coat is missing. I can't afford to take the risk that I've judged David wrongly, that he's not as well-intentioned as he appears.

"I don't know," I say, finally. "I don't know anything right now, including where my coat is. And that has to be my top priority — finding my coat, whoever took it."

"Then let's check everywhere. I'll help you. We'll find it. Two sets of eyes are better than just one."

"That may be true, David, but I need to take care of this myself. I'll see you in the morning."

"You're kicking me out?" he asks, hurt clear in his voice. "I didn't do this, Piper — I'm serious. I'd never do that to you, never *let* anyone do that to you. I want you safe, yeah, but I want you to be happy, too, and I know you wouldn't be if you couldn't be your seal-self. Believe me, please."

"I want to, David, but right now I'm too panicked to make any kind of rational judgment. I need to be alone, to try to figure this out on my own, with no one in this room but me, so that I know I've checked every spot it could be. I need you to go."

His shoulders sag, and I can see the light in his eyes diminish as surely as if someone had dropped a shade down over them. But I can't let his hurt feelings distract me. I've got to find my coat.

David moves toward the door, his reluctance clear in every step. He turns as he puts his hand on the door, looking morosely back at me, and my heart breaks, just a little. But I can't deal with this right now.

"I'm sorry, Piper."

He turns back and walks through the door, pulling it closed behind him, and I hear it latch, locked securely with him on the other side.

That's when the reality of this catches up with me, and I collapse on the bed, sobbing. Because I've lost my seal coat, and now I've lost David, too.

The next morning

I've torn my room apart. Every single piece of furniture that had a hidden compartment has been turned inside and out, upside-down and backwards, just in case it slipped back out of a niche or drawer. I've torn my bed apart, scoured the blankets, the sheets, the pillows, the sheer curtains and the frame they hang from. I've run through every item of my clothing. I've stood on that little bench to make sure I wasn't missing it stuck at the back of a deep, high shelf. I've even looked inside the air vents. It's not here. My coat is gone.

I literally stayed up all night looking for it, going over and over every single possible location multiple times. It's nearly sunrise, and I have to get ready for work now. Not because I'm planning to help David in the studio again today, but because I need to get my daily checklist items done before even *he* is awake, so I don't have to see him, talk to him, decide whether I trust him. Not until I find my coat, and with it, I hope, the truth of what has happened here.

I know I look horrible — tired and like I've been crying, which I have been, amidst everything else. No cold compress would be enough to take my eyes from red and swollen to anything resembling normal. I sigh in resignation while my hands tremble from both exhaustion and anxiety.

But, dressed for work, I head out to the highway, taking the long way from my room to the studio, using the front door this time instead of going in through the door off David's room, and stalking quietly down the hallway to the control-room door, peeking around the edge of the doorway.

Everything is as it should be at this time of day. No overnight recording session in progress, no early-morning composing by one amazing bass player who holds my secrets and my heart... and maybe my seal coat. I take a deep breath and jump to my tasks, loading up a new batch of recording drives for the band to switch in and out if they're recording multiple songs, which they could be now, if, as David said last night, they finished "Remember."

Longing hits me in the chest as I wish I could take the time to hear their final recording, even if it's not a final mix yet. But I can't. I have to get this done. And then one more thing, if I'm lucky.

The kitchen stocked, the bathroom checked, drives sorted, one last review of the control room and the live room, ensuring that all is in order, and I peek out the back door. David's surfboard is gone. The tide is up now, a swell coming in from a front off the coast. It's decent surfing weather, so it makes sense he'd be taking advantage of it. And now I'll take advantage of his absence to reassure myself that my heart knows better than my head.

I climb the steps to the kitchen and living area, stepping tentatively, just in case Alex had a need to make a sunrise omelet this morning. Hearing nothing, I head for the stairs to the third floor, where David's bedroom is, along with his brother's and the ones Hunter and Rhys occupy.

Someone's snoring, and as I pass Hunter's room, I realize it's him. He hasn't snored any of the times I've snuck out of or into David's room in the past, but as I glance through the door, which is slightly ajar, I see an empty bottle of liquor. That would do it. Though Hunter doesn't seem the type to self-medicate with alcohol... I'd ask David what was troubling him, but... Yeah.

I already know David's off surfing, so I quietly open his door and go inside, shutting it behind me. And now I sigh again, because I know this is a violation, going through his room. But weighing that against the need to recover my seal coat, there's no choice. I have to know.

My search is methodical, removing items from the dresser and setting them aside, then placing them back in, just as they were, before moving on to the next drawer. There's nothing in the closet but hanging clothes and a couple pairs of shoes, an empty duffle bag and a spare set of sheets and blanket. Only one place left to check... David's bass case.

The bass was down in the studio, along with his other instruments, but that one — his favorite Spector, in a custom deep purple color, with the slender Doug Wimbish signature neck — is the one he keeps with him in case he wants to play at a moment's notice. So, the case is still up here in his room.

I pop open the latches, begging the gods for I know not what... That it'll be empty, because David didn't take my seal coat... That I'll open it and find my coat, because then, at least, I'll have it back. That I'll find a wormhole inside that will allow me to transport myself back in time to last night, so I can take my coat with me to the gig, or at least see who took it...

Rubbing my thumb against Rónan's ring, I take a deep breath and then open the case.

At the same moment David opens the sliding door from the deck and sees me kneeling there, on the floor, next to his bass case, now opened, revealing its condemning contents — my coat.

"Piper! Thank god! Are you OK? Did you find your coat?"

I look down, and his eyes follow mine, getting huge as he realizes what I've found inside his bass case.

"No — Piper, I did not put that in there. I did not take your coat. I swear! Someone must have put it in there, but it wasn't me! Really, I swear!"

"How could you?" My voice breaks. "I told you how horrifying the idea of losing her coat is to a selkie. Why would you think this would ever be OK?"

"I. Did. Not. Do. This," he says. "Piper — look at me." And I do. His eyes are pleading with me, his mouth set, hard, and a deep crease between his brows that my fingers want to smooth away. But I don't. "I didn't do this to you. I need you to believe me. I came over last night to tell you about the song, and I came back to the studio — empty-handed — to get the thumb drive, and then I went straight back to your room. That's it. I fell asleep, and then you got there. Why won't you believe me? I thought we..."

He swallows hard and looks away from me, hurt in every bit of his posture. And even with my hands on my coat as it still lays in his beloved bass' case, I can scarcely believe what should be obvious and without question. He was in my room alone, without my knowledge, for I know not how long, and he left there and came back here, before returning again to fall asleep in my bed. And no one else had access to my room, aside from Rory, who I trust implicitly and who I know wasn't even there. And David had said he worried about my safety in the water. It makes sense that it was him. But it doesn't make sense in my heart, in my soul, and I am torn, despite the evidence.

"I have to go," I finally say. "The studio's ready for you to work in there today. I'll be back tomorrow. Leave me a note if you need anything special. I'm not sure what time I'll be in there." I say that, but if I have to get up and do my work at 3 a.m., just to dodge early-rising David, that's what I'll do.

If anything, David's shoulders sag even further, his mouth in a deep frown and pain... oh, such pain, etched into his face. And I'm the cause of that. Unable to absorb all of what's happened, all of what I'm feeling, I snatch up my coat, leaving the case open, vacant, looking like it's awaiting something to fill it now that my coat is no longer inside. I rush through the sliding door, which David never closed, having been surprised to find me here, searching his room...

Guilt eating at me for that, I race down the stairs and back to the refuge of Safe Harbour, where I take the steps required to remove David's access to my room before collapsing in my bed, exhausted now both physically and emotionally, with my seal coat cradled in my arms and my heart feeling broken and empty despite that.

CHAPTER 21

PLEASE FORGIVE ME

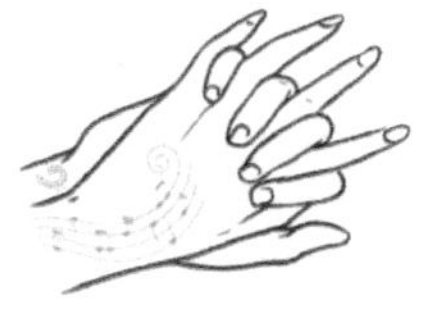

David

I can't believe she doesn't believe me. I mean, I can believe it, because clearly she doesn't. But I thought she trusted me. I thought maybe she even...

I can't think about that right now. It hurts too much, knowing that not only have I lost her for something I didn't even do, but that she didn't trust me after all. The first time her trust was tested, she gave up on me, on us. I start to see why none of the other guys' relationships have worked out. Relationships are hard. And that's before you get to the magical seal-person stuff or the fact that the guys — that we — spend so much time on the road, with trust between partners being tested every day. Maybe I've gotten off lucky that this is the first time I've fallen in love with someone...

And I never even said those words to her. Never actually told her I loved her. I did. I do. None of this changes that. But even if I could prove my innocence, could we ever re-establish that trust? Does she even trust me enough now that she's still comfortable with me knowing her secrets? Am I going to get knocked over the head when I'm sitting on the beach one evening and wake up having forgotten we ever met?

I picture her showing up to run sound for one of our gigs, and me asking Alex to introduce me to the new engineer, clueless that I know her better than nearly anyone other than my bandmates, and that she knows me just as well, because I'd forgotten her.

They couldn't do that, right? They couldn't erase her from my memory entirely. Too many questions raised if I don't remember her at all. Maybe they just erase my memory of the time we've spent together outside of the studio and the one gig. Is that a geographic restriction? Do I forget I saw her transform but remember making her come up against the door of the storage room? How would that even work?

My brain races in circles, stuck on the details and the hows, the science and logic of something that is not scientific and that defies logic as humans understand it. Humans. Because I'm human and she's not. She's 250 years old and a magical seal-woman, and she's my girlfriend. Or she was...

I collapse on the bed, staring up at the ceiling, watching the ceiling fan turn slowly counterclockwise, like a clock turning backwards, wishing I could undo the last twelve hours and just wait for her in my room. Maybe I send her a text telling her to come see me when she gets home, rather than going over there. Maybe...

"Dave — dude," Rhys says, peeking in with his hand on the partly open door. "We're heading down to the studio to work on one of Declan's songs. Come on! And why are you still in bed at 2 p.m.?"

"It's 2?" I don't remember falling asleep, but I can't imagine I spent eight hours staring at the ceiling, either. I shake off my confusion and follow Rhys down the stairs to the studio, stopping in the kitchen to grab a snack, since I apparently missed both breakfast and lunch. Piper left snacks in here.

Piper... I still remember her, despite fogging-out earlier. So, that's good. I think. I'm not sure how I'm going to feel if I never see her again. Maybe forgetting her would be better. Rory suggested it might be preferable. But no — I told Rory I'd never let them make me forget her. And I won't. I'll hold onto that feeling I had when I was with her, for the rest of my comparatively short, human life.

"Dave! What is up with you today? You're even worse than Hunter, and he's hungover," Declan says. "And you're just standing there, staring into the cabinet, like you've forgotten why you even came in here."

"Pretzels. That's why I came in here. I was in the mood for pretzels. Piper left pretzels for us."

"O... K..." He looks at me like I've grown a second head. "I think that's her job. No need to worship her for doing it."

"I'm not! I'm..." I don't know what I am. "I'll be in there in a second."

I decide to grab a protein bar instead. I don't know who brought those in.

I plop down on the sofa, chewing slowly but without tasting whatever I'm eating. It could be sawdust-flavored, for all that I'm enjoying it.

"OK — so let's listen to what we got done last night. Where'd you put that drive, Dave?" Declan says.

"Dave?" Alex prods, poking me in the shoulder when I don't respond.

"Hmm?"

"Where did you put the drive we recorded on yesterday? You were exporting the rough mix for Piper to hear, remember?"

"Yeah. Yeah. I did that. But I left the drive in the bay, since I figured we'd want to listen to it again this morning with fresh ears."

"It's not here," Alex says, scrolling through the files on the drive that's docked for recording. He swaps it out with the next one, finding it empty, too. And then a third. The growing anxiety in the room reminds me uncomfortably of Piper searching for her seal coat in her room last night. And probably again this morning, in my room.

"Would Steve have taken it into his office? For safe-keeping, maybe?" Alex asks.

"I don't know. I don't think so."

"I'll go check." He leaves the control room, heading down the hall to the offices. He returns a minute later with Steve right behind him.

"What's this about a missing drive?" Steve says.

"We'd recorded a rough mix of a new song yesterday, and now we can't find the drive. I've checked through all of these, and the tracks aren't on it."

"Has Piper been in yet today?" Steve asks.

"She was here early this morning," I reply, hoping this isn't headed in the direction I think it is.

"She sets out fresh drives every morning. It's part of her daily checklist," Steve says. "Maybe she picked up the other drive by mistake."

"Where would she have put it?" Alex asks.

"Standard procedure is to wipe the drives after they've been used, but that's only for ones where the work has been completed and the tracks aren't needed anymore. The ones in the basket. She knows better than to erase a drive for a project that's still in progress."

"If she picked up the wrong one, maybe she thought that one was ready to be erased. Would she have done it right away?" Alex asks, his tone getting a little desperate.

"Not necessarily," Steve says. "She usually does it as she has time between other tasks. And I'm not sure what else she worked on today besides the daily checklist."

"Well, let's hope she didn't take the time to wipe that drive."

None of this sounds right. Piper's not sloppy in her work habits. She wouldn't have grabbed a drive full of tracks and taken it to be wiped. Not even accidentally.

But then she was upset this morning, looked like she hadn't slept much, if at all, after spending at least part of the night searching for her coat and then coming over here extra-early so... so she could search my room, because she thought I took her coat...

And an even worse possibility occurs to me. Could she possibly have wiped the drive on purpose? Was the drive in the dock the one that had been full of a day's worth of work last night, but was now empty because she wanted revenge for her missing coat? Did she wipe my song — our song — on purpose?

"I'm going to call her and get her back over here," Steve says. "Maybe she's got a good explanation for what happened here."

I resist the urge to call her myself and warn her about what's going on over here. She's going to have to deal with Steve, and anything I say might make things worse, if she'd even pick up my call.

The other guys go into the live room to work on Declan's song, while Alex and I wait in the control room.

"What's going on, Dave? You've been out of sorts all day. Is something going on with Piper? Did you two have a fight?"

"Nothing's going on with Piper." Not even nosy "Mom" is getting let in on the fact that Piper and I are — were — seeing each other. I won't risk Steve firing her over it. She's got enough trouble right now, even though she's got her coat back. "I just didn't sleep well last night, and I was tired from surfing early this morning. I crashed out and was groggy after waking up."

Alex gives me a long, scrutinizing look.

"If you say so," he says, clearly unconvinced.

It's a long, uncomfortable five minutes of silence, with the two of us sitting in an otherwise empty control room.

"I just did what I normally do, Steve," Piper says, her voice carrying down the hall, clearly stressed out. "I replaced the drives in the basket with fresh ones. I didn't touch the one in the dock, since that's usually got tracks on it when someone is recording."

"Well, the one in the dock is blank, Piper, and no one else would have touched those drives. You sure you didn't make a mistake and take the drive with the tracks on it? You look a little tired. Were you running sound last night?"

"I was. But I was back home around midnight," she replies, giving a quick glance at me, since I know full well that she didn't go to bed anywhere near midnight, if at all. I let that fact go unspoken, of course.

"And you were back over here first thing this morning?"

"Yes. Before 6."

"So you had less than six hours of sleep? Why'd you need to be here so early today?" Steve is clearly grilling her now, his tone skeptical, slightly hostile. He glances over at me himself, as if he suspects that she was here early because of me, maybe even that she slept over here in my bed. Even though she didn't.

"I wanted to get things done early so that I wasn't in the way," she says. "In case the band wanted to do some formal recording with you. I knew they were working on rough tracks last night, and that's the next step."

"How'd you know that — that they'd done rough tracks last night?" he asks, again glancing at me.

"David had said they might get started last night. I just assumed they had," she says, shrugging. Her hands are shaking. Not obviously, but I notice. Because she's Piper and I'm me, and we're us. Even if we're not an us right now.

"So you came in here early, tired, after being out late at your other job," Steve says pointedly, "and you accidentally picked up a drive with tracks on it and took it to be erased."

"No. I didn't. I didn't take the drive out of the dock. I'm sure of it."

"Well, let's make sure," Steve says, heading down the hallway to the storage room.

Alex, Piper and I follow him.

"What are the labels on the drives still in the studio?" he asks, grabbing a basket of drives off a shelf.

"C, D and E," Alex says. "The B drive was the one in the dock last night. A was the scratch tracks."

Steve grabs the drive off the top of the pile in the basket and holds it up.

"The B drive. Right here. In the basket of freshly erased drives."

Piper's jaw drops, her expression shocked and horrified. Alex looks decidedly uncomfortable. Steve looks both satisfied and angry.

"But I didn't..."

"Piper, you're fired. Come back in tomorrow at 8 to collect your final check."

"But, Steve..."

"Steve," I interject. "We don't know what happened here. Piper is certain she didn't erase the wrong drive, and I believe her. She's very detail-oriented and conscientious. There has to be another explanation."

Piper is looking at me with a grateful expression, but it's tinged with guilt. Does she see the parallels here, of being accused of doing something she didn't do? I believed her. Why can't she believe me? But that's beside the point. I *do* believe her.

"What other explanation could there be? She's the only one who was in here today, and she did erase the drives. Maybe it was an innocent mistake, but it was careless and you've lost a day's worth of work, not to mention needing to re-create tracks that you no longer have a scratch track for, because that would have been erased from the A drive — A was the scratch tracks, right?"

He looks at me, knowing that I was the one who recorded the scratch tracks, with Piper's help. I nod, reluctantly.

He pulls out the next drive in the basket, marked with an A.

"This is an unbelievably careless mistake that could have been avoided if you hadn't been moonlighting, Piper, and whatever else might have caused you to be in here so early, short on sleep."

Again, he looks to me, his implication clear — that she was here early because she's sleeping with me.

Piper turns a deep shade of red, looking at her shoes. He's broken her down so much with this interrogation, the threat of firing her coming to pass, that she's shrinking into herself as I watch. I want to pull her into my arms, or at least stick her behind me so he knows he's got to come through me to get to her.

But I don't. I can't. It would only confirm his suspicions. And if we're going to recover from this unexplained set of truly shitty circumstances, he cannot have proof that he was right about us having gotten very, very personal.

"I've really got no choice to fire her, I'm afraid. I know you've been friendly," he says. "But I can't, as a business owner, as manager of this studio, keep her on staff when she's made a mistake of this magnitude. I'm a little surprised you're not demanding I fire her. Any other client would."

"Well, we're not just any client, Steve," Alex interjects. "And I'm both willing to take Piper's word that she's certain she didn't make this mistake and willing to give her some grace for what would have been an understandable mistake — a learning opportunity. Right, Piper?"

Piper's lip is trembling now as she looks back up at Alex, and I'm afraid she's going to literally do what she once said she might during an anxiety attack, and crawl underneath the mixing board to hide. But she pulls herself together and nods.

"Thank you."

"I'm not sure I can go along with this," Steve says. "It's too big a risk to the studio going forward."

"Have you ever made a mistake, Steve?" Alex asks.

"Of course," Steve says.

"So you know no one's perfect. Accidents happen. People make mistakes," Alex states slowly, decisively, practically begging Steve to try to contradict him. "And I'd hate to see you make the mistake of dismissing a talented young engineer in error, or over a simple mistake. And she is talented. So I'm afraid I'm going to have to insist you cut her some slack."

Piper looks at him, clearly grateful, but tense as her eyes slide over to Steve, who looks very uncomfortable.

"I'll take your request under advisement. Piper, you can stay on for now, but I want you to give your other job notice that they'll have to find another engineer."

"But..."

"I'm sure they'll need time to find a replacement, Steve," I point out. "And I'm afraid we also have to insist that Piper run sound for us while we're here and playing out to test this new material."

"Fine. But tell them to find a replacement, Piper. Sooner, rather than later."

She just nods.

"It's been a long afternoon for everyone. I suggest we all call it a day and start fresh tomorrow at noon — with a full night's sleep," Steve says pointedly, looking directly at Piper.

"That sounds like an excellent idea. Let everyone decompress, and we'll get back at it tomorrow," Alex says.

"Piper — can I have word, please?" I ask her, taking unfair advantage of the fact that she can't make a scene here, in front of Alex and Steve.

"Of course," she replies quietly, and I lead her over to the kitchen, shutting the door on everyone and everything except her and me.

Piper

I can't even look David in the eye.

Between feeling guilty over having searched his room and now grateful that he and Alex both intervened on my behalf... and then the little part of me that wonders whether I did, in fact, accidentally erase that drive... I mean, I know I didn't. I only erased what was already in the basket. But there it was.

"Sit down," he says gently, gesturing to the chairs at the kitchen table. "Please."

I do as he asks, still avoiding his eyes.

The silence is uncomfortable, and it lingers, until I finally look up from my lap and realize he's kneeling next to my chair.

"Are you OK?" he asks, grabbing my hands in his and rubbing his thumbs along the backs of my fingers. It's soothing, and again I marvel that this man thinks he doesn't read people well.

"I'm fine."

"You're not. But that's OK. We'll get you there."

"I'm sorry, David. I don't know what happened."

"Were you upset with me, thinking I'd taken your coat, and erased the drive because you were angry?"

"What? No! Of course not. I'd never..."

"— never do that, to me, to the band, and because you're too much of a pro."

I nod.

"I know that. I knew that. Because I know you. Just like you know me. And part of you, at least, knows I didn't take your coat."

"I didn't want to think so, David, but there it was..."

"But I know I didn't do it. That means someone has to have set me up. Someone with access to your room."

And that's when I realize he's probably right — this isn't just a matter of my coat going missing and turning up in David's bass case. Unless I have totally misunderstood David from the start, someone had to have taken my coat from my room, and they'd have done it with the express intention of framing David, knowing when it was found among his possessions that the only possible conclusion was that he'd taken it.

I have a sneaking suspicion who that someone might be. Even though he had no access, at least that I knew of, to my room.

Ramsay.

He's the one who told me David had been in and out of my room, even suggesting that something valuable of mine might go missing while David was there. What else could he have meant but to cast the blame on David? I should have known better than to have considered it. Ramsay lies, and he uses truth as a weapon, all the more powerfully when combined with his lies.

I'm going to have to confront him, make it clear that his ploy failed. And figure out how he got into my room to take my coat. I can't leave it there until I can be sure it's secure. As it is, it's stowed carefully in my backpack, which I don't normally bring to the studio with me but haven't let out of my sight since I walked out of Safe Harbour.

"I'll deal with it," I tell him. "I'll make sure nothing like this ever happens again."

"No — we'll do it together," David says. "Just like we'll fix this drive situation together."

"I can't, David. You should be working with Steve, or at least Sean. And Steve's never going to let me back into the studio after this. I'll be confined to restocking the kitchen and scrubbing the bathroom, making coffee."

He sighs, knowing I'm right.

"We'll figure it out. Together."

I don't get the chance to respond, persuade him of the folly of him standing up for me, because there's a knock at the door, and Steve opens it without waiting for an answer. I pull my hands free of David's, hoping Steve didn't see.

"Piper, why don't you head home," Steve says, making it clear that it's not a suggestion. "You should call the Pirate's Cove to let them know they'll need to get a replacement."

"Yes, Steve."

I grab up my backpack and slip past David before he can object. We've got no more room for mixing the professional and the personal, no matter how we feel about each other. My job is already hanging by a thread, and I'm about to lose the other one as a result. Giving Steve any additional reason to fire me would snip that final thread, and I'd be left with no job, having failed Rónan. And that I will not do.

In the meantime, I have a mystery to solve and a thief to confront, with David safely out of the line of fire.

CHAPTER 22

UNDERTOW

David

I re-read my text to Piper and add a line before I hit send.

Please.

I don't know if she'll listen to me, even if it seems like maybe she actually believes now that I'm innocent. But I need her to give me time — give us time — to get this sorted out.

Piper

David: *Do NOT call the Pirate's Cove and give notice. Not yet. If Steve asks, you left a message for the manager to call you back. Do NOT quit. Not on them and not on us. Please.*

I want to trust him on this, and guilt again washing over me for not believing him, I decide to do just that. Trust.

Which sets the scene for the confrontation I'm about to have. With someone I don't trust. At all.

I knock sharply on the door in one of the secondary buildings in the Safe Harbour compound. This is where Rónan chose to house the grey seal selkies, hoping they'd be less likely to cause problems with the rest of the Hidden Folk if they were removed from the central building and the rooms allocated to many of Rónan's nearest and dearest, and the community's most esteemed. The Elders are all housed in suites in the main building. My room is there, if more modest. And even Molly has her room there, though I suspect that was so Rónan could keep a closer eye on her.

Out here, in this building, it's more like a dormitory, intended for our bachelors among the Hidden Folk, but also a place Rónan chose to house those not entirely trusted. Since Ramsay fit both of those categories, there wasn't much room for him to complain about the accommodations. But now I question my decision to come to see him, instead of waiting to collect evidence or at least for the next inevitable moment when he seeks me out. But I'm here, and I'm doing this.

"Greetings, little one. What brings you to my humble abode today?" he says, his tone smarmy and self-satisfied, like a cat with a mouse.

He gestures for me to come into the small room, which is mostly filled by a twin bed, a chair and a dresser. There are few personal items here. A handful of old, weathered books atop the dresser, a bottle of amber liquor next to them, a sword — a sword? — hanging on the wall. That does not set my mind at ease. Few of the Hidden Folk arrived here with weapons, even among those whose families were well-established as warriors with their clans and peoples. Weapons are not forbidden, not even to one such as Ramsay, but his volatile nature and sense of entitlement make the sword's presence all the more concerning.

I step just inside the doorway, to better ensure privacy, but not so far that he can close the door behind me. He looks amused when I refuse to budge from that spot, despite his invitation. A nod, accompanied by a smug grin, as if to say, "As you wish," while dismissing my obvious reasons for concern.

"I know you took my coat and hid it among David's things. Your attempt to frame him for the deed failed. He has my trust, as I have his, and this is the last time I will warn you to stay away from him — and from me. My next step is a formal complaint to the Council, and it will not go well for you when I tell them what you have done."

"And your evidence of this misdeed you lay at my feet is?" he asks, clearly aware that I have none. He's covered his tracks well, and I have only circumstantial evidence to even suggest he was the one behind this.

"Your own words, spoken to me shortly before I discovered the theft. You implied something of mine had been taken, which no one else knew at that moment, except the perpetrator."

"Assuming you believe that human of yours."

"And I do."

"But will the Council? Or will they just erase his memory to eliminate the entire problem of his existence?"

"They wouldn't dare. He has done nothing wrong, and he keeps our secrets even more carefully than his own."

"Which would be? What in that human's pitiful handful of decades could possibly be so scandalous that it is on par in importance with the existence of Safe Harbour and our peoples?"

I don't have an answer for that. I deflect.

"That's none of your concern. But you run the risk of implicating yourself should it come to that. The Council will want to know how you came to be seeing him come and go from my rooms but allowed it to happen."

"Mayhap, next time, I won't."

"You won't what?"

"Allow it to happen. You're my promised mate, like it or not, and it wouldn't be outside the realm of my responsibilities to protect my mate — and my home — from an outsider. And if that outsider is a fragile, very mortal human, I doubt very much even the Council will have much care that I got a little too rough in my determination to defend us all and managed to snap his very fragile, very mortal, human neck."

Chills run down my spine, at both his concrete threat to David and his lethal tone.

"An unfortunate happenstance, but not unheard of in our history," he continues. "I'm sure the Council has had to cover up other such incidents, and the corpses that go with them."

I know that for a fact, though Ramsay has no reason to. And again I wonder whether he has more resources here than I was led to believe. Could he have a Council member on his side?

Someone with enough rank to override the security on my door and willing to do so to raise Ramsay's rank here, re-label him as a hero defender of Safe Harbour? For killing David?

Suddenly, I realize how badly I have miscalculated things in coming to confront Ramsay. My eyes drift unconsciously to the sword so prominently displayed on the wall, and he catches my glance.

"Or would it be more suitable to skewer your human? I'd even offer to duel him for your favor. I could scrounge up a sword for him to use. But then humans don't do much sword-fighting anymore, do they? He'd be at a decided disadvantage. I could fight him with one hand tied behind me, if you think that might improve his odds. A little."

His smile manages to be both smug and threatening now. Deadly, in fact.

"Or... if he were to decide that pursuing my mate was no longer desirable or useful... perhaps if she dissuaded him of his chances of success from this point forward, refused his advances... Perhaps then such extreme steps to protect my mate and my home would prove unnecessary."

Ramsay has turned the tables on me. Any advantage I thought I had in knowing his hand was behind the theft of my seal coat has evaporated under the weight of the open threat against David and the suspicion that Ramsay had help, perhaps of a higher rank than even Rory.

"I have to work with him. It's my job."

"You already know what I think of my mate having a 'job.' Soon you'll be spending your time raising my pups, *our* pups," he leers at me, his gaze traveling leisurely down my body. "You won't have time to pursue silly human pastimes. But, sure, for now, torment him by working alongside him, knowing he can't have you. His frustration will just serve to make my victory sweeter, whether that victory involves shedding his blood or not."

My hand flies, unbidden, at Ramsay's face, delivering a smack so sharp that my palm stings. He doesn't react, except to catch my hand as it drops toward my side, raising it to his lips as I struggle against him, and pressing a kiss to my palm.

"I do like my females feisty," he drawls. "Makes taming them all the more satisfying... For me, at least..." He levels that vicious smile at me once again. "So, what do you say, little one? Are you prepared to give up your pet? Or would you prefer to start digging his grave now?"

"Don't touch him, Ramsay!"

"So you'll rebuff him? Make it clear he is unwanted?"

I need time to think, to figure out a way out of this that will keep David safe. And so I nod my head, accepting that, at least for now, I will have to put real distance between David and me.

David

I'm sitting on the beach, trying to relax after all the craziness of the last twenty-four hours. And, yes, I'm wishing Piper was sitting here next to me. But she's not. I've got to fix this. I wrack my brain, looking for any idea to salvage everything that has come so perilously close to disaster. Nothing.

Eventually, I just end up watching the waves breaking on the beach, the rhythm of it catching me up like one of my favorite riffs. It sounds like... it feels like...

I've got it! I can fix this, maybe fix all of it.

I grab my cell phone out of my pocket and type a text to Piper.

David: *Come back over to the studio. I need your help.*

There's no immediate reply, but I run down the stairs, make sure there's a fresh drive set for recording, and then grab some cheese and crackers in the kitchen, since I missed two meals today and we're closing in on dinner now.

I hear the front door open and close — I assume it's Piper, but it means she's taking the long way, walking down the highway, rather than coming in through my room and down the stairs. And that makes me frown.

"David?" she calls as she gets closer.

"In the kitchen!" I call back.

She rounds the doorway, and I can't help myself — I walk right up to her and pull her close, hugging her hard.

"David! We can't do this," she says urgently, in a voice just above a whisper.

"Steve's gone for the day. The guys are all upstairs, chilling out, as suggested. No one is here to see. It's fine. Or are you still upset with me about your coat? You know I didn't do it."

"I..." she looks away. Maybe she is still upset about that. Was my going into her room without her that much of a problem for her? Again I question my ability to understand and read people. But I thought I understood her better than that. Maybe better than anyone.

"What did you need my help with?" she asks, not even subtle about changing the subject. Fine. We'll deal with the rest later. First things first. Priorities.

"We're going to re-record the scratch tracks."

"Why?"

"Because that was half of what was lost, and also it gives us a base to start from in replacing the recording that got erased. It'll make the guys' work easier when we go to re-record it."

She considers that.

"It'll also give you a chance to impress Steve with your efforts to fix this disaster, even though you weren't the one who caused it."

"You believe me?"

"I do."

I don't leverage that to get her to say *she* believes *me*. If she does, my dragging it out of her won't help, and if she doesn't, it'll just make things worse. She needs to know it in her bones, that she can trust me, that we're on the same team. And I invoke our mutual favorite TV team to do that.

"Let's go steal a studio."

CHAPTER 23

REMEMBER

David
A half-hour later

"I thought you were going to take a break for the rest of the day, like Steve suggested," Alex says from the doorway.

"Nope. I've got — *we've* got — work to do." I tell him, looking over at a clearly nervous Piper, who I'm sure is questioning whether she should be here at all.

"And what work is that?"

"We're re-recording the scratch tracks that were lost, so we can get a head start on re-doing the recording. I've already got the acoustic guitar part down. I was just listening to the playback."

"Let me hear."

"It's just the one track," Piper objects.

"Let me hear it," he insists.

She starts the playback of the simple single-instrument track, and Alex closes his eyes, listening intently. After the first verse, he's moving his hands in time with the music, replicating the keyboard part he created and laid down yesterday.

"OK — let's do this thing," he declares.

"What?" Piper says.

"Let's record this song. Now. We finished it in one night the first time. We can do it faster this time. And the engineering will be better, since it won't be one of us at the board," he adds, giving Piper a wink. Her mouth moves to object, but Alex is like a boulder rolling down a hill when he gets like this. There's no stopping him when he decides something needs to get done, and if you don't want to help, you'd better get out of the way.

I watch as Piper tweaks the EQ on his keyboard channels, blending the electronic piano with the synth, leaving enough sonic space for the guitars and vocals to be added later. He's Alex, and there's a reason he's been labeled a virtuoso, and less than a day after he wrote this keyboard part, he completes a perfect first take.

"How was that?" he asks. As if Mister Perfectionist doesn't already know.

"It was great!" I tell him over the talkback mic.

"Let me come in and listen to the playback." He pulls off his headphones and emerges from the live room, sitting down next to Piper as I offer him my chair at the console.

He nods along, eyes closed again, listening to the keyboard part in isolation. When it wraps up, Alex nods.

"Now, with the guitar."

Piper brings up the scratch track of my acoustic guitar, blending it carefully with the two keyboard channels, tweaking the EQ, until they weave together, the beginning of a rich tapestry.

"Wow. It didn't sound nearly that good yesterday," Rhys says from the doorway behind us. "Let me get the drums down so we've got a rhythm track to start from."

"Better to build it from the bottom up," Piper says, getting a smile and a nod from Rhys, who is all-business now as he climbs behind his kit. She even hops up from behind the console to tweak his kick mic placement, getting an enthusiastic thumbs-up from him when he hears the improvement in the sound profile for those low frequencies.

"She's good, this girl of yours," he calls out to me as she comes back into the control room. She shuts the door to the live room behind her, so I can't respond to tell him that she's not mine — publicly, at least, and maybe at all. She and I exchange a glance, but all I can take from it is that she's nervous, despite how well she's doing with the engineering tonight.

"I'm next," I note, and she nods.

"Rhythm section first, and everything else layered on top," she says, her focus back on the board.

Standing on her other side, Alex gives me a look and shakes his head, seeming to marvel at how much of a natural she is at this, how much of a pro she already is.

I'm tuning my bass when I hear Hunter and Kieran come into the control room, the sound carrying through the open door to the live room.

"What's all this?" Kieran asks.

"You all disappeared. We were wondering where you went," Hunter adds.

"We're recording a song," I call back. "Or re-recording one, anyway."

"Brilliant!" Kier says.

"I'm after Dave," Hunter adds.

Ten minutes later, even a cranky Declan has made it down to the studio, listening intently to the growing mix as Piper adds one channel atop the one before it.

"No one thought to come get me?" he asks.

"You always go last anyway. Diva," I point out. "Let everybody else do all the heavy lifting and then arrive at the last moment to claim all the glory." I say it with a smile, so he knows I'm teasing, trying to get him out of this mood he's been in since we got here.

"As is only appropriate. I'm usually the one singing the words, which is all people pay attention to."

A good-natured argument erupts, as each of us debates the importance of our instruments to the whole.

Finally, with all the instrumental tracks laid down and coaxed into place in the mix by Piper's skilled ears and hands, it's time for those vocals.

"Are you sure you don't want to do the lead vocals on this, Dec?" I ask him. "I'm fine with you doing them."

"You did great with them yesterday, Dave. And this is more up your alley, this sappy, romantic shit." He tilts his head over at Piper, who's once again deeply immersed in the mix.

"It's not sappy," I insist.

"Then own it," he says. "Own what you wrote. You sing it. I'll just do harmonies."

"Sibling harmonies," Piper says quietly, almost idly. "The timbre of your voices is the same."

"At least in this part of Declan's range. His range is a lot bigger than mine. A lot bigger than most singers' ranges."

Dec's usual smug expression returns to his face, giving me hope that getting this album recorded will get him out of this funk, where he's cranky and wired half the time and disturbingly quiet, almost melancholy, the rest of the time. He wasn't like this during the tour. It's just been since we got here. I have my suspicions as to why.

"Bigger is better. Ask all the girls," he says proudly.

Piper glances over at me and rolls her eyes. I chuckle and smile back at her. This is a good thing. She'll learn that very quickly, being around Dec.

I duck into the iso booth off the main live room, putting my headphones on and giving Piper a thumbs-up of my own, losing myself in the music as the playback begins, Hunter's acoustic guitar part leading gently into the upswell of the first verse, when the rest of the band joins in — Rhys' ticking drums, giving structure under the melody, the two joined together by that bass riff I've been playing since we got here, where it merges with Kier's ringing harmonics and Alex's floating keyboard layer.

My voice rings out in my own ears, odd to hear in this prominent place in the mix, but I close my eyes and focus on the flow of the song, through Kier's intense guitar solo, the vocal break and on, and then the richness of the mix drops away, leaving only Hunter's spare acoustic guitar part and my vocals. It builds again in complexity and intensity, until finally I open my eyes and look through the window at Piper, where she sits behind the console, willing her to look up at me as I sing this song — our song — to her, and only her.

The voice I hear over the water
Cold and empty it rings out over the silence
Feeling my pain

She looks up at me, our eyes locking with each other, her expression unreadable at first, until she blinks away a tear. And I sing my heart out to her.

It's never been only a dream
Or reality as it seems
As you reach for your soul's ecstasy
Remember to always be free
And I'll take you home through the wind
And I'll take you home through the rain
I'll help you along
In your weakness I'll help you be strong

I'm your guardian angel
Remember my name

It's a promise. My promise to her. That I'll protect her, her secrets, her people, her freedom, with my life, and that no one could ever make me forget her, so long as she wants to remember me. Together, we're stronger than anything that might challenge us.

Kier's guitar part erupts under me, carrying me along through the end of the song as she breaks eye contact and returns her attention to the mix. But she heard my promise. I know she did. We'll get through all of this. As long as we're together, we can get through anything.

Piper

Watching David pour his heart into this song, hearing him sing it like it's just him and me here, and not the entire band, I nearly lose track of the fact that I'm supposed to be mixing. I know what he's telling me. I can hear the promise in his song, and the tears pooling in my eyes aren't just from how deeply he's touched me with his music and his promise, but also with the knowledge that I have to push him away now. At least until I figure out a way to deal with Ramsay.

It's for his own good. I won't let him follow through on that promise to be my guardian angel, not when I'm the one who should be taking care of him, protecting him from Ramsay and all of the dangers that knowing my secrets, being with me, pose to his life. His very short, mortal life, as Ramsay keeps reminding me.

Remember David? His name is etched in my soul. And even if I have to hurt him, even if I have to lose him from my life to do it, I'm going to keep him safe.

I barely notice Declan following his brother into the iso booth, ready to do his backing vocals. A hand on my shoulder brings me back to myself, and David is there, squeezing my shoulder encouragingly.

"Let's bring this song home, maestro," he says with a smile.

I shake myself free of these thoughts, these feelings, focusing solely on the music and the mix, weaving the instruments and vocals together, Declan's backing vocals a shiny thread that makes the beautiful tapestry just a little bit more special.

This is different, mixing in a recording studio instead of live, for an audience. Mixing live is like... Well, I imagine it's a lot like flying an airplane — there's no track, and your destination and the path to get there can change in the moment, when you choose, or when conditions change. And when conditions change, you have to adapt, in the moment. There are no second chances, no do-overs, no fixing it in editing. You make a mistake, and you can crash the plane. You adapt wrongly to changing conditions, you can crash the plane. You have an equipment failure, you can crash the plane. You let the engine run away with you, out of control, you crash the plane.

And it's not just you on the plane — it's the band, your VIP passengers who will ensure you never fly again if you give them a bumpy ride; and it's the audience, the reason you're in the pilot's seat in the first place, because without them there to justify the cost of the plane, the fuel, the staff... nobody's going anywhere. You crash this plane, not only do none of the passengers reach their destination, there's a good chance somebody's going to get hurt, or worse.

Hurt how? A great engineer can't make the worst band in the world sound good, but they can make them sound better. A lousy engineer can make the best band in the world sound so bad people will walk out of the show. They can end a career before it even begins.

That holds true for recording, too. But working in the studio is a lot less about the rush of flying and knowing you might crash if you make a singular mistake. It's more about carefully planning, testing, bringing things together in the proper time and order, ensuring you have the building blocks — the ingredients — you need to make this masterpiece for everyone to enjoy. It's more like cooking a fine meal for a critic on a restaurant's opening night. Because you're going to have critics. You just have to hope the ones who don't like what you serve up are few and far between, and that the other people you have dining in your restaurant every day love your cooking. If they don't, you never cook again. But, right up until that moment you send the plate out to the table, you have the chance to change the dish, fix it, tweak it, make it special. And if you can do that, everyone wins.

So I set out to make my masterpiece. To take these amazing musicians, with their awards and their top-selling singles and their sold-out concerts, and bring their music alive for the people who will hear it and be affected by it, whether that's relaxing in their living room, driving their car, mourning at a funeral, dancing at a celebration or just holding on, trying to get through a single day to the next one. That's the magic of music, and that's why I'm here. Because it's the most potent magic that exists, at least to me. It takes all the other magical things in this world and makes them tangible for eternity. Even love.

It doesn't matter that this is just a rough mix for the band to work with once their producer arrives. I'm going to give them my best work, the version of their song that makes the magic sing in my mind, between my ears. If I do it well, maybe it will make the magic sing for them, too.

CHAPTER 24

I WILL

Piper

When I'm finally happy with the mix, I stretch and look around me.

Hunter is crashed out in one of the oversized armchairs in the control room, his long legs draped over one arm, his long blonde hair down the other side. He could have gone back to his room to sleep. He refused. Something is bothering him, that's for sure.

Alex and Kieran are stretched out in opposite directions on the sofa, looking like bookends — one a study in dark and light, sleek despite his shaggy hair falling into his eyes, and the other a cascade of bright colors, but soft, with his red-gold hair curtaining his face.

Declan went to bed along ago, saying he had something to do today but refusing to elaborate when the others pressed him on it. Rhys is laid out on the floor, a blanket pillowing his head, too tall even for the sofa to comfortably accommodate him, since he's a full foot taller than me. Tallest human I've ever seen in person. And a little... odd. But nice.

David... David is slumped over in the chair next to me. He refused to go to bed while I was still mixing, saying he wanted to hear the song the moment it was done.

Which it now is. I check the time and blink in disbelief, both at how late it is and how quickly we got this done. I scoot back carefully from the console, trying not to wake anyone up, use the bathroom, splash some cold water on my face and head into the kitchen to make a cup of tea. The water boils and dispenses from the little pod device just as I hear a noise behind me.

"Piper? What are you doing here?" Steve sounds more unhappy to find me here at all than surprised at how early I am.

"Just getting a cup of tea for David," I hedge. "I was doing my morning checks, and he asked for one." It's not coffee, but since Steve seems to think I'm better at that than engineering...

"You could have done your checks later. We'd agreed to start later today, see if we can fix this mess."

He looks like he's ready to start lecturing me again, but music suddenly erupts from down the hall. His eyebrows shoot straight up before he turns around and heads into the control room. I follow him, knowing someone clearly woke up while I was gone and decided hearing my final mix couldn't wait.

We find all five of the guys awake now, Rhys sitting in the chair I'd left unoccupied, his fingers on the controls. Of course it was Rhys. But they're all listening intently to the finished song. Alex sees Steve come in and gives him a cursory nod before returning his attention to the console as the faders slide on their own, following the course I'd set for them over the last several hours. Steve shows a moment of confusion before he finds a spot behind Rhys to stand and listen.

Still standing in the doorway, I look over and find David smiling at me, a bit of wonder on his face. Maybe I did a halfway decent job. But this is it — that moment when he hears this song, their song, his song (not ours, really, though he keeps calling it that), for the first time for real. A finished work. At least for now. It'll give them a place to start once Malcolm Fisher arrives.

As the final note of the song slowly fades away, a sense of peace, of rightness, settles over me. The mix is done. At least *my* mix is done. We'll see what Steve and Malcolm do with it. Theirs may be very different from my own. But this one... I'm claiming this one. This version of this song, David's song — it's mine and it is good.

"That was amazing," Steve finally says in the silence. "You all did this all overnight?"

"We did," Alex confirms. "Re-created what was lost, and even made it better, I think. Right, Dave?"

"Yeah, the other one was good. This one... Well, you said it, Steve — amazing, if I can say that about my own song."

"It's a great song, Dave — we just filled it out and polished it," Hunter says. "And on that note, I'm going to bed."

"Got a date tonight?" Rhys teases.

"Not if I can help it," Hunter says, rolling his eyes before heading up the stairs.

"I do not envy that man," Kieran says. "At least he goes to his doom with another future hit under his belt."

"That was a pretty polished mix there, guys," Steve observes, and I allow myself a small smile that he can't see.

"You liked it? I think we've got it dialed in," Alex says. "Frankly, I'm not sure we need to do anything else with it. It sounds pretty perfect to me. Piper — can you dump that off onto a thumb drive for me? I want to send it to Malcolm, see what he thinks. If he likes it, we can just move on to the next one."

My eyes get big. Is he talking about sending my mix to Malcolm Fisher as a potentially final mix of the track for their album?

"Piper — Alex asked for you to put a copy on a thumb drive," Steve prods as I stand frozen in place. "Can you handle that? Do you still need more sleep? I can call Sean in to help the band today."

"I've got it, Steve. Coming right up, Alex."

I pop open a storage cabinet and grab one of the thumb drives stored there, inserting it into the interface, exporting the finished mix and dropping it onto the drive.

"You did it!" David says, walking up behind me, beaming. "It's perfect."

"I'm sorry — Piper did what, exactly?" Steve asks. "A child could put a file on a thumb drive."

"No. I'm lauding her for her perfect mix of our new song," David says.

"*Her* mix? Piper mixed this?" Disbelief, outrage barely contained. Suddenly, my chest feels tight.

"Recorded, engineered and mixed it. We just played the song. She did the rest," David confirms.

"And wonderfully," Alex adds. "Couldn't have done it better ourselves, and I'm not sure anyone else could have, either. She's got a real ear for our sound." His look at Steve is pointed. As far as he's concerned, this is their final mix, the one that goes on the album.

"I see," Steve says slowly. "Well, congratulations on a job well-done, Piper. We'll have to discuss it. Later."

And there it is... *my* date with doom. Because maybe not today, maybe not tomorrow or next week, but this amazing windfall of being given the chance to work with aMUSEd is going to explode in my face.

David

I check down both sides of the hallway before I grab Piper's hand and pull her along behind me. The guys are listening to the finished mix for the sixth time, and Steve headed to his office to make some calls, so I'm going to take the opportunity to bring her up to my bedroom so we can talk, and maybe — hopefully — celebrate this together.

"David, what are you doing?"

"We are going to have a chat, while everyone else is busy with other stuff."

"David, I can't do this. Steve —"

"— is in his office, and since you already did the work he would have been doing right now, he has no reason to be anywhere else in the building. So, come with me. Please," I add when she doesn't take that first step up to the residence.

She visibly folds, following along behind me, up two flights of stairs, past Hunter's room, where the open door reveals not a sleeping guitarist but a drunk one, singing Nirvana's "Heart-Shaped Box" to himself. Loudly. Somehow, I doubt he's going on that date tonight. And maybe that's exactly what he had in mind.

"Hunt? You OK in there?" I ask.

"Spiffy!" he says cheerily. "Did I tell you I've got a date tonight? With cameras?"

"You mentioned it. Are you still planning on doing that?"

"Ask me in a couple hours."

OK then.

Piper and I move toward my room.

"Is he OK?" she asks, sounding concerned.

"No, I don't think he is. But he won't tell us what's going on, and it seems to be pretty harmless so far. But this is about as bad as I've seen him get. Even in our partying days, he didn't drink like this. He certainly wasn't doing it during this tour. I think this has something to do with Brighid."

"His friend? The one he left with the other night?"

"Yeah. That girl's been in love with him since they were kids. He swears he doesn't feel the same, but you watch them together, and they seem like a couple. They feel like a couple. Even after like two years not seeing each other — *this* time because we were on tour."

And that reminds me of part of what I need to talk to her about. I shut the door behind us, and we sit on the bed. Just sit. Priorities, remember?

That's just as well, because Piper seems hesitant. The confident, natural lover she'd been just a few days ago is gone, or at least hidden, buried under her anxiety. Which shouldn't be the case on the day of her triumphant debut as a recording engineer.

"Piper — what's wrong? You did a great job with the song! Amazing, even. And you've got your seal coat back. Come on — talk to me. I said we could fix all of this, together. And we have, even if we still don't know who framed me for having taken your coat."

Her eyes move to the backpack she hasn't let leave her side since that horrible night. I know her coat has to be inside. Is it possible she still doesn't believe me, despite what she said the other day? Has someone continued to try to turn her against me?

She takes a deep breath.

"Steve wasn't happy when you told him I'd done the engineering on your song."

"I think he was surprised more than anything. You blew everyone's highest expectations out of the water."

"No. Him saying he'd talk to me about it later — that wasn't good. When this went from us replacing your deleted tracks to me mixing a song Alex sent off to Malcolm Fisher — I leapfrogged not just over Sean but over Steve. That was literally Steve's job. He was supposed to be working with you today on that track, and on the final version for your album, with

Malcolm. And instead, his intern — a girl — stole his thunder, and his job."

See — this is why I don't do well with strangers. I don't think of things like this. I don't understand the nuance between being happy your intern did a great job and being angry she did it too well. And I don't realize the implications of that until after I've played a part in a mess like this. Because she's right. Steve is probably pissed right now. He's already agreed not to fire her, but nothing's there to stop him once we leave.

"I'm sorry. I didn't think about how that would complicate things for you. You just did so amazing — and Alex was right. That mix was good enough to send to Malcolm, and good enough, I think, to go on the album. You deserve the credit for that. It was amazing work. Steve should be able to see that. It's a shame if he can't."

"Thank you. But this is a big problem for me now. I've got to try to fix it, stay under the radar with him, do as he asks..." She looks up into my eyes, those big brown eyes of hers full of regret. "And that means we can't be together."

"What? No! Piper — you can't give up. Not now. We've already been through so much, and together can do anything. I'll talk to Steve, put some pressure on him to stop with this misogynistic bullshit."

"No. You can't. Please don't. Please," she says, tears filling her eyes. And I realize she's serious. She not only doesn't want me to intervene with Steve, she wants to break up with me before we're even done with the album.

"Why, Piper? This makes no sense. Are you still upset that I came into Safe Harbour without you? Or is it that you still don't believe me about your coat?"

She looks away from me, quiet.

"It's just not worth the risk, David."

"What risk? Tell me what risk. I'll deal with it. I'll make sure it's OK."

"My entire career is in jeopardy, David. This whole thing has been one disaster after another, and as much as I've enjoyed spending time with you, Steve's right. It's unprofessional. And if I have any hope of getting a job somewhere after he fires me, I'm going to have to address that. And the best way to do that is to start acting like a professional. Starting now. I don't know — maybe he'll get over my doing this mix. But I do know that if he realizes we've been together this entire time... He'll fire me on the spot, David. There'll be no coming back from that. I can't take that risk."

I can't think of a thing to say to get her to change her mind. If she's really unwilling to risk the slim chance that Steve won't try to fire her once we leave, if our relationship — the relationship I thought we had, that I thought we were building — isn't worth enough to her to risk even that much... Maybe Rory was right. Maybe she'd been mourning me from the moment we'd both realized we were falling for each other, falling into bed and in...

Well, maybe it was just me after all. It wouldn't be the first time I misunderstood how someone felt about me. From "Rain Man" to the girls who only showed interest in me to get to Declan. And now Piper. Who I thought I understood better than anyone, understood me better than anyone...

"We can keep working together, David. Or, if you'd prefer I keep my distance, I'm sure Steve would ask Sean to take over while aMUSEd is here."

She glances up at me but won't hold my gaze.

"No. It's OK. We work well together. I'd like to finish the rest of these rough tracks with you at the console, if Steve will approve it."

"I'm not sure he will."

"Well, I'm going to press him to do it anyway. If he's planning to fire you once we leave, it won't hurt to strong-arm him now. I'll make sure that's what happens. Let me handle that. It's the least I can do after getting you in trouble with him so many times."

She frowns, and I suspect it's over our relationship imploding and not the idea that she'll get to engineer more songs for us before she gets fired. I'm going to do what I can to make sure that doesn't happen once we leave.

Because suddenly my enthusiasm about maybe staying in this little beach town has waned.

CHAPTER 25

GOING WITHOUT

David

She left me. She gave me a hug — a sad hug, not even a warm one — and she left me, walking out the sliding glass door and down the beach, taking her bag and her seal coat with her, out of my room and out of my life. My personal life, anyway.

I'm not sure I've ever been this miserable. Rory said I might find forgetting Piper to be a blessing. This is why. She knew this pain. She's felt this pain. She lost her love in a totally different, irretrievable way, but nonetheless, she knows what it feels like, because she lost the love of her life after having him for a very short time.

Is Piper that for me? The love of my life? I think maybe she is. But when my lifespan is as short as it is in comparison to hers... Maybe that's fitting, that I might love her for the next fifty years, at which point she'll be three hundred years old and maybe thinking nostalgically about that musician she once called her boyfriend. I picture her showing up at my deathbed, looking exactly like she does today, visiting an old man who can barely remember his own name, let alone hers, and realizing she should have left that memory behind fifty years ago.

I'm deep in thought, my acoustic guitar resting idly in my lap, when I spot Hunter walking unsteadily down toward my spot on the beach. He offers me a crooked salute and appears, confusingly, to be headed toward town — through Safe

Harbour's beach. It's only sunset, so maybe the guard won't be quite as determined to keep him off their private property. But I can't bring myself to care right now. Safe Harbour is no longer any of my business. Hunter, on the other hand...

"Where ya headed there, Hunt?"

"I'm taking my friend here for a walk," he says, brandishing a bottle of Jameson that is clearly not the same one he was drinking from earlier, because there's more in it than there was in that other one. This is looking like a recipe for disaster, but I'm at a loss as to how to thwart that, barring wrestling Hunter — who's like five inches taller than me and outweighs me by probably forty pounds — to the sand on Safe Harbour's beach, where he's now walking south.

"Uh... OK. Be careful, there. You don't want to get in trouble for having that..." I offer, hoping that maybe he'll realize he shouldn't be drinking in public and just turn around. Maybe we can commiserate, me over the end of my first-ever relationship and him over... whatever the heck is going on with Brighid. Right now, that bottle of Jameson is looking pretty good to me, too.

"No law against public consumption in Delaware!" he shouts back at me, bottle raised in the air and the shoes he's slung over his shoulder banging him in the back as he plunges onward toward town.

I shake my head, wondering if I should follow. But Hunter's a big boy, and maybe falling on his ass on the boardwalk will wake him up to actually deal with whatever demon he's got eating at him. I make a note to be prepared to call Billy should it become necessary to bail him out of jail tonight.

It's ironic that I'm filling my evening with trying to write the saddest song I've ever heard, let alone written, within twenty-four hours of having recorded a love song where I sang my heart out, promising to take care of my girl. Who is no longer my girl. Wow, that was fast. This song — it's a broken heart in sonic form, only not nearly as elegant as I'd hoped when I started writing it. It's actually pretty pathetic, and I give it up as a lost cause after an hour, heading back up into the residence, hoping to find some dinner.

But Alex isn't cooking. He's on the phone.

"I know, honey. But I haven't seen him, and none of the guys have any idea where he might have gone. I'm sure he's fine. He's a big boy. I'll tell him you called. Four times."

He ends the call and looks over at me, seeming weary and a little morose.

"You haven't seen Hunt this afternoon, have you?"

"Yeah, actually. He headed down toward town about two hours ago. Not quite smashed, but definitely drunk."

I hear a shrill voice from the living area, and I cringe.

"He had a date with Holly, and her camera crew," Alex explains. "And they've been here for an hour, trying to get hold of him, but he's not answering calls or texts. She's been stood up on camera, so she's..."

The shrill voice gets louder.

"Stop calling me! You are just pathetic! Hunter would call you if he wanted to talk to you. This is pretty shamelessly stalkerish behavior for someone who's just a pity-fuck for a star like Hunter!"

I cringe, looking to Alex for an explanation.

"I gave Brighid her number, since I didn't have any idea where Hunt was and he was supposed to be going out with Holly."

He looks regretful, but he's simultaneously clearly very amused.

"What? She was driving me nuts!"

"Brighid?"

"No, Holly. I handed her off to Rhys to keep her busy, talking about his six-minute drum solo and that ridiculous new invention of his."

"The sock thing?"

"Yeah."

OK, now *I'm* amused. I kind of want to be a fly on the wall when Rhys explains to Holly the invention he's planning to try to put on "Big Fish Finds," which will never in a million years accept him or what he's come up with.

"You should have kept Bridge clear of her, though. Holly's as mean as a striped snake and twice as deadly. Brighid doesn't deserve that."

"I know — I didn't think it would get this far. I figured Bridge would stop calling her after the second time Holly hung up on her. But she's really freaked out over Hunter, said she had a feeling he was hurt or something was wrong with him."

"He *was* very drunk when I saw him earlier."

"Maybe she has a point."

"What about that app thingy — the one you used to locate Rhys when he wandered off at the carnival outside the venue that one time?"

"The phone finder? I think it's still on here, still connected to all our phones."

"It might be time to use it, before Brighid decides to come over and pull your arms off for not helping find him sooner."

"She wouldn't..." He looks down at his hands, rings on nearly every finger, bracelets on both wrists, and then over at me, just a hint of fear in his eyes. "Nevermind. Of course she would. It's Hunt. Her Hunt, whether he realizes it or not."

Forty-five minutes later, we're standing in the parking lot of an elementary school, next to the playground, staring down at our rhythm guitarist, surrounded by the fragments of a bottle of whiskey, a cell phone with a cracked screen and the remaining shreds of his dignity. And a mildly amused paramedic. After a minute, Hunter starts to stir.

"And here he comes! Back to the land of the living! How'd that walk with your buddy Jameson go for you, Hunt?" Sorry. I can't help it. He seems to be OK, but what an epic mess. Maybe the bonk on the head will bring him to his senses where Brighid is concerned.

"Hi, guys!" He says brightly, then immediately cringes in pain. "What happened?"

Suddenly, Hunter's first concern isn't his head, or his possibly broken hand — which has Declan swearing left and right over the impact on the album, our gigs — but Brighid. He wants someone to call her and let her know he's still alive, if damaged. Alex takes care of it just in time for Holly to arrive on the scene, making a big production in front of the cameras of how badly Hunter is hurt (which he's not) and demanding to ride in the ambulance with him to the hospital. This is not going to end well.

And it doesn't. Brighid flies through the E.R. waiting room, moving faster than I've ever seen her, her expression beyond worry, and she flies back out just as quickly a few minutes later, visibly upset, with Hunter calling out after her and the nurse telling him he can't leave yet. Because he needs his brace checked. The brace on his sprained left hand.

Yeah, Declan spent a while cursing after that news. With all of us back at our temporary home now, recording is officially on hold for at least a week, maybe as much as three, while Hunter's hand heals. I can't decide if this is terrible news or oddly welcome. On the one hand (no pun intended), it messes with our schedule, and I'm sure the label's not going to be happy. On the other hand, I've got one song in the can before Malcolm's arrival, but just three more written, Declan and me combined. Hunter's had writer's block since he won the Song of the Year award for the first single off our early EP. I'm starting to wonder if that little statue is cursed. Bottom line — we need the extra time to finish writing new material, so I'm not going to complain about the delay.

For his part, Hunter has been oddly... I don't know how to describe it. Antsy, maybe?

"Hunt? What are you doing?" I ask him as I come out of my room a few days after the trip to the E.R.

"Keeping my calluses in good shape," he says, looking like a kid caught with his hand in a cookie jar.

"I see... It's just — it kind of looks like you're playing guitar, with the sprained hand the doctor told you not to use for at least a week, let alone play guitar with."

"I'm not sure this qualifies as 'playing guitar,'" he says, laying aside his favorite green PRS with a frown.

"Then why are you doing it?"

"Because we need to get back to recording and gigging. ...And because I'm frustrated that Brighid won't speak to me," he admits.

"That was kind of an ugly scene at the hospital. The girl loves you. She was panicked about something even possibly having happened to you — and she somehow *knew* that it had and sent us to your rescue. And then she shows up and you're there with Holly, who's telling the entire internet how her 'boyfriend,' the famous guitarist, is being treated for a possible career-ending injury."

He looks both guilty and irritated.

"I'm trying to fix it. She won't let me."

Welcome to the club, buddy. Welcome to the club.

CHAPTER 26

STAND OR FALL

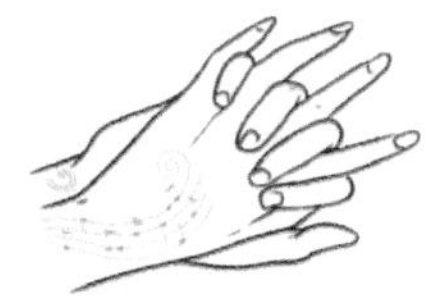

Two weeks later

Hunter's idea of "fixing things" leaves something to be desired. I've started to see why Brighid is upset with him, and that's before I got some of the details.

It all started with the band meeting we had a week or so after he'd sprained his hand, trying to make plans for working around his injury, which seemed like maybe he'd made it worse by not following the doctor's instructions not to play.

Before the meeting, Hunt had disappeared for more than a day, and we figured he'd finally made up with Brighid and was hanging out at her house. Pretty normal for them. So, when we hadn't heard from him shortly before the meeting was set to start, with Billy videoconferencing in, Alex texted him, tried to get his ass moving. We thought he was on his way, and then he tells Alex he hasn't even left Brighid's house yet. So, when he finally gets there, he's like an hour late, and Billy's irritated. Declan's *beyond* irritated, which was only going to get worse, because... well, you'll see.

I hear shouting from out on the first-floor deck off the living area, and I set aside my bass to go see what's up. That's the point where there's a bump — kind of like a really big bird hit the side of the house or something. Maybe an albatross, or a small pterodactyl.

"Hunter! What the fuck? Have you lost your damn mind?"

I swear, Declan says, "Hunter! What the fuck?" more often lately than he asks Alex to pass the potatoes. But, still, I get up, open the slider and look down onto the lower deck, where Hunt is standing by the door into the living area, Declan glaring at him. And then cursing at him, and the universe. That goes on for a while, and I'm not sure I really want to know what's going on.

But then Declan's bellowing for everyone to come down there, so I go back inside and follow them out onto the deck, where it quickly becomes clear that Hunter has gotten uncharacteristically violent with a patch of siding. Well, maybe not so uncharacteristically violent... He did bust down a door in a frat house once, trying to rescue Brighid from some creep. It's a safe bet this has to do with Brighid again.

I limit myself to a couple mild curse words, mostly after Hunter says he thinks maybe his hand *is* broken this time. This could scrap the entire album for months and send us back to New York, and I'm not sure I want to leave Mystic Beach. Not yet. Kier has to drag Dec back inside before he follows through on his threat to break Hunter's *other* hand. Rhys volunteers to call a ride to get Hunter to the hospital, while Alex seems like he's just over the Hunter and Brighid drama. He keeps trying to get them together, but it's never worked. I think that's mostly Hunter's fault.

I kind of want someone to get a happy ending here, and it's not looking like it's going to be me, so I sit down next to Hunt and wait. After a while, I have to ask.

"So, what happened?"

"I yelled at a goddess and punched a house."

"I see." Hey — a couple weeks ago I was dating a 250-year-old magical seal-woman. Who am I to judge? Maybe he's finally seeing Brighid in a new light. "Was the goddess Brighid?"

"Yes. I mean, no — not *my* Brighid. The actual Irish goddess Brighid."

OK. So more magical-seal-woman problem and less girl-of-his-dreams problem. I feel slightly qualified to consult.

"I see. And did Brighid — the goddess, not the girl — yell back?"

He's quiet for a long while, and I can see he's thinking things through, and at this point, I'm just curious, because there's got to be a doozy of an explanation for all of this, even if it doesn't involve magical seal-women.

"Yeah. I think she did yell back."

"Interesting." What? It *is* interesting. Here we are in this little beach town, and I learn that there's an entire colony, a refugee settlement, of supernatural, mythological and who-knows-what-else creatures, people... literally right next door. And my (ex-?) girlfriend's late foster-brother was a demi-god. So an actual goddess yelling at Hunt — literally or metaphorically — isn't exactly out of the realm of possibility. What is it about Mystic Beach that just throws both science and normal out the window? Is it in the name?

"This place is... odd," I finally say, not sure that "odd" even comes close to covering it. "Why's it called 'Mystic Beach'?" Hunt grew up here. Surely he has to know at least that much history, right? And now I'm curious, for my own reasons.

"A lot of unexplained stuff has happened around here over the centuries. Shipwrecks, pirates, strange fog and lights sometimes... there was a rumor about a swamp monster... Someone once said they'd spotted a mermaid, but I think that was just made up to attract tourists... Ghosts — the B&B down the road reportedly has a haunted bathtub. Witches — like actual curse-your-ass, cackling witches, not Brighid's Pagan friends and her customers at the shop. Though she did say she's had a lot more customers the last few years..." He shrugs. "Why?"

"Just wondering."

What? It's not like I can explain to him that our engineer is a magical seal-woman who I've seen transform with my own eyes. I was sworn to secrecy, and no matter how hurt I am by Piper breaking things off with me, I'm not going to even hint at her nature or the existence of Safe Harbour. I'd still throw myself in front of whatever threatened her, or them. Because, yeah, I still love her. Even if I never said it to her. And because I made a promise. I promised to keep the secret, and I promised I'd be Piper's guardian angel. If only she'll let me...

Is this just a woman thing? It's not like I have the relationship experience to even guess. And I honestly can't tell if she's still pissed at me for something I didn't do, or for the thing I did do that I didn't think was so bad, or if she truly is just putting her career ahead of her feelings for me. Because I'm still convinced that she feels the same way. Maybe Hunter understands women better. He's dated. A lot.

"So, what's up with Brighid? The girl, not the goddess. I'm assuming she's why you're punching houses and yelling at gods."

"I don't know, man. I thought we'd finally gotten ourselves sorted out. And then it all blew up in my face."

So, long story short, it turns out Hunt got tricked into kissing Brighid. And I don't mean like a peck on the lips. He made out with her, blindfolded and not realizing it was Brighid. And it seems like they both liked it. A lot. So, it's not just her. But Hunt had ruled out anything more than friendship with Brighid a long, long time ago, so after he realized it was Brighid he was kissing, it was kind of awkward, and she was a little pissed that he was dodging her and going out with Holly, which is why she wasn't speaking to him *before*.

Only *now* — well, Hunt finally got his head out of his ass and took the girl to bed. Finally! I don't know how long the rest of us have been waiting for that. But then something happened — he has no idea what — and now she's not speaking to him again, even though they'd apparently spent that missing day and change being very... intimate. Somehow, I suspect this is mostly Hunter's fault. Again.

"I don't know what I did, so I can't even try to fix it, even if I could get her to listen to me," he says, finally.

"Women are confusing."

That's the thought that comes to mind. Here, he's got Brighid, who's been totally in love with him for like fifteen years, and he finally realizes he feels the same, only to have her freeze him out with no explanation.

And I've got Piper — well, I *had* Piper — who's like a revelation for me, after spending my entire life waiting for an amazing woman like her to show up, and then all these crazy curveballs, which I managed to go with, and then she dumps me because her boss is jealous that his female intern did a good job and she wants to pretend our relationship never happened so he can't fault her professionalism. When we both know he's going to try to fire her as soon as we leave. It feels like an excuse, but I can't think what other reason she'd have unless she just doesn't trust me anymore. Or maybe a short-lived human is just too bad of a bet for an immortal. So, yeah — confusing.

"How so?" he asks.

"They act like they want you, and then they run. I can't tell if it's because they want you to chase them, or because they think you won't be interested if you don't *have to* chase them, or if they're just genuinely terrified of what would happen if you *did* catch them."

"There's something profound in there, man."

"What?"

"I'm not sure. But there is."

We're quiet for a second.

I put myself in Hunter's shoes — if I'd slept with my best friend after more than a decade of pushing her away, and if I'd decided after all that time that I was in love with her after all, I sure as hell wouldn't be sitting here, nursing a broken hand, if there was any way for me to prove to her that I did love her. No matter what it took.

"If you want her, you're going to have to fight for her."

Yes, those words came out of my mouth. The guy who doesn't fight for anything, except maybe to stand up to a blatant injustice. Fight for something *I* want for myself? I couldn't even stand up to Declan when we were kids. (Not that that's ever been easy. He can be very determined — single-minded, even.) And, lacking any real experience in relationships, I now consider myself sufficiently expert in the subject to offer Hunt advice? And that's the advice that comes to me? Go fight for her?

I'm a fucking hypocrite. I let Piper walk out the door after barely making my case for giving us a chance. I hadn't told her that I loved her. I hadn't told her I was thinking about moving here so I could be with her when we weren't touring. I'd promised to be her guardian angel and never forget her, no matter what they did to me, and yet a simple "This might destroy my career" was enough to deter me?

I'm in one of the biggest bands on the planet. I have a label CEO's direct number on my phone — a woman who owns part of this studio Piper's working at — and could arrange to find Piper a full-time job at any music venue she wanted to work at, because she's hella talented and anyone in their right mind would jump at the chance to work with her if I just put her work in front of them. Heck — I probably have enough money in the bank to buy Steve out with an offer so generous he'd never dream of refusing. I *can* fix this.

"I know," Hunt says. "I spent too many years fighting what she wanted, and now I've got to fight twice as hard for what we both want to prove to her that I really do want it."

I *do* need to fight twice as hard to prove to Piper that she should give us a chance, give *me* a chance. Because something's preventing her from doing that, and it's not just her job. I let her go too easily, too quickly.

"It took fifteen years to get you here. Are you going to wait another fifteen to fix it?" I ask him.

"Fuck no."

"Then you need to do something about it. Now."

"I've tried. I can't think what else to do."

"What would prove to her that you love her? You do love her, right?"

"More than anything."

"Then act like it."

And that's exactly what *I'm* going to do. Piper is the love of my life. It may be a short life compared to hers, but it's the only one I've got. And I want it to be spent loving her. It's about time I acted like it.

"Car's here," Rhys announces from the doorway to the deck.

"Who's going with me?"

"Yeh big baby," Kier comments from behind Rhys. "We got an XL. We're all going."

"Not me," I correct him. "I need to see a lady about a fur coat."

They're all looking at me like I've lost my mind. And maybe I did — when I let her walk out that door. But if that was crazy, then I'm feeling very sane right now, because I'm not letting her go. I'm going to make this right. All of it.

CHAPTER 27

WISH

Piper

David's been sitting on the edge of Safe Harbour's beach every night for the last week. He wants to talk to me, but within the confines of the studio, he won't broach a personal topic. He's going along with my stated effort to act purely professionally around him from this point forward. He's also looking for a loophole, hoping to find me when we're not working. So I just have to make sure to avoid him from the moment I step out of Safe Harbour until the moment I step inside the studio.

Ramsay's been watching me again. I've spotted him a few times, waiting casually along my route to or from the studio. He says nothing, and I ignore him, as best I can. Other times, I get that feeling of being watched, and I suspect he's hidden out of the way, or maybe one of his bully boys doing his dirty work for him.

"You've been a very good girl lately, Piper," he finally says as I walk past him. "No human pet in your bed. No back-and-forth in the wee hours from his bed. Not even your usual evening swim. He might yet live to grow old and die in his bed. And you might yet make a fine wife."

"Not for you, Ramsay. Not ever."

"Give it time, Piper. I've got big plans, for me, for us, for all of us."

He strides away, self-satisfaction overflowing from him.

That's about as genuine and direct as I've ever seen Ramsay, and that scares me. What does he have in mind? And what are the chances it won't be a disaster for me, Rory and all of Safe Harbour?

I need to think, and I do that best in the water. I dodged David well enough when they first arrived. I can do it again now. It's been too long since I've been in the ocean, and I can't stay away much longer.

I dive through the breaking wave, my seal coat wrapping around me as the darkness of the Atlantic Ocean here at night swallows me whole. It's no wonder David thought the swimmer he saw when he first arrived had drowned. I can hold my breath longer than any human free-diver ever has. Unlike humans, seals breathe out before we dive, utilizing the oxygen already in our blood and muscles while we're under the surface. My heartrate drops precipitously, much like those free-divers, but even lower, down from about a hundred beats per minute to just ten. I can easily cruise under the sea for half an hour like this.

In my human form, my swimming abilities are much closer to that of actual humans, though still beyond what they can do. The difference — that's one reason we selkies dwindle when we don't have our seal coats. We lose the ability to hunt as seals, experience the ocean as seals, dive deep and swim far offshore. Knowing that kind of freedom, losing it is soul-crushing. Those few hours without my seal coat, I'd already felt that growing — a kind of claustrophobia that has nothing to do with tight spaces, but nonetheless is a symptom of that loss of freedom. My anxiety around people is nothing compared to that.

David could never understand what it's like. And that's the reason him taking my coat made sense, in the moment. Half out of my head with panic already, it made sense. But my heart kept telling me he wouldn't do that to me. He'd reveled in seeing my seal form, his scientist's mind forced to expand its notions of the universe he thought he understood, his soul opening itself up to the magic of our kind, blending his human reality with his fascination with our seal cousins. It was beautiful to watch. It made the risk of letting him watch me transform worth it, and then some.

Just like helping him make his wonderful music was priceless to me. But that would come to an end someday soon, when he returned to New York, to touring around the world, while I would be trying to figure out some way to redeem myself and Rónan's experiment in integration. Molly really had been better suited to it, if you could trust her to control her... appetites. Rory keeps an eye on her now, as best she can.

And that was half the reason I hadn't taken this Ramsay problem to her once again. She already had too much on her plate. And I know if I tell her Ramsay stole my coat, that he has tried to frame David and also threatened him, she'll go straight to the Council to take him to task for it, demand he be forced out of Safe Harbour. But I don't have the evidence to prove that he's the one behind the theft. And without evidence, the Council could reject her charges, leaving her weaker in their eyes, vulnerable, politically and otherwise. Perhaps even ripe for a coup, especially if Ramsay has someone on the Council who, as I begin to suspect, is sympathetic to his cause and willing to assist him, if not openly.

And Rory... she's just as human and mortal as David. Ramsay could frame the failed charges as an insult to his honor (as if he actually has any) and decide to make her pay the price — the price that's mine to pay, if anyone's. And one he might decide to make just as fatal as what he'd threatened for David. But Ramsay covets me too much to kill me. So that risk, that weight, is mine to bear alone. And if I can do that until David returns to New York and his tour, I might just be able to save his life.

A late dinner caught and consumed, I give a careful look toward the beach from just beyond the breakers. No sign of David, Ramsay, the guards or anyone at all. Perfectly peaceful. And while nothing has changed during my long swim in seal form, I have a strange sense of peace, at least resigned to handling this Ramsay problem on my own. Risking David or Rory is not an option. This is an immortal problem, and I'm the one to handle it, even if a long-term solution still eludes me.

Shifting back into human form, I take one last glance around the beach and emerge from the ocean with my seal coat in hand. I close my eyes and take a deep breath, steeling my resolve.

"Piper."

David stands alongside me on the packed sand where the beach slopes into the ocean, impossible and delightful and fraught and looking determined, all at the same time. Have my seal instincts really dulled that much in the chaos of these recent weeks, or is it really that David's scent, sound and feel are so much part of me that I no longer notice when he enters my space?

"David. I'm sorry — I have to go. We cannot be seen together."

"Why? Steve's not here. The guys are at the hospital."

"Hospital?" I'm half-panicked, my first thought being that Ramsay had decided to take his frustrations out on one of David's bandmates.

"It's fine, Piper," he says, seeming to sense my fear. "No one's dying. Hunter just broke his hand."

"But... it was sprained, I thought..."

"It was. Now it's broken."

I wait for an explanation, because this doesn't make any sense. David sighs.

"Hunt... He gets kind of wound-up where Brighid's concerned."

"Because he's in love with her."

"Yeah. He is. But it's taken him forever to admit that to himself, even. And he's waited even longer to tell her. Actually, I'm not sure he's even told her yet. And he keeps fucking things up with her. I think it's because he doesn't think he's good enough for her."

"Is that what was bothering him? Why he'd been drinking?"

"Yeah, more or less. It seems like he finally realized what he wanted, and how much he wanted it — and what he wants is Brighid."

"Well, that sounds like good news, that they both want the same thing now."

"It would be, but things keep getting in the way. And she keeps shutting him out."

The look he gives me is pointed.

"I'm sure she has her reasons," I feel compelled to say, on my behalf and Brighid's.

"I'm sure she does. But whether they're good reasons..." Again, a pointed look. "Anyway... Hunt got frustrated, I guess, that she's not speaking to him again, and he kind of took it out on the side of the house, and his hand."

"Steve's not going to be happy if he's damaged studio property."

"No happier than Declan is right now, since a broken hand means that we won't be recording anytime soon, or playing out."

"So, you won't be needing me."

"The band won't. Not for a while. But *I*..." He takes a deep breath. "Piper — I didn't take your coat. You have to know that, despite how things looked. I'd never do that to you. I swear. I need you to believe me. I need you to trust me. Piper... I l—"

A light flashes across the water, the guard doing his patrol, and I step back from David abruptly. We've been standing here together for too long already. Even a moment is too long if Ramsay sees us.

"You should go, David. I can't... We can't... We just can't. I need you to understand that, keep your distance. Please," I beg, my concern for him bleeding into my voice and seeming to finally make an impression on him. I hold my coat against my chest, covering the parts of myself that he knows better than anyone ever has, that he has caressed and loved into the wee hours of the morning, and I take another step back.

Another heartbreaking look from him — both his heart and mine broken in this moment as things beyond our control keep us apart, and maybe for good. It needs to be for good. For his sake, if nothing else.

Two weeks later

"**P**iper."

I nearly jump out of my skin. David's sitting quietly on the sofa in the control room, even though it's three in the morning, and I walked right past him, so focused on getting my tasks done that I went straight to the door of the live room without noticing he was near. And he was clearly waiting for me. Why else would he be up and sitting in here at this hour? It's not like the band is recording overnight again, since Hunter's out of commission for at least another week or two.

"Hi, David. You startled me. I didn't think anyone would be in here at this hour." Hence why, for the last week or so, I've been doing my regular tasks well before the sun rises each morning. Yes, to avoid David. It's ironic that the one person I've ever felt totally at ease with is now the one I look to avoid.

"I needed to talk to you, and I wasn't sure you'd answer if I called."

"Of course I would answer! If you all need anything, it's my job to take care of it."

He frowns.

"Well, what I needed to talk to you about *is* work, so you can relax," he says, sounding weary. I suspect he's weary of my avoiding talking to him about us, as much as he's tired from being up so early, or so late.

"What did you all need? The band, I mean."

"We're ready to start recording some rough tracks again — one of Hunter's songs."

"Hunter wrote a song?"

"Yeah, and it's great. Our next single, I think."

"I thought you said he had writer's block, and his hand..."

"He did. But then he... well, it's a long story, but he and Brighid — it all blew up on social media, and he fucked that up, too. But then they finally talked, and..." He's practically beaming with happiness. "They're together, Piper — Hunter and Brighid are together and happy and in love. Finally. And his hand... somehow, it healed up way faster than they said it would. So, we've got a gig to play this week."

"Oh."

"'Oh?' That's all you've got to say? I stayed up all night to give you the good news, that we'll have another song for you to help us record. And that's all you have to say?" He shakes his head and sighs. "We'll need you to run sound at the gig, too."

"I never called them to give notice."

"Good! You shouldn't." He swallows hard, his expression softening again. "God, I've missed you." He grabs hold of my hands, starting that electric zing zipping between us. His tone is earnest. "I'm going to get this sorted out, Piper. I'm going to figure out how to deal with Steve. Just give me some time. Give *us* some time..." He leans in, and my eyes meet his, locked together like we had been so often, then his eyes sliding to my lips, clearly intending to kiss me, and I'm not sure I can deny him — deny us — that. Not right now.

I hear a door shut somewhere else in the house, and I start, pulling away from him.

"It's just Declan. He was out late."

"Oh." The silence is painful.

"Just give me some time, Piper, to fix this. If Hunter can fix things with Brighid, I can fix things so we can be together."

"I can't."

"Why not?"

"I just can't, David. Things are... they're just too hard. I can't do this. Don't — don't go to all that trouble for me. Please."

"Trouble? There's nothing I wouldn't do—"

I interrupt him before he can make more promises I cannot allow him to keep.

"Just let me know when you need me, David. The band, I mean. To work on Hunter's song, if that's what you want."

"What I want?" His voice fills with frustration. "What I want, I can't have, it seems. But we would like you to help us with these songs. So, yes, please, come over tomorrow morning. To work."

He shakes his head, frustration seeming to shift toward disdain. And it's then that I know I've finally pushed him so far away that there may be no coming back.

Having listened to Hunter's new song for the better part of a week as aMUSEd rehearsed and perfected it for their next live performance, I was unprepared for the emotion it unleashed when the band performed it for Brighid and the audience at the Pirate's Cove, under the thin guise of, as the marquee out front calls them, "Tattletale Signals." (Yes, I rolled my eyes at the too-obvious Telltale Signs reference. Declan again.)

"Shepherd Me Home" is a pastoral wash of a ballad that stirs in me such longing for the shores of *my* home that, for a brief moment, I wonder if I made a mistake coming here, to Mystic Beach. I could have found refuge elsewhere, but there was Rónan, and the promise of a new life in a new place, with the past no longer weighing us down. It had turned out to be much harder than that, even before we lost Rónan, but then there was David, and it felt like maybe, just maybe, I'd found a new home — one that was human-shaped. Human, period.

And now I feel dislodged, adrift with no land in sight. Can I live the rest of my life — of eternity — feeling this way? Would I even want to?

As Hunter leads Brighid in a romantic dance during Kieran's extended guitar solo, I glance up at David, finding him looking back at me, the same bittersweet mix of longing and frustration on his face as had been that night on the beach. Tonight hadn't been easy for either of us — now ironically awkward precisely because of how comfortable we had gotten with each other since that first show aMUSEd had done here, instead of just because the both of us, separately, were awkward with everyone. Everyone *else*, now. We'd become the exception to that rule for each other. Or we had been.

Brighid and Hunter, meanwhile, are totally in sync, even more than before, despite the fact that this whole night has been full of surprises for her — including the moment Hunter removes the brace on his previously broken hand and shows off not just his restored ability to play guitar, but the new tattoo he'd acquired in honor of his soulmate.

Could this have been me and David if Steve hadn't insisted we keep things professional? We'd failed, but it had also forced us to hide, another secret kept from the world. Hunter seems determined to declare his relationship with Brighid to the world now, after trying to keep her out of the ugly spotlight of social media and failing, from what I understand from the band's conversations in the studio this last week.

I wish, idly, that David and I had had that option of declaring our feelings publicly.

Hunter has declared himself with that tattoo on his hand — a woven Brighid's cross that shines with magic for those with eyes to see. Gods-touched, that, and the pair of them. The same kind of energy Rónan had, and even more so when he was with Rory. Soulmates in every sense of the word, both of these couples, despite the tragic ending for one.

And as I watch Rory watching the happy couple with a pained smile on her face, that's a bucket of cold water over my daydreaming. I may have been stupid to let myself fall in love with a human, but if I had it to do over again... Yes, I would have. But I would have spared David the pain I see in his eyes now as he watches me from the stage. That I will always regret.

CHAPTER 28

THINKING OF YOU

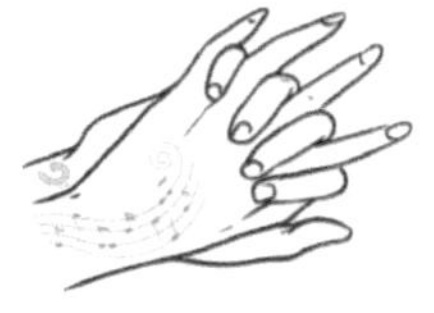

Piper
The next night

If things had been awkward last night between David and me, tonight they are only more so, as the private party I'd been asked to run sound for at the Pirate's Cove turns into a small-scale invitation-only aMUSEd concert with an opening act that includes Hunter getting down on one knee and proposing marriage to Brighid.

"The two of us have always belonged to each other, in every way that mattered, and I know now that we always will," he says, gutting me neatly with his words. I'm one of the few who doesn't look confused when he asks her to marry him "again." These two are promised to each other throughout time and space, their union already sanctified by entities older and more powerful, by far, than I. It is obvious to me, if perhaps to no one else here.

Again, David and I exchange a loaded glance as Brighid, of course, accepts Hunter's proposal.

Is this what David envisioned for us when he spoke of overcoming obstacles together? As much as circumstances threatened to tear Brighid and Hunter apart, I know there is no comparison to what David and I have standing between us. It's more than a long-distance relationship or the pressures of life on the road. It's deeply-held secrets, others' lives on the line if those secrets were to be revealed and David's own life under serious threat if we are even seen together.

We had gotten lucky that night on the beach. Ramsay hadn't seen us. In fact, I've only spotted him twice since then, both when he was standing casually outside the bachelors' dormitory with his podmates. The cursory nod he gave made me just as nervous as his threats had. Is he so reassured by David's absence from my room that his demeanor has shifted? Perhaps he hopes to win me with a less aggressive stance now that David is no longer pursuing me. It seems like an improvement, but I'm still on edge, fearing what he has planned — for me, for David and for Safe Harbour.

As I settle in with my mix on the first song of aMUSEd's set — one of their biggest hits, since they're only performing tonight in front of their extended family of friends, Rory included — there's a sharp crack of wood on wood as a bar stool is tipped over hard onto the deck behind the bar. Even with my earplugs in, the sound carries, grabbing not only my attention but that of nearly everyone in the place, since I'd kept the sound system volume low to avoid drawing an uninvited audience.

"Callie!" Declan cries out as he watches the woman who'd been sitting on the stool scramble away and then sprint for the parking lot. He chases after her, dropping his mic to the deck with a noise even more jarring for me than the bar stool's crash. I cringe, picturing the potential damage to the microphone capsule inside, and promise myself I'll examine it closely at the first opportunity.

The band stops playing as the mic hits the floor, and Declan races past me and around the corner, the anguish in his voice as he calls out for the woman again slicing me, nearly as far to the bone as Hunter's words of love to Brighid had.

It mirrors my own pain, and I realize then what David had avoided telling me about his brother's past, which is now exposed to everyone here. Declan has loved and he's lost. And he's buried that pain deeply, for a long time, I would wager. And now... now it's a festering wound, reopened, gaping. The only question is whether reopening it will help heal the confident frontman or destroy him.

As he returns, unsuccessful in his efforts to bring his lost mate with him, I withdraw to the shadows of the restaurant at the edge of the deck, watching as David joins Declan at the bar and works to console him. These two are often at loggerheads, but they are brothers, and David is — as I know well — inherently kind. Brighid's hound — familiar to me from his time in the studio with the band — also offers his support, as dogs are wont to do, and Declan accepts that a bit more willingly.

Declan is already drowning his sorrows with whiskey, but the gentle hand he lays on the wolfhound's massive head speaks to the vulnerable man underneath the bravado he'd prefer was all the world saw of him. On that first night, running sound for them, I had mistaken it for an insecure and inexperienced musician aiming to prove himself. Now I recognize it for a close cousin of the veneer of false confidence that I've taken on in order to do my job. Only Declan's hidden anxiety isn't for his performance, which he knows all too well is stellar. No — it's for his heart, broken and barely protected by that veneer, underneath it full of terror at the idea of letting any woman close to him again, lest he lose her.

Oh, Declan. Such sorrow... The ties that bind...

Perhaps David and I were lucky that we were not already bound as tightly yet as those two. Perhaps.

As if summoned by my thoughts, David turns from Declan and catches my eyes with his. I look away, busying myself with the tablet that controls the sound system, turning on some background music since the band's performance has been cut short. But David isn't deterred, coming to lean against the wall next to me. He says nothing, and after a minute I can't stand the silence nor not knowing what is to come tonight. For the band, at least.

"Are you going to be playing more?"

"Probably. I don't know," he says, leaving me to sigh in frustration. I would prefer to get some distance from David and call it an early night if they are not going to be on stage.

"No one here is going to report back to Steve that you were talking to me," he assures me. I can't tell him that Steve knowing we were talking is a much lesser concern than Ramsay knowing.

"It's a bad idea nonetheless."

"Piper..." He heaves his own frustrated sigh, then grabs my hand, pulling me behind him to the other side of this corner of the restaurant, hidden from the others on the deck. In the comparative privacy, he presses me up against the wall with his hard body, his hands gentle on my cheeks, his lips threatening to claim mine.

"You don't have to do this. I'll fix it. I can still fix this," he says, desperation and determination blending in his voice.

"It's better this way, David," I reply, standing firm. "For both of us. You'll be leaving soon, and I can't leave Mystic Beach. And I can't live with the risks involved. *You* can't live with the risks involved." He'll assume I mean the risk to my career, not to the lives of those precious to me, and I hope that misapprehension will ensure he leaves here once the album is done and go safely back to New York. It's the only way I can think of to ensure he will be safe. Safely away from me and these dangerous secrets.

"It's worth it," he says, his fingers tracing up my neck.

And then he closes the distance between us, brushing his lips across mine. I can't help it — I melt into him, eyes closed, my mouth opening to his, his hips pressing me against the wall, his hardness against my belly.

I'm so overwhelmed by the assault on my senses that I don't register the tablet slipping out of my hand until I hear it hit the wooden deck. I push him away, grabbing the iPad back up, praying that it is not damaged, since it belongs to the venue, not to me. David grabs my wrist, checking for damage himself before he tugs on my arm, trying to pull me back to him. I pull my wrist free of his grasp, firm with him in the face of this renewed intimacy.

"It's not worth it to me, David. I won't risk it. I can't."

And I walk away from him, knowing the pain in my heart tonight is mirrored in his brother's and, now, in David's as well. I tell myself that David in pain is better than David potentially dead at Ramsay's hand. But based on what he said and did tonight, I suspect David would argue with me.

CHAPTER 29

NOT SURE YET

David
Three days later

"I'm sorry to bother you, Ms. Matthews, but I had a question about the studio."

You have no idea how long it took me to psych myself up just to make this call. It wasn't just the weekend that forced me to wait. That I'm doing it at all should tell you how determined I am to fix this.

"Oh? What can I help you with? Is there a piece of equipment you're missing?"

"No. Nothing like that. I was just wondering whether it might be possible to buy a stake in the studio."

"Oh! I guess you like it down there, then?" She sounds amused, almost warm, which is a change from her normal all-business attitude the few times we'd talked before we'd arrived here in Mystic Beach.

"I do. And I'd like to see a few changes here that an ownership stake would help me pursue."

"I see..." she says. "Well, there are three partners, myself and Steve included. The third partner... They're tied up in some legal issues right now, so I can't imagine they're going to be entertaining any buyout offers. And, to be honest, I'm not sure you can afford to buy that big of a share."

"I don't want a big share. Just a significant stake in it."

"Well, you'd need fifty-one percent ownership to make unilateral changes, David. I own forty-five percent, as does the other major partner. Steve holds the remaining ten percent."

"And you're not interested in selling me, say, eleven percent?" She chuckles.

"Steve's being a problem, is he?"

"In some respects, yes. He's blaming Piper for the loss of some tracks we did, and I don't think it was her fault. I'm afraid he's going to fire her — he already did, actually. But Alex talked him down, for now."

"These weren't the tracks for the song you sent Malcolm Fisher, were they? It would be shame to have lost those."

"No — those weren't lost. It was the rough mix we'd done the day before we recorded that. With Piper being blamed, I thought having her help re-recording them would help make up for it, even though I don't think she really was to blame."

"Piper helped with this song? Presumably without Steve's permission?"

"Well, I'm the one who called her back in to help. And she didn't just help, Ms. Matthews — she recorded, engineered and mixed the entire thing by herself! We just basically played our parts and let her have at it!"

"Piper did this on her own? This mix Malcolm called 'extraordinary'?"

"Did he?" I can't help it. I've got a huge smile on my face.

"He did. And that's high praise from him, as I think you know by now. And I'd have to agree with his assessment."

"I didn't realize you'd heard the song..."

"I keep on top of my label's projects, David. My hearing a finished song at this point is a little unusual, but Malcolm had very good things to say about it. He wanted to hear it in the studio before he decides whether it can go straight onto the album, but I expect it will. Congratulations, to you, your bandmates, and to Piper. This success helps make up for Mr. Graves' injury. And his unexpected deviation from our public relations plan. Our extensively discussed and vetted public relations plan."

Her tone is definitely less positive now than it was in discussing my song. Hunter is clearly on her shit-list.

"But given the extenuating circumstances..." she sighs, clearly nonetheless on Hunter's side as he deals with the trauma of his childhood, now revealed to the world. "As to your inquiry... your best move, I'd suggest, if you really do want to pursue this, would be to offer to buy a portion of Steve's holdings."

"I'm not sure he'd sell to me, even if the price was tempting."

"Because of Piper?"

"Indirectly, yes."

"Well, you won't know until you make the offer. So I'd start there. I'll have my assistant text you with what I would suggest would be an appropriate amount to start negotiations, if that would help."

"It would. Thank you so much!"

"My pleasure, David. I'll wish you the best of luck. You'd be a fine addition to our ownership team."

She ends the call, and I'm left wondering whether I can manage to even make Steve an offer without sticking my foot in my mouth yet again.

The next day

"**Y**ou want to buy into the studio? I'm not sure that's a good move for you, David," Steve says.

"Why not?" I've checked with my accountant. I've got way more saved up than I should need to buy Steve out, according to the numbers Marina Matthews sent over.

"We've already had concerns about professionalism while you've been here. Having you as an owner would make that exponentially more problematic."

"Why? Because Piper is an intern here?"

"We wouldn't want to have the perception that there was favoritism here due to her *seeing* an owner."

"We aren't '*seeing*' each other, Steve." That's entirely true right now, as much as I'd like to change it.

"Oh? Because I'm at a loss as to why you'd be going into the storage room with her for a rather lengthy period, if you weren't *seeing* her."

Steve taps on his tablet and offers it to me, the screen filled with a video showing Piper and me entering the storage room all those days ago, then cutting to us coming out ten minutes later, slightly disheveled.

Uh-oh.

"You have video cameras recording us? Do you know how creepy that is, Steve?"

"It's right in the contract for the studio rental, David. Business areas of the studio are subject to security monitoring, as well as the exterior of the property as a whole. I can pull out the pertinent sections of the contract, if you'd like to see it."

"That's not necessary."

"And then there's this…"

He taps on the tablet once again, showing me video of myself in the live room, pressing Piper up against the closed door to the control room, our faces too close even for friends and my fingers in her hair. I don't think anyone seeing it would believe that we weren't "seeing" each other. I haven't got a leg to stand on here.

Steve's expression is smug. But I'm not prepared to give up this fight.

"Favoritism could also be an issue for you, Steve. The other intern here is your son."

His smile falters a little.

"That's not the same. I don't have anything to gain with Sean."

"Well, since Piper and I are no longer *seeing* each other, thanks to your unfair treatment of her, I have nothing to gain, either."

He sits back in his chair and ponders this news. I've told him he's won the battle in our wrangling over Piper's and my relationship. I've also neutralized his argument for why I shouldn't try to buy in.

"I'm still not selling you any of my share of the studio."

"Why not? I addressed your concern."

"Because, David — you've attempted to strong-arm me over Piper ever since you arrived. You may have forced me to hold off on firing her — over behavior I now have proof of — but once your album is done, I refuse to have you interfering with my business. And make no mistake — this is *my* business. I'm the manager, and I'm the owner who handles operations. None of the others have ever questioned my judgment, aside from Piper being hired as an intern, which I think has now been proven to have been a bad idea. Lesson learned. It won't be repeated."

"What do you mean by that?"

"Just that I knew a female engineer would prove a distraction to the bands. And she's been much more than that. The girl's been a thorn in my side from Day One — first you and your interference, then her erasing those tracks, and now she's usurping my engineering jobs, as if her taking the Pirate's Cove job Sean was supposed to get wasn't enough."

"Piper didn't erase those tracks! And she only worked on that song with us because I asked her to, so we could fix the problem you were blaming on her!"

"Which you felt you needed to fix because she's got more than a professional relationship with you. You've proven my point. As to her not being responsible for erasing those tracks — why do you think I ended up looking over the security video from the last couple weeks? I watched her do it, David — I don't know if she was angry with you for breaking things off with her or what, but she's right there on the video picking up the drives on the morning after you recorded that song the first time and taking them to the storage room to be erased."

He proffers the tablet yet again, showing me a frame of security video capturing Piper with her hand by the dock where the completed tracks were supposed to have been ready for replay.

"Do you want me to pull up that footage, too?"

Piper had denied she'd erased the drives on purpose, even though she was angry with me that morning. The question was whether I believed her. She hadn't believed *me*.

"That won't be necessary."

Nothing that he could show me would change anything. The angle of the camera didn't show the dock itself, and even if it had, it still could have been an honest mistake and not sabotage. It all came down to whether I believed her — believed *in* her.

Two hours later

“G o.”

“Gryff, I need a favor.”

“You miss me too much down there to let me relax?”

“You never relax, Gryff.”

“Good point. What can I do for you, David? You need more tips on your stroke, now that you’ve got weeks at the beach to practice?”

“No. Haven’t spent as much time in the water as I’d expected. Been in the studio a lot already.”

“How’s that going?”

“Good. Except an issue that I’m hoping you can help me with.”

“Tell me what it is, and I’ll see what I can do.”

“I just found out that the studio here has security cameras that record footage going back weeks.”

“Makes sense. Place like that can be seasonal, and you might not discover that something’s missing immediately.”

“Well, it isn’t something that’s missing — it’s something that inexplicably showed up.”

“Oh?”

“Yeah. I think someone broke into my room here — well, let themselves in anyway, since I had left the sliding glass door unlocked when I went down to the studio.”

“David...” he growls.

“I know, I know. But other than this one suspicious incident, I have no reason to think we’ve had any security issues.”

“Assuming that’s the case — and I’m tempted to come down there and sit on top of the lot of you, regardless — you want me to get hold of the security video for that day? Hour?”

“I don’t know exactly when it happened. Probably within a 24-hour period.”

“And you’re sure they came in through the slider?”

“I’d think so, but I can’t swear to it.”

"OK. I'll see what I can dig up. This would be easier if I had the studio's permission, though. As it stands, I'll have to talk to a buddy of mine..."

"Well, if you need permission, I know who could give it to you..."

Four hours later

My phone rings. It's not who I was expecting to call.

"Mr. Carter."

"Ms. Matthews?"

"I understand that you have some security concerns about the studio."

"We just had the one incident."

"And nothing was taken?"

"I don't think so. Just something left."

"I see..."

"Did Gryff find something?"

"Mr. Gryffin did. I'm sending over a still from the security video of the day in question."

My phone beeps.

The man in the image isn't anyone I recognize. But then I don't know anyone who lives in Safe Harbour except Piper, and Rory. His hair is down to his shoulders, probably somewhere between dark blonde and medium brown, judging by the tone of it in the black-and-white picture. His features are sharp, giving him a predatory look that is only enhanced by his furtive behavior as he enters my room from the deck, with Piper's seal coat draped over one shoulder.

Gotcha!

Now I can prove to Piper that it wasn't me, and maybe we can do something about this guy who's got it in for me and would do something so cruel to Piper to set me up.

CHAPTER 30

STILL AROUND

David
The next morning

The swells bob up and down under my paddleboard. It's peaceful. Just me and the seagulls watching the sun rise over the horizon.

The ocean's been either flat or choppy most of the days we've been here, and I haven't gotten to surf much — not that I'd have given up time with Piper to surf. But that's not exactly an option now, is it?

I get that she's scared — for her career and much more besides. Having her seal coat go missing had to have terrified her. But I have the proof now that it wasn't me who took it. She should already know that I had nothing to do with it, but when I show it to her this morning after she comes into work, it will remove any doubt in her mind, once and for all. And if it's not doubt that's keeping her so distant... Can't she just forgive me for overstepping and going into her room that night, and let us just have this time together? We can dodge Steve, play it cool around him and Sean, and even around the guys in the band. No one has to know we're anything more than friendly colleagues. It would be fine. I know it would.

But she won't risk it, says we're not worth the risk. I'm not sure she believes that, but it hurts to think she might. We're... — together we're more than either of us is alone, more than the sum of our parts, and I'd risk nearly anything to have that back. I've waited my entire life to find it, and now that I know what it feels like, I can't give it up. As long as Piper and her fellow refugees were safe, I'd do anything to have us back together again. Yeah, I'd even be willing to give up the band.

Speaking of which... Declan's single-minded effort to find Callie has kept him out of the studio since that night. He's too wound up to write, and he's too busy with his search to even try. He's scoured every inch of the internet for even a mention of her, with no luck, and he's pestered Brighid so relentlessly for information that she finally threatened to put a hex on him that would make his dick fall off. Not that I think she would. Probably. But she was already pissed off by what she'd found out about his past with Callie, and she warned him that she protects her friends from those who would do them harm. I know Dec better than to think he would do anything to hurt Callie ever again. He considers this a second chance with her, and he's determined to make things right. If he can find her.

My legs trail in the water as I clear the swells nearest the beach and get ready to stand up, paddle in hand. I'm already enjoying the warm sun on my shoulders, having opted not to wear my rash guard today, but being in the studio has left me yearning for a solid workout — and, no, marathon sessions in bed with Piper didn't have quite the same impact, though they're way more fun. And now I don't even get to do that. Since we haven't had even one new song ready to do scratch tracks, I haven't even seen her since that night, though I've seen evidence that she's been in the studio when she knew I was unlikely to be there. But today — I'm going to insist she come over to the studio as soon as I'm back from my session on the paddleboard, clear the air about what happened to her seal coat.

I sigh and roll my shoulders to loosen them up before I get started, and that's when I feel something brush against my leg. I smile. Could it be that Piper has been missing me as much as I have been missing her? Dare I hope? Maybe a morning swim in her seal form is exactly what Piper needed today, and it's given her time to reconsider, before I even show her my proof.

I peer over past my knee, but I can't see even her spotted gray coat in the murky waters of the ocean here. Anything down past mid-shin is cloaked in the depths. I wait for her to surface, but there's no sign of her. My board gets bumped from behind, and

I turn to catch her at her little game, but again there's no sign of her. When something brushes against my other shin, my surfer instincts kick in, and I pull my legs up onto the board in front of me. It would be my lousy luck to let my guard down because I'm hoping to see Piper and instead turn into brunch for a tiger shark. I can paddle back in from a seated position, no problem, or I can stand up and paddle. Either way, with my legs out of the water, I look a lot less like a seal relaxing on the surface — a.k.a. shark bait.

That thought would normally give me some peace of mind, but now it just reminds me how vulnerable Piper is out here on her own. I wonder how many human husbands of selkie women hid their coats not to keep them tied to their human families, but to protect them from the threats in the water. I'd never do that to her, even though she thought for a while that I might, but it makes me wonder how many other men have had that thought and put it into action, just trying to keep their selkie woman safe.

Right now, though, I'm focused on getting myself out of the water safely and away from whatever that was. I'm going to feel really silly if it's just Piper playing tricks on me...

I stand up on the board and dip my paddle in the water, turning the board toward shore and then shifting to the long strokes that will move me efficiently across the water. I get maybe ten yards when my paddle gets caught on something and it, and I, go tumbling into the water. With whatever it was that bumped me.

I'm not exactly religious. Science has always been my core belief, music a form of prayer, as such things go. But right now, I'm making entreaties to whatever powers are listening, up to and including the late demi-god Rónan and his all-powerful father, whoever he might have been.

I have the wherewithal to keep my grip on the paddle, and as I reach the surface, I'm scrambling to get back on the board and out of the water. Pain lances across my back as something solid hits me from behind. Survival instincts kick in, and I reach to make sure I'm not bleeding, with a chunk chomped out of my back to drain my lifeblood into the water and draw sharks for miles. Tender, painful, but no broken skin that I can feel. My focus returns to getting back on the board, and I manage to get an arm over it before my leash is jerked down hard, sending my head spinning with pain. I fall away from the board again but kick hard with my right leg to push myself back in range. I manage to lay across the board, paddle in hand, but as soon as I do, something yanks on the paddle and I'm catapulted headfirst into the water.

I aim for the surface, pulling hard with my arms, kicking with both legs — including, painfully, the one that *had* been secured to my board by what is clearly now a broken leash. I can see light filtering down from several feet above me, but that light is suddenly blocked, and full-on panic sets in as I recall Rory's visit and realize what's blocking the light isn't my board, or Piper, or even a hungry shark — it's a very large adult male grey seal. Or at least what looks like one at first glance. As it stares down at me, I see the same kind of intelligent awareness than I first saw in Piper as a seal, but with none of the innocent curiosity. Instead it feels much as if it *were* that hungry shark, or maybe a genetically-altered hyper-intelligent shark that considers itself the top of the food chain, in or out of the water. And I am very much in the water...

With no warning that I was going under, I'm running out of breath, and if a seal can give a predatory grin, this one is doing it. It reminds me all too well of videos I've seen of leopard seals hunting penguins. It dives down toward me, and I make a run at the surface for all I'm worth. I kick out with my uninjured leg as it comes within reach, connecting solidly with its jaw. That gives me just enough leeway to break the surface and drag in a lungful of air. I spot my paddle floating nearby and lunge for it, managing to get hold of it just as another solid impact to my back drives my breath out of me. I drag in another lungful of air to replace it, falling instinctively back into the training Gryffin gave me to help improve the efficiency of my swimming stroke and my ability to hold my breath.

I feel the water move around my left calf, and I ignore the part of my brain that reminds me that male grey seals can reach nearly 10 feet in length and more than 800 pounds, blindly making a strike for the massive creature with the paddle, connecting hard with something. I try to use whatever time that buys me to get back to the board, but just as it comes within reach, the seal grabs my ankle in its mouth and pulls me back under. Through the pain, I hold on to the paddle for dear life, because it's the only thing I have to defend myself with.

I jab the seal in the belly as hard as I can, and it moves back away, appearing to reconsider its plan of attack. I take a tentative stroke toward the board, expecting the seal to come at me, but it keeps its distance long enough for me to once again get my torso across the board. I scramble up, waiting for the seemingly inevitable attack, but there's nothing. And the seal has now disappeared. And so has the end of my paddle, apparently snapped off with that last blow I gave the seal.

Well, here's a dilemma...

I'm a long way from shore now, and I functionally have no paddle — though believe you me, I'm holding on to what is now effectively a carbon-fiber spear — but I'd rather keep my hands, arms, feet and legs inside the ride vehicle at all times, because I'd like to, well... just plain old keep my hands, arms, feet and legs. Which, judging by the pain in my ankle, could still be an issue. That moment of Piper grabbing my hand with her teeth when she showed me her transformation flashes in my mind. The damage those teeth could do to the hands I need to make music... Yeah... Not paddling back to shore with my hands in the water.

I look around and see no sign of the seal. Maybe my jab with the paddle did some actual damage? I also realize I'm only drifting farther from the shore as the tide continues to go out. I need to make a move now, or I'm going to be swept out to sea.

My ankle is bleeding from several punctures, and I picture the trail of blood that would follow behind it like tasty breadcrumbs of the sharky variety if I were to try kicking my way back to the shore. And that's going to take a lot longer with an injured leg.

I look down at my hands, the tools of my trade, and I admit to myself, reluctantly, that they won't do me much good if I'm dead from hypothermia or dehydration and severe sunburn after I'm stuck on this board at sea for hours or days. So, paddling ashore it will have to be. I look for the seal again, and seeing nothing, I decide to go for it. I tuck the ersatz spear firmly under my arm, take a deep breath, repeat my pleas to any available deity, or half of one, and start paddling briskly for shore, which is still farther away than I'd like. Which would be zero, in feet, yards, meters or Sheppys.

I cringe every time my fingers hit the water, picturing them coming back up as gnawed-off nubs. But I keep paddling. Until the board rockets up out of the water, hit hard from underneath, and it — and I — go sailing through the air. The paddle is lost before I hit the water, and with a broken leash, the board isn't within reach either. I make a split-second decision to just swim for it, picturing Gryff's instruction on an efficient stroke and trying to keep my mind in that setting. Nothing to worry about. Nothing to fear.

Except drowning with an 800-pound weight attached to my ankle by a sharp set of teeth, as I'm pulled back under. I've got a full breath, but I'm using oxygen like crazy from the exertion of swimming and now trying to battle my way free and back to the surface. No matter how many times I've practiced remaining calm underwater, my body knows this is life-or-death, and it fights like it. I kick at the seal with my other leg, aiming for its eyes and connecting hard enough that it lets go. But before I can get to the surface, it comes at me again, full bore, slamming into my solar plexus, and all thought of holding my breath is gone. My diaphragm spasms, and in an instant, I'm drowning.

Chapter 31

DROWN

Piper

Something is wrong. I'd gotten used to David being curled up around me when I wake. Even though we've been estranged for weeks, it still strikes me as wrong that he's not here with me now. Maybe that's what woke me. If it is, I'm just going to have to get over it. David and me together is a thing that cannot happen, not if he's going to be safe. Ramsay can do whatever he wants to me. I don't care about that. The Council won't let him threaten Safe Harbour. But David... I have to keep him safe. It's my fault he was ever in danger.

I stretch, gauging whether I have time to grab some more sleep before I have to get ready for work, since Steve wanted me to work on inventory with Sean today. I probably do. But as unsettled as I feel, is it likely to happen? I snuggle back down, trying to ignore the sense that my bed is too empty, and...

Panic-pain-fear!

Something is wrong. Something is very wrong. With David.

I dart out the door and run over to the studio house, racing up the deck stairs to his room on the second floor, where I find the sliding door is closed but unlocked. His flip-flops are sitting by the closet door, but his board shorts are missing, an empty hanger left in the spot he'd been hanging them to dry. Shoeless and in his swimming gear, he's got to be out on the beach. And if

David, who's nearly as at home in the ocean as I am, is panicked while out there — something is beyond wrong.

I'm halfway down the stairs to the ground when I realize two things: I'm naked, and I don't have my seal skin. I race back to my bedroom and grab the skin out of its hiding place, and then run the fastest I've ever run, toward the ocean, toward David.

I dive into the face of the first oncoming wave and make the quickest transformation into seal form that I've ever made, gliding through the water with powerful strokes of my flippers pushing this hydrodynamic body at top speed. My hearing underwater has a much wider range than it does in air or than humans do in either element, and I can hear the sounds of a struggle not far offshore. I turn toward the sound, panic of my own overlaying what I felt earlier, because I know what that sound has to mean.

Ramsay.

Ramsay has David. Is trying to kill David. And I will not let that happen. I will give in to Ramsay if that's what it takes to save David. But I'd much rather Ramsay was dead instead, and as I ram into his belly with every ounce of force I can gather, that's the result I'm hoping for. Ramsay releases David, and I push him up to the surface, praying to the gods that he is still alive. The loose limbs and lax expression on his face don't bode well, and I grab him gently by the wrist, pulling him across the surface, making sure he remains face up so he can breathe. If he's breathing at all.

As I reach the breakers, I dip under the water and transform back into human form. I wrap my coat around David's chest, supporting him with one arm as I use the other to bring us the rest of the way onto the beach, with both of us washing in on a wave. I turn his head to the side and listen for his breath. Nothing.

I try to remember everything I've ever seen or read about humans drowning. Doctor, white coat... Noah Wyle in a white coat in the new "Leverage" series, which David needs to live to see. I know Noah Wyle had also played an emergency medicine doctor. I even watched a few of those old shows of his so I could understand the "Easter egg" they'd stuck in the new show. I scrounge through my memory. Patient not breathing... what was it... that CRP? thing!

I pinch David's nose and put my mouth over the one I've kissed so many times, forcing breath into his lungs. Again. That spot on the chest... I press down. "Stayin Alive." I read about this when I was going through the music of the disco era. Music is going to bring him back to me. I push with the beat as the tune repeats in my head. As a bass player, David would appreciate the consistency of my rhythm. I want to laugh, but that seems inappropriate. Maybe even a little unhinged.

David suddenly drags a breath into his lungs, coughs hard and begins to vomit up seawater. I turn his head to the side, offering thanks to every deity I can think of. He begins to wake, and I try to lever his much larger body up off the sand.

"David — come on... Help me! We need to get you to the healers!"

He coughs again and nods absently, his fingers running over my seal coat where it lays across his belly, where I now see a bruise. Rage erupts in my mind. Ramsay tried to kill David, and almost succeeded. May yet succeed, if I don't get him to the healers.

"David Carter — move!" I order him, and David begins to sit up. "Come on — up!"

With my help, David manages to get his feet under him, and I tuck my coat over my shoulder before I slide it under his arm, supporting him and moving us up the beach toward the hidden gate. We stumble through the secret door and down the hall, up the steps and through my door. I lay David on the bed, tucking my skin under the pillow behind him, and turn him on his side.

"David — I'm going to get help. You stay with me, OK? You're not allowed to leave me! You're going to get better, and we'll watch the new 'Leverage' together. You can't miss out on that! You're going to love it!"

I run my fingers down his cheek and kiss him on the forehead. Barely taking time to grab my robe, I rush out the door and down the hallway to Rónan's rooms, which Rory has taken to using when she's worked late in his office.

"Please let her be here. Please let her be here. Please let her be here..."

The lock opens at my touch, and I fly through to the bedroom, where I see Rory laid out on her side, her hand on Rónan's empty pillow. A chill runs down my spine. I cannot lose David.

He can't die yet. Not for a long, long time to come. I was ready to give him up to keep him safe, but he has to live!

"Rory! Wake up! Please! I need help!"

She snaps awake and sits bolt upright.

"Piper? What's wrong? Are you OK? And why are you naked? Did you get caught transforming again?"

"Ramsay tried to kill David, drown him, and he nearly succeeded! May yet if we don't get him to the healers!"

"Fucking hell!" she swears. "Where is he?"

"In my bed."

"Get back in there and keep an eye on him. I'll get some help."

I throw the robe around me as I race back down the hallway, and I find David as I left him. He coughs reflexively and I race to get a trash can, just in case he vomits again. He doesn't. I wet a cloth and clean him up. His eyes are closed and he's panting, as if he's still short of oxygen, and my mind races as I try to avoid thinking how close Ramsay came to succeeding. I crawl into the bed with David, carefully wrapping my arms around him.

"New 'Leverage,' huh? I guess I'll have to stick around for that..."

His voice is hoarse, barely a whisper. But there's a hint of a smile on his face.

"Yes, you will. No leaving this earthly plane, David Carter. I'll follow you to the Summerlands and drag you back here again, and I'll be very irked with you if I have to do that!"

"You'll have to tell me about this Summerlands sometime. It sounds nice. Can you surf there?"

I can't tell if he's making a joke or is just that far detached from what's happened that he's fixated back on his surfing. After nearly drowning.

"What happened?"

"Got attacked by a massive-ass seal..."

"Ramsay."

"You know him?"

"He's tried to force me into becoming his mate, per some old promise between his clan and mine."

"'Tangled up in old covenants.' So that's what she meant..."

"Who?"

"Rory."

"You talked to Rory?"

"She came to see me after you told her about us." He pauses to catch his breath. "Wanted to make sure I was good enough for her little sister." He manages a small smile now. "Not that it did me a lot of good in the end, but I think I passed."

"You did indeed, David," Rory replies from the doorway. "Though I suspect you may be wishing now that I'd sent you packing back to New York with your bass, your tail between your legs and your normal life awaiting you."

"Nope."

Rory's eyebrow rises.

"You sure? You realize you nearly died just a handful of minutes ago, right?"

"I'm tougher than I look."

Rory shakes her head and chuckles grimly.

"It would appear so. Now, tell me exactly what happened."

"I was out on my paddleboard, and something bumped against me, and then I got pulled off into the water. Once I was underwater, I realized what had bumped me was a massive seal and that it probably wasn't a normal seal... And from there, it basically tried to drown me."

"And almost succeeded, it seems. If Piper hadn't... Wait — if you were out there alone, how did Piper know you needed a rescue? And I thought you two were broken up?"

"We are," I say firmly, just as David says, "Not if I can help it."

He and I exchange a look, both exasperated with each other.

"You two can have make-up sex later," she says impatiently. "Now, how did Piper know to run to the rescue?"

They both look at me, and I shrug.

"When I woke up, something felt wrong, and I ran over to check on David, and when I realized he was out on the beach and maybe in the water, panicking, I ran out to find him."

Rory gives me an odd look, and glances at David, and back at me. Scrutinizing.

"When I got to them, Ramsay had David held underwater, and I rammed into him as hard as I could to make him let go. Then I pulled David into shore and did... CRP?"

"CPR," they both correct me.

"Where did you learn CPR?" Rory asks.

"One of the actors on the new 'Leverage' used to play an emergency doctor on an old medical show."

"'E.R.'?"

"I think that was it. Noah Wyle? They made a doctor joke on one episode, had him pretend to be a doctor. They mentioned it in the after-show. So I watched a few episodes of his old show. I just tried to do what I saw him do."

Rory shakes her head.

"And here I thought you were just watching TV to practice your American accent..."

"Wait — so the new 'Leverage' saved my life?" David asks. "Because of an inside joke about Noah Wyle's old show? I guess I should be glad they made him pretend to be a doctor and not a librarian. Or that you weren't so enamored of Christian Kane and his music that you watched 'Buffy the Vampire Slayer' and 'Angel' instead. I'd be dead now instead of un-dead. I mean, not dead."

"Let's not get ahead of ourselves, David. You're not entirely out of the woods yet," Rory cautions. "I've done a couple stories on 'dry drowning,' which can happen after any kind of drowning incident. If circumstances were different, you'd be on your way to the real-life E.R. right now, but there's no way to explain your injuries without putting a spotlight on Safe Harbour and its resident population of 'seals.'"

She points to the damage to David's left ankle.

"Unless you got attacked by a dog on the beach and managed to nearly drown afterward, there's no other explanation for your condition."

"The healers?" I ask.

"On their way. I had to swear them to secrecy, and I'm still not sure we don't need someone with more expertise in human medicine..."

She gets a thoughtful look, but there's a commotion behind her as three of the Hidden Folk healers arrive. I hop up out of the bed, but I keep hold of David's hand.

"I always knew you were trouble, Piper NicGilleMhoir," Morgan, the senior among the healers, says in Welsh, shaking her head, with its iron-grey braids, and giving me an eloquent look. "Dragging half-drowned humans into Safe Harbour..."

"Leave off, Meddyg Morgan, os gwelwch yn dda," Rory tells her in a respectful tone tempered by assertive authority. At 27, Rory still outranks Morgan, via her place on the Council, despite the healer's three millennia, and Rory's doing a tightrope walk of politics, addressing "Doctor Morgan" in her native

Welsh, including "please." Apparently, Rory's a quick study where languages go. "Piper did the wise thing, considering that he was attacked by one of our own and nearly killed outright."

"Ramsay?" Morgan asks.

She and Rory exchange a look, and Morgan nods curtly, moving to David's side.

"Aeronwen, tend that ankle. Make sure it's clean, first thing. Gods only know what kind of things Ramsay's had in his mouth..."

Morgan shoos me out of the way

"Angharad, take his hand, fix those abrasions on his wrist and ensure he stays with us."

The flaxen-haired twins take up their posts as instructed, leaving me to stand and watch.

"Young man, I'm going to check your lungs and heart," Morgan says in English. "Close your eyes and relax. Breathe easy."

David follows her instructions, and Rory pulls me away, out into the hallway.

"Piper — I'm going to have to call an emergency meeting of the Council. Ramsay will be found and called to account for his actions. Regardless of his likely justifications for this attack, he has put us all at risk, and I will advocate for him to be removed."

I sigh in relief. This might be the one thing that would keep David safe, aside from sending him back to New York, broken-hearted and resenting me.

"Don't think you're off the hook, though. Assuming they agree, there's still the matter of David being aware of your secret, and ours. And now he's been seen inside the compound, by those with no ax to grind. So, there will be a reckoning for you both, and me..."

"How bad is this?"

"I won't lie to you. It's not good. But a precedent has been set, and you're looking at her. Here's where we hope my efforts in the last year have been appreciated."

She frowns, looking uncertain. Rory's hardly ever uncertain. And when she is, she doesn't often let it show.

"If things go badly, you may need to get him out of here. Make sure you have your phone on you at all times. Here's a credit card, in case you need it," she says, pulling a card from a deep pocket in her skirt. "And I know I don't have to tell you, but keep your coat nearby and hidden."

"Aeronwen, help your sister hold him steady!" Morgan's urgent tone makes my blood run cold.

"Take care of him, Piper. Make sure he stays here with you. I'm going to go convene the Council, and make a phone call..."

What I see when I get back to David's side is alarming. The twins are holding his hands and shoulders down against the mattress while Morgan holds her hands over his chest, a soft light radiating from them. His wrist is free of the abrasions from my teeth, thanks to Angharad. His ankle is free of blemishes, indicating that Aeronwen had also completed her work. My hand trails over his skin there, marveling at the effectiveness of their skill.

David suddenly relaxes into the bed, and Morgan gives me a speculative look that reminds me of the one Rory leveled on me and David earlier.

"Keep your hand on him, Piper. I'm almost done."

A few minutes later, Morgan leans back, her shoulders falling in a posture of fatigue. David appears to be sleeping peacefully.

"Are you well, Meddyg?" I ask.

"Your manners are impeccable, youngling," she says, "even if your judgment is questionable."

She gives me a shrewd look.

"I am well enough, and I will recover. I cannot promise the same of your mate here," she adds, and I simultaneously register surprise at her calling David my mate and dismay at her prognosis.

"He is out of immediate danger, Piper. But humans are more at risk from drowning than are we. Our blood disperses seawater from our lungs into our blood more effectively, with less risk of complications to the cardiac system."

My surprise must register on my face.

"Yes, I have been studying human medicine. I haven't lived this long without learning to adapt and to integrate new knowledge. But I do not have the skill to completely reverse the infiltration of seawater in his blood. He remains at risk of a relapse — what young Aurora called 'dry drowning.'"

"So what do we do?"

"We may need human medicine to fully treat him. I made a suggestion to Aurora. She'll have to decide, with the council, whether that's an appropriate step. He's fine for now. Stay with him. Hold his hand. Remind him he is wanted here, that he is loved." She shakes her head. "Impulsive child... It's been a millennium since anyone in your clan took a human lover. And longer than that since such a lover was in the midst of a selkie enclave with full knowledge of what we are. But if we are to keep him... Well, that's a decision above my rank."

She pats the back of my hand.

"Give him your touch. It soothes him and will help him recover. Get him out of those wet clothes, keep him warm. Sips of water or tea if he wants it, but only sips. We will return this afternoon to check on him."

She and the twins leave me alone with David, shutting the door behind them, and I do as instructed, stripping him out of his board shorts, leaving his side only to get a dry towel to put under him and a fresh sheet and blanket to pull over him. When I'm done, I hide my seal skin under my pillow and crawl back into the bed next to him, laying my head on his shoulder and lacing our fingers together.

His breathing is steady, his heart beating strongly, and that soothes me enough that the physical and emotional toll of my morning finally catches up with me, and I fall asleep tucked into his side.

CHAPTER 32

TREASURE IT

"Piper." A hand nudges me awake, and I open my eyes to find Rory looking at me from across a sleeping David. "The Council has requested your testimony as to what happened today. I need you to come with me."

"I'm not leaving David."

She gestures toward the doorway, and the twins come in, one on either side of the bed by David's feet.

"Aeronwen and Angharad will stay with him while you are with the council. And while it was phrased as a request, there is nothing optional about it. They were quite firm about that, even after I explained that your presence was also needed here. Ramsay has demanded a formal hearing — both of the charges against him and those he would make against you, me and David. Your testimony is required."

"Let me get dressed, and I'll be right there."

A few minutes later, clad in a formal robe embroidered with the symbols of my clan, my hair tamed in a tail gathered low on my neck, I gaze down at David's sleeping face, my heart pulling me to stay with him, no matter how things have been between us of late.

"He'll be fine with us, bach," Aeronwen says, the endearment underscoring her genuine caring for me, as well as her care for her patient. Even if I'm not fond of being called "little." The twins are many years my senior and four inches taller, so it isn't an unwarranted remark. "We'll care for him as if he was one of our own."

"Thank you. Thank you both for what you have done for him, for us," I say, taking her hand. "I owe you a debt."

"No debt is ever owed for healing, Piper," Angharad replies. "And if you can rid us of the plague that is Ramsay and his pod... they give even the grey seals a bad name." She grasps my hand tightly, and I'm struck by this oddly overt expression of solidarity from the normally restrained twin.

I nod solemnly. It seems I was not the only one subject to unwanted attentions from those three.

"**S**he has broken the very rule of secrecy her own foster-brother swore me to when I was granted asylum here! I caught her red-handed bringing her human lover in and out of this refuge, and I saw her put her transformation on display for him, as if it was some kind of entertainment for the curious!"

Ramsay's tone is full of disgust — dripping with it as he says the word "human" — and I half cringe to hear his tirade as I walk into the council room. But this is Ramsay, and as superior as he feels to me, to all of us, really, he has no room for criticizing the behavior of others, not here. I hold my head high as I move to stand behind Rory's chair at the council table.

"She has displayed tremendously poor judgment, and I would very much like to resolve at least that part of the problem for you — by taking her as my wife and insisting on proper behavior from the girl. Clearly, discipline must be applied here if she is to become a responsible member of my clan."

He gives me a meaningful look from the open center between two curved sections of table that together form an O shape — symbolic in that it has no head or foot, with all members of the council being equal, at least in name.

"Ramsay, you have been told repeatedly that you have no claim to Piper. Those old customs were rejected when our refuge was established here, and you agreed to abide by that, as well as our rule of secrecy, when you accepted a *provisional* place here with us."

Hamish's tone is pointed as he emphasizes the provisional nature of Ramsay's residence in Safe Harbour, giving a scratch to his bulbous nose — a casual gesture that seems anything but when matched against the seriousness in his pale grey eyes.

"And you see how well the dismissal of those traditional practices has worked for you," Ramsay retorts. "Humans sneaking in and out of our females' bedrooms, a girl given license to behave in ways we never would have accepted in our homelands, with her 'job' and her time spent in drinking establishments with all manner of human males pawing at her... which I saw happen barely a week ago, with my own eyes — shameless behavior, approved and encouraged by this human female." He points his chin at Rory. "This insidious effort to undermine our traditions must be halted before it does further damage to our culture!"

"Ramsay — I would caution you against building your case upon outdated traditions that deny our females equal rights," Aoife cautions, the weight of two millennia as clan historian behind her. "Your clan may have subjugated your women into this millennium, but that is not the tradition in most of the selkie clans, even among the grey seals. And many of those in our community have long-established matriarchal hierarchies among their people. You will find no sympathy here for your misogyny, so best you abandon it now."

Ramsay grits his teeth but says nothing in reply.

"Have you anything further to add in your defense?

"My defense? I undertake to defend my mate — the mate I was promised long ago," he emphasizes as council members begin to object, "protect her from a predatory human male, and to protect the secrets of Safe Harbour from an outsider, a *human*, and you ask me to defend *myself*? Against what charges? Acting in the best interests of everyone here? Moving decisively when everyone here appears to have accepted lax security as a default when our lives are at risk if we are exposed? I understand this is not the first time that a human has trespassed onto our lands and inside this refuge."

He gives Rory a scathing glance, and she sits, impassive, as if the complaint has nothing to do with her.

"You are establishing a precedent here that will quickly spiral out of control, with younglings finding human mates and bringing them into our refuge. There is no question that someday, one of them will let it slip to human authorities what manner of creatures reside here, under their very noses, and then we will all be in danger. If no one else will defend our lives against this threat, then I will do so, gladly. It's time the vacuum of leadership in this place was filled."

His expression is pure arrogance, seemingly certain that his rank among his clan and his aggressive posturing will be enough to not only successfully make his case, but based on his rhetoric, maybe even to earn him a spot on the council or perhaps even as Rónan's replacement.

It's an idea I had never credited as even possible, and yet he seems to consider it inevitable.

"Well, I, for one, thank you for your candor, Ramsay," says Nolan, giving a nod of his sharp chin. "Your words will be taken into consideration as we discuss the appropriate steps to resolve these matters before us today."

I hadn't even considered that Ramsay's arguments might find support among some of the council members. We had our rules, but Rónan had been adamant that we must change with the times and adapt to the ways of our new home, and most had seen the wisdom in that. I knew not all of our people agreed with all the changes that had been made, but Nolan, on Ramsay's side in this? Could Ramsay end up the victor, and Rory, David and I risk becoming victims of his claims against us?

Ramsay's smug grin when he looks over at me suggests he thinks he's won. He strides confidently through the council chamber doors and down the hall. A shiver goes down my spine.

"Piper NicGilleMhoir — come before the council to testify," Hamish invites, the expression on his gnomish face unreadable.

I move to stand in that center space, suddenly feeling anxious with all these impassive faces surrounding me, no wall to my back, nowhere to hide from their judgment. Rory gives me an encouraging smile, making a show of slowly inhaling and exhaling, reminding me without words to follow that example.

"Piper — you have heard the core of Ramsay's charges against you. What have you to say in response?" Hamish asks.

"I'm not sure why I'm being called in to face charges, when Ramsay was the one who has continually harassed me and just hours ago attempted to murder a human that I work with." There — bravado re-established, if by the skin of my teeth.

"Do you deny that you brought that human inside the refuge at Safe Harbour, breaking the rule of secrecy under which we all abide here?"

"I do not deny that I brought him inside our walls. But I had permission to do so, and the circumstances were extraordinary, with only one similar case in our entire time here — and Rory has more than proven her value to our community."

"Aurora's history with Safe Harbour has been well-established," Aoife acknowledges.

"But that should call into question her neutrality in this case, if anything," Nolan says. "I would request that she recuse herself from voting on these charges, on both sides."

"I will recuse myself from voting on Piper's fate, and mine by extension," Rory agrees readily. "I will not do so regarding the charges I have laid against Ramsay," she adds firmly. "In my pro-tem oversight role here at Safe Harbour these many months, I have had to document his repeated efforts to intimidate and harass Piper, and others, and I will not abdicate the responsibility I bear in ensuring the safety and security of those members of our society. I will not cast a *deciding* vote on Ramsay's fate, should it come to that, but I will nonetheless cast my vote, once we have fully discussed the circumstances and their implications on our larger population and on our future here."

"That is acceptable to me," Aoife says.

A round of nods and acceptance spreads around the council table.

"Now, Piper, if you would please tell us how we come to be here today, with an unknown human under our roof, in need of healing, and, as Ramsay tells it, fully and intentionally informed of the nature of our community and of your nature as one of the sluagh rón?" Hamish asks.

I told them nearly everything. I left out the timeline of gaining Rory's approval for David to be let in on our secrets. I emphasized that he and I held each other's secrets, ensuring that both of us would stay silent, I argued. Though I left out the allegation that Ramsay had stolen my seal coat, due to my still lacking the evidence to prove his guilt, I corroborated the harassment by Ramsay that Rory had, thankfully, documented, as well as filling in the details for the council of what had happened today, with Ramsay's attempt on David's life.

In doing so, my anxiety grew exponentially, both over how close Ramsay had come to killing David and the fact that he now lay in my bed, still at risk of losing his life over my secrets, Safe Harbour's secrets.

"Fellow council members, I would suggest we've heard enough from Piper to discuss both sides of this case and make a decision, and she has had a very traumatic day and is fretting over her friend's health," Rory acknowledged when I'd finished my story. "I'd like to conclude her testimony and send her back to relieve the healers who have tended to David Carter in her absence."

"Agreed," Aoife says. "Thank you for your time, Piper. We'll discuss this and send word when we have reached our verdict."

I nod and offer an uneasy smile to the rest of the council before leaving the chambers. I only just let the doors close behind me before I break into a run to get back to David.

"His color is still off, but he is well-enough," Angharad confirms when I rush through the door. "Your urgency is not required, though he has been more restless since you left his side. It seems your presence soothes him, even in sleep."

I take the hint and crawl back into bed with David as soon as the twins have walked outside and closed the door behind them. I rest my head on his shoulder, listening to the sound of him breathing — both reassuring in that it is concrete evidence that he has survived today's threat to his life and concerning, in that I can detect the smallest difference from the sounds I had gotten used to hearing in the weeks prior to our separation.

Rory's concerns about "dry drowning" are at the forefront of my mind as I wrap my arm around his waist and give in to exhaustion, prayers for his life and health flowing through my mind.

CHAPTER 33

MIRACLE

Piper

"Mother of twelve gods! David?"

I awake to find a familiar face peeking into the bed.

"Is this where he's been disappearing to all summer?" she asks quietly, clearly aiming not to wake him. "And... I'm sorry — I don't think we were ever introduced. I'm Brighid, Hunter's fiancée."

"Piper."

"And since David appears to be naked, in what I presume is your bed, I'm going to assume that you two are... together?"

I'm not sure what the real answer is to that question right now, but I nod, my cheeks heating.

"That explains a lot. And now... Rory tells me someone — David, clearly — nearly drowned?"

"Was nearly drowned. On purpose."

"Unless you were the one who tried to drown him — which would be entirely justifiable if it was his brother instead — I can get the other details later. Right now I need to know what's been done, what his condition has been."

"He wasn't breathing when I pulled him out. I tried... CPR?"

She nods.

"And he coughed, vomited and then woke up enough for me get him in here."

"And then your healers did their work?"

I have no idea what she knows about us or why Rory has decided to bring her into a protected enclave — only the third human inside since the construction was completed — especially while the council at this very moment debates our fates over *David* having been brought into our secret.

"Piper, I know this place is a secret, and I know there are more secrets here that I'm not aware of. That's fine. I don't need all the answers. But I need to know what's been done to him, what his injuries were."

"He was attacked in the sea. There was a bruise on his stomach."

Brighid looks for my permission and then slides the sheet down to David's waist, running her right hand over his belly.

"And the healers repaired that damage... I see..."

I can almost hear her thinking, questioning how this is possible. She reaches into her bag, with its mermaid design in a border of Celtic knotwork, and pulls out a pale blue cloth, laying it over David's chest. She closes her eyes, puts her left hand over him and begins chanting. Irish! She's chanting in Irish!

A glow begins to grow under her fingers, seeping into David's skin. His color returns to its normal tan, his expression relaxed and comfortable, as if it was just another night spent sleeping in my bed. Then he starts coughing. She grabs the trash bin from beside the bed and pulls him up to sitting.

"Cough, David. Spit it out. All of it. You're a surfer, not a merman."

He does as instructed before flopping back on the bed, looking tired but healthy.

"Bridge?" he asks, his voice weak and hoarse.

"Welcome back, bass-man. Glad to see you survived."

Looking over at me, she explains.

"I've known David since we were 15..."

"Nope — 16. I was 16. I'm older than Declan, remember?"

She chuckles.

"A year older and far more mature," she agrees, rolling her eyes before a smile steals over her face. "We met on the beach just a little ways south of here, down at the boardwalk in Mystic Beach proper. That was the day aMUSEd was born."

"Thanks to you..."

She blushes.

"You would have gotten here with or without me," she says, folding the cloth and tucking it back in her bag.

"Not from what Hunter's said, now that he's told us what happened to his mother."

Her expression is sad, like distant grief recalled... a feeling I know well.

David's hand brushes my arm.

"Piper lost her brother about six months ago."

Brighid looks thunderstruck.

"Rory! Oh, my gods... That's why..." She turns to me, her expression just as solemn as it was in remembering Hunter's loss. "I'm very sorry, Piper. I didn't know him, but I've seen how much Rory misses him. She's been very kind to me recently, and the wisdom she's shared from her own experience is part of the reason Hunter and I ended up together after all."

"You speak Irish." I don't know why that's what comes out of my mouth in this moment, but it is.

"I do. A bit. Cúpla focal agam..."

"Why?"

"Why not?" she replies with a chuckle and a shrug.

"Bridge is a witch," David supplies.

"Priestess of Brighid," she corrects. "I'm only a little witchy. On an as-needed basis."

"You were needed today."

She nods.

"How are you feeling, David? Better?"

"Tired, a little sore, but otherwise pretty much normal. Now I see how Hunter's hand healed so quickly. Twice. That's some fierce juju you've got there, Bridge. No wonder Declan was worried."

She rolls her eyes again and frowns wryly.

"I would never harm him — and you should know that, David. It goes against my moral code, as a priestess and as a healer. But your brother..." she sighs. "That's neither here nor there. As for today... the others did most of the work. I merely gave a helping hand. Just do me a favor and try not to get drowned again. I'm not sure I could do it a second time," she admonishes him. "And I'm not sure the guys could find a new bass player in your league, let alone one who could put up with Declan."

He chuckles and leans up to rearrange the pillows behind him.

"Is that...?" she says, looking behind him, where my seal skin now peeks out from under a pillow. She looks over at me, back at the skin, back at me and then at David.

"I'm guessing David was attacked by a seal. A male seal."

David's jaw drops.

"How..."

"I'm a priestess of an Irish goddess, David. I know what a selkie is. Though I'd assumed they were a myth. But then a lot of people assume witches and the old gods are a myth, too. I never would have expected I'd meet a selkie on the Delaware coast, regardless."

"You can't tell anyone. Not even Hunter," David warns her urgently.

"I wouldn't dream of it. Hunter doesn't get all of my secrets, David — especially the magical ones. He knows the things he needs to know, but I keep too many other people's confidences to share them freely with him, and he prefers it that way. If Catholic priests had wives, they wouldn't break the seal of the confessional for them, and it's no different with me. Though I think you'd be wise to let the guys know you and Piper are together..."

"That's a whole other can of worms..." he says.

"I'd get fired. Steve already wants to fire me. David still being here is the only thing keeping him from doing it."

"I see..." she says. "Were you aware Herself is known to champion fairness to women in judgments? Sexism in the workplace would be right up Her alley to address."

I nod.

"We do not have any priestesses of Brighid among us here. We lost one... before we arrived, and our people follow so many gods..."

"I can make an entreaty, if you like."

I give my assent, and David reaches across my shoulders to hug me reassuringly.

"It's going to work out OK. I'm going to make sure of it, one way or another," he says.

Brighid smiles and shakes her head.

"You two are so stinkin' cute... I'm going to die of sugar overload just sitting here. Just do me a favor and let the guys in on *this* secret sooner rather than later. Trust me — having the people around you seeing you happy and rejoicing in it with you is one of the best feelings in life."

David leans over and kisses the side of my head, and all thoughts of keeping him at a distance fade into the background of my mind. Every moment is so precious. Nearly losing him today has reminded me of that in a way that has shaken me to the core.

"Putting my healer hat back on here. David — I was joking when I said not to get drowned again. But that's also a deadly serious issue. Literally. Your body's been taxed once already like that, and your lungs and cardiac system will take a while to fully recover. In their current state, I'd be concerned another incident might be fatal. So maybe stay out of seal-infested waters for a couple weeks? No offense, Piper."

"None taken. But Rory's dealing with the problem right now. I hope."

"Alrighty then. If you can point the way to the exit, I'll be on my way. Tell Rory if she needs my help here again to just call. And you have my sworn word as priestess that I will not breathe a word of any of this."

"She wouldn't have brought you inside if she didn't trust you implicitly."

I stand and walk her to the door.

"Is he really going to be OK?" I ask when we get outside.

"I think so. I suspect your healers did the bulk of what was needed. I'm just a human, a pair of hands for Herself. She does the work."

"Well, thank you for coming, for helping."

"You're quite welcome. It was lovely to meet you, officially, even if the circumstances were less than desirable. I like you two together. You'll be good for him."

"That's what Alex said."

"Busybody..." she replies with a laugh, shaking her head. "We've got to get that man a girlfriend, so he'll stop fussing over everyone else's love lives..."

"Which way did Rory bring you in?"

"Up off the beach," she says, picking up a pair of sandals from near the bottom of the steps. "I was at my shop downtown, getting ready to open for the day."

"David told me you had a shop."

"Yeah — Dream Weaver: yarn, needlework supplies, ethically sourced crystals, herbs and incense, holistic healing, spiritual counseling, tarot readings, witchy stuff," she adds with a laugh.

"That's why Rory called you! You're a healer."

"I am. Under Her blessing. Though I suspect it's a lot less impressive than what your healers do."

"You did for David what they couldn't. And that's all that matters to me right now. I need him safe."

"I can see that..." she says, her expression thoughtful. "Stay close by him for a while, a couple days at least. We need to make sure he doesn't relapse, but I think having you close by will do him some good. Call in sick to work. I'll tell Hunter that David wasn't feeling well and is holing up in a hotel room for a couple days just as a precaution."

I blink in surprise.

"What? It's true, after a fashion. If they assume he just didn't want to share a cold, that's on them."

She chuckles.

"Make sure he rests. I'll put together an herbal tea for him. A couple cups a day, with honey. I can send some with the tea if you don't have some already."

I flush, remembering David licking honey off my finger.

"We have honey. Definitely."

"OK. I'll be off then. Just have Rory call me if anything comes up."

I show Brighid out through the side door and the hidden gate. She winks at me, making a zipping motion across her lips, and heads off toward the water.

Back in my room, I change out of my formal robes and into a tank top and leggings. Then I slide in under the blanket with David, snuggling up next to him. I sigh in relief as his arm wraps around me.

"So... New 'Leverage'?"

"'Leverage: Redemption.'"

"Ooh... Sounds awesome."

"It is."

I put the show on the TV and angle it toward the bed before climbing back in beside him, snuggling close.

I came so close to losing him today. I never thought when I woke up this morning, missing having him there with me, that I'd be hauling his nearly lifeless body into that same bed before the sun even reached its zenith.

"Hey — don't cry. I know it's sad, but I'm sure it gets funny and clever, just like the original," he assures me, wiping a tear from my cheek.

I burst into tears and a sob erupts from my throat.

"Oh, Piper..." He pulls me against his chest. "I'm right here. I'm not going anywhere, no matter what. That's what I've been trying to tell you."

"You almost died! And it's my fault!"

"Was that you chewing on my ankle and pulling me under?"

"No."

"I didn't think so. You're not so... menacing. And way cuter, with that cute little button nose and those soulful eyes." He kisses the end of my nose. "So it's not your fault. In fact, you were the one who saved me! My hero! And not a hint of anxiety! I told Rory you were fierce, and there you went and proved me right. We make a good team..."

CHAPTER 34

CARELESS WHISPER

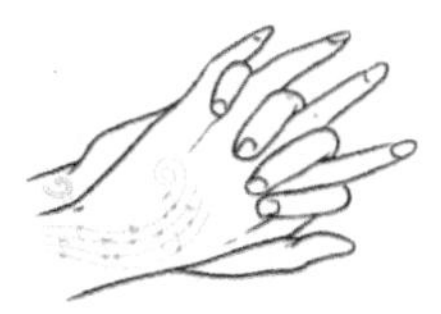

Piper

We settle back in and watch our show, nodding off together until there's a knock at the door. Rory lets herself in and takes a seat in the armchair by the bed, heaving a big sigh.

"So..."

"What happened?"

"Well, first off, here's your tea. Brighid sent it along, said you had the instructions, and something about honey?"

David and I exchange a look and start laughing.

"I don't want to know," Rory says, shaking her head. "I mean, I already know, but let's pretend I don't."

David looks confused. I raise a questioning eyebrow at Rory.

"Sure — why the heck not?" she says wryly. "He's already carrying around secrets that could get us all killed. What's one more?" She shrugs.

"Rory is an empath," I explain. "She feels other people's feelings. She can tell when people are lying, or when they're sad, or angry or in love..."

"Or when they're afraid — even at a distance, if it's someone I'm close to."

"That's why they couldn't erase your memory."

"It is. And we'll get back to that. First — practicalities... Ramsay has been permanently banished."

I gasp.

"What does that mean exactly?" David asks.

"He is not only no longer allowed to be here, he's anathema — not to be given succor, no matter the circumstances. He's stripped of all clan rights within the community, and his honor price is now zero."

"Honor price?" David asks.

"Under ancient law, which the Irish called Brehon law, penalties for wrongdoing against others were weighted based on the victim's honor price," Rory explains. "A king's honor price would be higher than a common man's, a poor man's lower than a rich one's, an esteemed member of the community higher than one with a history of wronging his neighbors... It's not exactly the egalitarian ideal we aspire to in this country, but then we haven't exactly managed to perfect that ourselves. Yet."

I'm reminded that all of this was new to her a year ago, and now she metes out these penalties.

"Piper's honor price is very high," she continues. "She was not only Rónan's foster-sister and his ambassador in this integration effort, but in their home, she was... well, a princess is probably the closest equivalent."

David looks at me in surprise. I shrug. Maybe someday I'll tell him about my family, my clan, but not today.

"Ramsay insists that his ancestor was promised a match between the two clans, and that that promise came due with my birth," I tell him. "It's an antiquated custom even among my people, and I rejected his overture. Rónan had already set aside any such agreements when we arrived here, so that was the end of it, at least as far as the rest of us were concerned. Ramsay begged to differ."

"And Ramsay, as Piper's story suggests, is of high rank in his clan. The equivalent of a duke, perhaps," Rory notes. "His honor price would normally be very high, though less than hers, and the difference between the two would leave him at a disadvantage were she to make an official complaint to the Council. But Ramsay is an outsider here, a later arrival with no status in the community, and with a more recent history of not following our tenets. So his honor price was already quite low."

"OK, I get that," David says. "But how does that end up with him getting banished?"

"Ramsay's recent actions against Piper — the harassment, the attempted blackmail, the crude comments — they're all documented, since I kept a record whenever she mentioned them to me."

"You did?" He looks worriedly over at me, seeming to realize that there had been a history of problems with Ramsay well before this morning. "I wish you had said something, let me protect you."

"What happened today was exactly why I didn't tell you David. I knew what Ramsay was capable of. I wanted to ensure he didn't turn his viciousness on you."

"And that's why you pushed me away."

I nod solemnly. "I'm just not sure why he went after you now, after I'd stayed away, all except that one night on the beach..."

"Piper — did you and David spend any time together in the last week, outside of the studio?" Rory asks.

"Just at the two performances aMUSEd did at the Pirate's Cove."

"And did the two of you... Did David show any interest in you either of those nights?"

"I tried to talk to her after Declan's meltdown. I may have kissed her," he says, clearly reluctant to admit to it in the current context. "But it was a private party! There was no one there except the staff and our friends."

"And yet Ramsay told the Council he'd seen a human male 'pawing' her at a drinking establishment in the last week."

"He was there! Ramsay was watching me, and he was there, and saw David kiss me!"

"I would assume so, Piper. But that's no longer a concern. And yes, to answer your question, David, I was keeping track of Ramsay's infractions as I was made aware of them. There was going to be a point when he crossed the line, and I wanted an airtight case for him to be kicked out of Safe Harbour. Not formally banished, but no longer living here. One or two more incidents, and I would have gone to the council anyway."

"Stealing Piper's seal coat and framing me for it wasn't enough?"

Rory looks agog.

"He did what?!" She looks at me with alarm.

"Piper didn't tell you?" David asks.

"Uh... No! What the heck, Piper! I'd have ended Ramsay myself if I'd known he'd done anything like that. Why didn't you tell me?"

"It was the night you were staying at Lyric's so she could write. I knew you couldn't leave her kids to come help me, and at the time, I wasn't sure who'd done it."

"And Ramsay wanted you to think David had done it — like the movie, like the legends of the seal-wives?"

I nod.

"What does this guy look like?" David asks. "I mean, when he's not a big-ass seal with a murderous glint in his eye."

"Tall, lean but muscular, light brown hair down to his shoulders. Same glint in his eyes," Rory supplies.

"It *was* him!"

We both stare, now confused over what he's talking about.

"I found out there was video footage from the security cameras at the studio. I was going to show it to you today, see if you recognized this guy. On the video, a guy matching that description sneaks into my room while we're in the studio that evening, with Piper's seal coat in his hands. He must have put her coat in my bass case. And when she didn't find it here in her room, she came looking for it in mine..."

"And caught you red-handed, just like Ramsay wanted... only you were innocent."

"Yeah."

My cheeks feel heated.

"So is that why you broke up initially? Because you thought David took your coat?"

I avoid looking at either of them.

"She said it was because she was afraid Steve would fire her, since he'd told her to keep things professional between us."

"Well, that was stupid of him. That never works."

"Well, Steve's pretty stupid where Piper's concerned. Already fired her once."

"He did?"

"There was a problem with a recording the band had done," I explain. "I can't imagine how it happened, but I was the last one in the studio before they realized there was a problem, and..."

"Steve blamed you. Of course he did," she says, rolling her eyes. "I told Rónan to send you to college. I warned him Steve wasn't open to women working in his profession. Receptionist, sure. Engineer? Nope. And with his son being the other intern... Rónan thought it was nice to keep things in the family — Steve's son, his foster-sister — they'd be that much more invested in the studio's success." She shakes her head. "Instead, all the negatives of nepotism, with a side of misogyny."

"Wait — Rónan set up your internship?"

I was afraid he'd respond this way when he found out.

"She's fully qualified, David," Rory hurriedly clarifies. "She's studied hard. That was never the issue. It was her work history, her identity documents. Rónan wanted to be sure he had some control in case there was a problem."

"No! No — I didn't mean to imply that she hadn't deserved the internship. She's amazing at it! I just didn't realize he was connected to the studio."

"Connected? He owns — owned — nearly half of it."

"You walked into the studio like you owned it..." he muses, looking at Rory.

"I kind of do, but not really, David. It's one of Rónan's investments that I haven't had the time to stay on top of. I figured it was in good hands, between Steve and the other owner..."

"Marina Matthews..." David says quietly.

"Marina Matthews...?" Rory prods. "Are you saying your label is the other big investor? I haven't even looked at the documents — mostly because I can't find them in his bass-ackwards Welsh filing system," she says with frustration. I have to chuckle. "But Rónan never said anything about a record label being the other owner."

"It's not. Marina Matthews owns her share personally, or so she told me... — which you cannot tell anyone now, because she asked me not to, and I just... did... anyway..." he adds slowly, as if just realizing how easily he spilled that secret.

"Maybe you all should wipe my memory after all, because I seem to be lousy at keeping my mouth shut."

"No harm done, David," Rory assures him. "Marina would have known Rónan was aware of her identity. And I'd have eventually realized it myself. So, the only one this is news to is Piper."

"No — I already knew. I went over the paperwork with Rónan when we first started discussing my internship."

"There — you see: no secrets spilled at all. Not that this is even on the same level as the other ones you now know... And now that we've gone off on that revelatory tangent..."

"Ramsay. How did he end up banished?" David asks.

Chapter 35

Every Time

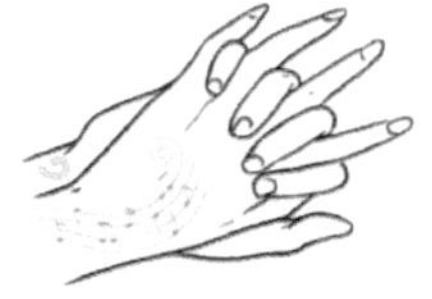

Piper

"I went over, very pointedly," Rory says, "with the other members of the Council what happened today — that Ramsay had tried to kill a human and would have done so if Piper hadn't intervened, despite his overwhelming size advantage — and reminded them that a drowned man washing up on our beach with a seal bite to the ankle would have had wildlife officials, police and scientists down here scrutinizing every single seal in the region. It wouldn't have been safe for any of the selkies to go out on the beach, let alone the water."

"And they didn't like that idea."

"They did not. They were ready to evict him at that point. But they gave him a chance to speak in his defense. As you heard earlier, Piper, he gave a very slanted take on what — *who* — he was owed, and claimed that Piper had taken a human lover and that he was just defending his promised mate and protecting the secrets of Safe Harbour from an outsider."

"I *had* taken a human lover. And David *does* know our secrets."

"And I confirmed it when Ramsay told them you'd said I'd given my approval. Which I have. If retroactively. During our deliberations, they made it very clear they weren't thrilled, but I emphasized that I had vetted David — using my battle-tested skills," she adds with a derisive look, "and had concluded definitively that David had a vested interested in protecting the secrets of both the selkies and Safe Harbour, and could be relied upon to do so. I vouched for him, which makes me responsible for his actions in the context of the dispensation he was functionally granted. So, don't fuck up, David, or someone's likely to decide I need to be dead — urgently this time."

"I don't know what to say, Rory, except to thank you."

She gives him a curt nod.

"I don't understand — how does that result in Ramsay getting banished?" I ask. "If anything, it would support his case that he felt justified. Nolan certainly seemed to support his cause."

"Well, ignoring the fact that he acted on his own, without council sanction, with some bizarre notion of taking over for Rónan..." She shudders with obvious revulsion. "Which, despite how he phrased it to Ramsay, Nolan found very disturbing, I have to say... Ramsay could have brought enough scrutiny on us to have destroyed everything... He also failed to take into account one very notable thing."

"What?"

"He freely admitted to trying to kill David. He didn't have any way to know David was David Carter, rockstar."

"Well, no. Ramsay hasn't made a single effort to integrate here. He prefers the old ways, selkie ways, not human," I point out.

"What rank is inherent to a harpist, Piper?"

"Harpists are the only musicians to carry the rank of noble, regardless of whose household they are or are not part of."

"Since David is a bass player and guitarist — a player of stringed instruments — I argued to the council that he was already of noble rank, making Ramsay's attack on him all the more serious of an offense."

"That was smart," David says, "though I don't know that my skills are the equivalent of a harpist."

"Be that as it may, David, that was what I argued, and that argument was accepted by the council. And then I went a step further." Rory turns to me. "How high is the honor price for a bard, Piper?"

My mouth forms an O.

"You see where I'm going with this?"

I nod. Clever, Rory. So clever...

"And how high is the honor price of one of the most favored bards amongst all the clans?"

"As high as a king's in some cases."

"You've lost me," David admits.

"I simply made the argument that you, David Carter, are a bard. As a songwriter, you are the modern equivalent. As part of one of the most popular and highest-earning bands in the world — especially as a primary songwriter — you are equivalent in rank to a legendary bard. As such, your honor price is a good bit higher than even Piper's. Perhaps as high as Rónan's. Attempting to kill you, even without the insults to Piper and putting Safe Harbour at risk, called for an éraic — a man-price — that so far outweighed Ramsay's honor price that the council was unanimous in choosing to banish him, lest he bring any more trouble down on our heads.

"I didn't even have to remind them that a dead human on the beach is a far cry from a dead rockstar on the beach. We'd have had journalists from around the world traipsing across our beach and climbing the fence just to get to the spot where the body was found."

I shudder at the image she's painting. We came so close to disaster today.

David hugs me tight against him.

"I'm sorry to be a downer, guys. But I need to know you both realize you're playing on an entirely different level than David is used to. The stakes here aren't an album that bombs or an embarrassing story in the tabloids. It's literally life-or-death."

"'Splash.'"

Rory looks at David, puzzled.

"The movie. Piper and I talked about this the night I found out."

"Ah... Yeah, not a good scenario. And you two have a double-edged complication..."

"What do you mean?"

Rory sighs.

"I've talked to Morgan and to Brighid, who both confirmed what I observed of you two earlier..."

"Rory, you're scaring me. Is there something wrong?" I ask.

"No. It's quite right, in fact. Just unexpected. David, close your eyes."

He looks to me for confirmation, and I nod. He closes his eyes. Rory holds a finger to her lips, gesturing to me for silence. She walks around the bed, picking up a box of matches from next to the candle on the bedside table. She lights one and brings it slowly toward David's shoulder, where he sits propped up on the pillows. I'm ready to stop her from burning him when her hand drops down, moving the flame next to my seal coat, and I instinctively start to reach for her. But David's hand snaps up, grabbing her wrist with all the honed strength in his bass-players' hands.

David's eyes pop open, and he's staring at his hand, and Rory's, like he has no idea how they got there. Rory blows out the match.

"You can let go now, David," she tells him. He releases her, and she returns to the armchair with perfect aplomb.

"What just happened?"

"I scared Piper — apologies, sweetie — and without her saying a word, making a sound or moving an inch, you knew she was scared, and why, and instinctively took action to protect her. Kind of like she did with you this morning."

"So, I'm an empath?"

Rory chuckles.

"Yeah — no. And be glad of that, because you've got enough on your plates. No — you two are what I call 'life-bonded.' You're tied together, soul to soul. Some people call it 'soulmates' or 'twin flames,' but this is a very specific state... Brighid said she's seen people talk about it as the partners' chakras linked together, energetically, in multiple locations, but she hadn't seen it in another couple until she saw the two of you together. Morgan said she's seen it in selkies just a handful of times in three millennia..."

"Wait... the healer lady — she's one of the ones who's..." David is in disbelief. I nod. "But she looks like she's what... 70?"

"Yeah, it's trippy, isn't it?" Rory tells him with a chuckle. "The twins are... what, Piper?"

"I believe they were born in the late 700s."

"They look like they're my age! And you're telling me they're 1,300 years old?" he asks.

"And still in their apprenticeship with Morgan," Rory notes.

"And she takes orders from you? A 3,000-year-old magical seal-lady healer... No offense."

"None taken. And, no, Morgan is a law unto herself. She likes to let us think she's taking orders and complying with our rules, but we all secretly know she does exactly what she wants. It just happens that it usually coincides with what we ask her to do. And if it doesn't, she's too wily for us to figure it out." Rory chuckles, and I smile.

"And she agrees with you that we're... life-bonded? And Brighid?"

Rory nods. She closes her eyes. After a minute, they snap back open, and she looks... shaken.

"What's wrong?"

"Nothing. It's nothing," she assures me, a little too quickly, rubbing her hip. "Nothing involving the two of you."

"So... what's this mean? You said it was a double-edged complication?"

"Yes, because it means you'll each know if the other is in trouble — and probably some more... pleasant... emotions," she adds with a smirk. "It also means it's highly unlikely that they could ever wipe David's memory of you, Piper, regardless of they what they tried. And they know that now, so they won't try. Be glad of that," she says, shaking her head. "But it also could mean that you'll share pain. If one of you were to break a leg, the other might find themselves unable to walk. Shared headaches... any number of things. It's somewhat uncharted territory, especially between a human and a selkie. All of this is by way of me telling you both to be careful. You're not invulnerable, either of you. I'm sure you two would have made up eventually, even without this near-death experience, but if David *had* been killed..."

"Piper might have died as well?"

"I don't honestly know. I don't think anyone does. But it's a possibility you should be aware of."

"But Piper's immortal."

"She is."

"And I'll live maybe a hundred years, tops?"

"Unless science progresses a lot faster than it has been, yes."

"So what happens to Piper when I'm an old man on my death bed?"

"I don't know. I suspect we'll find that out on your death bed, though I may not make it long enough to see it, if I don't get some sleep."

"You work too hard, Rory," I tell her. "You can't do your day-job and Rónan's work both, not by yourself."

"It's temporary, Piper. Once I get his files straightened out in some kind of form I can explain and everything running on schedule again, I'll have Hamish take on more of the load. We'll get things delegated enough that it'll run smoothly on its own."

"It never ran smoothly on its own when Rónan was doing it, so that would be a big accomplishment."

She chuckles, if a little gravely.

"I'll do what I can, Piper. Thanks for the concern. But that's all for another day. This one has had its way with me on all fronts, and I am overdue for some after-care. Starting with a nice hot bath in that ginormous tub in Rónan's room."

"His one self-indulgence, that son of a sea god..." I observe. "Whether it was from stress or overexerting himself with construction tasks, he always recovered better in warm water..."

It's too close to home, reminding us both that his body lies somewhere in a cold ocean.

"And on that note, I'm getting in that bath. You two..." She looks back and forth between us, seeming suddenly fragile. "Enjoy your time together. Every precious moment of it. You never know how much time you'll have until that last grain of sand drops through the hourglass." She closes her eyes, turns away from us and walks out the door.

"Piper," David says after a moment. "I know you said we weren't worth the risk but..."

I grab him hard in my arms, crushing his chest to mine and his lips, too.

"You're worth it. Worth anything, David." I look deep into his eyes. "I'm sorry. This was exactly what I was trying to prevent. Ramsay said he'd kill you if I didn't push you away. I guess after he saw us the other day, he decided to go after you at the next opportunity he saw."

"So it wasn't that you didn't trust me? It wasn't just Steve?"

I shake my head vigorously.

"Steve's a problem, but it was Ramsay's threat that pushed me to end things between us."

"And now that he's banished?"

"I still don't know how he managed to get into my room, and until I do, I'm not sure we don't have another enemy amongst us here," I tell him. "I'm not sure the risk is over. And then there's Steve... And you're still leaving once the album is done."

He brushes his fingers down my cheek.

"We'll figure it out, Piper. The secrets, your job, what happens after the album is recorded — I've got some ideas I'm working on. We *will* figure it out. We can make anything work, as long as we're together."

I nod my agreement, and we settle down in the bed once more, both of us at peace, now that we're together again.

CHAPTER 36

LOVE YOU MORE

David

Piper and I spend a blissful three days together in her bed, recovering and then reconnecting on both an emotional and a physical level. I'm feeling pretty good, all things considered. Like the fact that I nearly died. And might have taken Piper with me if I had, apparently.

Yeah, that's scary. Nothing gives you pause about keeping yourself safe like knowing that you might kill the woman you love if you don't eat right, look both ways before crossing the street and avoid running with scissors, or if you piss off eight-hundred-pound seals. Forget falling down and breaking a finger, and how that might force the cancelation of some tour dates — this is literal life-or-death stuff, and that point has been driven fully home, thanks to that asshole Ramsay.

Rory stops by to tell us he — and his posse — have been escorted off Safe Harbour property and onto a boat headed for... Well, she wouldn't tell me where they were headed, but I got the impression it was an uncharted island somewhere in the North Atlantic, where they had relatives. Piper and I shared a sigh of relief at that news. No more threats from Ramsay. Now we just have to deal with Steve. And figure out how we can make a relationship work when I have to go on tour in a few months and she can't, or won't, leave Safe Harbour.

I've decided I'm going to try again to persuade Steve to sell me his share of the studio. At this point, I've already pissed him off, so it's not like I can make things any worse by giving it another try. It's not like he'll try to kill me or anything. So, hey — that's a lot less intimidating than it was a few days ago. I haven't mentioned it to Piper yet. I don't want to get her hopes up.

But these three days together have persuaded me entirely that I don't want to be without her. We lost too much time trying to get Steve off Piper's back and with her trying to keep Ramsay from coming after me. Neither of those efforts succeeded, so it was just time that we could have been spending together that we can't get back now. I'll have too much time away from her when we're touring. I don't want to miss a moment while I have it.

"You have recovered admirably, young man," the healer, Morgan, tells me on this third day. She's stopped by briefly each day since Piper first brought me into her care, half-drowned. OK — more than half. I know that. I keep reminding myself, just so I'll be that much more careful in the future, that much more mindful of the precious time I have left. "Piper has excellent taste in robust young human males, it seems. Perhaps I should find one of my own. Unless she wishes to share," she adds, smiling almost mischievously.

I'm not sure how to take that.

"Meddyg Morgan... Stop teasing him, please," Piper says, trying not to laugh herself. "He has no idea what to make of selkie humor, let alone selkie humor set in the mores of many centuries ago."

I exhale the breath I didn't realize I was holding and do my best to smile politely back at the healer.

"I thank you, ma'am, for your help. I'm not sure I'd still be here if you hadn't..."

"No thanks needed, youngling," she says. "Your soul will be sufficient recompense now that you've signed it over to me."

"Morgan!" Piper wails. "Stop that! He's going to think you're serious!"

Morgan tosses her long iron-grey braids behind her and smirks.

"Apologies, David. I'm an old woman with few chances to visit with outsiders. You'll have to forgive me if I take my entertainment where I can find it."

"You're forgiven. So long as you warn me the next time that you're teasing. Otherwise, I might embarrass us both."

"He's awkward with people, Morgan, kind of like I am."

"Ah... that anxiety problem?"

"No, ma'am. Autism."

"Ah. I see. I've been reading your human medical journals. They call it... neuro—"

"Neuro-diverse. My brain just works a little different from most people's. I don't read social cues well. I can get overwhelmed when there's too much sensory stimulus, like light or noise."

"That has to be challenging when one has a career in modern music. So much of it seems composed entirely of noise," she adds, chuckling.

"Morgan — David's music isn't noise!"

"It *is* loud sometimes, though," I acknowledge. "But music is my center. I find myself there, even when the rest of the world seems like chaos to my brain."

"Spoken like a bard," Morgan says. "It has been long since I've had the chance to enjoy the company of one such as yourself, young David. I would very much like to hear your music."

"Piper, do you have a copy of 'Remember' on your phone?"

She nods, cuing up the song.

Morgan tilts her head, listening intently from her spot in the armchair beside the bed. Her expression is thoughtful, but it's hard to determine whether she's liking what she hears.

When the last notes fade away, I look carefully at her, waiting for the verdict. The judgment of this three-thousand-year-old woman on the music I wrote just weeks ago, recorded in a modern studio, with modern instruments and a modern aesthetic.

"Extraordinary," she says finally, wiping a tear from her cheek. "A romantic ballad written by half of a life-bonded couple for the other."

"Piper recorded it."

"Ah, yes. Piper's modern career. This is not a thing we had when I was young — recorded music. It was always a great privilege, to witness the performance of a master bard, whether a storyteller or songster."

"David's band is amazing live, Morgan."

"Would that I could..." But she shakes her head, rising from the chair and heading toward the door, leaving the thought unfinished. "Take care, David. You are not yet fully recovered, mind you. I know young Aurora and the healer-priestess have warned you. Take heed of their advice." And she walks out the door, shutting it behind her.

"Morgan doesn't leave Safe Harbour," Piper says. "She is too precious to us and is unused to modern ways."

"She seems quite interested in modern medicine and music."

"Yes. But we bring those things — the journals and what entertainment she likes — to her."

"Does she... Does she swim? In seal form?"

"That I could not tell you. I only know I've never seen her in seal form. As Rory said, none of us know exactly what Morgan gets up to. And what we do know is only because she wishes it."

"I like her."

"She likes you. It is a great compliment."

"So, she was kidding about you sharing me?"

Piper roars with laughter.

"Yes. She'd never approach part of a mated pair. It's just not done."

"And we're a mated pair?"

Piper's cheeks turn red, and she avoids my gaze. I pull her chin up so she's looking at me.

"I love you, Piper."

"I love you, too, David."

I claim her lips, just like I'm claiming her, whether I call her my girlfriend, my mate or...

CHAPTER 37

ALL IS FAIR

David
Two days later

I'm sitting in a chair in Steve's office, his desk between us. His expression is hostile, and there's no question what the social cue is here. He wants me to leave. Piper is down the hall, tweaking the EQ on Rhys' drum kit ahead of another planned recording session tonight.

I informed Steve that Piper would be working on the rough tracks with us, at least until Malcolm arrives to begin the formal recording process. Malcolm can decide whether he wants Steve to engineer and mix the album, but I've put my foot down about the rough tracks as we work out the arrangements and instrumentation for the songs. Piper will be the engineer on those.

It's not unheard-of for a band to bring their own engineer into a studio. Often, the producer has an engineer they prefer to work with, or the band might. And since this is just rough tracks, I'm pressing for that prerogative, for Piper. And the other guys are fully on-board, after the work she's done already on "Remember" and "Shepherd Me Home." So, Steve is not a happy camper right now.

"Steve, I recognize this is a situation you're not happy with. But we're the clients, and this is what we want. If it makes it any easier for you, I'll increase my offer to buy you out — by, say, thirty percent."

"David, you could double your offer, and I wouldn't take it. You may have the upper hand here as the client right now, but this is still my studio. Piper's days here are numbered — to exactly the number of days you're here, or until Malcolm Fisher or Siren's Song tell me she's no longer needed on the project. Then she's out on her ass, and you can do with her what you like. As long as it's not in my studio."

"Steve, you can find a job working anywhere in the country. You could even find one where Sean can continue his internship unimpeded by Piper's presence. But she's not leaving Mystic Beach, and that means I'm not inclined to leave it, either. Take my offer and find a better situation for yourself and your son. Please."

"Listen, you—"

Steve's cell phone rings, interrupting the ugly tirade I know was coming.

"I've got to take this. If you'll excuse me for a minute."

He gestures toward the hallway, and I decide to do the polite thing, as disinclined as I am from being polite to this asshole.

"Good afternoon, Marina," I hear him say as I pull the door shut behind me. "Yes. I've got you on speakerphone now."

"Is David Carter there?" I hear her ask, her voice amplified over the phone speaker.

I freeze in place, wondering why she's asking about me.

"He just left my office."

"Bring him back in. And bring Piper in as well. And if Sean's there, bring him in, too."

"Marina, I don't know what this is about, but—"

"Now, Steve. You forget just how small your slice of the studio is."

There's a moment of silence, and then the office door opens. Steve scowls to find me still so close to the door, knowing I likely heard his exchange with Marina.

"David, if you'd come back in please. And bring Piper."

"And Sean?"

He glares at me.

"Yes. I think he's out at the reception desk."

Which he is, his feet propped up on the desk, texting with someone on his phone.

"Sean, you're needed in the office." He gets up leisurely, smirking at me, like he knows something I don't. It reminds me uncomfortably of the look on Ramsay's face on that security footage as he prepared to frame me for the theft of Piper's seal coat. Is Marina about to override my demand to have Piper work on our rough tracks?

I stop to collect Piper on the way back down the hall.

"We're needed in the office, Piper."

She looks concerned, and I don't blame her. Too many lectures and threats have been delivered to her in that room. But, this time, I'm going to be there with her. We'll stand and face whatever is coming, together.

"Is everyone here now, Steve?" Marina asks, her voice no less imperious for that it's carried over a tiny speaker.

"David, Piper and Sean are all here with me, Marina."

"Good. Piper, David — have a seat."

Sean's sitting in one of the two chairs in front of Steve's desk, his legs stretched out in front of him, looking very comfortable.

"Sean, get up," Marina snaps, and we all look around the room, realizing that Marina must be watching the security video live from her office.

Sean follows her order, moving to stand next to the desk. I gesture for Piper to sit down before I take the other chair myself.

"As you may now realize, I'm utilizing the security camera in Steve's office as my eyes for this meeting, unplanned as it is," Marina says. "The video surveillance system was something I hadn't fully considered when I began looking into the recent issues at the studio. But it was brought to my attention this week that we have a large number of such cameras throughout the studio area, as well as outside."

"It's standard practice for a facility this valuable, Marina. You know that."

"I do know that, Steve. But I was curious as to how it was that David became aware of it, and just what insight it might offer into recent events involving aMUSEd's work and your interns."

Sean fidgets a little, as if he's just now realized that Marina has oversight over him, as well as Piper, and that maybe he's on the hotseat, too.

"I showed David proof from the security video that Piper was in the studio on the morning the recording drives, and aMUSEd's rough tracks with them, were removed from the control room and erased. He had questioned whether she was responsible for it. I was concerned that their... relationship... might have influenced Piper to erase the tracks. On purpose."

"No! I would never!" Piper's outrage is clear. I had hoped she'd never realize that Steve had suggested she might have acted in anger or revenge. But that ship has sailed.

"Piper, there's no need to defend yourself here," Marina assures her. "I know you didn't erase the tracks on purpose. In fact, you didn't erase them at all."

"What? Now come on, Marina — I understand you have a soft spot for Piper, likely in no small part because David's gotten so inappropriately attached to her, but she's right there on the vid—"

"Steve — shut it," she orders, and Steve's so taken aback that he does exactly as she's asked, after first picking his jaw up off the floor. I try not to smile. "Now, I want to give you the benefit of the doubt here, that you showed David a frame or two of the video that showed Piper in the control room, near the recording dock, thinking that it genuinely proved that she'd been the only possible culprit. I want to give you the benefit of the doubt about that. And maybe that's really what happened. But, if so, you were careless in your investigation, because you missed a key piece of evidence."

Steve's tablet beeps with a message.

"I've sent you another piece of surveillance footage, taken the same day, but an hour or so before Piper arrived at the studio. Please show it to Piper and David."

Piper and I stand and lean over Steve's desk to watch the video. The timestamp is the same day, the same morning, but about eighty minutes earlier than the one Steve had shown me a frame of last week. There's a hand reaching toward the recording dock, removing the drive from the bay, and it's not Piper's, but clearly that of a man. I peer more closely at it, seeing only a hoodie with the hood pulled forward, disguising the man's face. He takes another drive, writes on the label, the letter B legible even on this small screen, and puts the first drive — also labeled with a B — into the pocket of his hoodie. Then he inserts the C drive into the recording dock, leaving the A drive and the newly labeled B drive in the basket of drives to be erased.

Piper's eyes are wide as she realizes what is happening on the video.

The man in the footage turns to leave the room but fails to take into account that he's turning his face toward the security camera as he does so.

"Sean!" Steve yells in surprise, standing up from his chair, at which point we all realize that Sean has been steadily creeping toward the office door since Piper and I stood to look at the video. "What the hell have you done?"

"You wanted her gone! I was making sure you had reason to fire her that would stand up, even if she's fucking the guys in the band," Sean says, not a trace of remorse in him. "First she stole my job at the Pirate's Cove, and then she pussy-whipped David into letting her work with the band here. She had to go!"

"Steve — I take it you informed Sean the prior night that you'd realized Piper and David were involved? And that she'd been serving as engineer for David's scratch tracks?"

"Well, I wasn't happy about the lapse in professionalism, and Sean was the senior intern. If either of them was working with the band that closely, it should have been him."

"Regardless of what the client wanted?"

"It's my studio."

"And that's where you're wrong. Steve, you're going to sell me six percent from your ten percent of the business."

"Why would I do that?"

"Because I speak for the other ninety percent of the ownership, and I'm telling you it's what you're going to do, unless you'd prefer to be dealing with a lawsuit from your soon-to-be-former partners."

"Lawsuit? Marina, I understand Sean's caused a problem here, but that has nothing to do with my stake in the studio!"

"You gave him access to the studio, didn't you?"

"Well, yes. Of course. He and Piper both have access."

"But Piper didn't use that access to destroy the property of one of our biggest clients. Nor is she your son."

"So you're going to demote me down to four percent ownership, by threatening me with a lawsuit?"

"No. I'm removing you altogether from this partnership. You're going to sell your remaining four percent to David, at fair market value."

"I repeat, Marina — why would I do that? David's favoritism of Piper is entirely unprofessional."

"And your favoritism for Sean was the height of objective management?"

"You can't force me out, Marina. I have ri—"

"Steve, ask Sean what he did with the drive he stole. Ask him what he did with the tracks on it. The unreleased tracks recorded by a multi-platinum recording artist on my label."

We all turn to look at Sean again.

Now, he has the grace to look ashamed.

"What did you do?" Steve shouts at him. "Answer me, Sean! What did you do?"

"I know a guy who runs a site..."

"Oh, god..." Steve says, visibly paling and falling back into his chair.

"And he paid Sean quite handsomely for these stolen tracks, from what I understand. Isn't that right, Mr. Gryffin?"

I only now realize that she's had Gryff sitting with her this entire time, since he's undoubtedly the one who uncovered all of these revelations we've heard today.

"More than Sean makes in a year."

"Which is a pittance compared to what those tracks are worth, I should point out," Marina says. "Original studio tracks? Not even digital copies of the originals? They'd have been on every pirate site on the web and dark web within days. Fortunately, Mr. Gryffin is very good at his job, and very expedient. He recovered the stolen drive before the tracks were distributed. So, no harm done. Except, of course, that Sean will have to pay back what he was given for the property he stole."

"But I already spent—" Sean starts.

"I'd suggest you take some of the proceeds from the sale of your ten percent share of the studio and help Sean repay his 'friend,' Steve. These pirate types aren't all harmless computer geeks, are they, Mr. Gryffin?"

"No, they are not. It would be best for Sean's continued health if this one was refunded his money. With interest."

Sean swallows, loudly enough for us all to hear.

Steve closes his eyes, defeated.

"The additional six percent share will put me at fifty-one percent ownership, Steve, so I'll be making all major decisions going forward, while our other partners sort out their legal matters. And David's input as part owner will be valuable, despite his minority share. In fact, I'd like David to oversee the transition in ownership until we can have a full ownership meeting. If that's OK with you, David?"

"Uh... Sure. I can do that. But Malcolm is going to need to hire another engineer, since Steve's done here."

Steve looks a bit like a slapped mackerel. And I try not to gloat. Really, I do. But you know — those social skills... I'm well-known for lacking them...

"Malcolm has already agreed to help us hire a new manager for the studio, and he'll be helping with studio operations until we find someone to take the position going forward. As to the engineer for your album... Malcolm and I agreed that Piper is the best candidate for that job."

"What?" Piper exclaims, genuinely shocked. "You want me to engineer the whole album?"

I beam with pride in her. I knew Malcolm had been impressed with her work, but this is far more than I ever expected to come of it.

"Yes, Piper. You've earned it. Malcolm called your work 'extraordinary,' in fact. And I agree. You have quite a gift, young lady."

I nearly laugh to hear Marina call Piper a "young lady." Piper's probably six times Marina's age, and the last person I heard refer to Piper as "young" is herself 3,000 years old, so it wasn't inaccurate then. But Piper is, as she said, equivalent in maturity to her apparent age. And this is a big responsibility for her as a relatively inexperienced engineer.

"I'd even call you a prodigy," Marina adds. "So, with that in mind, I'd like to offer you the role of in-house engineer at the studio, on a permanent basis. I can't wait to hear what you can do with all the bands who come through there."

Now it's Piper looking like someone's smacked her with a fish. And I can't help myself. Professionalism be damned! I pick her up and twirl her around, giving her a kiss of congratulations.

"Enjoy the celebration, you two. You've got a lot of work cut out for you, including getting the rest of those songs written and arranged for the new album. Don't forget that, David!"

"I won't. I have a feeling I'm going to be very inspired for a while."

"Good. Inspiration is a valuable gift. Make use of it when it is given to you. Now, if you'll excuse me and Steve, we've got some technicalities to work out. I'll have my lawyers draw up the ownership transfer papers, David. And Mr. Gryffin has sent down an associate to help ensure Steve and Sean get sent off on the right foot."

Sean grabs the doorknob, appearing intent on escape, only to find a very large, very intimidating-looking man on the other side of the door.

"Sit down, Sean," Steve says wearily.

Piper and I clear the way for him and head out into the hallway, shutting the door behind us. Back in the control room, Piper emits a little squeal of excitement, and it's so cute I can't help but pick her up again, carrying her into the live room, where I shut the door behind us and kiss the daylights out of her. After a few minutes of that, I suddenly remember the other security camera, and pointing it out to Piper, I give a wave to whoever might be watching, pull Piper's legs around my hips and proceed to carry her up the stairs toward my bedroom.

"David! What are you doing! The guys will see!"

"And? Steve's gone. I'm in charge, at least until Malcolm gets here. And you're officially the engineer at this studio, with no one to answer to except Marina, Rory and me. And while I'd never take unfair advantage of that, I am definitely going to be taking *fair* advantage of it."

She laughs heartily, that comfortable understanding blooming again between us. Me and my girl.

"Guys! I'm taking my girlfriend up to my bedroom so I can make love to her for the rest of the day and night," I yell into the living room. "Put your earplugs in if you don't want to hear it, because we're celebrating!"

"Get a room!" Alex yells back.

"We've got one! Two, actually!"

Piper giggles as I carry her up the second flight of steps.

"We'll have to celebrate in *your* room tomorrow! Make sure we're doing this girlfriend/boyfriend thing properly!"

"Aren't you going to tell them why we're celebrating?" she asks, laughing.

"Later. Time is precious, and I know how I want to be spending my time right now."

I kiss her hard, before either of us can think about how precious time will be for us in the future.

CHAPTER 38

IN YOUR ROOM

Piper

I slide down David's hips until my feet hit the floor, keeping my arms wrapped around his neck.

"I love being able to call you my girlfriend," he says. "I love *being* your boyfriend," he adds, the sun filtering through the sheer drapes over the sliding glass door flashing in his pale blue eyes.

"It feels good not to have all of that hanging over us anymore," I agree.

"I'm going to show you how good you can feel," he replies, running his hands up my sides, underneath my top. His fingers slide into my bra, tweaking my nipples, before he slides around my back and unhooks the strap. He strips the top over my head and slides the shoulder straps down off my arms, leaving me bared to him. He stands back just briefly, taking me in. Then he dives into my chest, sucking one nipple into his mouth, while he fondles the other breast with his hand.

My eyes close as I let the sensations wash over me, reveling in finally being able to enjoy being with David, no threat hanging over us from either side, no fear of discovery, not even a need to be quiet as his touches heighten my arousal beyond the point of staying silent.

"Oh, gods..."

He sucks harder on my nipple, pinching the other lightly in time with the draw of his mouth. He releases them, only to lick up across both nipples, one after the other, soothing and further arousing.

He steps back again, but not to look at me. Instead, he steps away, sliding open the big glass door behind the sheer curtains, opening the room to the sea breeze. The curtains shift as the air blows through them.

"One of these days, I am going to make love to you outside, with no roof over our heads, just to show the entire world how I feel about you," he says, looking back at me as the cool breeze makes my nipples tighten, the skin of my breasts pebble with goosebumps. "I don't need anyone to see us. But I want the sea and the sky and the sand to take note, to bear witness to how much I love you, how much I love giving you pleasure, losing myself in you, body and soul."

"Oh, David... I feel... I feel the same way."

"Then one night I'm dragging you out on that deck and making you come until you beg me to stop, and then I'm going to plunge myself so deep inside you that they won't be able to tell where I end and you begin."

I shudder, pausing only a moment before I throw myself at him, my legs tight around his hips, my arms around his neck, pulling us so tightly together that I can feel him press into my slit straight through our clothes.

"Off. Now. Clothes off. All of them," he breathes urgently.

He pulls his shirt off over his head, and I grab for the waistband of his shorts, undoing them, sliding them down over the bulge already threatening to escape his underwear. His breath catches as my hand brushes over his erection, and he grabs for my waist, stripping skirt, leggings and panties off me in an instant, tossing them aside before stripping out of his boxer briefs while I watch, just as he did me after releasing me from my bra. The strong curve of him makes my mouth water, and I push him back on the bed, crawling up between his legs and taking him into my mouth.

"Suck, not blow, right?" I tease, sliding him out of my mouth before caressing him with a gentle breath. His cock jerks, and I watch his eyes roll up into his head as he struggles to maintain control.

"I'm not sure you're going to be able to for long, either, at this rate," he says, his voice a quiet growl of concentration. "I want inside you so bad, Piper."

"You can wait. I want to enjoy this, touching you with the sunlight streaming through the glass, the breeze on your skin as it moves across the spots I've made wet with my mouth."

"I bet that isn't the only part of you that's wet right now," he says. "I want my fingers inside you, stroking you, just like you're stroking me with your tongue."

I give him a calculating look and rearrange myself, placing my legs on either side of his chest while I suck his tip back into my mouth from above.

"You are just fucking amazing, Piper. Have I said that yet?" he asks. "This beautiful pussy of yours, that mouth..."

"And my engineering skills?" I ask with a smirk as I look back at him over my shoulder.

"I think you could make a man come with those alone," he says, stroking my lower lips with his callused fingertips. "But I'm the only one I want coming from your talents."

"That makes two of us."

I suck him back into my mouth, taking him deep, to the back of my throat.

He pinches my clit, and I swallow, causing him to moan. I take a deep breath, relishing his response before I lave him with my tongue along the ridge of his cock.

His fingers slide inside my warmth, brushing against that one spot, bringing my hips instinctively toward him,

"Ride my hand, Piper. Suck me and ride my hand."

I split my focus, my pussy seeking the stimulation of his fingers, driving deep inside me, while I mirror my movements around his dick, pulling hard with my mouth and circling his balls with my hand. We get a rhythm going that rivals any tango for passion and immersion in the rhythm... this rhythm that is purely us... and I feel my peak nearing, slowing my mouth's touches against his incredibly hard cock.

"I want you inside me when I come," I tell him, sliding off him and turning to kiss him, slowly, sensuously, our mouths as wet against each other as his fingers have made me.

David sits up, tweaking one of my nipples as he moves aside and pushes me down on my back. My spine arches toward him, and he sucks the other nipple into his mouth once again, biting it lightly as he sheathes himself deep within me in a single stroke. My fingers grasp his head hard against me, begging him for more, and he sucks harder, pressing his teeth against my nipple as my arousal rises once again toward a peak. He sucks in time with his strokes within me, drawing on me until I'm ready to burst with sensation.

"Come with me, David. Come inside me. Fill me up with you..."

His pace speeds up, the collision of our bodies getting rougher, the sensation of flesh slapping into flesh, the warm, sharp intensity of his draw on my breast heightening the sensation. He looks up at me and bites down harder, his icy blue stare needle-sharp with intense longing as he plunges inside me once, twice, again, harder, faster, and I keen loudly as the wave crests and breaks within me, grasping at his cock inside me, enveloping us both in bliss as he pours himself into me, body and soul.

Lying in each other's arms in David's bed, the afternoon sun casting shadows across the deck outside, I feel content. No longer caught between so many pressures from all sides, with a new life opening up before me, with so many possibilities, and David present in all of them.

"I missed this. I missed you," I tell him. "I'm sorry I couldn't tell you, couldn't find a way for us to be together that was safe. I hated hurting you like that."

"It's OK, Piper. I understand why you did it. I still wish you'd told me what was going on, so we could have faced it together. But look — it all worked out. Even better than I could have hoped. I mean, I'd talked to Marina Matthews about buying a share of the studio. I never thought she'd muscle Steve out and offer me a stake when she did it, let alone hire you as the in-house engineer."

"You really want to do this? Buy part of the studio? I mean, she's got a majority share now. You don't have to spend your money to ensure I get treated fairly, let alone get this job."

"Let me be very clear, Piper — you earned your shot. I didn't ask Marina to hire you to replace Steve, or even to engineer the entire album. I never thought that was something she'd go for. But Malcolm was so impressed with your mix that he sent it over to her, and she was so impressed... Well, you see how impressed she was. I did tell her I felt you weren't being treated fairly, or employed to the best of your abilities. But that's it. The rest... that was all her."

"Or Brighid."

"What do you mean, 'Or Brighid'?"

"Your friend Brighid. Hunter's mate. She said she'd make a plea to her goddess on my behalf, for fairness."

"And you think it worked, that this was divine intervention?"

"I'm not sure how else to credit all of the amazing things that happened today. Sean got caught, I got vindicated and Steve is no longer in a position where he can prevent me from doing my best work, or keep us from being together."

David looks thoughtful.

"Hunter's broken hand did get healed basically overnight. And Brighid pulled me back from the brink, even after your healers did their best... Maybe there is something to this goddess thing," he says.

"I've seen a lot of things you wouldn't believe, David. I know what magic is, what the gods can do if they wish to intervene. I think we've been blessed."

"Well, I know I have been. Just having you in my life is a blessing. All the rest of this — just icing on the cake."

"So, now you're going to own part of this studio."

"I am. I wanted something here in Mystic Beach that was mine. A foothold, setting down some roots here."

The look he gives me is meaningful.

"You want to come back here after the album's done?"

"I want to stay here, with you, for the rest of my days," he says, taking my face between his hands and looking deep into my eyes.

I ignore the longer-term implication of him spending the rest of his days, limited as they are.

"You have the tour. And your life in New York."

"First thing tomorrow, I'm calling my landlord to cancel my lease. I'll start looking for a place here — for us — right after that. That is... if that's what you want. Us being together here, I mean."

"And the tour?"

"I've been thinking about maybe taking it easier for a while. Maybe seeing if the guys can find someone to tour with them. Instead of me."

I'm touched. And horrified.

"No! You can't quit the band! Not to stay here with me!"

"What if that's what I want? I'd already been thinking about maybe retiring down here, doing some work in marine science. This would just be moving that plan ahead a couple decades."

"But your music, David! You love music."

"And I can still do music. I'm going to own part of a recording studio, after all. The guys can come here to write and record, and I'll do our albums. They can just find someone else to go on the road with them."

"They're going to hate me, David. For tearing the band apart. Your fans will hate me."

"I don't care what anyone else thinks. That may be one of the first times I've ever said that, but I mean it. Besides, they won't hate you — they'll see that we're in love, and they'll be happy for us."

"Maybe... But — I can't ask you to do that David, not for me."

"You didn't ask. It's what I want. I want to spend my life with you."

"I want that, too." But I leave the rest of my thought unsaid. That the rest of my life can't be spent with him, because I could literally live forever, and he is, as much as we'd both like to pretend otherwise, very much mortal. In a hundred years, he'll be gone, and I'll likely be here, alone.

Desperation erupts in my mind, and I crush my body to his, wanting to meld us together so we'll never have to be apart again. Is this what it's like to be life-bonded, as Rory called it? The sadness that percolates beneath her practical surface, the anguish of Declan's call to his fleeing mate... If David and I are truly tied together at a level beyond the physical, how much worse will that pain be for me when David is gone? Assuming I even survive that loss in the first place.

CHAPTER 39

LIGHTNING CRASHES

Piper

There's a light tapping on the glass of the sliding door behind me, and I turn slowly over, careful not to wake David. The light rain that started up a few hours ago has become a downpour, a classic summer thunderstorm here on the Delaware coast. Lightning flashes across the sky, silhouetting a figure against the glass. I hop up out of the bed, ignoring my nakedness, because I recognize that figure, and being unclothed is the least of my worries upon seeing it here.

I unlock the door and slip outside, into the pouring rain, pulling it closed gently behind me.

"Angharad! What are you doing here, outside Safe Harbour and out in a storm like this?"

Her healer's robes are drenched, loose strands of her blonde hair plastered to her forehead as the long braids drip rain back onto the deck in front of her, in a spot I know is farther from Safe Harbour than she has been at any moment since she and her sister arrived here with Morgan.

"I'm so sorry, Piper!" she cries, nearly hysterical. "I should never have agreed to do it. I should have warned you, gone to Aurora, the Council... But then it all worked out, and he was gone, and we were safe. I thought we were safe, finally!"

I grab her by the shoulders and shake her hard, aiming to break through the burgeoning hysteria.

"Angharad!" Her eyes go wide, as if she's just now realized where she is. "What is wrong? What is going on?"

"It's Ramsay, Piper." She's close to hyperventilating. "He had my coat, Piper. He said he'd burn it to ashes if I didn't help him! And if he had mine, I knew he could get to Aeronwen's, too. I couldn't let him harm her. Even if I could have survived him destroying my coat, I couldn't let him take that from her. She spends far more time in seal form than I do. She spends hours in the sea every day. She has since we were younglings. It would have killed her to lose her coat. So, I... I did what he asked."

What Ramsay did to me and to David is terrifying enough. But his threat to Angharad... No wonder she was so relieved that he was facing banishment.

"What did he ask you to do? Did you do it?"

She bites her lower lip, reluctance to admit whatever infraction she's committed under his threat radiating from her.

"Angharad!" I shake her again. "What did you do?"

"I took your coat. He demanded that I go in your rooms, find your coat and give it to him. I'd never... Piper — I'd never willingly harm you, but he promised you'd get it back soon, swore he wanted to make you his wife and would never harm a hair on your head nor your coat, but that he needed to get you to see he had your best interests in mind."

I look at her with skepticism. How could she possibly have thought Ramsay would ever have anyone's best interests in mind, other than his own? But then I recall that Angharad, much like Morgan, had rarely left the confines of the village where she and her sister lived, until they came to Safe Harbour, and even now... The deference shown to the healers among her clan is absolute. No one would have thought to have offered either of them insult, let alone threatened them. This threat from Ramsay was unprecedented for her.

"And then I saw that he had given it back to you, that day when your mate... your human mate... was nearly drowned. And I knew he'd fulfilled his promise where you were concerned. He'd made sure you got your coat back! I nearly confessed to you that day, but I decided mayhap it had all turned out for the best — you were back with your mate, you had your coat and Ramsay was banished! I thought it was all over, that we were all safe."

I take a deep breath. She's right that it all seems to have turned out for the best in the end. Lightning flashes again, followed by a crack of thunder that makes us both jump.

"Why are you here now, Angharad? Why did you come to find me here, outside Safe Harbour, in the middle of a storm, if you'd already decided not to confess what you'd done?"

"Ramsay's back, Piper! He's back here now!"

I'm not sure how this can even have come to pass, especially when Rory ensured he got on the boat tasked with taking him far from these shores, back to his clan.

"And... and..." she sniffles, her hysteria ramping up again in a way that kicks my anxiety over the top and straight into dread. "He has that sword. And Aeronwen had gone for her swim before the storm rolled in... He said he'd kill her, Piper! Not just destroy her coat, but 'slit her from crotch to throat,' do horrible things to her... And I... You'd left your coat back in your room again, and I still had access, even though Ramsay can no longer get inside Safe Harbour. So I gave him your coat! Again! And... gods... I'm so sorry, but he let Aeronwen go back inside, safe, when I handed it over to him."

Nausea overwhelms me, and I bend over, lightheaded, dragging air into my lungs, trying to think.

"What did he say, Angharad?" I demand when I can finally see straight again. "He had to have given you a message for me. What did he say?"

"He said if you wanted your coat back, you'd meet him, alone, at that abandoned tower to the north of here. He said if he scented even a whiff of human — your mate or Aurora — that he'd burn your coat to ashes and kill whoever was with you. And if you aren't there by midnight, he'll just burn your coat and come after your mate directly."

I have no doubt Ramsay means to deliver on that threat. David and I have already cost him everything he might have had here. Rory saw to his banishment. And now this is a fight I have to fight on my own. It is a threat I must end myself. Alone.

I send Angharad back to Safe Harbour and her sister, swearing her to silence on all that she has told me. I race back to my rooms, digging deep into my closet for clothing I haven't worn since before Rónan's death — thick pants and a vest of heavy leather, studded with pieces of iron and lined with light steel chain. I lay it out on my bed, looking nervously at the clock, watching the time I have tick away.

I take a deep breath and, wearing my robe, tread quietly down the hall to Rónan's rooms, letting myself in without knocking and peeking carefully into the bedroom, just in case Rory is here. It's early yet, and if she's at Safe Harbour at all, she's likely in Rónan's office. But what I need is here, in his rooms, in a secret cache at the back of his closet. I rub my thumb against his ring as I reach for the panel that will release the door, stepping inside and taking a moment to marvel at what he managed to collect here for our defense.

The walls are lined with swords, long and short, heavy broadswords and feather-light sabers. A cupboard holds daggers of various lengths and styles, some meant for dual-wielding in both hands or in conjunction with a sword. Maces, battle axes and iron-tipped spears fill another cupboard, while a small collection of firearms is stored in a drawer, with a second drawer beneath, full of silver, steel and iron-coated ammunition.

Rónan made sure I knew how to fire these modern weapons, but my experience is with the modest longsword my mother insisted I be trained to use, so I could defend myself when all else failed. And that's the weapon I reach for now, pulling the slightly downscaled longsword and its sheath from its spot on the wall, where it has rested since the last time I needed to take up arms in defense of my home and my family.

I had hoped to avoid this, knowing that I am no match for Ramsay, with my scaled-down sword against the massive longsword I saw that day in his room. But I am the daughter of Gillebride MacGilleMhoir, clan chief, and foster-sister of Rónan MacMurchadha, savior of Safe Harbour, and I will not allow the threat of Ramsay to continue to loom over my people. Banishment has not been enough to vanquish him, but he will get no quarter from me now that he is declared without honor and without man-price.

I want my coat back, but even more than that, I want David safe, and Rory, and all of Safe Harbour. And if I must spend my life in ensuring that, I will do so.

David

The crack of thunder is so loud, so close, that I sit bolt upright, half expecting to see the pine trees in front of the deck on fire from a lightning strike. They're not, but the lightning flashes again, striking farther away but lighting up the sky so thoroughly that I can see the individual raindrops pouring down. And the empty expanse of mattress next to me, where Piper should be.

Piper.

I feel uneasy with her not here. Is that what life would be like if I went back out on the road without her? Always feeling something was amiss, that there was something looming over us? Maybe it's the opposite side of the comfortable joy and warmth I feel when she's nearby. Or...

Tension-concern-resolve.

That's not me. Those aren't my feelings. At least I don't think so. But I am feeling them. Is this what it was like for Piper when I was fighting for my life just a few days ago?

I jump out of bed, rushing down the hall to make sure she's not in the bathroom.

"Uh... Dave? Why are you standing in the hall? Naked?" Rhys has just reached the top of the stairs and is staring at me.

"Eyes up here, Rhys!" I tell him, reaching into the unoccupied bathroom for a towel, which I wrap around me.

"Where's your girlfriend? I'd have thought if you were running around naked you'd have her with you..."

I can't decide if he's implying he's looking forward to seeing Piper naked or if he's just confused that she's not with me, since they know the two of us came up here together. I shake my head, because the question is the right one. Where is my girlfriend?

"I don't know. I'm looking for her."

"Did she dump you already? That sucks, man. She's awfully small, but she's really cute, and a hell of an engineer. If things don't work out with my dream-girl, do you think I could..."

"No."

"But if she dumped you..."

"No, Rhys. She hasn't dumped me, and no, you can't date her even if she did. She's mine."

He nods amicably.

I turn and head back into my bedroom, dropping the towel and throwing on the first thing that comes to my hand — cargo shorts and an old Fixx fan-club T-shirt given to me years ago by an aMUSEd fan who shared my love of the band. I'm sliding on my flip-flops when someone starts banging on the sliding door.

"Piper! I was just coming to look—"

It's not Piper. It's Rory.

"She's not here with you, is she?" she asks hurriedly, her blonde hair dripping with rain and near-panic obvious in her voice and expression.

"No. I just woke up and she was gone. I was going to come over to Safe Harbour to look for her."

"She's not there. And I'm afraid I know exactly where she's gone."

"Where?"

"To confront Ramsay."

"Ramsay? The guy who was on a boat for some island in the middle of the North Atlantic?"

"Yeah. Apparently, getting onto a boat doesn't guarantee a selkie stays on that boat. Especially when he feels he's got unfinished business back here."

"OK — what's going on? Is Piper OK?"

"I'm going to say she's probably not. Or at least she won't be OK for long, if we don't get moving. Can you use a gun, David?"

"A gun? Why..." I shake my head. The answer is obvious. "No, I've never even held a gun."

"Here — ten-second lesson. Two hands, like this," she says, pressing a small handgun into my palm and showing me how to grip it. "Safety on, safety off. Keep your finger off the trigger until you're ready to shoot. Most important: Never point it at anything you don't want to destroy or kill. Press the trigger, don't jerk on it."

"O...K... I'm not sure this is a good idea, me with a gun."

"Would you prefer a sword? A dagger?"

"Actually? Yes."

She grabs the large backpack behind her, withdrawing a dagger longer than my forearm.

"Buckle up, boy wonder — we're going hunting for a psychopath."

CHAPTER 40

UPRISING

Piper

The rain has seeped below the edges of my leather armor, into the layer of comfortable cotton beneath. It's making this trudge down the beach even more challenging, and I'm suddenly glad all the work carrying heavy equipment around the deck at the Pirate's Cove has helped me build up muscle and endurance well beyond what my nightly swims could do.

The rest... well, there were weeks of training with Rónan, but that's been nearly a year ago. I'm no longer at the peak of my form. But I can do this. Or so I keep telling myself. I look down at my watch — it's nearly midnight, but I'm nearly to the World War II tower that's just a short distance to the north of Safe Harbour.

Lightning flashes again, and I can see the tower silhouetted against the sky. When the light fades, I see a bright spot inside the silhouette — not a flashlight or lantern, but what's clearly a fire, dancing as the storm winds blow through the open window port on the tower. Ramsay. Perhaps preparing to toss my coat onto that fire, knowing the horror that would pose for me. But not nearly the horror of losing David. I suspect Rory was right to be concerned that I would follow him to the Summerlands should Ramsay take his life.

I have no choice now but to defend my mate, with my life, because losing him might well cost me my own, and if it didn't, I'm not sure it would be worth living.

I climb up toward the top of the tower, doing my best to stay silent, my hand resting lightly on the sword's grip at the top of the sheath strapped to my back.

"Looking extra-yummy, Piper," Ramsay drawls as I finish the climb, licking his lips to emphasize the point.

He's crouched down on the other side of the fire he's built up here, my seal coat in his hand, and his sword laid out across his lap.

"So glad you could join me. I'd have hated to have burned your coat without you here to witness it. Or me being able to witness you watch it turn to ash. I'm going to enjoy that, savor the look on your face as your days as a seal come to a final, crushing end. Just as you ended my carefully laid plans for Safe Harbour."

"What plans were those, Ramsay?" I ask, starting to circle the fire in the center of the room as he stands, sword and seal coat each in one hand, mirroring my movements. "No one was ever going to let you assume Rónan's place as our leader. You were dreaming if you thought they would. You're without honor, without redeeming value to anyone in that community, and now you're officially anathema here. You should have stayed on the boat and found a deserted island along the way, where you wouldn't cause trouble for anyone else."

"Stewart and Wylie were too weak, too cowardly to join me, but I wasn't going to leave here without getting my revenge, Piper. On you and your mate. And once I've dealt with you, he's next on my list, your *human*."

"You will not touch him. Not while I live."

"That's exactly what I had in mind," he says, lunging at me lazily, sword in one hand and still holding my coat in the other.

He's playing with me. That's clear. The question is why.

"Why me, Ramsay? Why are you so fixated on me, so determined to have me? You could have found a mate among your own clan, built a life with your own kind. Why pursue me, a harbor-seal selkie, when you could strengthen your own clan by building an alliance there?"

Ramsay grimaces at me.

"The females remaining among my clan are all weak, low of status. Too many of our females were killed during recent battles. And I needed a mate who was worthy of my status. You were promised to me, Piper NicGilleMhoir. With you, I could have restored my clan's status, built an empire reaching even to these shores, once your foster-brother was destroyed. And if he hadn't been killed as he was, I would have ensured he died soon enough, leaving me as the heir apparent, husband of his cherished foster-sister. But then that human whore of his had to step in, usurping a role that was never hers to claim. She'll find that out tonight, too, after I take care of that human pet of yours."

I strike out at Ramsay, unable to contain my anger at this threat to Rory and to David. I narrowly miss slicing his midsection open, as he dodges my blade by twisting aside. He doesn't bother to raise his blade in defense, and that's both troubling and promising. He doesn't consider me enough of a threat to make a sincere effort at defending himself, expecting I will be easy to defeat when he's done toying with me.

For all that he appears to genuinely consider my father and Rónan to have been strong leaders, he underestimates what they taught me of swordsmanship. I am not one of the subjugated females of his clan. I am not only trained but experienced in battle. I may quail at the idea of pressing a local cover band to better their stage setup, but I will run him through without hesitation if he gives me an opening.

I make three more runs at him, each time pushing Ramsay closer to actually defending himself in earnest. He is learning quickly that I am a force to be reckoned with, despite my size. But at this rate, I'll wear myself out before I can get a real chance at shedding his blood and ending his miserable life.

"Come on, Ramsay. I weary of this dance. Here you are, this warrior among your people, and you can't even disarm a young girl nearly a foot shorter than you? Your ancestors would be ashamed."

The taunt works, and Ramsay drops my coat to take his sword in both hands, taking aim at my head and striking downward. I dive under his arm, making a grab for my coat as I do. But he sees the move coming and smashes a knee into my diaphragm, driving the breath from me, and my hand closes on empty air inches from my target.

"You wanted this, Piper?" he asks, brandishing my coat just out of my reach. "Well, one thing we agree on — I weary of this dance. It's time to end this so I can take care of your humans and move my plans forward, unimpeded."

And he tosses my coat onto the fire.

David

I feel ridiculous, racing down the beach, barefoot, behind a Rory who — in her black-on-black outfit of leather pants and tank top — looks more like a spy, or at least a cat burglar, than she does the curvy reporter dressed for Casual Tuesday that I first met. I ask myself what she, what Piper, has been through in the last year that she seems so comfortable in this role of armed rescuer. The long dagger strapped on my back doesn't make me feel any less ridiculous in comparison. I'm a bass player, not a knight or an action hero.

But Piper's in danger, and I swore I'd be her guardian angel. And if that means acting like a gender-swapped Lara Croft before I fall on my ass, so be it. I'll throw myself on my own blade if need be, but it's more likely I'll end the night spitted on Ramsay's. As long as Piper lives, I can accept that. It seems like the guys will have to find another bass player, after all.

"Stop being self-defeatist, David," Rory says, panting hard as she comes to a stop on the beach ahead of me. "Your need to defend Piper is your strongest weapon. Your selfless love for her is what will ensure our success. Know that. Rónan would not let her be harmed if he were here, and I will not either. Between the two of us, we can assure her safety. Never doubt that."

She's read my emotional state so accurately that I know she's got to be doing her empath thing. I am kind of glad that isn't something I have to deal with. Those few moments of feeling Piper's emotions when I first woke up tonight were intense. I'd hate to think what it would be like if I was feeling everyone's emotions when they were around me.

"Don't feel sorry for me, David. You learn to deal with it, filter it out. That may be something that you and Piper will find useful. But first we have to save her, make sure Ramsay is no longer a threat. Remind me to start a treadmill routine if we survive this."

She takes off again for a short distance before she angles up the beach, approaching one of the old World War II artillery towers. As she looks up toward the top of the tower, I see the flickering of flame from inside. Rory gives a glance back at me.

"Ready? We're going to have to come at him together. Just stay close to me. Don't get between us. I don't want to accidentally shoot you instead of him. But if you get an opening, stab — don't slash. Aim for the vital organs. They may be immortal, but disemboweling him is still likely to prove fatal."

I blink in disbelief that I'm getting ready to engage in a fight with an immortal creature of legend, armed with a really big-ass knife. And then I picture Ramsay looming over Piper, threatening her with the same fate Rory would clearly like me to hand him, and I'm fully prepared to stab and hack his treacherous ass into small pieces that I can then feed to the seagulls.

I nod back at Rory, and she takes off into the tower. I make it one step before I'm blinded with pain, my skin feeling like it's on fire, and I drop to my knees in the sand, collapsing into unconsciousness.

CHAPTER 41

LONELY AS A LIGHTHOUSE

Piper

"Get away from her, Ramsay!"

Confusion reigns as I open my eyes to find Rory, her hair flattened to her head with rain, standing several feet away, clad in black, pointing a gun at Ramsay, who looms over me from behind.

"Ah! The healer cracked, and did her job as expected — even if she didn't realize she was still doing my bidding!" Ramsay says with a satisfied laugh. "Perfect timing, Pretender Aurora! Now Piper can watch as I destroy her foster-brother's human lover, knowing I'll be doing the same to her own. It's a shame I don't have time for a little fun before I put an end to you, but I've got big plans, you see. Plans that will be made all the easier once you're out of the way."

"I said, get away from her, Ramsay," Rory repeats, her tone deadly.

"I've already destroyed her coat, 'Rory,'" he says mockingly. "She's barely even a selkie anymore. Are you sure you wouldn't rather I put her out of her misery?"

My coat?

Memory flashes horror into my mind, as I see my coat laying atop the flames of the fire Ramsay had built in the center of the tower, smoldering and then... Blackness. And now that feeling creeps over me again, that claustrophobic terror when I couldn't find my coat. Only now, that fear is a relentless reality. I push up onto my hands, crawling toward the fire, no conscious intent, just knowing that the thing I need more than oxygen is in that fire.

"Piper, get away from there!" Rory shouts.

Ramsay howls with laughter.

"See — she's ready to throw herself on the pyre with the ashes of her seal form. Killing her would be a mercy, you know. You really should consider that before you decide which of us to use that weapon on. It could be that she'd prefer you ended her even before you put me in your sights."

My mind howls with pain — not the burning pain of the fire that I felt as it consumed my seal coat, but the existential pain of unmeasurable loss. Irretrievable loss. Is this the pain Rory has felt every day since Rónan died? Is this what I will feel when David's life ends?

And that's the thought that pushes me to full awareness. David. If Rory... if Rory and I don't destroy Ramsay right now, for good, he will kill David.

"Piper, come over here, behind me," Rory urges, keeping her tone calm. "Circle around the fire and come to me."

I stare into the fire, finally understanding that my seal coat is gone — ashes. There's no coming back from this. I sit up, kneeling, my hands in my lap. One deep breath. Another. I look over at Rory, taking in her concerned glance as she tries to keep Ramsay in her sights.

I turn to look at him over my shoulder, watching him edge closer toward her, sword ready, as if he expects to stop a bullet with the blade. I can tell him it won't work. I saw so many die a year ago, on both sides, trying to face modern human weapons with only swords, daggers and spears in their hands. But he wasn't here yet. He won't know that. He'll charge recklessly at Rory, thinking he's fast enough to overtake her before she can fire.

My thumb goes to rub against Rónan's ring, the cool metal reassuring, reminding me of him, and his strength, his determination, his love for her, his self-sacrifice. Rónan didn't teach her to shoot. That's another one of her useful story assignments coming into play. I'd have paid to watch the two of them in a quick-draw contest, assuming they weren't actually shooting live ammunition. They were both deadly with a handgun, especially once Rory got past the idea that even an empath might have to kill in cold blood. To defend herself and our people. To the death.

And as Ramsay falls into the trap of his own arrogance, charging at Rory, I leap to my feet, slamming into him once again with everything I have, and then some, knocking him from his feet toward the wall of the tower. Only there's no wall there. Just window. And he goes tumbling out into space, grabbing hold of my wrist as he realizes he's falling, clinging for dear life, and pulling me out the window after him.

David

There's a thump nearby, and my brain struggles to make sense of the noise. Is Rhys sound-checking his kick drum again? Did Hunt find another reason to punch the house? My eyes crack open, and I realize I'm lying on my side on packed sand, surrounded by dune grasses, a wall of concrete the only other thing I can see. I sit up gingerly, my head screaming with the worst headache I've ever had. Nausea rushes over me in a wave, and I pant with the exertion of trying to keep it under control, trying to stay upright, breaking out in a sweat.

I push to my feet, wondering why it feels like I've got my bass strapped to me but there's no bass there. I brush my hand across my chest, finding a leather strap that I trace back over my shoulder until my hand hits metal, and my brain suddenly puts together the pieces. I have a big-assed knife strapped to my back. Why...

Piper! But there's a gaping void in my chest where my heart used to be, like some horror movie where the monster just reaches through the person's ribcage and yanks their beating heart out and shows it to them. I look down, expecting to see a bloody mess and a cavernous opening, but no — just that old

Fixx T-shirt. It doesn't make the pain go away. I stumble forward toward the wall, tripping over something as I do.

I look down to see a brown leather boot, attached to a leg clad in heavy leather, and my eyes follow the shape. But there's something wrong. There's too many limbs. Some long and heavy and others shorter and smaller, and my brain struggles to make sense of what it's seeing, until I see the dark brown hair and the soft lips and the sweet, feisty pixie face of the woman I love, lying with her limbs entangled with those of the man from that security video. Ramsay!

But she's not moving. Piper's not moving. Piper's not moving!

I fall to my knees again, my fingers brushing over her cheeks, so pale... and...

And now there's movement. But it's not Piper. It's Ramsay, pulling free of Piper's body, pushing her off of him, grabbing for something shiny near his outstretched hand. A sword. I don't have a sword, but I have a big-ass dagger. And my fingers grab hold of the dagger, drawing it from the sheath, knowing I will end this man, this supposedly immortal creature, so that he will be as pale and still as my Piper is now, because he has done this to her. He's taken her from me, from this life. And I will take his life in exchange. It's not a fair exchange, but it is a just one.

I lunge at him with the blade, and he scrambles up, sword in hand, only just brushing aside my strike at his heart. He takes a moment to look at me, take in what he's seeing before him, and he sees death in my eyes — his death. And he does the only smart thing he's probably done in his entire long, miserable life — he runs.

And I take off after him, my bare feet offering the advantage over his booted ones as we race over the loose sand toward the water.

"David! Stop!" I hear Rory yell from behind me, but it's of no consequence to me now. The only things that exist in my world now are Ramsay's back and the knife in my hand. He's taller — his legs, his strides longer. And maybe he spends a lot of time in the water. Maybe he swam a good distance when he jumped off that boat mid-route. But I spend hours working my ass off on stage every night, and I surf and paddleboard and skimboard, and I'm running not for my life but to avenge Piper's. And every stride I take, I gain on Ramsay, until we're at the edge of the water, and I throw myself at him with a roar.

He turns, his face etched with horror as the knife comes at his heart. He drops the sword, grabbing for my hands, the hilt of the knife, whatever he can grab to keep the sharp blade at bay. And my weight — all the solid muscles of my arms, honed with so many thousands of hours with my bass, my shoulders strengthened by so much paddling, my legs strong from swimming and surfing and keeping time with my feet for hours on end, night after night — my weight hits him hard in the chest, sending him over backward into the breaking waves.

Ramsay uses the buoyancy of the water to lever my arms and the knife away from him, continuing to scramble backward into the water, trying to dislodge me from him as I press the blade back toward him. The water pulls me sideways as the wave recedes, and I lose my footing. But I keep hold of the dagger, diving instinctively toward Ramsay as he pushes through the breakers and out into the swell.

It's pitch black above and below the water, and I'm operating purely on instinct. Ramsay's selkie instincts should give him an advantage here, but he doesn't have his seal coat with him, and his advantage is limited. He also just fell forty feet to the ground. The fall may have killed Piper — I can't let my mind absorb that, not yet — but immortal or otherwise, he has to have some internal injuries. He wouldn't be alive himself if he was human, and I suspect it's adrenaline that's fueled his attempt to escape me.

And I'm not just any ocean-loving surfer. I've been trained by a Navy SEAL. Maybe not for combat in the water, but to dive deep, swim to the edge of my limits and hold my breath long past when the average human would drown. And if that's what it takes to put an end to this plague on Safe Harbour, this murderer of the love of my life, so be it.

And that's my last rational thought as Ramsay comes at me from under the water and tries, again, to drown me. My body goes into survival mode. It's him or me now, and I'm the one with the weapon. I lose track of how long I've been holding my breath, my focus solely on planting this blade in his vital organs, just like Rory said. He kicks at me, scratches at my arms, even tries to bite me, but none of it stops me. I angle the blade toward his heart and push it... forward, forward, forward, until it hits bone and lodges in his chest.

Ramsay's eyes go wide, and he puts up one last bit of struggle, cracking me in the skull with his elbow as he tries to twist free. The last thing I see as my vision goes dim is Ramsay's lifeless body floating away from me.

CHAPTER 42

OUTSIDE

Piper

"**P**iper! Piper! Wake up! Tell me you're OK. Tell me Ramsay isn't the only one who walks away from that fall!"

My eyes blink open, and I try to roll over, off my back, but... Ow. My entire body aches.

"Oh, thank god!" Rory says with a sigh. "Can you move? Can you stand up? Walk? We've got to go find David."

"David?"

"He took off after Ramsay. I'm pretty sure he planned to kill him, because it sure looked like you were dead there for a minute."

"David's chasing Ramsay?"

"With that big-ass dagger your brother insisted I carry on me last year."

"Help me up!"

She pulls me up to standing, staring at me like she's seen a ghost.

"Are you supposed to be able to walk away from a forty-foot fall?"

"It's been known to happen. Our bodies go through a lot with the transformations. They can take a lot of trauma, as long as our vital organs aren't compromised. I think Ramsay cushioned my landing, though."

"Good. Maybe he's got some internal injuries and will die from those before David gets to him."

"No — David's going to kill him." I know that as surely as I know my own name. "He wants to kill him. Nothing's going to stop him. Oh, gods, Rory! Nothing's going to stop him! He'll get himself killed trying to kill Ramsay, because he thinks I'm dead."

"Then let's go find him before he does that. The getting himself killed part. He can kill Ramsay all he wants."

I lean on her, my body still recovering from the fall, but I'm determined to find him, to find David and keep him safe. After all we've been through, he can't die like this. I'm really not sure he won't take me with him, and I don't even want to consider life without him. So, he has to live.

Rory and I get to the water, but there's no sign of anyone. Not Ramsay and not David.

And twice in one night, I've lost something that means the world to me. And it's only then that I remember what the other thing was.

Two hours later

"**S**he's just sitting there. She doesn't respond when I talk to her. She won't eat or drink anything. She won't even let me put some dry clothes on her."

None of that is untrue, though I'm fully conscious of Rory talking about me to Morgan like I'm not even in the room.

"It's shock. Frankly, I'm surprised she's alive at all. She's the only selkie I've seen in a millennium who survived the destruction of her seal skin," Morgan replies. "It happens so rarely. But it's usually too much of a trauma for them to survive, and the ones who last even a few days afterward... They preferred not to have."

"No. That is not going to happen. I promised Rónan I'd take care of her, no matter what. There's got to be some way to fix this."

"There might be some hope of getting her through this, but if, as you say, she's also lost her bonded mate..." Morgan's voice trails off, but my semi-conscious mind screams with pain even beyond the existential torment over the loss of my seal coat.

"We looked for him... for any sign of him... for... his body..." she whispers, thinking I can't hear her say it, "for more than an hour. I finally had to get her back here to treat this..." Rory throws her hands up.

"Send out everyone you can safely put out on the beach, in the water," Morgan suggests, though her tone does more than suggest. "David risked his life to save her, to ensure Ramsay was no longer a threat to Safe Harbour. Tell them that. They'll look for him, even if he is human."

"I'll gather everyone I can. But I can't leave her here like this..."

"Call the priestess. Bring her here. If we find him, we may need her."

"I can't bring Brighid in here, with us not knowing if David is... if he's still alive. He's a friend of hers. She's going to want to tell his brother, his bandmates. They'll bring in police, search-and-rescue, the Coast Guard, and then we've got a dangerous mess that we can't control."

"Bring her in without telling her why. Just that her help is needed, urgently. We can contain her once she's here."

"Fine. But she's a friend of mine as well, and I don't like doing this to her."

"She'll forgive you if we find the bard and bring him back to them. And I fear we may not be able to do that without her help. And she can stay with Piper while you organize the search. Meanwhile, I need to talk to Aoife."

"What? What can Aoife do here?"

"Offer me some ideas of how we might ensure Piper survives."

Survive? Do I want to survive this, if I can't truly live? No seal coat, no David... I...

"Sleep, Piper," Morgan says, touching her hand to my forehead, and the world fades away.

"**W**as she injured?"

"I sent her into unconsciousness as a precaution. It was a long fall, but her body seems to be mending on its own. Her spirit..." Morgan's voice again, trailing off. "The loss of her coat is bad enough, but her bonded mate... the bard..."

"What's happened to David?"

"We're not entirely sure yet. Aurora is leading the search."

"Oh, gods... I've got to get out there, help them. Get his brother, Hunter, the guys... the police..."

"You can't, dear. I'm afraid we can't let you."

"You can't *let* me? Am I a prisoner here now? Do you hold no tradition of guest-right among your peoples?"

That makes me smile. Morgan should know better than to tangle with a priestess of Brighid, let alone one who's a friend of Rory's.

Morgan sputters. I'm not sure I've ever heard her make that sound before.

"We do, priestess, as I'm sure you know. But we've had to adapt to circumstances since we've come here, and present circumstances require that you, too, adapt. By staying here, I'm afraid."

"Just tell me he's not in the water. Not so soon after nearly drowning already. I warned him, warned them both..."

"We won't know until he is found. In the meantime, my concern is over Piper. If we are to save her..."

"What can I do? Tell me — I might as well be useful while I am here."

"I consulted our historian, to see if she'd heard of any cases where a selkie survived the destruction of her coat. I know of a precious few, but I don't know the circumstances, so I have no knowledge of how it was done, or if it was just pure will that kept them alive."

"And what did Aoife say?"

"She didn't have any answers. She said a number of things had been tried — even some too dark to consider now... The murder of one selkie to steal their coat as a replacement for another's."

"So this... this Ramsay — if we were to find his coat? Could Piper use it?"

"Doubtful. If he is already dead... The magic of the coat dies with the owner."

"So that murder?"

"Slow and torturous. And it did not work in the end."

"What else has been tried?"

"She'd heard tell of people — humans — trying to become selkies by burning their coats and drinking the ashes."

"Did it work?"

"They died. The ashes acted like a poison."

"What about selkies? Is it poisonous to them?"

"No, but I can tell you from the amount of seal-coat hair that many of us manage to inhale or swallow over the years, between our own coats and those of our mates and pups... it just passes through our systems."

"So drinking or eating something with the ashes of her coat in it wouldn't do any good."

"No."

"Did you collect any of the ashes, just in case?"

"There was no reason to, and we've been occupied with other things since she and Aurora returned."

"Of course. But I can go get them now, if it might prove useful."

"I can't let you leave."

"Not even if I give my word I won't say anything about David?" Morgan hesitates.

"Your sworn word as a priestess?"

"Yes."

"Go. Come straight back. We may need your gifts if we find him."

"T his is not at all what we agreed to, priestess." Morgan's tone is hushed but irritated.

"I gave my word I wouldn't say anything about David. I didn't say I wouldn't talk to anyone about this. About Piper."

"And you think this friend of yours can help? This Siobhan?"

"I do. I was thinking about what you said about humans and the ashes of a selkie coat, and that while they're poisonous to humans, they are not to selkies."

"Yes. But the selkie digestive system doesn't absorb anything from our coats."

"Exactly! What if we were to inject the ashes into her body?"

"She wouldn't gain anything from putting them into her blood, any more than from eating or drinking them, since she's already a selkie."

"I don't mean inject them into her blood — under the skin. A tattoo lasts a lifetime. Some of the ink gets absorbed, but most of it remains, just under the skin, part of the person forever. Even modern removal methods don't remove every trace of it."

"And your friend can do this — tattoo with ashes?"

"She can and she has. It's not common, but some people do get memorial tattoos using the ashes of their loved ones, incorporated into the ink. I think if we have her tattoo Piper using the ashes of her own coat... It's worth a try, isn't it? I mean, if you're right, and she's unlikely to survive without her ability to transform, don't we owe it to her to at least try it? Siobhan's waiting for us at the shop."

There's a long pause.

"We can trust your friend?"

"You have my word."

"Which you neatly worked around in telling her in the first place."

"I want to try," I finally say.

"Piper! Are you OK?"

"I am not, as I think we all know. But since you won't let me help look for David, I would like to try Brighid's idea. I've seen her friend's work. She does more than ordinary tattoos."

"What do you mean, Piper?" Morgan asks.

"Magic. Her tattoos are magic."

"What's this?" Morgan asks.

"Siobhan is... special. She has a gift with ink, with the intersection of art and music. She can engrave a song into someone's skin, and it becomes part of them."

"Tell her about Hunter's tattoo." I don't know all of what happened, but I know that tattoo is magic.

"My fiancé, he'd broken his hand. We tried a healing, but it didn't work. Something was missing, another step. Siobhan tattooed his hand with a Brighid's cross, while he sang her a song... our song, about our past life together, centuries ago. And his hand was healed."

"Potent magic. A commitment to you, and your goddess, and to his music, all in one. And you think she could do this with the remains of Piper's seal coat?"

"I know she can do the tattoo. I'm not sure whether it would be the kind of magic needed to restore Piper's ability to transform."

"Piper — the bard's song. Your mate's song. Your song. Do you still have that recording device of yours?"

"It's on my phone," I explain to Brighid.

"That's the other ingredient you need. Take her to your friend, with the ashes of her coat and the song of her heart. And bring her back to us whole."

"**Y**ou sure you can do this, Siobhan?"

Brighid is less sure of this idea now that she's not having to persuade Morgan to let us try it.

But I have at least two reasons to want this done. And even if it fails to restore my selkie nature, I need to have it done.

"I don't see why not. I'm not sure what the end result will be, but I can ink the song into her skin, and I can do it using ink with the ashes incorporated in it. I've already mixed the ink with the finest bits of what you gave me, sorted out the bits of wood ash so it's pure ash from the fur and skin. Now I just need the song. Are you happy with the design and the placement, Piper?"

"Yes. It's perfect. No more waiting. I have things to do."

Siobhan chuckles, though I'm quite serious, since what I have yet to do is a matter of life or death.

"Put the song on repeat, then. And let's begin."

The first chiming chords of David's song — our song — ring out over the speakers in Siobhan's shop. She closes her eyes, seeming to absorb the sounds like oxygen from the air, and as David's voice joins with the guitar, she opens her glowing amber eyes and sets needle to skin.

I close my own eyes, remembering the last time I swam in seal form without Ramsay's threats and Steve's judgment weighing on me, when I was happy, full of delight that David saw me, knew me... loved me. And I immerse myself in the sounds of David's song, and the feel of the water as I swim around his legs, the sight of the amazement in his eyes as the world he knows is re-written in a new, expanded form, full of mystery and magic.

"Piper, you're done."

Siobhan's voice stirs me from dreams of David and swimming beneath the sea.

She wipes down the wide expanse of skin on my back, now engraved with the image of my seal-self, floating on what appears at first glance to be waves in the ocean, but, when considered more closely, reveals itself to be waves of music — notes and staffs and sonic patterns curving and bending, following the patterns of David's song, our song, my song... It's my song now, too. Part of me forever, just as he is, and, if the gods are kind, just as my seal-self is now once more.

"That was... Wow," Brighid says, exhaling with amazement. "I mean, I know you did the same thing with my back, and with Hunter's hand. But... this is the first time I've seen you do it where I could see it as it was happening."

"Most people can't see it," Siobhan says. "But you're not most people."

"No. And I'm not sure I've ever been more grateful for that, outside of my relationship with Hunter," Brighid replies.

"I've actually been meaning to talk to you about Hunter's tattoo — the one on his shoulder, with the muse. I think I know how to finish it off for him, if he's ready. If he's ready to ink the face of his real muse into his skin."

Brighid blushes.

"The guys all have that tattoo, except..." Her voice trails off as she decides not to speak David's name. "You think Hunter's going to want to change his?"

"Yes, I do. It was the reason Olivia designed it like she did. She knew they'd evolve as people, as musicians, and someday they'd want to fill in her face. Each as the universe bids them to do. But we can talk about that another time."

"Now, Piper — this is your first tattoo," Siobhan says, turning back to me, "so I need to give you the after-care instructions.

Make sure you follow them. Keep it clean. Treat it like an open wound. I'm going to put a protective film on it, and you should leave that on for a full day, then take it off and allow the air to help it heal up. You can wash, but stay out of open water for three weeks. Got it?"

"Definitely," I say, sitting up, letting my top fall down over my back. "No swimming in open water. Got it."

"Piper, I still need to put the bandage on. Lie back down."

"Sorry. No. Thanks for the help. I'll pay you later. Right now, I need to go find my mate."

And I jump off her tattoo table and race out the door into the still-pouring rain.

There's a song in my head. No, in my soul. And in my skin. Let's be accurate. The song in my heart and my soul is in my skin, and now it's in my head, leading me onward down the beach, away from Siobhan's shop, past Safe Harbour and the studio, past Rory and the Hidden Folk scouring the sands and the waves, so focused that they don't even see me race past them... past the tower where I nearly died, where my soul burned and the love of my life went into the water, determined to destroy the monster that had nearly killed me.

I strip off every stitch of clothing, bared to the wind and the rain, and then to the water, as I dive head-first into the oncoming wave. My back burns, but it's not the searing pain of flame consuming my seal coat — it's the comforting pain of salt in a wound, making me feel alive. The damaged tissues of my skin swell, sealing closed over the ink, the ashes of my seal coat.

Siobhan offered her expert advice for caring for my new tattoo, but I'm not human, and my natural environment is in the ocean. I breathe out, as I do every time I swim deep under the water as a seal. I close my eyes, remembering how the water feels rushing over my coat, the sounds magnified for seal ears, every bit of sensation shifting, redefining my existence in the space of moments.

And I open my eyes, seeing the world anew, muzzle and whiskers pointing the way, flippers pushing me smoothly through the water. Just as I was always meant to be. No — one thing is missing. Yes — that. I can smell it, feel it, almost taste it, pulling me along like a fish flashing its scales in the water in front of me. I give chase. The pursuit is all that exists now, all that matters. Through the waves, along the sandy bottom, over and around creatures great and small. And there... it's close... right there.

I haul up on the rock jetty along the swiftly moving inlet. The tide has just shifted. What was being pulled in is now being pushed out again. Fast enough to take any unwary creature far out to sea. But I'm not unwary. I know these waters, and there is no place in this ocean where I am too far from land. Nor is there any place in this ocean where I would not find my quarry. The song in my mind builds to a crescendo, promises made and promises fulfilled. And now is the time for me to return the favor.

I clamber across the rocks, my bare feet nearly as sure under me on this slick surface as my flippers would be. I know this place, and I know this creature, this man, lying upon the rocks. And he is mine. It's time to take him home.

"Piper! Oh, my god! How did you...? Nevermind. Let me help you."

I glare at Rory, growling, my seal instinct, to protect my mate, fading more slowly than I am used to. She raises her hands, palms out, as if signaling surrender. I recognize the gesture and return my focus to moving a semi-conscious David up the beach and into my bed, where I can keep him safe. For good this time. No one will take him from me ever again.

I pull the blanket up over his body to fend off the chill I can already feel on his skin, and I climb in with him, warming him with my body heat. He starts to shiver, and I pull him closer.

"Piper, we need to tend to David. Can we do that?" Brighid asks, and after a momentary glare at her, I recognize her intent to help him, nodding once but not relinquishing my hold on him. She moves to the other side of the bed as Morgan joins her, both of them fussing over David. Morgan raises her hands over him, seeming to assess his condition, while Brighid lays her head over his chest, looking at me with fear in her eyes.

"He lives. He will live. I will not let him go," I tell her.

She nods and pulls back from the bed, whispering in conversation with Morgan, who looks no less concerned.

"Piper, bach... He is not well. It was too soon for him to be back in the water," Morgan finally says. "I will do what I can, but..."

"I will not let him go, Meddyg. I told him I'd follow him into the Summerlands and drag him back with me, and that is what I will do."

She gives me a look of alarm before adding a sharp nod. She sets about her work, Brighid alongside her, again chanting in Irish, though this time there is desperation in her prayers. I lay my head on David's shoulder, my nose alongside his neck, inhaling his scent. He still smells of seawater, but there's that comforting David scent underneath, and I drift off to sleep, waiting for him to come back to me.

CHAPTER 43

DUST IN THE WIND

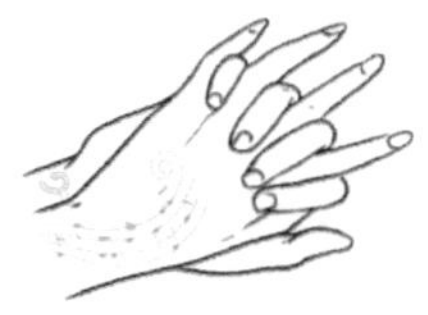

Brighid

"This is not working..." I'm not even sure what the appropriate thing is to call the elderly healer.

"Morgan, child. We are beyond formalities here, you and I. And you are correct. It is not working. I am afraid I have exhausted my abilities just to keep him stable. A second near-drowning was too much for him. He is human. He does not have a selkie's constitution, nor did he have that ring that I suspect made all the difference in Piper surviving her fall. Now that she has had her selkie abilities restored, she'll be fine. Except his death could still take her with him."

"We need to get him to a hospital."

"It's too late for that, dear. If we'd found him a few hours earlier, perhaps it would have been enough. As it stands, he has perhaps a handful of hours left."

Any professional distance I managed to maintain thus far in this whole crazy episode deserts me entirely. I sob. And Morgan pulls me farther away from Piper and David, lest I wake her. Waking him, I'm afraid, seems unlikely.

"I have to go get his brother, his bandmates, Hunter, at least — my fiancé. They need to be able to say goodbye to him."

"I regret to say it, but that cannot be allowed. No one else can be allowed to know Safe Harbour exists. We have far more to protect here than the selkies. The council would never grant permission."

"Then let me take him back to his room at the studio. I can say I found him on the beach while I was walking over from the shop."

"Do you think Piper will allow you to so much as move him from her bed?"

I recall her response to my even approaching them earlier and realize that is never happening.

"I realize this is totally uncharted territory for you all, but... how she was acting earlier? That territorial display, for lack of a better word? Is that normal?"

"No. It's not. But what you've done is incorporate her selkie nature in her human form. She no longer has two distinct forms. There was bound to be some confusion in how her instincts from both forms are expressed. As it stands, if we try to take him from her, it's entirely possible she'll shift into seal form and take off our fingers before she lets us touch him. She might even try it in human form."

I want to think she's joking, but I can see she's not.

She pats me on the hand, clearly sympathizing but unable to offer a solution.

"Sit with him. It could be he'll wake, and he might want to see a friendly face. And you can pass along a message to his family, even if we can't have them here with him at the end."

I can't think what else to do, so I sit down in the armchair next to the bed, holding David's hand and praying with all that I'm worth, to my goddess, that, despite appearances, he can be brought back to us — for Piper's sake, and for that of his friends and family.

"**B**ridge. Bridge." It's a quiet whisper, just a notch above silence. But it's enough to pull me from my prayers.

"David! Oh, goddess bless... You're awake! They won't let me bring Declan and the others. I tried to persuade them. I know this place is secret, but they just won't listen, even though..."

"Even though I'm dying?" He smiles, and I find that almost as frightening as his unconsciousness had been. "It's OK, Bridge. I kept Piper safe," he says, looking over at her where she sleeps on his chest. "And I kept them safe. And that's what I promised I'd do. Even if it killed me. Which it seems it has." He tries to chuckle and then starts to cough, which he stifles in a clear effort not to wake Piper. "It's OK. I knew what I was getting into. There was always a chance I wasn't going to make it out of this alive. It was worth it."

"How can you say that?"

"Because I met the love of my life, and I had some amazing days with her, and after thirty years of waiting for her, thinking I might always be alone, I can be content with that. It's not what I'd have wanted, but I wouldn't have missed this for the world — having her, as briefly as it lasted. Tell the guys that. I mean, don't tell them how it all happened, but make sure they know how much I loved her and that they take care of her. She's going to need that. Promise me."

"Of course, David. We'll all take care of her. But don't you want me to move you over to your room at least, so you can tell them that yourself?"

"No. I'm good here. With Piper. I just want to stay with..."

His eyes drift closed, and I grab for his wrist, checking to make sure his heart is still beating. It is, but his breathing slows just a tiny bit, and I know nothing can save him now but divine intervention.

I sit on the padded bench in the funeral home, leaning into Hunter, who squeezes my hand and kisses my temple, trying to console me. He knows I tried. He knows I did everything I could to bring David back to us. He found me on the beach, leaning over David's body, and he wrapped me up in his arms and let me cry, though he knew so little of what had happened.

I look up at the casket, David, quiet and serious, as usual, wearing his favorite Fixx T-shirt, his purple Spector bass tucked in alongside him, a floral arrangement accented with seashells by his head. But something's missing. Something he'd want here with him at the end... No. Someone.

I turn to look, trying to figure out who's missing from this scene. The band's all here, somber and sad. But when I turn back to look at David, he's not there. Instead of a casket, there's an urn. Full of David's ashes. There's a crack of thunder outside, and a window blows open, the wind tipping the urn, spilling ashes like a river from its neck into a pool on the marble floor. The wind scatters them, shaping them, arranging them like the grains of sand in a mandala, only the patterns aren't that of a mandala. No, it's aMUSEd's logo, the faceless muse with her long hair flying out behind her, filled with music notes and a lyre, a scroll, a quill pen and all the other traditional symbols of the muses.

I look to see Hunter's response to this strange turn of events, and it's like time has frozen. No one and nothing else moves. Just me and the scene before me. And the wind rises again, not disturbing a single fleck of ash in the design, but depositing more, in a masterful portrait of a woman's face, filling in the muse's visage.

Piper. Of course. David's muse is Piper.

CHAPTER 44

SAVED BY ZERO

Piper

"**G**et Siobhan! Now!" Brighid shouts, alarmingly loud for Brighid.

It wakes me from sleep, and I sit up, realizing that I'm still naked after my transformation back from seal form, and that David is awake, too, though his breathing is labored.

"Why? What for?" Rory asks, alarmed.

I lean down to kiss David on his lips, simultaneously joyous to see him awake and terrified at the sound of his breathing.

"To save his life, I hope — gods willing..." Brighid says.

Less than a half-hour later, Rory had managed to pull together an emergency session of the Council, made her case that an exception must be made — no, two exceptions — and, somehow, gotten a unanimous vote to approve both of them.

"Explain this to me, please," David says, his voice still barely above a whisper, his breathing shallow. "You did what to Piper?"

"All that was left of her seal coat was ashes," Brighid says. "Morgan said no one was on record in selkie history as having restored a selkie's transformation ability after their coat was destroyed, but that some humans had tried to obtain that power by drinking or eating the ashes of a selkie's coat."

"And that worked?"

"No. They died. But they were human, and Piper is a selkie. Just one who can't transform."

"So you had her drink the ashes of her own coat?"

"No. I had a different idea. I remembered that Siobhan had told me she'd done some memorial tattoos using the ashes of deceased loved ones mixed in with the ink. And since Siobhan does magical tattoos..."

"Wait — that tattoo she did on Hunter's hand? That was magic?"

"Yes. Her magic uses music and ink, blending them together to become more. We'd already tried healing Hunter's hand. But it needed... Like a magical kickstart. Hunter needed to actively accept what was being offered."

"So you decided to have her try to put Piper's seal coat back, but under her skin?"

"Basically, yeah."

"And, it worked?"

Everyone looks at me, waiting for an answer.

"I can transform without my coat now. I just went in the water after you and thought like a seal, and I was one. And when I needed to change back to bring you home, I just did."

"It's the first time we know of that anything *anyone* has tried has worked to restore a selkie after their coat was destroyed," Morgan says. "It may be it's particular to Piper's circumstances — her ring, that she'd just survived an almost certainly fatal fall." David cringes. "That she has a bonded mate, that she's bonded to a human, that she was fearful of losing you and determined to find you. There's no way to know why it worked, no way to know if it would ever work again, or whether it might prove fatal to whoever tried."

"Piper has her transformative ability back. That's all I care about. She won't dwindle, won't fade away. And no one can ever steal her coat from her ever again, because it's part of her," David says.

"I hadn't even thought about that. That's a big plus," Rory says.

"But it doesn't matter — there's no point to it all if David dies."

Everyone looks at me, expressions grave.

"That's why I called the council together," Rory finally says. "If David was a selkie, he'd be immortal."

"But you already said that trying to become a selkie had been fatal for every human who'd tried."

"That we know of. And none of them used a magical tattoo made with selkie coat ashes to do it, let alone those of the coat of their life-bonded selkie mate."

"And you think since I'm dying anyway, we should give it a shot and try to make me an immortal seal-man."

"David, this has to be your choice," Rory tells him. "There are no guarantees, despite the success we had in Piper's case, because you are not a selkie. It could be just as fatal. You need to be certain."

"And if I don't do this?" he asks, wheezing slightly, looking to Morgan for an answer.

She frowns and shakes her head.

"And if I die? If we don't try it and I die, what happens to Piper?"

"You're fading now, David," Morgan says. "It may be — there's a chance, a slim chance, that it's a gentle enough passage that Piper would survive, despite your bond."

"And if we try it, and it's fatal?"

"There's no way to know. It could be that because she's a selkie it would have no impact on her. It could be that what poisons you poisons her, and she could die with you, despite the fact that she's a selkie. It's even less sure now, because she's not exactly a normal selkie now."

"What does that mean?"

Rory looks at me and sighs.

"Her seal nature seems to be bleeding over into her human form. She's more aggressive than she was. More territorial."

"Oh, screw it. Let's not pussyfoot around things here. He needs to know. *She* needs to know," Brighid says. "Piper about snapped their fingers off when they tried to help get you inside, and again when we tried to get her move to away from you so we could try to treat you. There's a..." She looks to Rory for help.

"Feral — there's a feral quality to her that wasn't there before."

"And that's a problem?"

I turn to look at David, finding him looking back at me.

"It was always there. It's just not buried as deep as it was before. She's still Piper. Just even feistier." He smiles at me. "Don't mess with me, and she'll be fine."

"And you're OK if — assuming we can manage this at all — if you end up the same way?" Brighid asks. "Are you going to end up biting your brother the next time he's being a dick?"

"Would that be a problem?" David asks, smirking.

Brighid bursts into laughter. "OK. I've changed my mind. Piper's a good influence on you, even now. No worries."

"Joking aside, David. This is uncharted territory," Rory warns. "So uncharted that it's actually officially against the rules here. Most of the individual selkie clans would kill a human who even tried it."

"So if I do this, I've got a target on my back?"

"No. The Council voted to make an exception for you. If this works, you become one of the Hidden Folk, officially, one of the citizens of Safe Harbour. As Piper's mate, with her selkie abilities shared with you, you'd be part of her clan. Re-establish her clan, in fact."

My eyes go wide. David looks at me, sensing a change in my demeanor.

"I was — I am — the last of us. There are other harbor-seal selkies, other clans. But I'm... I'm the last of the GilleMhoir line."

"That's what you meant when you said you were alone."

I nod.

"You're not alone anymore, Piper."

He pulls my head down to him, kissing me on my lips, and I kiss him back, knowing that he's right. If this works, he and I will build a life together. If it doesn't... No. Neither of us will ever be alone again. In this life or the next.

"Is this what you want, Piper? Do you want to take a chance on me, on us? I won't do it if you don't want me to."

I lean in and kiss him, nipping at his bottom lip before brushing my lips over his and then smiling as our eyes meet.

"Let's do this," he says.

"**I** feel absolutely ridiculous," Siobhan says as she's led, blindfolded, into my room.

Rory stands behind her, a big bag in her hands.

"I'm sorry, but this is a necessary precaution, for you and for us," she tells Siobhan. "Whatever you see, hear or do today, you can tell no one. I need you to swear to it."

"Of course. This never happened," Siobhan says as Rory pulls the blindfold from her eyes.

"Piper! You didn't let me put the bandage on your tattoo! Is that why..."

She looks at my back, where the blanket has shifted, leaving it bare.

"What the ever-loving—! Can someone explain to me how Piper's tattoo is completely healed?"

"Uh... No," Brighid says.

"Your tattoos don't all heal up this fast?" Rory asks, not entirely managing to keep a straight face.

Siobhan gives her a scathing look.

"Woman, you do magical tattoos," Brighid finally says. "Do we really need to get into this right now? Time is kind of of the essence."

Siobhan now pauses to take in the rest of the scene.

"He doesn't look like a tattoo should be the first priority for today."

"He's dying, Siobhan," Rory says plainly. "We've got one last 'Hail Mary' — pardon to the Pagans — shot to prevent that, and you're it."

"Me? You want me to do what? Tattoo him to save his life?"

"Exactly," Brighid confirms.

"Oh, boy."

"Now, about those ashes we used earlier..."

"**C**an you do it?" Brighid asks.

"Yeah, I can do it. It's the same as Piper's tattoo. You sure you want me to do this freehand? Looking at the album cover art on my phone?" Siobhan replies.

"You're an amazing tattoo artist. I've seen your freehand work," Brighid says. "You can do this."

"I'm asking *you* this, David" Siobhan says, "because assuming this works, you've got to live with this tattoo for the rest of your life."

"I trust you."

Siobhan takes a deep breath and lets it back out slowly.

"Shoulder? Same as Hunter's?"

David nods. "But my left shoulder instead."

"And with Piper as the muse?"

"She *is* my muse."

"Same music?"

David looks to me, questions in his eyes.

"It's what she does — the music is part of the magic. She needs a song to ink into your skin."

"What did she ink into yours?" he asks.

I sit up and turn around, showing him the tattoo on my back, the first time he's seeing it. His fingers trace over it, across the seal, through the waves and down the staff, tapping the notes.

"This is 'Remember.'"

I nod.

"How did you know that, bard? It's not literally the music to your song," Morgan asks. "Even I can see that."

"Have you touched it? Touched her tattoo?"

"I have not. And I will not. I think that is for you and your mate alone."

Siobhan looks up at Morgan with surprise. Morgan gives a nod of respect.

"Brighid — is this what it's like when you touch Hunter's tattoo? Do you... Do you ride the song like this?"

"I see the vision I saw that is connected to it, and, yes, in the back of my mind, I hear 'Shepherd Me Home,' It's us, blessed, together — then and now."

"Then let's get this done. I want to see Piper's face when she touches my tattoo, when she comes face-to-face with herself in the form of my muse."

He smiles at me, and I fix it in my memory, knowing that it's possible neither of us will survive this. If this is the last freemory I have of him, it will be a happy one.

"Let's go steal forever."

CHAPTER 45

OCEAN BLUE

David

Siobhan sets up her tools and ink on an adjustable metal table Rory brings into Piper's room from elsewhere in Safe Harbour. Her wild long white hair tied back behind her, she's prepared and sterilized everything that wasn't already, including my arm, with me propped carefully at the angle she needs to do the tattoo.

She gives a nod to Piper, who starts up the music from her phone, filling the room with sound that's nearly a match to the quality of the monitors in the studio. I squeeze Piper's hand and smile at her before closing my eyes to focus on the music.

In my mind, it's not the moments in the recording studio that I see — writing the song on my acoustic, working with Piper on scratch tracks, having the guys play their parts — it's every happy moment I've had with Piper, from the awkward moment we first met through realizing how much we both love "Leverage," that breakfast, the honey, the taste and feel of her finger in my mouth, the picnic on the beach, learning about her, then learning her secret, making love to her for the first time, reckless moments in the storage room at the studio, the rush of having her ride me in my bed with the guys downstairs, the delight of seeing the magic of her transformation, swimming with her soft fur brushing against my legs, stolen moments in the live room, the entire spans of days spent together since, telling her I love her, hearing that she loves me, planning a future here with her and our studio, even waking up here with her seawater scent and her wonderful warmth bringing me back to life.

If the moments of your life flash back in your mind before you die, these are the ones I want to remember. These are the ones that are set to the soundtrack of this song in my head, in my heart, my soul, and now my skin — making my song, our song, her song, part of me, and part of my life with aMUSEd.

If this doesn't work, if I've played my last note with my bandmates, my brother, then I go to my grave with the symbol of all we have created engraved in my skin forever, the visage of my own personal muse brought to life on the arm that holds the neck of my bass, creating the rhythm of my every waking moment. And if I live... if I become the magical creature Piper has always been, immortal and as at home in the sea as on land... her mate, forever... I can't imagine anything better. I've had a decade as a rockstar, making music people love, and still, I can't imagine anything better than this.

Piper

I watch as Siobhan uses ink and ash and needles to turn David's left shoulder and upper arm into a living canvas, the symbol of his band coming to life in vibrant color.

Hunter's tattoo has the faceless muse holding out his favorite green guitar to the viewer, as if in offering. But as Siobhan begins humming along with the melody of "Remember," it's not a guitar she adds to the design that now bears my likeness, not even a bass guitar. Her eyes half-closed, she's wrapping David's shoulder in the tresses of this muse, shifting the design from hair full of symbols to a wavy mass of water. But not just water — water and waves like she's etched into my back, following along with the rhythms of the song, as if the waves themselves are the song.

And when the waves smooth out across the back of his shoulder, transitioning onto his back, she shapes the likeness of a harbor seal, its coat tawny and spotted like mine, but darker, more brown and less silver. No one asked her to do this. She didn't mention it to David. And, looking at her carefully, using my eyes that can see more than most humans, I can see she's in a trance, floating herself on this sea of music that David has created, following the tide and the wind and the waves where they take her, her hand and her gift. Not a dedicated priestess, this woman, not like Brighid, but gods-touched nonetheless.

I offer a prayer of thanks, to the other Brighid, who has watched over her namesake and us through her, and to whichever gods have brought us together like this, surviving all that has challenged us and threatened to divide us. I don't know if that unknown father of Rónan's is behind it, or perhaps Rónan himself, wherever his soul has landed. But I offer thanks to them all.

The buzzing of Siobhan's needles stops as the last notes of the song fade from the speakers, and I turn the music off, looking anxiously at David. He remains pale, his breathing still shallow. And then it stops. He stops. He stops!

"No!" I scream, shaking him hard, my hand narrowly avoiding the fresh tattoo. The tattoo that did nothing! Nothing!

Rory pulls Siobhan away, still half in a trance, as Brighid and Morgan lean over David's chest, both of them, eyes closed, holding their hands above him, a dull glow emitted, but not spreading as it had before. They exchange a look before stepping back.

"No!" I roar again, pulling David down flat on the bed and beginning to breathe for him again, make his heart pump for him, for me, for us. My thumb rubs over the waves engraved on my ring, Rónan's ring, just like the waves Siobhan engraved into the skin of David's back, like the waves that I dove into, following his scent, his song, his soul into the ocean to find him, finding myself in the process, in the shape of a seal.

I grab his arm and throw it over my shoulder, not caring a wit that both of us are naked, and I lever him out of that bed with every ounce of strength I possess.

"Piper!" Rory objects, chasing me down the stairs as I half-drag David with me, down the hall, out the door, kicking open the hidden gate and then carrying him down the beach to the ocean, still pitch black in the stormy night. My hair is drenched before I reach the crest of the beach, the skies seeming to cry for David and me both, while my eyes remain dry. Because I am not done. I am not letting him go, my David, my mate, my life. If I can't breathe life back into him on land, I'll do it in the water.

And I drag him through the breakers and into the swells behind them, pressing my lips to his over and over again. There's no response. Growling in frustration, I yank the ring from my finger and slide it onto his ring finger, a perfect fit.

Strong as the ocean
Deep as the sea
Song on the waves
David's song...

But if it's Rónan's ring that made the magic work, it's not working now. I roar wordlessly at the sky, at the universe, and...

"Come back to me, David!" I yell at him, loud enough to be heard over the breakers and the rain and straight into the Summerlands if that's what it takes. "I will come in there after you! So you'd better come back, right now!"

There's no reply, no sound of his breathing, no heartbeat from within his chest.

I dive under the water, seeking the one place I feel nearly as at home as I do with him, and I swim until I see the sky light up overhead, lightning turning the water into a lantern all around me. Coming back to the surface, I see David's body floating on the swells, and I dive once more, skimming along the sand on the ocean floor, then rising beneath him, nosing at his shoulder with my whiskers, tracing the song in his skin. I start to sing along, the melody etched in my soul as surely as he is.

My song. Our song. David's song.

The voice I hear over the water
Thrilling me now to let go
Touching me
Taking my hand as I lead in the dance of my soul
Feel the wind as it slips through your fingers
Just like the sands of time have come and gone
Never looked back
Timeless
Senseless
Faceless

And you know it's only a dream
Fly so high over the rainbow
Colors before never seen through eyes forever blinded to the
whole mystery
And should you go off on your own
Never lose sight of your home
When you think that it's all just a game
Remember my name
I've taken you home through the wind
And I've taken you home through the rain
I've helped you along
In your weakness I helped you be strong
And I carried you home at the end of the day
Now, too soon, the feeling is gone
In the daylight it all looks so wrong
Just a false sense of reality
The voice I hear over the water
Cold and empty it rings out over the silence
Feeling my pain
It's never been only a dream
Or reality as it seems
As you reach for your soul's ecstasy
Remember to always be free
And I'll take you home through the wind
And I'll take you home through the rain
I'll help you along
In your weakness I'll help you be strong
I'm your guardian angel
Remember my name

It's not a song a human could hear, sung at a frequency well above the range of human ears, but my ears — my seal ears — hear it, cherish it, declare it to time and the tides and... to David. To his soul. And I take his fingers gently in my mouth and pull him along behind me as I swim out to sea.

CHAPTER 46

SUMMERLAND

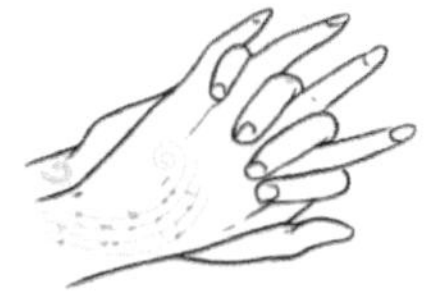

David

The waves swell gently under my board, a beautiful summer sunrise coloring the sky. The most beautiful one I've ever seen. It's not surfing weather, but it's quiet and beautiful, a picture-perfect day at the beach. After waiting for this vacation for more than a year, I could honestly sit here like this all day.

Maybe I'll go work in the studio later. There's this song I keep hearing in my head, and I want to get it down before I forget it. Yeah, that's it... A song about memories. Happy memories I want to hold onto forever. Dark brown eyes, silken hair, a pixie face softened with gentle curves. A girl I met at a gig once, I think. The kind of girl you want to call your girlfriend. Not that I've ever had one of those. The guys keep teasing me about that, saying I'm looking for a mermaid.

No, no mermaid. Just a girl. But one who gets me, who understands me without me having to explain what I meant or apologize for saying something stupid. She just gets me. Yeah, that's what I'm looking for. And if she loves the ocean, even better. Because one of these days I'm going to finish up my degree, and then I want to work with dolphins or something, maybe volunteer with a rescue group responding to seal strandings. Yeah. That sounds good.

We're solid enough in our career that I can ask for more time off, longer breaks between tours. The guys will understand.

Hunter wants to spend more time here in Mystic Beach, with Brighid. Those two need to get their shit straightened out. I mean, if I had a girl who looked at me like Brighid does Hunt... But what are the chances of that?

Probably better to daydream about the kind of happy memories I'll put in a song. How did that go, again?

I hum along to the melody in my head, trying to think of the words that go with it. Something about finding your way home through a storm, my guardian angel watching over me... I need one of those.

Something brushes against my leg, and momentarily I panic. Something about the song... Do sharks like music? Should I stop humming it because it brings all the sharks to my board? Ha! Or should I sing louder and scare them away? But that doesn't feel like a shark. I've touched a shark before. There was that lab class... This feels like...

I stick my fingers into the water, brushing against something... soft, warm, furry. Definitely not a shark. Not even a dolphin. Hey, at least it's not a shark nibbling at my fingers. Oh, wait — it *is* nibbling at my fingers. It's nice, though, like that big dog of Brighid's... Wait. That's not right. Brighid doesn't have a dog. And why would it be nibbling at my fingers all the way out here, under the water?

I lean over to see what's nibbling on my fingers and get pulled over into the water. Suddenly, I'm face-to-face with a seal. Is it that one I saw on the beach the other day? Has she followed me out here? Or is it that I followed her? Doesn't matter. She makes me smile. Seawater floods my mouth as I forget to hold my breath, exhaling and kicking along behind her as she swims off, turning to look at me every few yards.

She dives deep down, and I follow her. Gryff would be proud of me. I worked pretty hard to be able to swim this deep and stay under this long. How long *has* it been, swimming after that pretty tawny silver seal like this? It seems like a long time, but I haven't run out of oxygen yet. She speeds up, heading toward shore, and I chase after her, kicking my feet out behind me, like flippers, slicing through the water so gracefully.

Ooh... What's that? Such a pretty silver fish! And the seal, she comes back to me, chasing after it, and I chase after her, after them. We change places, back and forth, one of us closing in on the fish, then dropping back to let the other one lead. It's fun, playing like this. I'm not even hungry, but chasing this fish with her is the most fun I've ever had.

It rushes into the breakers at the beach, trying to get away from us, and I lose sight of it. I turn back out toward the sea, looking for my friend. There she is. Right in front of me. She pokes me in the shoulder with her nose, tickling me with her whiskers, tracing the spots on my fur. I like this girl. And she likes me, brushing her nose against mine. Seal kisses. I think this is the happiest I've ever been. And I kiss her back, my mouth opening against hers, tongues tangling, arms wrapping around her.

A wave breaks over our heads, and I pull her against me so we come out the back side of the wave together. It's dark, but I'm comfortable here with her, my girl, my girlfriend, my... Piper. Her name's Piper.

"David!" She sounds just as happy to say my name as I am to say hers.

"Piper. Hi."

"Welcome back."

"Did I go somewhere?" I ask.

"For a little while, I think," she says, treading water within the circle of my arms.

"Did you go with me?"

"No. But I came to get you, to bring you home."

"So we're home now?"

"Yeah, we're home."

"Good. I like it here, with you. I want to stay here for a while. No more touring for a while. OK?"

"Yeah. We've got a studio to run."

"Oh. Right. We were going to steal a recording studio. No, wait — I *bought* a recording studio. Part of one, at least."

"You did. And I've got an album to engineer."

"And you're going to kick ass doing it! Declan and I need to finish those songs. And Hunt... Hunt's got one we can record, too. The one he wrote for Brighid."

"He does. 'Shepherd Me Home.' Remember?"

"I remember. I remember it all."

She pulls me hard against her, and wraps her legs around me, kissing me hard.

After a few minutes, we come up for air, still treading water in the swells.

"Piper?"

"Yes?"

"Was I a seal?"

"You were."

"Oh."

I think about that for a second.

"That was fun. Can we do it again?"

"Anytime you want."

"Cool."

"But I think we should probably go back inside now. Brighid's probably freaking out, not knowing what happened to you."

"Right. Don't want to piss her off. She threatened to make Declan's dick fall off."

Piper giggles.

"I don't think she really meant that," she says.

"Don't tell him that. It'll help keep him in line while he figures out how to get Callie back."

"I wouldn't dream of it." She smiles up at me.

"I love you, David."

"I love you, Piper."

It takes a few more minutes for us to make it to dry land. I think we're making up for lost time. Even though it feels like we now have all the time in the world. Together.

EPILOGUE

Piper
Two weeks later

"I'm not sure, Piper. You feel different to me. After three millennia, I know what a selkie feels like to my healing skills, and you... It's like you're a blend of selkie and human, or at least mortal." Morgan shakes her head.

"Are you saying I've lost my immortality?"

"I don't honestly know. I think you should be prepared, just in case that's what's happened."

"So I could die tomorrow?"

"I wouldn't think it would be tomorrow. But it could be you'll live two thousand years and pass away in your sleep, looking exactly like you do today. Or you could live two hundred years, and die in bed with your grandchildren around you, looking like I do now."

"Oh. And what about David?"

I gesture at him, where he sits in a comfortable chair next to Morgan's treatment bed.

"I have no idea what standard to measure him against. He doesn't feel like a selkie, but neither does he feel mortal. Mayhap it's that you both have the magic of your seal coat in you now... that you're sharing it in half-measure, shared across two people instead of one."

"So, we're the same?" he asks.

"Not exactly, but you're different in similar ways. If I had to guess, I'd say you'll live a much longer life than you would have naturally. Perhaps just as long as Piper now. But I don't think you're immortal, either of you." She shrugs. "I'm sorry to deliver such bad news."

"It's not bad news, Meddyg. The only bad news would be if I was still immortal and David was mortal."

"Or the other way around," David adds.

"Then I will be happy to have delivered two pieces of good news today."

"Two?" David asks.

"You mean about David and about me?"

"Well, no. But also yes. There is the news of your indeterminate mortality, which we will call good news, as you suggest. There's also news about the future of Clan GilleMhoir."

"Meddyg?"

"Congratulations. Your clan of two will soon be three."

David turns to me, his eyes huge.

"I thought it was the wrong time of the year," he says.

"Well, it's a month or so earlier than it would normally be for a selkie. But Piper is no longer a normal selkie, and you are no longer a normal human. You are a rule unto yourselves. From the moment you were both changed, it was an unknown frontier. But I can feel a new spirit growing within Piper — though I would not hazard a guess as to what its nature will be. Other than your babe. Is this unwelcome news after all?" she asks, looking between us.

I turn to look at David, holding my breath.

He takes a deep breath of his own and looks into my eyes. And breaks into one of the biggest smiles I've seen on his face. Even bigger than it has when we've gone swimming together in seal form these last two weeks. And my smile gets just as big.

"It is not, Meddyg Morgan," he says. "It is quite happy news indeed. And now, if you will excuse us, I would very much like to go celebrate... with my clan chief and the mother of my child."

He sweeps me up from the bed and carries me off to my room — our room now. His hand slides up under my shirt, across my lower back, while I grip his upper arm. Ostensibly, it's to steady myself during the short walk down the hall; but, really, it mirrors his touch, carrying our song into each other's minds — a duet of two souls made one. And now three.

"Let's go steal our future."

David
A week later

"**M**arina, Rory, I wanted to talk to both of you about plans for the studio going forward."

"Of course, David," Marina says from the screen of the laptop in the middle of the conference room table between Rory and me. "I'm interested to see what changes you think need to be made, since you're the one who has experience working here as an artist."

"Well, it occurred to me that you've got the residence upstairs, with six bedrooms, which works fine with a band full of bachelors. Now that I've moved in with Piper and Hunter's mostly staying at Brighid's, there's even room for Malcolm. But as Hunter has already shown us, there may be times when an artist wants to have family members with them while they're recording. At some point, we're not only going to run out of bedrooms for everyone, we're going to have artists who want a more family-friendly atmosphere." I've had good reason to think this through in the last week.

"This town is perfect for a family vacation, and I think if we could offer our artists the option of family quarters, as well as just housing band members in the main residence, we'd open things up to an entirely new range of clients. Not every artist wants to be isolated and tortured. Studies show that happy artists are more focused, make better music, and if they're not kept separated from their families while they're recording — after spending all that time on the road, where they're also separated from them — you're going to get albums done faster, with better end results. It could at least be an option for those who'd want it."

"That's a creative idea, David. We've got enough land to build another residence — something more suited to families with children. Maybe we could look into expanding into a villa-style compound, with a central courtyard so the artists could easily get to the studio, day or night, regardless of the weather, any time of year."

"Rory? What do you think?"

"I think you've thought this through very well, in great detail," she says carefully. "Is there anything you want to tell us?"

Trust the empath to know something was up. She looks over at Piper, who's sitting beside me, taking notes.

Piper and I exchange a glance. She nods, and I take her hand in mine, running my thumb over the ring that is once again on her index finger.

"We'll be adding a new member to the aMUSEd family before next summer," I tell them both. "And I don't mean a new bass player to tour with the band, though we may need to discuss that at some point down the road."

"You're pregnant?" Rory asks, looking at Piper, appropriately, since she's the one who's carrying our child. Pup? This is all still so... odd. But wonderfully odd.

Piper nods, looking unsure of herself.

Rory jumps up from her chair and grabs Piper up in a hug.

"I'm so happy for you, Piper! Rónan would have loved being an uncle. And David." She grabs my hand and squeezes it. "Congratulations."

"Yes, congratulations are in order, for you both," Marina adds. "We'll discuss touring and release schedules as we get closer to completing the new album. We'll make whatever accommodations are necessary. I'm going to let you all go celebrate. I assume you'll be letting the band in on the good news?"

"Yes. We were planning on telling them later today."

"Then go do that. We'll schedule another meeting to discuss the details of the expansion plan, and whatever other ideas you have going forward, David. The future is looking very bright for Mystic Studios."

"Mystic Studios?"

"I've decided to change the name. A fresh start for us all, with everyone on the same team, working together. If we're all in agreement?"

"It's a great name!" I tell her with a smile.

"I think Rónan would love it," Rory says quietly, but with a small smile. "He always loved the name of the town. It just fits."

"That's the thing I found about this place, ever since we got here," I say. "Things just fit. They fall into place like the universe just wanted us to be here. Like it's where we were always meant to be."

"Perhaps that's exactly the case, David," Marina says. "Perhaps that's exactly it."

Epilogue 2

Declan

David pulls Piper into his arms from behind, placing his hands on her belly, even though she's nowhere near pregnant enough for either of them to feel a baby kicking or even for there to be a "baby bump." He smiles down at her, and she smiles back up at him, and I repress the urge to walk out of the room.

They're so stinkin' happy, so stinkin' cute, the two of them — their new matching tattoos, their brown hair just a few shades apart, though David's has those bits of blonde he always gets when he's been spending time on his surfboard or paddleboard. Will the baby get Piper's brown eyes, or David's pale blue ones, I wonder.

And just like that, the future of aMUSEd is called into question. Because I can't imagine David is going to willingly leave his pregnant girlfriend to tour the world for a year or more. Hunter was already talking about shorter tour legs, longer breaks in between, maybe buying a jet of our own, just to get home more quickly between legs — home being here in Mystic Beach, as far as he's concerned, and not in New York, where all six of us have lived for nearly a decade now. It feels almost symbolic that I'm now the only one of us who doesn't have a tattoo, and specifically the aMUSEd muse inked permanently into my skin.

The irony there is that everything seems to changing — except me.

Maybe Marina Matthews is happy to accommodate the changes, but she's not the one who's going to have crying babies on her tour bus, if Hunter gets his way and brings Brighid on the road with us. And Marina Matthews is not the one who's going to have to find a bass player in my brother's league who can tour with us if David decides to quit touring altogether. If we can even find one that good who's also willing to deal with... well, me.

Yeah, I'm a dick. I own it. Most of the time, anyway. But the guys are used to it. Trying to break in a new bass player? That's a problem I don't need. I've already got enough problems, and that was before we even got here to Mystic Beach. I thought it would be fine, coming back to the town Dave and I had vacationed in as kids. Sure, I've got some memories here that don't exactly make me smile, but it's a vacation, and a vacation where we get to record our music and play out when we feel like it. Best of both worlds. Right?

But as soon as we got here, as soon as I saw that same stretch of highway, the same little town with its boardwalk and cute little shops, the quaint little restaurants...

Yeah, my whole outlook soured. Half the time I'm pissed off that things aren't going my way, and the other half, I'm wallowing in self-pity that I have to be here, where the worst thing I ever did haunts me every single damn day.

And that's the bottom line. I fucked up. Twelve years ago, I fucked up so badly that it changed my entire life. And, yeah, not just my life. I'll own that, too. I fucked up hers, too. Badly enough that I never expected to find her here when we came back for the summer.

Calliope Angelica Martino. Callie. The love of my life. From the moment I first saw her until this moment, right here. That's never changed. As much as everything else has changed, that hasn't.

I gave her up once, thinking I was doing the right thing. For her, at least. But finding her here again... Why does it feel like fate wanted to bring us back together, to give us a second chance? All I know is I can't get her out of my head, now that I've seen her again. But then she's never really been out of my head. Or my heart. And it's past time I told her that.

AUTHOR'S NOTE

Thank you for reading "Smoke on the Water." I hope you enjoyed this latest edition in the Mystic Beach fantasy/rockstar romance series. Please consider taking a few moments to give it an honest rating or short review on Goodreads and on Amazon, or wherever you like to leave your reviews. Even a few words can help tremendously! Authors (especially independent authors) rely on reviews to sell books, and they're doubly important for a new author. If I don't sell books, I can't afford to keep the plot bunnies that are multiplying so rapidly in my head, creating new books in this series and beyond. (Note: I am knee-deep in plot bunnies. Hungry ones. Send help. Professional help. Preferably an editor.)

(Also, I have cats. And they don't eat plot bunnies. Nor does the teenager who sporadically emerges from his bedroom and is eating me out of house and home.)

Great. Now I'm hungry...

"Smoke on the Water" is the fourth course in the eight-course meal that is the series, and it contains a hefty dose of what you'll get when you pick up each of these novels: talented and charismatic musicians, strong and complex women, fantastical creatures and circumstances, a deep love of music, some seriously steamy love scenes, a quirky little beach town, a mystery or two, an occasional life on the line and plenty of drama on the romance front.

This is a summer that changes everything for aMUSEd, a band that is comfortably at the top of their game. And the universe has decided that it's time to shake things up for these six talented men.

If you haven't already, make sure to sign up for my e-newsletter, the Mystic Beacon. When you do, you can pick up the Mystic Beach fantasy rockstar romance prequel novella "Good Golly Miss Molly," Molly and Logan's story; the Brighid and Hunter pre-prequel short story, "Here Comes the Sun"; and the new seasonal Brighid and Hunter bonus novelette "Spooky" **free**, just for signing up. (You won't get a second newsletter if you're already signed up.)

If you want to know all of what's happening with the members of aMUSEd and the... odd things that happen every day in Mystic Beach, the *Mystic Beacon* will magically appear in your email inbox on a semi-regular (but not *too* frequent) basis. You'll get backstage pass to the world of aMUSEd, with inside information on upcoming releases, teasers, behind-the-scenes details, giveaways, maybe even some original music and a surprise or two. Be ready for guest blogs from some of the members of aMUSEd and some exclusive stories on the band from our intrepid Mystic Beacon reporter, Aurora "Rory" Carmichael (provided she can find the time to do her day-job amidst the fantastical things that few even know happen in Mystic Beach).

And be sure to follow me on social media, at <u>https://www.facebook.com/AislinnArcher</u>; on Twitter <u>@AislinnArcher</u>; and on <u>Instagram</u> and <u>TikTok</u> @aislinnarcher. We'll have some goodies there, as well as on my website at <u>AislinnArcher.com</u> and <u>MysticBeachRocks.com</u>.

Thank you for reading, and I'll look forward to chatting with you about the characters of Mystic Beach, all of whom are near and dear to my heart. (Yes, even Declan...)

Aislinn

What's Next

The next book in the Mystic Beach Fantasy Rockstar Romances is "Remind Me," Declan's story. You've just gotten a taste of where Declan's romantic life stands at the point where "Smoke on the Water" ends, as well as Piper's unique insight into Declan's past. The dual epilogue to the second book in the series, "Dream Weaver," also included Brighid and Hunter's engagement party, as seen from Callie's view as she discovers the man who broke her heart at 17 has returned to Mystic Beach. And that's where we'll pick up with Book 4, "Remind Me," set for release in early 2023.

Note: "Smoke on the Water" is the third book in the Mystic Beach Fantasy Rockstar Romances, and the first that is a true standalone. If you haven't already read the series-opening duet, "Once Upon a Dream" and "Dream Weaver," Brighid and Hunter's two-part story, that should probably be your next stop. The timelines of "Dream Weaver" and "Smoke on the Water" overlap, so some of the events in "Dream Weaver" have been referenced herein, but "Once Upon a Dream" also contains the backstory of our band, aMUSEd, and how they got here — both literally in Mystic Beach and in a more general sense of their careers.

Once you've read at least "Once," and perhaps also "Dream Weaver," you may also wish to venture into the first of the Mystic Beach Fantasy Rockstar Romance interstitial novels, "Down to the Sea," which is a side story for Brighid and secondary character Aedan "Mace" Mason that takes place between the second half of "Once" and the beginning of "Dream Weaver."

But be aware that "Down to the Sea" is not a happily-ever-after novel. Rather, it is a story of personal growth and a near-miss romance that almost was. It sets the stage for "Dream Weaver," as well as for the next interstitial novel in the series, and for Mace's own book, forthcoming at a later date.

RETURN TO MYSTIC BEACH

<u>The Mystic Beach Fantasy Rockstar Romance series</u>

Once Upon a Dream (Brighid & Hunter duet, Part 1)

Down to the Sea (Brighid interstitial novel, 1.5)

Dream Weaver (Brighid & Hunter duet, Part 2)

Smoke on the Water (David & Piper)

<u>Coming Soon</u>

Remind Me (Declan & Callie)
Mad World (Rhys)
Drawn to the Rhythm (Kieran)
Carry Fire (Alex)
and more to come...

<u>Bonus Content</u>

Good Golly Miss Molly (0.5)
(Molly & Logan, series prequel novella)

Here Comes the Sun (0.25)
(Hunter & Brighid sweet pre-prequel short story)

Spooky (2.75)
(Hunter & Brighid seasonal bonus novelette)

The Mystic Beach Mysteries
(Aurora Carmichael contemporary fantasy series)

Coming Soon
Safe Harbour

Visit Aislinn Archer's website at http://AislinnArcher.com now to subscribe to the Mystic Beacon newsletter and get your FREE bonus content. *As a subscriber, you'll get early access to details on new releases, sales, exclusive content and more. You can unsubscribe at any time, but I hope you'll stick around for the fun!*

Suggested Playlist

Why does David Carter love The Fixx? Well, partly because I do. They were my third favorite band (meaning the third band that was my favorite, and I'm only up to about five now) and are still one of my all-time favorites. But mostly it's because so much of their music has themes related to the ocean (which is just one of the reasons I love their music), and this book (other than perhaps Mace's books) has the strongest beach theme of the series.

When I made aMUSEd's first cover setlist, I asked myself what David would ask for. I already knew he'd love anything related to the sea, plus The Fixx does have some great bass lines, despite being known for their keyboards, guitars and vocals more than anything. But I figured their New Wave feel would nicely complement the other thing David loves: funky bass lines of any era. He gets his share of those, but it's The Fixx's music that really shines as part of the suggested playlist for this book. So many songs just fit.

Read Between the Lines — The Fixx
   I Believe — Robert Plant
   No Mermaid — Sinead Lohan
   Seals — Seven Nations (If you aren't seeing seals playing in the surf in your head when you listen to this, I'd be very surprised.)
   My Spine (Is the Bass Line) — Shriekback
   Love is a Battlefield — Pat Benatar
   You Know Me — The Fixx
   Letting the Cable Sleep — Bush (Coiling cables like Piper teaches David to do in this chapter is a real thing. Unfortunately, it is not a skill I ever mastered. After having Al attempt to teach me about fifty times, I gave up, because I never could do it up to his standards, so he always ended up recoiling them himself anyway. It's a running joke for us at this point. David learns way faster.)
   Breakfast at Tiffany's — Deep Blue Something
   Rules and Schemes — The Fixx
   Reach the Beach — The Fixx
   Shred of Evidence — The Fixx
   Human — Rag'n'Bone Man
   Never Get Old — Sinead O'Connor (The first spoken-language part of this song is in Irish, some of which I can actually understand these days, though I could understand nearly none of it when I first heard this song. But my favorite part of it is that it talks about music being the only thing that never gets old. I suspect Piper and Morgan would agree. David may too, someday. We'll have to see.)
   Eyes Can't Hide — Caitlin Parrott
   Precious Stone — The Fixx
   Don't Be Scared — The Fixx
   Red Skies — The Fixx
   Trouble Me — 10,000 Maniacs
   The Flow — The Fixx
   Cruel Summer — Bananarama
   Please Forgive Me — David Gray
   Undertow — Ivy

Remember — Al Cook (This is the first Al original with lyrics you're getting in this series, since "Changes," from "Once Upon a Dream" is an instrumental and the one I used in the playlist for "Dream Weaver" is an Alice-in-Chains cover. [The lyrics of Mace's song for Brighid in "Down to the Sea" were written specifically for that scene, by me, so I get all the blame for that.] But there will be more Al songs to come. I already have the perfect one picked out for Rhys' book. I've also finally talked Al into releasing some of his songs for purchase on iTunes, starting with "Remember." So, if you like it, you should be able to buy it very soon. [There's also a video up on YouTube that incorporates footage from the recording sessions.] You should note that he wrote this in 1993, before we'd even met, and despite the fact that it has nothing to do with selkies or psychic memory wipes or deadly secrets, when he recently re-recorded it, I realized it was a near-perfect fit for this book. From there, I basically just incorporated the song into several scenes, with a couple words added to the story here and there to make it even more of an organic part of the book — though the keyboard part exists solely in my imagination. The lyrics are unchanged from his original version. Yet more Mystic Beach serendipity.)

I Will — The Fixx

Heart-Shaped Box — Nirvana (credit to Dan Debuque, whose amazing solo slide-guitar cover of the grunge classic inspired Hunter's take at age 15 and again here)

Going Without — The Fixx

Stand or Fall — The Fixx

Wish — The Fixx

Thinking of You — Christian Kane (I somehow left this chapter out when I was first doing chapter titles. When I realized it, I decided to scrounge through the music used in "Leverage" to see if there was a match. But most of the show's soundtrack is instrumentals written by master soundtrack composer Joseph LoDuca. And then there was this... Yes, actor Christian Kane of "Leverage"/Eliot fame, as well as the "Buffy the Vampire Slayer" spinoff "Angel," is also a legit country music singer/songwriter, and this song figured in an episode where he goes undercover as a country music singer/songwriter, with a villainous John Schneider nonetheless. I adore the stripped-down acoustic version of this song that they used in the episode, and the album version is amazing, too. It also just happened, yet again, to fit my story — a wistful, almost sad, but totally romantic ballad.)

Not Sure Yet — Andy Lange (This is another of the rare non-instrumental songs featured in "Leverage." It's a bittersweet theme for Nate and Sophie in several episodes, with an overall tone of being hopeful everything will work out OK. And once again, it just fit.)

Still Around — The Fixx

Drown — Smashing Pumpkins

Treasure It — The Fixx

Miracle — Seven Nations (I not only had to find a song that fit here, I had to find one that just says Brighid. So, once again, my favorite Celtic rockers stepped up to the plate and hit a home run.)

Careless Whisper — Seether (A little more edge than the original.)

Every Time — Lia Rose

Love You More — Alexi Murdoch (We'll probably see more Alexi Murdoch on my book playlists. His voice just does amazing things between my ears. And he's *so* deep.)

All is Fair — The Fixx

In Your Room — Depeche Mode

Lightning Crashes — Live

Uprising — Muse (I insert here my usual reminder that my fictional band aMUSEd is not named for the real band Muse in any way, shape or form, but for the classical Muses of artistic inspiration. But I do love Muse, too. So when this song popped up as I was looking for a song for a different chapter, the image of Rory and David setting out on their Ramsay hunt just fit perfectly with the mood. So here is some Muse.)

Lonely as a Lighthouse — The Fixx (This one is off the band's new album. Yes, yet more ocean theme! Check it out.)

Outside — The Fixx (On my list of favorite songs ever.)

Dust in the Wind — Kansas (I really want Al to cover this one. But it also fit perfectly with Brighid's vision that gave her the idea of how to save David.)

Saved By Zero — The Fixx

Ocean Blue — The Fixx (This is the song that first got me thinking David has to be a Fixx fan. It's one of my all-time favorites among all their songs, and one of my all-time favorite songs, period.)

Summerland — The Dolmen (The Summerlands is a common concept along Celtic Pagans, though the idea of it as a Pagan "heaven" is a little more complex of a topic. It might also be called "Tír na n'Og," which translates as "The Land of Youth" in Irish. But Piper threatening to drag David back out into this life if he dared leave her was something that just had to happen. And I just went with calling it The Summerlands. And David's idea of heaven? Sitting on his board on the ocean, on a beautiful summer morning, meeting sea creatures, of course. It just fit.)

(Epilogue) Happy Landings — The Fixx. (This song's hopeful tone, of the sun coming out after a stormy night, is one I wanted to have for David and Piper and their little clan-member-to-be, as well as for the studio going forward. And if you're wondering how this selkie family is going to address the issue of touring — remember, they're not exactly normal selkies... and that'll all unfold at a later date. If you've been waiting for aMUSEd to go back on tour, that day will come!)

(Epilogue 2) Still Got the Blues (For You) — Gary Moore (Live in London) (We've got a story yet to unfold for Declan and Callie. But this is one of two songs I've had in mind for them pretty much from the start. The first is "Always Something There to Remind Me," by Naked Eyes, which has been shortened up to "Remind Me" as the title of Declan and Callie's book, with its first-love/second-chance romance storyline. And then there's "Still Got the Blues (For You)," which could really be said of either of them, since, clearly, both of them are still reeling from the impact of their past with each other, twelve years later. This amazing modern blues-rock song from a legendary Belfast guitarist and singer is one of my favorites among Tranzfusion's massive repertoire [it's actually one of the newer songs they play, having been released in 1990], and Al just... well, he kills it on lead vocals, every time, as does Hank on guitar. I'll post video of one of their performances of it, so check my social media accounts for that. I hope that gives you all the more reason to stay tuned for Book 4 and Declan's story.)

P.S. — That The Fixx fan club T-shirt David wears when he runs off to help Rory save Piper and take out Ramsay? It's a real T-shirt that I have around here somewhere. (Though Al may have also stolen that one. That would explain why I can't find it...) And it's actually one I designed. Back in my more active days with the fan club online, the call was put out for a T-shirt design. With my then-fledging graphics skills, I submitted a design that was one of two they ended up selecting to be produced for the fan club. Cool, huh? Nowadays, my graphics skills are mostly used designing my book covers. The Fixx is actually one of the well-known bands I've spent the most time with, in person. They're great people, in addition to being amazing musicians — especially live. Go see them if you can. I've met them several times and hung out with them a couple, and my fledging-rocker spawn first saw them live at age 8, in my hometown, when he was gifted one of Jamie West-Oram's well-used guitar picks. We both treasure it.

Acknowledgments

The first person I have to acknowledge for helping bring this book into reality is my best friend, Al, who was the inspiration for aspects of several of the characters in this series, not the least of which is David's under-appreciated skill as a bass player and his love of Spector basses. A full-time professional musician and sound engineer himself, Al taught me enough a decade ago that, even though I'd given up on that dream, I really could work as a live sound engineer, and he believed in me in that respect almost as much as our Brighid believed in her Hunter. He even got me a job and insisted I get paid for it once I got good enough. Al trusted my ears (which are the most important tool in the engineer's toolbox) for helping perfect his own mixes, and he taught me how to put my ears to work for a band and their audience.

So, Al's the real reason we have Piper and her struggle to be respected as an engineer and a female in what is still often a man's industry. (Yes, I was actually told, at 17, that I couldn't work with younger bands, because they'd get distracted. And, yes, I lost track of how many times people expressed surprise at seeing a female engineer. Thankfully, we're much more common than we used to be, but there's still a long way to go. Shoutout to my fellow Soundgirls: You all rock!)

Al also graciously gave me permission to once again use one of his songs as part of this book, only this time, with what he gave me, the song itself became part of the story — a major part of the story, in fact. How well it fit is pure serendipity. The gift the muses gave him almost 30 years ago has given once again, regifted and multiplied in the process.

Snippets of real-life have once again been pulled as inspiration for some of the elements of this story, though the outcomes are different, and the names have been changed and the credit dispersed to protect the guilty and confuse the innocent.

I have to again acknowledge Al's real-life bandmates, the legendary Ocean City, Md., classic rock band Tranzfusion, going on 40 years of rocking people's socks off, for which Al has been around for nearly a decade of that. There may be a few conversations and scenarios herein that were inspired by real-life interactions with the band members, their families and fans. All of whom are wonderful, I promise. Come out and see them sometime. Tell Al he's extra-famous now!

I'm not going to thank them all by name, but the special people in my life who deal every day with a world not built to accommodate the neurodivergent — you've been an inspiration to me in more ways than one. From ADHD and ADD to the autism spectrum, I've seen you tackle things I can't imagine dealing with, armed with only the desire to just be yourselves, and you do it on a daily basis. I hope I've done some of your story justice and will continue to do so going forward.

As for my friends, family members and readers dealing with social anxiety: Hi! This one's totally on me. No one ever told me I had social anxiety until I was hit so hard with it that a lot of seemingly simple tasks were no longer simple at all. I was the classic "shy" kid. Only what we used to call "painfully shy" seems like a very mild way to describe what I deal with on a daily basis and have since I was little. In my job as a journalist, I've had to learn to picture myself putting on my "journalist hat" just to ask simple questions of people I already know. Dealing with strangers is sometimes impossible, and don't get me started on phone calls. Yikes!

When every cell in your body tries to tell you your next word or action could be life-threatening, you learn to function even when fight-or-flight is permanently switched to flight. Just like Piper, you glue your feet to the floor and do what has to be done, or what you can do, which sometimes isn't at all the same.

If you're lucky, no one's the wiser. If you're not, you get the extra worry of knowing that everyone is likely wondering why you're acting so strangely, which only ramps up the pressure and the likelihood that you'll embarrass yourself. It's a great example of a self-perpetuating cycle. So, if you ever see me in person, or even talk to me online, know I'm doing my best to approximate normal human behavior. Feel free to pretend I'm doing a great job of it. It may be easier for both of us that way.

I can't go a moment longer, either, without acknowledging the late, great Dame Templar Patricia Kennealy Morrison, author of the Keltiad series of Celtic-influenced sci-fi/fantasy novels. I'm not sure we'd have a book about a selkie and a rockstar without her. Patricia was a role model of mine from the first moment I picked up one of her novels, and the more I learned about her, the more I realized we had in common, from our love of Celtic lore and languages, our drive to tell tales based in that lore, our religious beliefs, Mensa membership, our trade as journalists, and music journalists specifically, and last, but hardly least, our soul-deep love of rock music. Patricia was also incredibly generous to me with her time and self, during not just one point in my life but two of them, and I forever will appreciate that. I miss knowing she's out there in the world, but I am so glad she's reunited with her love. (And, yes, Piper Morrison is named for Patricia.)

Thanks are also due to my soul-sister, Melissa, and my new friend Chris, who've both reminded me that I've got a community of like-minded folks around me, even though it sometimes seems like I'm the one oddball in a huge crowd.

I want to again thank all my friends who supported me in adding professional fiction writer to my professional journalist identity. From serving as alpha readers and editors to just plain encouraging me to keep at it — 12 years after an app glitch ate most of my notes for the first Aurora Carmichael/Mystic Beach novel — you made things a lot easier, and I appreciate it.

Once again I have to thank my Mystic Beach rockstars, who once again pitched in with reading, giving feedback, hunting down pesky typos and being incredibly supportive when I needed it. Ce-ce, Julia, Bene, Sandy and Jill, you've all been amazing! And once again, a shout-out to my urban fantasy writers' group, including L.A. McBride and Heather G. Harris, for your ongoing support and insight.

Thanks also go to all of you, my readers, who've so enthusiastically greeted these characters and these stories.

You've kept my creative energies high, which is the fuel that lets me get these stories on the page.

Last, but definitely not least, I have to thank my family, both by blood and otherwise, for getting me where I am today, that I could start writing about these characters with whom I've fallen totally in love.

I will again add here my thanks to Herself, who has kept pushing me along on this journey, even when I was plagued by doubt and second-guessing us both. She knows I've appreciated it, but it feels important to publicly acknowledge Her role in this work coming to life.

Next up in this series is Declan's story, "Remind Me." We're going to find out exactly what happened to make our ri-dick-ulously talented lead singer who he is today, flaws and all. You may find out that he's a little deeper than he lets on. A little. Maybe. He's definitely misunderstood, though that's mostly his own fault. Time will tell whether he'll get a taste of his own medicine or his just desserts.

And don't miss Rhys' story, which will follow that. We'll get to visit with some familiar Mystic Beach characters, including Rory's friend Lyric (who, along with Amber, has a cameo in the new Hunter and Brighid seasonal bonus novelette "Spooky") and see whether the wild happenings in Mystic Beach can help tame "The Madman" behind aMUSEd's drum kit.

If you were intrigued by Rory and the Hidden Folk as this later chapter in their story played out, make sure to keep an eye out for "Safe Harbour," set for release in early 2023 as the kickoff to the Mystic Beach Mysteries, a sister series in the contemporary fantasy genre. That story is where Mystic Beach and the aMUSEd series was born, and if you'd enjoy seeing the balance between fantasy and romance flipped toward the fantasy side of the scale, you're going to love what's to come.

ABOUT THE AUTHOR

Aislinn Archer is an award-winning journalist, columnist and photographer, music and tech journalist, and editor, as well as a semi-retired live sound engineer.

She is the author two interconnected series spanning the paranormal fantasy and rockstar romance genres, set Coastal Delaware, where she lives. She is a member of Mensa and the Order of Bards, Ovates & Druids. Aislinn is an Irish language learner, persistent advanced-beginner guitar and bass player, photographer, foodie, gadget guru, jewelrymaker and lampwork glass artist. She is a voracious reader of the urban fantasy, fantasy and rockstar romance genres, and dedicated music fan across many genres. She loves attending concerts and spending time on the beach.

For updates, freebies, sneak peeks and inside details, sign up at http://aislinnarcher.com/home/subscribe/ and follow Aislinn at https://www.facebook.com/AislinnArcher; on Twitter @AislinnArcher; and on Instagram and TikTok @aislinnarcher. Visit her website at AislinnArcher.com.